It is 1993. South Africa is on  the brink of political transformation and in Walmer Estate, a busy suburb on the slopes of Devil's Peak, fourteen-year-old Alia Dawood is about to undergo a transformation of her own. She watches with fascination and fear as the national drama unfolds, longing to be a part of what she knows to be history in the making. As her revolutionary aspirations strengthen in the months before the election, her intense, radical Uncle Waleed reappears, forcing her parents and sister Nasreen to confront his subversive and dangerous past.

Nadia Davids' first novel moves across generations and communities, through the suburbs to the city centre, from the lush gardens of private schools to the dingy bars of Observatory, from landmark mosques and churches to the manic procession of the Cape Carnival, through evictions, rebellions, political assassinations and first loves. The book places one family's story at the heart of a country's rebirth and interrogates issues of faith, race, belonging and freedom.

An Imperfect Blessing is a vibrant, funny and moving debut.

AN IMPERFECT BLESSING

Nadia Davids

Published in 2014 by Umuzi
an imprint of Penguin Random House South Africa (Pty) Ltd
Company Reg No 1953/000441/07
Estuaries No 4, Oxbow Crescent, Century Avenue, Century City, 7441,
South Africa
PO Box 1144, Cape Town, 8000, South Africa
umuzi@randomstruik.co.za
www.randomstruik.co.za

© 2014 Nadia Davids

All rights reserved.
No part of this book may be reproduced or transmitted in any form or by
any means, mechanical or electronic, including photocopying and
recording, or be stored in any information storage or retrieval system,
without written permission from the publisher.

First edition, first printing 2014
This edition 2015
1 3 5 7 9 8 6 4 2

ISBN 978-1-4152-0769-7 (Print)
ISBN 978-1-4152-0574-7 (ePub)
ISBN 978-1-4152-0575-4 (PDF)

Cover design by Gretchen van der Byl
Text design by Fahiema Hallam
Author photograph by John Gutierrez
Set in Trump Medieval

Printed and bound by Paarlmedia, Jan van Riebeeck Avenue, Paarl,
South Africa

For John: all that is past, and all that is to come

And somewhere also the children

who laugh and play as if untouched by history
or by the heavy hands of their parents' gods.
You sit, bent over your table,
head in your palm and notepad at hand,

in your mouth
a whole night's talk
like cool, euphoric stone
and your tongue its reticent home.

– RUSTUM KOZAIN, *The Blessing*

1

Friday, 8 January 1993

It was her longest summer yet. And it had been (almost) without wind. For the months of November to February to be filled with days of warm stillness, unhurried by the wind that always began innocuously – a small sigh, a nothing, and then abruptly a full-skied shriek – was as rare as it was loved. *A windless summer*, Alia thought, remembering how often she had said those words as prayer, not as fact. Hers was a city of winds and storms, of fierce sun and chilling fog, of long cold rains and terrible droughts, of unexpected hails and gales, and sometimes all those things in one day. A city of unease, Cape Town. A moody city. A place of rock and water. Rock and water. The mountain and the sea had long ago broken and brokered its shape, but history had pushed back at the natural rim of the coast and formed a place out of careful division.

Alia lived in a neighbourhood called Walmer Estate, a small universe at the foot of Devil's Peak. The streets ran on long steep slopes bound for the harbour and the homes that ran beside them tilted forward as though they were being tugged by an invisible pulley. Walmer Estate was full of opposites. It was a place of large light-filled houses and stingy gardens, of overcrowded smelly flats and open fields, of little girls in burkas hurrying down sharp hills to madressa and teenage boys clustered outside corner shops, smoking cigarettes, admiring each other's sneakers and contraband denim. It was where wind-stunted shrubs and stooped trees leaned gratefully against five-foot tall graffiti commands to defy the state. Where old women sat on stoeps in faded house-dresses saying terrible things about their neighbours one day and weeping like hired Greek mourners at their funerals the next. It was where men never quite outgrew those first longings for German engineering, and that rite of passage, the purchase of a Mercedes Benz, new or used, could happen well into middle age.

If asked, no one could tell you who "Walmer" was, or if the land had once been an estate and anyway, everyone pronounced it "Warmer" and they took "Estate" to mean that they lived somewhere a little loftier than others. Its residents were often accused of nurturing a certain arrogance; living on a hill (any hill) will do that to you. But Alia thought it was more than that. The hills were one thing, the wind was another. She believed it made them all mad. And tough. Mad and tough.

The wind was a constant, more common than life, more frequent than death. For Walmer Estate children it was first among the elements. Before sun or rain, they learned how the air could move. They knew that a thin breeze from the north could cool your cheeks in the summer, but that a berg wind driven over the mountains could tip the temperature just a few degrees up until you felt as though you were wearing a hot, slightly billowing dress. The crazed south-easter came in the in-between months, ruining springs and autumns, breaking all those fragile beginnings. They called it "The Cape Doctor" because it chased the dirt and mess of the city and the sky to other places. For Alia it was a bitter medicine, because nobody, *nobody*, had it worse than in Walmer Estate. There, the streets were nothing more than tunnels carved out for the wind's passage. It used corners as spots of convergence and argument. It tipped over rubbish bins making homeless cats ecstatic and dirt-men dread their rounds. It pulled at hair and skirts, caring nothing for modesty or health; it grabbed bags and made old women's angina play up when they walked between the bus stop and home. It snatched children's balls, flung them down streets and never returned them. It did not need the mysteries of night to terrify. Walmer Estate winds could haunt in full daylight, surrounding houses and holding the occupants hostage.

Alia remembered once when she was very little having to clutch onto a telephone pole just to keep feet and ground connected, and that her sister had looped two small arms around her waist in the faint hope that their combined weight could anchor them. At first Alia had laughed, but when she stopped being able to hear her own voice, when she saw her sister's face pulled tight with fear, she understood it was not a game, that they could go adrift, be blown all the way up the mountain and spend the rest of their lives eating berries and dodging spirits.

A windless summer then. At least until the early hours of this 8th January when the inevitable bad luck that plagued this area hit.

Just two roads behind Alia's house stood the highway and the mountain veld. There had been no rain all summer and the bush had dried out into a stretch of almost featureless colour, just alternating shades of browned leaves and grey rock. In the weeks ahead there would be reports of a flicked cigarette, a piece of glass caught in the sun, an unidentified braaier. No matter. The wind had come and the fire came with it.

~

Two homes, with nothing but a thin highway between them and the mountain, had been the first to catch alight.

It was an act of nature. Or God. Or fate. Perhaps all three. What everyone did know was that the tree had crashed onto the roof of one house and tipped up the foundations of the other. It had stood between those two homes for just over sixty years and with the disregard that nature has for walls-as-boundaries had sunk its roots deep into the ground of one property and curved itself over the gables of the other. The two houses had been locked in a no-speaking spell for almost thirty years. A slight had passed between the oldest man of each house – who had said what had been lost somewhere in the dim decades of the argument, but the cudgels of the fight had been taken up with great enthusiasm by the next generation (and the next). A promising friendship between the youngest daughters of each family broke off, the sons began ignoring each other when they backed out of the driveway, the children obeyed the cement line between the two properties as though it were an electric fence. Chalk outlines of hopscotch and the whirr of skipping ropes were tempered to heed the delineation and the mothers turned their scarved heads away from each other instead of breaking the rhythm of the day to talk over the washing line. Birthdays, weddings, twenty-firsts and newborns went unacknowledged.

Today the two households stood waiting for the fire department, their faces lit by a strange animation of combined lights: day and fire. It was an awful assembly. Neither group looked at each other but each could feel the other's throbs of resentment. Everyone clutched at the stuff of forced migration, pots, hastily grabbed clothing, favourite toys, folders stuffed with important documents. Someone had turned on a tepid hosepipe and began half-heartedly to wet the cars. Then the wind shifted direction and began to tug at the burning palm. The two families watched the tree, each member striking a different pose of anguish, the men raising their hands to clasp their heads, looking nervously at the blazing veld, the women grasping squirming children towards them or peeping out from fingers they had clapped over their eyes. When the tree finally crashed onto the roof it had been sheltering for all those years, their cry was unanimous.

The fire department and the newspaper reporters arrived at the same time. The firemen leapt from the truck while the engine was still running, shouting at everyone to stand further back. The chief, busy screaming instructions at his men, ignored the son of one house who kept tapping at his shoulder, asking, "Now listen here, just whose fault is it *really* that the tree fell?"

The flames were doused, leaving the bark wet, burnt and dripping, and the roof-tiles smashed and despondent. An old man still in his dressing gown, his expression tragic and sour, turned towards his neighbours and shuffled forward. For a wild moment it seemed as though he would say something, offer some wisdom earned from years of wind and fire and terrible arguments. The two families waited as one for him to make his aching way towards the cement line. He stood with his back to his own tribe, cleared his throat, let the phlegm gather and rattle, and then calmly spat at the feet of the others.

The reporters began to round up the victims. They staged pictures of them standing staring at the damage, holding onto the detritus of their households. They tried to pull all the children into a single frame and to gather up suitable quotes from the adults. When all they were met with were glares from the grown-ups and huge eyes and shaking heads from their offspring, the writers pushed for the usual resigned and doleful moans about living in the shadow of the mountain. Still nothing. The silence grew large and awkward, until suddenly, everyone began to talk at once.

"The people next door are dangerous and selfish."

"We have been saying for years that that tree should have been cut down, and *now*?"

"Roof broken!"

"Pipes damaged!"

"Who is going to pay for that?"

"They have always been a lazy bunch."

"Why didn't they get their useless son to climb up and trim those branches if they were so concerned?"

It was rare to get this kind of venom in the midst of tragedy. Usually people found solace in a shared brush with death. The reporters dutifully wrote down each surname: "Hassan," said the one group. "Hassan," said the other. It was only then that the newspapermen's investigative training kicked in, and they realised that they were one family.

~

Alia Dawood was not quite a Hassan, but enough of one to feel a slow flush of shame when her father, Adam, walked into the house on the Friday after mosque, his hands full of the afternoon papers, his head full of the details whispered between prayers that the article couldn't carry. "Smack bang on the front page," he said triumphantly, throwing the paper onto the table next to the chopped tomato salad. "*Incredible.*" He turned gleefully to his wife Zarina. She refused to look up and focused instead on checking the rice and fanning back an oppressive mix of two heats, summer and fire. The ash of the burning mountain was creeping in steadily through the window's small opening.

"It's disgusting," she said finally and then moaned, "Oh *God* – I hope no one knows we're family."

"Everyone knows," said Alia cheerfully.

"At least we didn't have to evacuate this time."

Her mother always found something to be grateful for. It was a trick she had learned as a child, an act of self-preservation. In the swirl of the strange and busy days of her youth she had learned to imagine the worst and appreciate even the slightest reprieve.

Alia's sister Nasreen wandered into the kitchen, her hair lying in a fat wet ponytail down her back, a damp swimsuit visible beneath a thin T-shirt nursing her shape.

"Were you just swimming now?" asked her father sharply.

"Ja ... So?"

Nasreen had been doing this for about a year: answering her parents in sulking one-syllabic words, daring them to fight with her, shrinking back when they did, staging elaborate political arguments that drew attention to everyone else's shortcomings.

"It's Jummah!" said Adam, outraged. "How can you *swim* when it's Jummah?"

"I-get-in-the-pool-and-I-flap-my-arms-about."

She delivered the syllables flatly, letting the words lean in and against each other, as though every one of them were an indicator of heroic patience.

"Don't get smart with me."

Nasreen offered a shrug and began scratching her way through the fridge for the previous night's leftovers. This was another new tactic: refusing to eat with the family, or pushing her food around her plate when she did. Her father sat, his elbows on the table, his chin propped up onto a steeple of his own making. Zarina, sensing the beginning of another fight that would end with slammed doors and hours of hungry sulking, recalled the front page. Nasreen glanced at the newspaper while her father attempted to reconcile with her by making fun of the Hassans.

"Christ! I can just *see* Uncle Salie ... 'These phucking people-next-door! What have they ever done for us but bring us grief? I'm having the most terrible headaches, it's like a tight band around my brain.'"

Nasreen refused this old game. Twisting her mouth into a dismissive pout, she addressed her grievances at the orange juice. "No one cares. *God*, it's not as if there aren't more important things to write about right now. What a waste of everyone's time. Doesn't anyone in this family have any perspective?"

But Alia scrambled to take her father's bait. "My heart! My heart!" she said, breathing rapidly, impersonating one of the aunts. "It's not for *me* to judge, but what people do on the dunyia WILL be judged on the Yawm ad-Din!" Alia hunched her back over into the curve of someone who spent their days stirring pot after pot and strained her neck to look at her family from the corner of a squinted eye. She punctuated her testimony with an imaginary spoon, her breath landing hard on the Arabic words. Her father popped pieces of papir into his mouth between bouts of chortling; Alia was a good mimic, if a cruel one. Nasreen began to search for a glass to pour her juice into, making work of opening and closing the cupboards. She sighed loudly. "Where are the glasses? Have you moved them again? Why can't they just stay in one place? Why does everything have to be so *jumbled*?"

"Well," said Adam, his face wreathed in a grin, "perhaps you should think about staying at the Hassans? Number five or number seven would be happy to have you ... looks like they will be needing some interior decorating advice soon."

Adam delivered a series of nudges against Alia's ribs that declared them comrades while Nasreen looked at her sister from over the rim of her glass, eyes narrowed, filling with accusations of betrayal. Alia caught the look and shoved the newspaper and the nudges aside, but Nasreen had already turned to her mother, complaining, "You *know* I don't eat chicken curry, you're so selfish," and beat a wet retreat, the slap of her feet muffled by the carpet.

From the kitchen everyone heard a bedroom door bang shut. "What is the matter with that child? What kind of person doesn't eat chicken?" her father said.

"Leave it, Adam." Zarina's voice was distracted as she dished up.

"*I* waited all month to have chicken when I was her age."

"Really?" Alia said, honing in on this bit of information. Her father spoke about his childhood so rarely; there was a story about the bioscope, something about a comic book and a lucky escape from a neighbourhood gangster, but waiting for chicken was new. She leaned in close to the promise of her father's history. But Adam had already lost interest in his meatless days and was bemoaning the imam's Friday sermon. "Absolutely unbel*ievable* ... incredible stupidity ... banging on about how rampie sny is unIslamic." He returned to the newspaper. "Look here, Zina," he said, tapping a heavy forefinger against a photograph. "*Another* one of Rashaad's pictures. That boy has done nicely for himself."

Zarina offered it a cursory glance but Alia made a diligent study of the image: a young child in a squatter-camp rested on a makeshift wheelbarrow piled high with Coke cans and plastic bottles. His feet were bare, his toes squelching into the mud of the unpaved, puddled road. Standing next to him, also barefoot, in an overlong cotton dress, a large, untidy bow fixed on her head, was a little girl of about six.

"Is he recycling?" Alia asked interestedly.

"What? *No*, man. He collects this stuff and then he makes something out of it ... hang on." Adam thumbed through the paper and found a further spread, this time dedicated to the fruits of the boy's labour: the cans had been razored into thin petals and then bound together by scraps of wire to make a multi-coloured metal bouquet that he held up against his chest like a corsage. "Hell, that now takes some ingenuity," said Adam admiringly and then began to read aloud. "Matthew Sibon— Sibongi … ag, never mind, Matthew *Something* Mda is up at four every morning – four, mind you – to get to the rubbish heaps in Khayelitsha so that he gets first dibs on any cans and wire." Here he paused to look meaningfully at his daughter. "I'd like to see you get up at four for anything, never mind to do that." He cleared his throat before continuing. "Mda, eight years old, has left school – *sjoe*, but it's a shit life for them – in order to help support his family. Their mother is a live-in domestic and their father is a miner in the Transvaal. The children are looked after by their grandmother." He put the paper down with a sigh and leveraged a look at Alia as though he hoped a lesson had been learned.

"How far is Khayelitsha from here?" It was the only thing she could think of to ask.

"Thirty, thirty-five minutes. It's just a little after Uncle Omar them in Athlone."

"Why have you never taken us there?"

"Why do you want to go?"

"Well," said Alia piously, looking down at her hands, "we should know what it looks like."

"You can see what it looks like from the photos." Adam reached for another helping of the curry. "This is really nice, Zina, it's got a real kick to it." Zarina smiled in reply and offered to warm him more rice, but Adam started, suddenly aware of the time, realising he was late to reopen his fabric shop. He darted from the table with an admonishment to his daughter that she should finish her food and a final assurance to his wife that the fire could not, *would not*, spread further.

When he'd gone, Alia left the kitchen and wandered

through the house, her body filled with that bored, anxious restlessness peculiar to adolescents. It was the summer of 1993, the year at its own beginning, and Alia was on edge. The whole country was on edge; everything felt as though it was on hold. The careful plotting of the interim government to negotiate power from one group to another was daily reading for its citizens. They had drawn a collective breath and were holding it and none had exhaled just yet. "You're coming of age *with* the country," Alia's uncle had said to her a few months earlier at a family lunch, "nothing could be more exciting." Alia had smiled at him – wasn't that what she was supposed to do? – and made eyes across the table at Nasreen, who was looking at their father's brother with the fixed stare of someone who had just received a benediction.

Problem was, thought Alia, dragging her feet through the house, it didn't feel like she and the country were in this together. She had been born too late. Too late to be a part of the graffiti and the chanting and the defiance. Too late to know what it felt like to lend flesh to a crowd, to spit at the police, to gather in secret corners at school. Too late for all that. And she felt more than a little robbed. The nation's new beginning had been long in the works, a beginning paid for with someone else's blood. She opened the glass sliding door that led onto an enclosed balcony, sat for a moment on an uncomfortable wooden bench, began inspecting the plants for ash from the fire, quickly lost interest and went back inside.

Near the front door was a formal portrait of her father as a boy of perhaps three. It was a photograph that had been blown up until it was almost a metre tall and then painted over in muted tones of white and pink and finished with a light dusting of golden brown on his rounded cheeks and baby locks. He stood, in a pale, grey-blue tunic, one foot placed in front of the other like a young lord in a gallery of ancestors. His hair fell to his neck and his mouth was slightly open as if he was about to ask a question. The photograph was held in an oval mahogany frame festooned with carved bunches of wooden grapes. Alia saw this picture everyday, but what always surprised her, what gave her pause and wonder, was the colour of her father's eyes. They were, like the tunic, a soft grey-blue. And they were not the eyes of an infant, where colour changes as rapidly as sleep patterns, but the eyes of a child when features have settled. When she asked her father why, he gave a short, barking laugh. "That was Van Kalker's style, the photographers down in Woodstock. They made everyone look white in their pictures. Why do you think they were so popular?"

Alia passed the portrait and, as always, flicked her eyes to acknowledge the paternal blue ones. This photograph, like all those of parents at their beginnings, presented her with that strange mystery, the capable parent at his most vulnerable.

She opened the front door and felt a warm blast of berg wind: part air, part fire. In the distance, the jagged outline of a small city centre undercut the still blue of a harbour made tall by cranes and ships. Everything felt slightly dirty, her eyes watered, and the smell of burnt wood settled on her hair. She sat on the brown brick step that separated their driveway from the pavement. The wind had dropped again, just a little, and a thick grey smog settled low over the area. The smell of burning brush and trees made the day seem hotter and bits of debris and ash were swirling in little eddies and whirls down the street. Alia had not yet started smoking, but sitting in the midst of all that ash and the distant threat of danger, knowing she couldn't beat it, made her want to join it.

The end of a windless summer and the weekend before school began. She waved her hand to cool down her face, feeling a little trapped between the sulks inside the house and the burning air outside of it.

"Howzit, Alia?"

She looked up to see her friend Farouk from next door, peeling a lemon. He did this frequently, picking them off his tree, the sourer the better, sucking at them, grimacing, saying it was a test of endurance.

"Howzit, Farouk."

There was not much else to say. They were as comfortable with each other as two old women. But then Farouk surprised her. "I saw the paper – that was your family, right?"

"My mother's cousins," Alia qualified.

"Funny."

Alia made her way over to him and took refuge in the thin shade of the lemon tree. The street stretched in front of her with wraith-like wisps of heat rising off the tar. Striding through the mirage came another neighbour, Mikhail, fifteen and immaculate. For a moment, it seemed as though he was wearing a cowboy hat, roguishly placed, precisely angled, like the star of an old Hollywood classic. Alia blinked, the hat was not there, but the aura of sly command remained and shimmered. Mikhail came from a family of tailors and it seemed to Alia as though by some genetic inheritance, by some historical osmosis, he had been gifted with the talent of being perpetually neat, freshly ironed. His house was on the corner of their street and had a wrap-around balcony, perfectly positioned to watch whoever drove up, down or through the area. He considered this a responsibility and with responsibilities came judgements in the form of little titbits of gossip that he parcelled out. He walked over to the two under the lemon tree, lifting his chin to Alia and offering Farouk his greetings, shaking his hand, pressing his own against his heart, wishing him a good Jummah. Farouk responded to this as he did to everything in life – with total equanimity. Lemons and God were equally welcome on a late Friday afternoon in the shadow of a still burning mountain. Mikhail turned his body so that he gently but effectively blocked Alia from the conversation. Alia didn't mind, she didn't like Mikhail much, but sometimes thought it was a shocking waste that someone so beautiful could be so dull. He turned to face her as though he had heard the unspoken judgement.

"Everyone was talking about your family by mosque today." Mikhail leveraged this at Alia like an accusation.

"So?"

"*So*. I'd be *kak* embarrassed."

Before she could respond, he turned to Farouk. "Where were you, bra? I thought you said you were going to start coming?"

"Oh ... ja. Next week, next week," answered Farouk, squinting while he sucked at his lemon. His eyes flicked upwards at the effort. "Oh my God. Look at the *sun*."

Three pairs of eyes looked to the heavens and witnessed an image from the Last Days. The smog had moved in tiny increments across the sky and covered the sun. It was the first time any of them had been able to look directly at the star. It was weird and worrying. Hidden behind the pollution, the sun could no longer blind, but it had lost none of its terror. Alia fancied she could see it spinning and that it would, at any moment, drop to earth. The three of them moved, unconciously describing a little triangle, their silence broken by Farouk's despondent voice, "School on Monday."

A different kind of foreboding settled over them.

None of them went to the same school. Farouk and Alia went to same-sex private schools on different sides of the city; Mikhail went to a government school within walking distance. It was something none of them talked about very much. The schools said more about the parents' differing politics than any of them felt equipped to discuss without fighting. Private schools were enclaves of privilege, white schools, sell-out schools, schools for those whose family had an eye on the future prize, and in this country, where the front-line was on the playground, school was no place to make the wrong political choice. His friend's schools, superior in facilities and education, were a sore spot for Mikhail, who was innately competitive. He had been to their functions, the food fairs, discos, sports days, and had seen the tightly plaited heads of girls who longed to be class captains, the arrogant stride of boys who were little gods on the rugby field, the manicured lawns, buildings wound with ivy so that the grounds looked like a tiny university, and he had felt the unfairness of it all sharply, keenly. Mikhail thought now of the cricket pitch at Farouk's school, of his friend's clumsy execution of a googly and of the graceful arc of his own bowling. The unnamed gloom of the afternoon had turned sour and found a purpose.

"At least my school's got girls."

He flung this, a little unfairly, at Farouk, who, knowing he could do nothing to refute the truth or question its relevance, merely nodded and sighed helplessly at his own hard luck. Farouk looked so downcast that Mikhail's conscience spoke for him. "I'm going to HAL's on Saturday, the back to school party. Come with."

Mikhail walked away, always somewhere between a saunter and a shuffle. Alia waited for Farouk to be outraged on her behalf. When he wasn't and Alia saw a look of gratitude slide over his lemony mouth, she exploded. "I can't believe he didn't even *ask* me to go with! He is such a *sexist*! This is such *bullshit*!"

Farouk sighed. This had been a thorn in Alia's side for years now. Her interaction with these boys had been her first indicator that life inside her home was an acceptable blueprint for life outside it. Over the years Farouk and Mikhail had refused to let her ride their bikes, play with their tennis rackets, or even have access to their Nintendos. At ten she began to suspect it was because she was a girl and when she confronted them they seemed a little surprised that she needed confirmation. Alia was not above blackmail, a card she played now on Farouk: "If you don't take me with you, I'll tell your dad you're going."

Farouk didn't mind if Alia came or not, he just needed a watertight reason to give Mikhail and this was it. "Sure," he shrugged, "meet me here tomorrow at two."

~

Nasreen sat in the refuge that was her room, body on bed, turned cat-like towards a patch of afternoon sun. She was eating an apple and painstakingly making her way through a library book, difficult to read, but worth the librarian's impressed glance. She looked regretfully at the fruit; she was really hungry but just couldn't stomach the oily goose-pimpled sliminess of the animal skin in the chicken curry. Her friend Emma had suggested once that maybe she had a texture disorder. When she relayed this to her parents, they said nothing at the time but had taken great delight in recounting the story to their friends. "And then she said," they would chorus, "I've got a *texture* disorder."

There was a knock at the door, followed immediately by the entry of – who else? – Alia. Nasreen hoisted the book to shield her face, hoping that this would be subtle enough to communicate her need for privacy. But Alia insisted on interpreting it as an invitation to sit down. She leaned in close, making a study of the title, *Nausea*. It was a slim volume with a crazed landscape on its cover; a clock dripped off a table, another hung off a pale, thin tree branch. Alia tapped repeatedly at the title, each tap darting the book just an inch away from Nasreen's eyes, asking, "What's it about?"

"It's not about anything." Nasreen was unable to explain in words what she thought she might just be beginning to understand. "It suits my mood."

"Why? Because you didn't eat lunch?"

Nasreen forced herself not to answer, thinking that to engage might be to unnecessarily prolong. But Alia had settled onto the bed, she was clearly in it for the long haul. They sat in silence while Nasreen's eyes raced conspicuously across the page. Eventually she admitted defeat, stopped mid-sentence and looked at Alia, waiting.

"I'm going to HAL's tomorrow," her sister offered.

"Gross. Why?"

She could see this was not the response Alia had been hoping for, but she was so close, she was *verging*, she thought, on understanding this book, almost able to grasp this man's waning interest for everyone and everything—

Alia pressed on. "I'm going with Mikhail and Farouk."

Still reading, Nasreen split her focus for just long enough to say, "And they're letting you? I am shocked."

Alia didn't reply but remained stationed on the bed in a demanding fusion between sulking and need that Nasreen promised herself she would not give in to. When Alia sighed loudly and shifted position, Nasreen fixed her eyes with elaborate concentration on the page, smiling slightly while she read as though she and Sartre were in complete agreement.

"Can I borrow something? I don't have anything." Alia was up now, opening Nasreen's cupboards without asking permission (this after the previous week's catastrophic fight in which *asking permission* had been part of the treaty their mother had drawn up). Nasreen stayed on the bed but skimmed a remote finger over her favourites, managing to vet certain pieces before Alia could claim them, finally saying, "You can take the purple cross-over top," and then, knowing HAL's to be an unforgiving place, she generously co-ordinated the rest of the outfit. "Wear it with the Levi's. And your black beetle-crushers."

Alia took the top with something more than gratitude and Nasreen returned to her book remembering her own first afternoon at that club – all those months ago! – its cheesy disco, its disappointments, the lame pick-up lines, the cattle-like stupidity of synchronised dances, and felt a wave of pity for her sister flood through her. She finished the apple and tossed the core out the window and into the neighbour's garden below.

2

SATURDAY, 9 JANUARY 1993

This place, he thinks, *this place*. He doesn't come here often.

When it happened he had been not quite seven. Old enough to remember everything without understanding any of it. The talk had been in the house for months.

We have to leave.

Everyone on the street got a letter.

Ask the Abasses if we can use their truck.

His mother had gone into a frenzy of organisation. She packed and repacked the contents of her kitchen. She kept Waleed's clothing in an old suitcase stowed in the hallway as though he was always on the precipice of a long trip. When he thought of his family then, it was usually through the memory of an old and recurring dream; in it, they all walked a tightrope, his mother with an oversized copper pot on her head, long wooden spoons dangling from her ears and belt, one plump foot placed gingerly in front of the other. His father and brother Adam carried a couch between them, looking at each other warily over its braided arms. He trailed behind with an over-stuffed suitcase and a collection of old comics. Beneath the rope, policemen circled, their painted clown faces tilted up like so many moons, uniforms pinched into tight waists. They beat miniature drums and pointed comic plastic guns up at the family. There were other dreams too, more prosaic, of dust and rubble and the floor giving way and the roof being blown off.

We have to leave.
Everyone on the street got a letter.
Ask the Abasses if we can use their truck.

None of it meant anything until he came home from school one day and saw his mother and a few other women from his street standing clustered together on a neighbour's stoep while a giant wrecking ball smashed away at a house on the corner. Each time the ball hit, the women flinched as one. Years later he would think of those women with their scarved heads, their dark dresses and their synchronised cries and movements as a travelling Greek chorus, plucked somehow from the open-air ruins of a theatre in Thebes and placed on the slopes of Devil's Peak, to wail and lament and prophesy.

Within a few months most of his street was gone. He became used to picking his way over and through rubble and debris, making half-gone houses into new play places. When his family eventually left District Six they didn't have to go far, just a ten-minute walk away. *We are lucky*, his mother used to say.

They moved in with his grandmother in Woodstock and when the old woman died, his father inherited the house. With the new neighbourhood came new behaviour. Nothing happened in a straight line anymore. Nobody had simple answers.

Just because.
We moved just because ... don't you like it here?
Be grateful you have a roof over your head.
We are lucky.

His father began to plan meandering journeys that would avoid driving past what was now just an empty stretch of land between Woodstock and town.

Everything required a twisted route. Visiting family in the BoKaap meant the rattling Peugeot would wind its way through the dead ends and one-ways of Woodstock, past the grey commerce buildings of the downtown Foreshore until it curved into the city centre. Anything but that straight road that opened at the four-way stop, with Nicros behind them, Zonnebloem School in front, Holy Cross to the left and the dread of the District in front, where nothing would grow. ("No nothing," his mother said, "for years, nothing.")

Waleed's father had been a carpenter, a man who spent hours coaxing new life from dead trees with a gentleness his sons never knew. The man was not a gifted liar and so his children learned early the line between hurt and fiction.

We have to go to Auntie Marrel to drop off this plate first.
I forgot to pick up cigarettes from the bubi.
Just because, okay?
Just because.

But there were Saturdays without a car, days when his father was making deliveries and he and his mother and his brother had to take the bus into town to do the weekly shopping. The three of them would stand at the stop watching bus after bus, with empty seats in front, pass them by. His brother would scowl at his shoes and his mother would retreat into a strange and aching silence. Once, when it was just the two of them, the wrong bus did stop, an accident, a trick of the light, his mother made pale by the glare of the sun. Waleed had charged through the open doors before anyone could stop him. He sat right behind the driver, entranced by the man's sharply creased uniform, his masterful control of the over-sized gears, and the machine that spat out bits of coloured cardboard paper for the tickets. The conductor, his head speckled with a dusting of grey, had come up to them and said, "Please, lady, I don't want any trouble. I think there are some seats upstairs. Just take your boy up there."

Fozia, who had never been very good with personal space, curled over to whisper fiercely, "Don't you know your own people?" before turning to Waleed and saying, "My seat is specially reserved. The one at the top has the *best* view, you crazy to want to sit here, you will miss all the fun. Besides," and here she confused her son by addressing the conductor directly, "can't you see how dirty it is down here? It's filthy. It *stinks*."

Waleed charged ahead, trying to take the bus steps two at a time. He got to the top and saw that both front seats were occupied, the one he had imagined for himself taken up by a girl in tight red bell bottoms, her dark hair in an ironed-out flip. He began to run back and forth between the rows of dark green plastic seats before turning to wrap his body over the top of the rail, hopping impatiently from one foot to the other while he waited for his mother to join him. When he looked down the spiral staircase he saw three things: an old lady's foot in a thick, white orthopaedic shoe, a mesh of brown pantyhose that clung to a swollen ankle and a walking stick with a rubber bottom. Behind this came his mother, murmuring encouragement, her hands held out as if to catch the older woman. The woman's breath came in short heaves and on the fourth step she leaned a little against the bus wall, took a tissue from her cardigan sleeve and wiped furtively, as if embarrassed, at the beads of sweat that had gathered on her upper lip. When she got to the top deck, she collapsed into the chair closest to her.

Waleed's mother hurried after her, "You okay, Auntie?"

"Fine, fine. Thank you. I guess I got my exercise for the day." A laugh. But what was funny?

Waleed looked at the woman's legs, snaked with puffy veins, and in a loud whisper asked his mother, "Is her seat *also* reserved upstairs? She should ask to be downstairs. Must I go tell him? Must I tell the driver? I'll go now—"

His mother said nothing, but tugged him up the length of the bus to the middle of the back row.

"We can't see anything from here! That girl is in our seat! Why don't you go tell her to get up? Didn't we pay for it and everything?"

"You just sit still," she answered in a tone he knew not to challenge.

When the bus passed the District, it seemed to move with a cruel slowness. Even the screeches of the gears felt exaggerated, a mechanical opera of grief. Fozia clutched her son's hand. She did not look out the window once. Her face, usually so full of movement, had the glaze and stillness of a statue.

But Waleed looked. He tried to hold the ruin in his gaze. The bus gathered speed somewhere between the Moravian Church and the beginnings of the city centre and for a moment the earth blurred. The bricks, the dirt, the cobblestones, the untouched palm trees, the undemolished mosques merged, and for an instant, he swore he saw a Khoi man running, his feet barely touching the earth, his arms flowing mid-gesture into his bow and arrow, poised to take flight, a leather bag filled with water knocking lightly against his hip.

Today, Waleed had not taken the bus. He had walked here from Observatory, his body adrift without the signs that marked his childhood, those small parameters of his beginnings.

You can walk the length of Muir Street.
You can't go to the British Bioscope.
We buy our meat from the Adamses.
We only go to the doctor in Hanover Street.

There had been a few exhibits and talks to memorialise this place, but he hadn't attended. He dismissed it, all the storytelling, all the pooled remembrance. "Easy," he told friends who were moved by the worship of witnessing, "too easy. Let me tell you a story and everything feels better."

Instead he came back here, where it was difficult to pick feet over rocks and where abandoned plastic bags made the place branded and filthy.

He looked to the mountain and saw that yesterday's fire had left deep pits of black all over its slopes. The smog had cleared and across the harbour he could see the Island, adrift in an impossible ocean. Beyond that, the thin rim of the horizon, the still point between sky and water. To look at it was not to know it. To look was not to see the rounded triangles of the slave ships' cotton sails with their cargoes of death and spices, of rum and rape. To look was not to know the Island with its hidden prisons, its quarries of bright and blinding stone, its tiny cells only just opened. To look was not to know the recent – too recent – joy of those men, salt-sprayed, prison-aged, elated, as their feet touched the mainland. What Waleed did know was that somewhere, in some dark century, in a grief that tunnelled down through the ages, that sometimes gripped him by the throat, there once had been a man or a woman, a great-great-great-great grandparent who had sat in the hulls of one of those Dutch ships, sick with vomit and terror, lifted high on the apex of a wave mad with salt and height. That someone who had given him blood and bone had once turned, their ankles straining against iron shackling, to speak to another, to ask for water in a language since lost.

3

Saturday, 9 January 1993

Alia's room was one of messy beginnings. Everywhere there was the evidence of another incomplete project. Above her bed were three rickety pine shelves, the result of four hours of hard labour one Saturday. They could hold just a few light paperbacks successfully and she was always slightly fearful that they would crash onto her forehead in the middle of the night. A few weeks earlier, she had taken her curtains down and replaced them with a couple of saris, bright bolts of cloth pinched from Zarina's store cupboard.

Alia knew what sort of room she wanted and it wasn't this one. It was as if the room, like her personality, was something she couldn't quite get right. She had only just moved out of her pink phase and had been trying on this new image, but it was a thin, fragile garment through which, or so she thought, everyone could see.

Today, the Saturday of HAL's, the floor was clothed. She had been hearing about the club for years, but it was only recently that the idea of a room of flashing lights, loud music, boys and too much eyeliner had become as tempting as an afternoon with book in hand, body on bed. She had reached into the middle cupboard and had scooped everything up, gathered it towards her and dumped it in the centre of the room. Nasreen's instructions: jeans, purple cross-over top and beetle-crushers were laid out reverently, bodiless, on the bed. But there were other things to be considered. The purple top was long sleeved, the day was hot, and she had heard that HAL's in the afternoon, packed to capacity with heaving, sweating bodies, was a fetid place. Alia had a fierce mistrust of her body. The recent betrayal (still too difficult to talk about except with other girls) had not yet been soothed and she had begun to think of sweat marks as secondary little pockets of shame.

An older cousin had told her that black was the colour that hid all the body's sins: fat, sweat, blood, clumsy food stains, skin yellowed by long winters. At two o'clock Alia found herself clothed entirely in the sinless colour; an unintentional Goth. Everything conspired to make her look like a spider. Her skinny frame (she was still almost hipless) was made more so by her hands and feet that had experienced a growth spurt independent of the rest of her body. She had lengthened herself with the two-inch flat rubber soles, shoes her mother had paid for with resigned defeat and that her father had laughed at outright. "Those have to be the ugliest things I have ever seen. They look like orthopaedic shoes for cripples."

"*Disabled* people, Adam, please."

Alia glimpsed herself in the mirror – a very young widow – and decided to play towards the lank-haired, kohl-lined girls at school who walked about in a deep funk, their private angst poured out in bad poetry in the school paper and the graffiti on their satchels. She took an eye-pencil and began to shadow her rims and lids with unskilled hands. The shock at seeing them darkened and jumping out at her like two smudged holes was enough to make her stop.

"You look like Morticia Addams." Nasreen was standing in the doorway. "Please don't go Goth. It's so annoying. It's for white kids who need to validate their non-problems."

Alia pulled an Indian print bag towards her and began

tumbling in things she thought she might need: a ten-rand note, eyeliner, a box of cigarettes she didn't smoke.

"It's to hide sweating," she answered, embarrassed.

"Oh, that's all right then," said Nasreen forgivingly. "Listen, you'll probably hate it – just tell Mikhail to bring you home if you're not having a good time. Or call me, I'll make a plan."

~

Mikhail's older cousin, Shaheen, was driving them to HAL's and an ugly silence had sprung up between him and Alia. Mikhail, perfectly attired in a pair of pale blue, baggy Aca Joe jeans and a white Levi's T-shirt branded with huge lettering that ran from just below his collarbone to several inches over his hips, had taken one look at Alia's clothing and laughed. She had retaliated by telling him that the gel he'd massaged into his head had softened his brain, and Farouk, who had on tight-fitting pants nipped at the waist with a Lacoste belt (irrefutably the worst dressed of the three), had attempted to broker a peace by saying, "So do you guys, like, know who the DJ is?"

It was an unforgivable question, badly timed, full of the right intentions and the wrong content. It betrayed his ignorance, reminded Mikhail of the school Farouk went to and made Alia, who didn't know the answer either, retreat into a shamed, sulking silence. Mikhail answered because he didn't want Farouk to reflect even more badly on him later. "It's *Raheem*," he said, pronouncing the "i" in "it's" like a "u", his voice heavy with disgust.

Shaheen rested his hand lightly on the steering wheel of his father's BMW. He coaxed the car's power-steering with the gentlest of short arcs, stroking the soft, rounded leather left or right. His seat was pushed back into a reclining "v" so that he sat in a slumped attitude of studied nonchalance, head peering just a few inches above the door lock. He had only just mastered the art of driving, smoking and adjusting the volume all at once, and it was a skill he showed off now, exhaling a lungful of Rothmans-addled air, while he fiddled with the volume to show off his subwoofers. God's name dangled from the rear-view mirror and two bumper stickers declared his mother's primary beliefs: one said ISLAM A WAY OF LIVE and the other – a stab at the national negotiations after Mandela's release – bore the legend JUSTICE BEFORE PEACE.

Mikhail's cousin was a slicker, darker version of him. Shaheen didn't have any younger brothers and believed in passing down all his hard-earned knowledge to this, his closest blood. He turned down the volume and said to Mikhail, "If you want to smoke, there's a staircase at the back door, and then upstairs there's a roof deck. No one will mind if you go there." Mikhail nodded coolly, answering with a head that matched the r&b ragga beat.

Shaheen drove his car in mad bursts of speed and sloth, both designed to show off. When he charged down Roodebloem Road towards Woodstock Main Road he moved with sudden breaks and sharp turns, made his wheels squeal above the stereo and considered it a victory when his passengers were breathless and slightly nauseous at stop streets. He laughed when Alia's hand reached instinctively towards the handbrake but as they turned into Salt River Main Road, he slowed to a snail's pace.

A double row of parked cars lined the long street, each with a competing sound system. Doors were flung open and long Levi-clad legs jutted out of them. Boys in alternately oversized T-shirts or tightly fitted vests arranged themselves in careful poses, snapping at Zippo lighters, coaxing a recalcitrant hair into place with long-lasting gel, fingering the twenty-rand notes in their pockets. Shaheen slowed to a halt, leaning out the window to greet a friend. "A*weh*, Riyad! You looking good."

"Howzit, Shaheen." His friend smiled into the car, questioning the mismatched coterie of Alia, Farouk and Mikhail. "Who are your friends?"

Shaheen winked at Riyad as if to distance himself from the group. "This is my cousin Mikhail, my mommy's sister's son."

Mikhail reached his hand out to Riyad, clasped it in a double-binded move and briefly touched the flat of his palm to his chest. "Hoezit, Riyad," he said, with the exact amount of deferential camaraderie he should.

"And this is, er … sorry, man, I forgot your name again."

Shaheen had seen the way Riyad's eyes swooped unforgivingly over Farouk's outfit and decided to affect a little self-preserving amnesia.

Farouk, ignorant of the social slap, blithely pumped Riyad's hand up and down, saying, "Hello, great to meet you! Hi!" His accent clashed with the setting almost as badly as his clothing.

Riyad's eyes finally settled on Alia. She was glowering in the back of the car, overcome by the feeling that this had all been a terrible mistake.

"Hi. *Hi*," she said, "we've actually met."

Riyad executed a shrug of disbelief and Alia was reminded, once again, about Cape Town's social coding. The first and often hardest lesson was *never* to be the first to admit to knowing someone, or even to having met them. She considered now the city's array of rhetorical insults masquerading as questions:

"Who is *he* to act like he knows *you*?"

"*What* are you and *who* am I?"

"Who are *you* to talk to *me*?"

Social power was defined by how many people you knew, how many people you pretended *not* to know and how many people claimed to know *you*. One of the most potent social insults was to pretend not to know somebody to their face. It didn't matter if you had passed them on the street every day for five years, visited their house, if they had eaten your food or used your toilet. If a slight was to be delivered, it was usually done through this: non-recognition. It was like saying "You just don't exist." It could happen when driving; people passed each other in the street and, masked behind sunglasses, lightly sailed past each other delivering snubs behind the excuse of concentration and the brightness of the light. "That *bastard* didn't greet me," the insulted would rail; "I just pretended I didn't see him," the insultee would shrug with exaggerated nonchalance. Alia knew not to take Riyad's quizzical stare too seriously, but she was already too annoyed to play the game. "Oh for God's sake, Riyad! You are friends with my cousin Rania. I've known you for years ... I *swam* at your house last month."

Riyad looked shocked. "Oh *ja*, *ja*, sorry, man. I didn't see you properly in there."

The queue to the club snaked around the block. HAL's. An institution. Founded in the early seventies by the enterprising Parks brothers – Yusuf ("Peanut Kop" for his head which dipped in an unfortunate indent somewhere in the centre), Hassan ("Milky" for his fair skin) and Noordien (too suave for a nickname). The Parks brothers were a marvel, managing to be both a part of and apart from the community. All three had an excellent ear for the whining cadence of Arabic recitation, they were always first in line to fetch relatives at the airport returning from the haj, they affected suitable outrage when they found out anyone (even their Jewish friends) ate pork, but they were also notorious womanisers, gamblers, dancers. "They were," Yusuf would proclaim, drawing himself up to full height, "raconteurs." They mixed a mean vodka and lemonade (not for themselves, but for the customers) and could shake their asses to any disco beat. They strutted through the streets of Cape Town, heels clicking on the sidewalks, loud-as-fuck printed shirts, each of them behaving as though the Brothers Gibb had been inspired by *them*, not the other way around.

One night, the brothers Parks had watched a smuggled copy of Kubrick's masterpiece. In a darkened basement, a group of bell-bottomed, wild-haired, smoke-muddled twenty-somethings gathered to listen to a computer beep towards its own demise. The boys left, clutching towards themselves Kubrick's message of a new spiritual frontier and morphing it into something they understood: a place to boogie.

They sat up all night talking about the kind of club they wanted. Nothing dark and dingy. Nothing that referenced the outside world. No fucking policy about who could come and who couldn't. Open to everyone. "Well," Noordien interjected, "everyone who dresses right." That's right, they decided. No fucking T-shirts, no casual shoes, not even for whiteys. "Especially for whiteys," snarled Hassan. Fitted clothing, shiny material, glittery makeup, high heels for women, Cuban heels for men, fast cars driven at a slow pace, a black and white checked dance floor, and every session would open with the reverberating strains of Richard Strauss's "Also Sprach Zarathustra". *Deeeeeeee deeeeee deeeee dum dum dum dum dum*. Hassan saw himself standing in the DJ booth waving his hands in mock orchestration while the crowd gathered. That was the seventies.

Today the club held inter-generational memories. Alia's uncles and aunts had all come here and told her how they had bowed at the altar of disco. A decade later her older cousins had pumped their fists in the air to Afrika Bambaataa and Run-D.M.C., imagining a link between themselves and the ghettos of New York City.

Mikhail climbed out of the car and inspected the long line and its patient queue with disgust. He turned to

Shaheen. "Can't we skip it or something? Don't you know someone?" Shaheen understood. Waiting in line would have been an admission of failure. Groaning deeply, he exited his car, nodding at Riyad to watch it. His self-appointed role as older brother was beginning to chafe. He told Mikhail as much as he made his way towards the bouncer, head down, legs loping in a cool, deconstructed ramble, while the other three traipsed after him, trying to keep up – in more ways than one. Shaheen worked his magic, smiling while he talked, lighting up a cigarette and offering it to the doorman. The man smiled all three of them in, ignoring the mutterings of the patrons nearest the front. "Naai! What kind?"

Alia, Mikhail and Farouk wound their way down the corridor towards the promise of music.

~

Waleed left the District feeling the waste of the morning and early afternoon lying thick and heavy in his head and mouth. He left as he had arrived, defiantly on foot, one of the city's few pedestrians by choice, walking with a hunched, slightly loping gait, a stride that was testimony both to the hours he spent curled over his desk and to the ghost of the loose-limbed rol he had tried to copy from neighbourhood gangsters as a boy. Now, as then, he had three or four books in his bag. One was always his own, a notebook filled with his writing, the others a careful selection, designed to lend that notebook depth and worth, the works of poets and writers of fiction: comrades, unmet and unseen, who also inhabited worlds of dust and worry and sleeplessness, for whom rest was never really rest, just an unconscious pocket of space and time in which words and ideas jostled for solutions.

Waleed walked the city, believing somehow that these books anchored him, evened him out, granted him quiet companionship, and sometimes even an absurd sort of protection. He knew that this place was dangerous for dreamers, and that without the additional weight of the books he could be knocked off his feet by the wind, that there could be hours of stultifying boredom on public transport, that a bookless bag could not be slammed as effectively over the head of a would-be thief.

He had gone to the District thinking that perhaps he could finally write something about it all, arrange words that would speak to … what? Some sort of homage? A rant? (Maybe. He spent most days with one eye on the past; focused fury could easily be reached.) But predictably nothing had come, just that taunting mirage between intention and product. He was tired and hot and fed up and *hungry* for something – food or writing, it was difficult to know which.

His mind turned to the notebook stowed away in his knapsack, all those white pages, reproachfully, resentfully empty. It had not left the safety of his bag for several weeks. *This is the problem*, he thought miserably as he made his way from the grassy knolls and rubbish-strewn pits of the District back to the relative safety of the tarred road: he had always cherished the *idea* of writing, the romance of late nights and strong coffee, the ecstasy of a well-tuned sentence or a phrase that references five things at once, that sense of invincibility that comes when things charge and move and arrive unbidden, when the world is brought to heel, when the violence of the outside is contained, order is enforced, logic is remade. But those days were fragile and few. Mostly there was just this, walking, and the dreaded realisation that the promise a notebook held when it was first purchased was in constant danger of becoming an elaborate and cruel joke. Lovers and friends were always giving him notebooks as gifts, hoping perhaps to appear, even as a faint trace, an outline, in his stories. He was the kind of writer that people claimed as their own discovery. His coterie of followers – mostly friends, a few acolytes from university and a smattering of coffee shop readings – was small but devoted. Waleed told himself that this was just as it should be; better a gathering at his grave of three who understood the work than an assembly of hundreds of chattering idiots.

The wind was beginning to pick up again, dragging a knot of plastic bags, whistling and sighing, over shrubs and stones. Waleed decided that in lieu of writing, food would have to do, so he caught a minibus taxi back to his own neighbourhood, Observatory.

His area sat in the dipped foot of the city, a valley of sorts, where some of the old architecture had survived. It was a little enclave of what the country might have been. On the Main Road, Victorian buildings stood just two stories high while thin pillars divided the street into small squares. In between the squares were shops that made a large part of their revenue from the sale of incense sticks, and smoky pool bars where the smell of dagga mingled with booze. One got the feeling that the area was charmed by its own shabbiness. In a city full of extraordinary poverty and spectacular riches, this place sat smack bang in the middle. Its occupants were a part of a gentler revolution of artists and academics whose collective conscience was pricked badly when they moved to Rondebosch or Tamboerskloof.

In Observatory everyone was robbed regularly, homes were broken into at least twice a month and cars were routinely stripped of sound systems and wheels. But Waleed's neighbours tended to shrug and place these incidents on a continuum with society's unequal distribution of wealth. Those who were parents used the moment to teach their children not about the moral vacuity of stealing, but rather the crisis of capitalism.

Waleed was comfortable in this place, more than any other. There were aspects of his first home in it (the District, with its turn of the century architecture, its nosiness, its knowingness), but more than that, Observatory was a tiny version of the world he would have built given the chance.

Just off Main Road there was a small public parking lot and around it another little collection of shops and bars. Some were Victorian houses turned public lounges, warm and wooded and roomy, others were fast-food joints where you could buy newspapers, milk, deep-fried snacks, hot chips and Rizla. There were several such places throughout the city and everyone had their favourite. Fati's Kitchen was Waleed's. Its sign was scripted in a faintly Eastern font, the "F" thick and curved with the dot on the "i" looking as though it should be resting above a pair of almond-shaped eyes. It had once been vermillion-red on a white field but years of sand and sun and wind had faded it to a turmeric stain against a backdrop of brown-flecked plastic.

Auntie Fati herself stood guard at the counter, a general at her post. Before her, encased in glass, was a buffet of deep-fried food, the sticky confectionery of Indian sweetmeats decorated with hallucinogenic greens and pinks, samoosas and baajias golden from hot oil, koesisters dusted with ground cardamom and desiccated coconut; the stuff of cardiac nightmares. Behind her, the fridge was packed tightly with psychedelic rainbow rows of fizzy Double-O cooldrink. Fati's hair was divided along a strong parting line laid flat by coconut oil. Her body was all hilly peaks and soft landings but she moved with surprising quickness on little feet that were always shuffling across the shop floor.

There was a line.

"Always a line," Waleed sighed to himself, and nodded in greeting to Fati.

He tried to use the time productively, picking his thoughts between choices: Mutton or vegetable roti? Gatsby or chip roll? Maybe he should pick something up for Anna?

Ahead of him was a stoned Rasta whose thickly coiled dreads were piled into a translucent black net, snakes in a bag. His eyes were red rimmed and swollen, widening only when they settled on a samoosa or a gulab jumun. The man seemed partially paralysed by the selection, struggling to decide between savoury and sweet, hovering near one, committing to it unequivocally, then seconds later abandoning his choice. Waleed watched him tap at the glass to point at an onion baajia and noticed his dry and puffy palms traced with faint white tell-tale lines that marked him as a button-kop, a mandrax addict.

Behind the Rasta was a group of five white girls, no older than eighteen, come straight from university. Waleed looked at them and thought of that irritating phrase that was already gaining popularity, The Nelson Mandela Generation. He noticed their differences, though they did not. Was this what getting older was about? They were dressed in gear he remembered vaguely from 1977, bright bellbottoms, those dreadful stack-high clogs, short iridescent skirts, fringes that fell over khol black-lined eyes, fifteen thin bangles an arm and inexpertly applied nail polish. *Inexpert on purpose?*

One girl tugged at her fringe, clipping it back with knowing fingers and no mirror and turned to the Rasta, voice raised. "Could you hurry the fuck up?"

Fati had been drumming her fingers on the countertop for some time. She shot the profaner a look and said, "Language, please. This is my shop, and I won't have it spoilt by your filth."

The Rasta smirked, giving her a conspiratorial grin, but she turned on him too. "*You.* You are currently dancing on my last nerve. If you cannot make up your mind, you are going to have to stand in the back of the queue."

Waleed realised he had lost his appetite. It was as if the encounter, the collision of three of the country's worlds – the Rasta, the white students, the shopkeeper – had all been too much. He turned around and left, feeling his body walk with some certainty, while his mind was curiously absent. He had only a vague, slivery notion of where he was headed and then he found himself in a taxi, this time bound for Walmer Estate. What a stupidly circuitous day it had been. Home. The District. Home. And now Walmers. Waleed looked round the kombi, taking, as always, rapid notes: an old man, his blazer frayed slightly at the edges, his left sleeve's button dangling from a weak thread, a teenage boy whose gelled curls looked like onion slices tossed in dressing, a woman cuddling her child towards her, arms thickly muscled beneath fat. He jumped off at the corner of Coronation Road and made his way to the home of Rashaad, a childhood friend who still lived with his mother. It was a place he was guaranteed a (secret) joint, a plate of food, and someone with whom to commiserate about those girls at Fati's Kitchen.

~

The matinee was in full swing. Raheem (The Love Machine) was on the decks exhorting the crowd in a fake American twang that reverberated from mike to speaker and back again. "All right Cape Town! We getting down this afternoon-noon-noon ... Can I get some noise from the ladies? Where are the ladies? Ohhhhhh-hooooooooo! And remember-member-member, no smoking on the dance floor-floor-floor."

Alia stood transfixed at the edge of the steps. The floor's black and white check was obscured by hundreds of rapid feet and swaying bodies. Two boys had leapt onto a table and were moving as loosely as if their limbs were held together by high-viscosity oil. A girl with hair tightly scraped back and a butt squeezed into white jeans cinched with a bronze studded belt was dominating the left corner. Her stomach strained against her black bodysuit while she tripped her feet double time against the beat. Her friends had formed a respectful circle around her, nodding and clapping and shouting as though her prowess reflected well on them all. Mikhail's baggy Aca Joe jeans and outsized Levi's T-shirt were a uniform. Alia felt as though she was seeing his outline in one of those rooms filled with mirrors where an image is replicated in a dizzying ad infinitum. Confined to a corner, as if the dance floor was an abstracted grid of the city and they were still obeying a now abolished law, was a group of black teenagers: they danced with their backs to the rest of the club, their movements a seamless blend of American music video sequences and 1950s kwela.

Farouk adjusted his golf-collar and grinned into the crowd and Alia realised with gathering dread that not even her beetle-crushers could make up for the Gothy whiteness of her get-up.

The song climbed towards its peak and the crowd flung their arms into the air as if to catch its spirit. The DJ mixed the follow-up song with such stealthy skill ("Che-che-check the beat out" and then moments later "Don't worry, be happy") that people whooped in appreciation. The synthetic murmur of a late '89 disco track filled the room. The tune bounced out of the speakers and into the feet of the dancers whose faces were wreathed in smiles of nostalgia; when you are sixteen even tunes from four years ago feel like a retrospective.

The fragile troika that was Mikhail, Alia and Farouk was already beginning to crack. Mikhail announced his intention to dance and did not invite either of his friends to join him. He moved like a shark through the crowd, greeting boys he knew and girls he had jolled with. He took up position somewhere in the middle of the floor and began to lean and tilt, too cool to actually perform any steps. Alia folded her arms across her stomach with a disapproving air, jealous of his supreme lack of self-consciousness, and said to Farouk, "He's dancing *next* to the beat."

Farouk laughed. He was immune to both Mikhail's attempts at distance and the beginnings of Alia's black mood, and he pulled lightly at her arm, trying to lead her to the floor. She shook her head and stalked off to a serendipitously empty booth. Hunched over, overcome with envy, she watched Farouk glide and groove. In a peculiar twist of fate, despite his clothing, which had already earned him the nickname "Carlton" (*The Fresh Prince of Bel-Air* being newly aired on South African television), Farouk could indeed shake a leg. The crowd, in which there was a strict and unforgiving hierarchy of coolness, began to look at him as though his clothing was a choice, not a disaster.

Alia checked her watch – how much longer would they have to stay? – and decided that this would be a good time to start smoking. She reached into her bag and drew out the box of Camel Mild. Her fingers trembled a little as she ripped at the cellophane. She went through three matches before she managed to light up successfully. She coughed and wheezed and spluttered, her eyes watered and she panicked, justifiably, that her thick mascara and liner were going to smudge. With her eyes squeezed shut, it took her a few moments to notice the boy standing in front of her, cooldrink in one hand, tissue in another. The objects, in tandem with his solemn pose, made him look (with the exception of his Malcolm x peak cap) oddly nineteenth century.

"You look as though you may need these," he said.

"Thank you." Alia reached gratefully for both. She gulped down the water, blew her nose and put out her cigarette, while he lit one with courtly ease and shouted obligingly, over her gulping, snotty ministrations.

"This is sort of a weird place, isn't it? All that standing in line, only to get in here and sit to one side and shout to be heard. Not exactly a jazz bar on the Left Bank is it?"

Here Alia, who had been nodding, looked at him, puzzled. He said quickly, "I'm Nicholas, by the way. *Nick*, you can call me Nick. If you want to."

They shook hands formally.

"Alia." She listened to his accent and made some rapid deductions. "Where do you go to school?"

"Canterbury," he answered, confirming her suspicions; the brother school to her own, populated by boys in khakis and boater hats.

"Oh," she smirked and inflected the word just enough to let him know she was judging him. His confident beam seemed to dim just a little and he began to gabble in a nervous way she recognised as her own.

"I hate it, it's an awful place. So elitist. I mean we still have cadets. Can you believe that?"

"Cadets?"

"It's like pre-army training. We have to march and polish boots and all that shit, and a master has a loudspeaker where he shouts commands."

"Jesus."

"I know."

"Why don't you just refuse?"

"We get caned. Six of the best."

Alia moved along her booth to make room for Nick. But instead of sitting, he said, "Do you want to dance?"

"No."

"But this is a great song," Nick persisted.

Alia chose a sceptical expression as her defence and Nick pressed on. "I mean it. Listen to the lyrics." He began to chorus them, distinguishing the words from the garish sound of the synthesizer. "Democracy is just a word / Often used but seldom heard / The army / Fights for money / But we fight for peace."

Alia got up and felt her arm hairs rise a little. "Is it South African?" she asked, hoping he would tell her that it was, that it was banned, that he knew for a fact they were listening to a smuggled copy of an underground recording and that this moment actually constituted an illegal gathering.

"No," said Nick, "it's a British band. Norman Cook."

Alia and Nick faced the dance floor with the detached wonder usually reserved for safari game drives. Both stuck their hands into jeans pockets, and rocked back and forth, studying their feet and the view ahead. They were rescued by Farouk, who looked both damp and euphoric from his recent gyrations. "Howzit, man." He slapped his hand into Nick's. "I didn't know you were here."

"Oh. Hi." Nick returned Farouk's handshake a little limply.

"You know each other?" Alia shouted above the music that had morphed into a disco classic that assured everyone that the beat would indeed go on.

"School," answered Farouk. "We played rugby against each other last term." He turned to Nick. "Great game, broe!"

Nick looked outraged. "I didn't play. I just served you guys oranges at half time. I was only there because I had to be – it was that or another detention, and I really wanted a weekend off."

Nick said this to Alia as though she was entitled to an explanation while Farouk groped towards a reply. "Detention, ja … *fully* … what a las, hey?"

Alia spied Mikhail coming towards them. Unlike almost everyone else, he didn't have to fight to get through the crowd; he had that special gift of being able to attract and repel people at whim. They parted as he stalked through, improvising moves to accommodate his path as if they were the chorus line in a Broadway show and he was the overpaid lead. When Alia tried to explain it to Nasreen later, "It's like he has this private magnetic force field or something," her sister snorted, saying, "It's called being popular."

Mikhail looked a little taken aback, as though he had not expected Alia and Farouk to know anyone else here. Introductions were made and Mikhail, having nothing to contribute to tales of meetings on a rugby field at half time, one boy wet and muddy from a tackle, the other crisp and fresh carrying a tray of oranges, filled the awkward gap with one word, "Coincidence."

Except it wasn't really. Not in Cape Town. Communities were drawn in tight legalised circles; coincidences were never surprising, they were inevitable. In addition, the city was a gossipy place that thrived on its own intimacies. People traded information like currency; long before the dot-com era Capetonians understood that personal knowledge was a form of wealth. If Nick, or Farouk, or Alia, or Mikhail went home and asked their parents about each other's families, a barrage of stories (some censored, some not) would be unearthed.

Nick's presence complicated the dynamics of this already mismatched coterie. He had taken an immediate (and wildly unfair) dislike to Farouk, offended by how easily the other boy negotiated school and the club. The two spaces were, in Nick's view, entirely incompatible. Farouk was blissfully unaware of this and proceeded to talk to him at length about "Simon's tackle" while Nick alternated between trying to win over Mikhail and make conversation with Alia. Mikhail stood with them, but kept looking around for another group to join. He had long ago made it a policy to dislike anyone who went to a private school. He had made an exception with Alia and Farouk because they had grown up together, but he didn't have any room left in his moral roster for newcomers. Alia kept glancing from Mikhail to Farouk and dragging her eyes up to Nick's cap, hoping that the politics of it would soothe Mikhail's stance, but she was met with blank indifference. Mikhail didn't know who Malcolm x was, and anyway, he didn't believe in branding his clothing with anything but a well-known, preferably American, label. Alia was feeling protective of Nick because she had, in the space of just a few minutes, developed a full-blown crush on him.

Leaning against the railing that separated the dancers and the sitters, she stole glances at him, studying his profile while he spoke to Mikhail (Nick was dropping the few Afrikaans phrases he knew, attempting, and failing, to find people in common). Beneath his cap, his hair was cropped in short, tight curls, so short they lay almost flat against his head while the front and sides were shaved at clean angles. He looked from certain angles like a marble Roman bust. It was too early to tell if he was going to be a beautiful man, but he was a beautiful boy. Terrible things could happen between now and then, features could overtake each other and destroy the delicate symmetry, limbs could stunt, promising calves could never bulge, a face could remain stuck in a cherubic phase so that the adult always looks like an ageing child. But for now, Nick was what Alia's grandmother would have called "easy on the eyes". He was laughing (too much) at something Mikhail had just said when Alia noticed that his eyelashes were wet and spidery-looking, like a girl's. She found herself inspecting them, wondering if he might be wearing mascara.

Nick was asking her something. She shook her head, shrugged and pointed to her ears.

He repeated himself, now almost shouting, "CAN YOU JAZZ?"

"CAN I WHAT?" she shouted back.

"JAZZ," he repeated unhelpfully.

Mikhail, who had not stopped casting his eye about for a better group to join, overheard the exchange and began to laugh with forced hilarity. Alia shot him a reproachful look, which only served to spur him to greater heights of cruelty. He began to speak over the beginnings of her question, his voice alive with sarcasm.

"Can she jazz? Ma broe, she will *rip up* this dance floor." He pronounced "dance" like Raheem did, with an American accent. He raised a finger to his chin, shaking his elegant neck from side to side, absurdly like an older, sympathetic aunt and began down a well-worn path of teasing. "Shame, but it's now not her fault, hey, she now always had difficulty with a disco beat. Now come! Now come!" he taunted. "Show us your styles there, Alia. Let's see you jazz! Nick, you mus' ma just druk her vas. Take her to the floor and you can lekker jazz up a storm together!"

Farouk was watching the exchange as he had done for years, laughing at Mikhail, feeling sympathy for Alia. Eventually the latter won out and he placed his hands on her shoulders and pointed her in the direction of five couples, who executed a series of smooth-sliding steps, hyphenated somewhere between a salsa and a waltz.

"*That's* jazzing," he said, "what they're doing. My parents do it all the time."

Nick joined in, his attempts to curry favour with Mikhail over. "Sure, it's like a Sunday afternoon thing in Cape Town. You braai, you push back the furniture, you pour the brandy and Coke—"

Here Mikhail spat out, "Only Christian parents do that," and looked at Nick accusingly.

Alia stared out at the gliding couples, watching girls twirling about their partners, boys controlling spinning bodies with the last extremities of their fingers. She noticed something and started to ask Nick about it.

"Why do they look so solemn? Why are they not even looking at each other?"

Nick took a long drag of a newly lit cigarette. "It's all about looking cool. You have to try and look totally nonchalant about how skilled you are. The better the dancer, the more uninterested they look in what they're doing."

"I'm out!" announced Mikhail. A club was for finding girls to jol with, not standing on the sidelines *talking*.

Alia watched him stride off and with him much of the afternoon's tension, while Farouk shook his head and let out a whistle, directed at no one and nothing in particular.

Reaching his hand into his pocket, Nick pulled out a little plastic moneybag with a small head of marijuana. "Do you guys smoke?" he asked the remaining two.

"No, broe," Farouk said quickly, and then apologetically, "I have allergies."

But Alia eyed the baggie greedily. "I do!" she said. "I mean, I haven't before, but I will. We can go upstairs, to the roof-deck. Mikhail's cousin says there's this place after the landing."

For the first time Nick allowed himself to look scornful. "I know about it," he said.

Alia walked in step with Nick, thrilled both to be alone with him and on a mission laced with such rebellion. They snaked through the crowd, passed the queues at the toilet, picked their way up the rickety stairs and flung the heavy emergency doors open into the bright light of the afternoon.

The deck was peopled by three little circles of smokers: the first was taking in the vast view of industrial Woodstock and the sheltering mountain, the second was making miniature examinations of each other's sneakers, checking for signs of fakery, and the third was focused on the serious business of rolling joints against a light breeze.

Nick made his way towards the last group. Five boys greeted him with great excitement, telling him his arrival was "blessed" because they had, just that moment, rolled their last. They were all tall and lanky and slightly unkempt, but had managed to convert their collective awkwardness into a confidence built up almost exclusively around rolling perfectly turned out joints.

In just two years they would be ravers in fitted tops and wide-legged bells, dropping ecstasy and acid like it was no one's business, but for now it was about progressive electronics and weed. These boys were perched somewhere between home and the world. They still hung hard at HAL's but they had also leapt onto white pastimes like rollerblading and Pantera and plugged into black subcultures like Rastadom and graffiti. They all rocked Mikhail's uniform but with personalised twists; one was wearing a New York Yankees shirt (though he had neither visited the city nor ever watched a baseball match), another sported a leather bracelet with red, yellow and green beads.

"This is Manfred – the *Man*," said Nick, beginning introductions, "Edgar, Dave, Sean, and AJ. Guys, this is Alia."

Alia noticed that Nick's accent was beginning to roughen up around the edges. These boys were from his neighbourhood and he had a different voice for them.

"Irie, Alia," said Manfred, fist-bumping her and handing her the joint.

"Right, right," said Alia. "*Irie*."

She pinched the joint between her thumb and index finger, forming two cheeky hollows when she took her first drag.

"Nice one, sistah," said Dave admiringly. "You smoke it like the Man – he always inhales like it's his last joint on earth."

Manfred, who moved even in stillness, shifted his head from bop to nod, gleeful and agreeing. Dave had just raised the group's favourite and most painstakingly embroidered topic. AJ, the quietest in the crew (and by his own measure, the coolest), offered his view. He did it in a low voice so that everyone would have to lean in slightly to catch what he was saying. He suggested that a joint should be smoked like a cigarette, that this was Africa, place of bounty, that there was no need to crowd around a single rollie like uncivilised Londoners, hoping, no, *begging* for a toke. There were standards. A sense of pride, honour. Edgar, large and loyal to AJ unto death, nodded deeply. When the joint came his way, he dwarfed it with his giant fingers and demonstrated his friend's belief, taking leisurely drags while carrying on his conversation until Dave, with a wide grin, took it off him, saying, "Gimba! You hogging it now, broe."

The joint was duly passed to Nick, who held it with brief deference before passing it on to Manfred, who proceeded in Dave's expression to "hit it like a motherfucker".

Alia watched this all unfold, her body encased in a sort of fascinated glow. The dagga had settled nicely, but with just two drags in her system, she wasn't sure if it was the weed – or the mere thought of it – that was tingeing everything with this aura of breezy-hazy defiance. Nick was deep in conversation with Dave and Edgar about a rumour that Depeche Mode was coming to Cape Town. "No way, broe! No fucking way!"

"I don't care what it takes, I am front row, ma broe – golden circle—"

"I'm there with you, brother ... front and centre—"

"Everything counts—"

"Because I am—"

"Your personal—"

"*Jesus!*"

Stoner chatting followed, a projection into that magical moment when they would pay long-awaited homage to Gore and Gahan until AJ broke the reverie gently. "Don't get too excited. They may only come next year and then only after the election, and then only if Mandela wins. Can't see them coming if the Nats get in. Can't see anyone wanting to come ever if that happens."

Nick shook his head as if to clear it, the effects of the weed slowing his outrage just a little. "There is no way. *No way* they are going to get in. Impossible."

"You say that," said AJ soberly, "but at least four people in this circle have parents voting for them."

Everyone began to look at each other suspiciously.

"Statistically anyway," AJ qualified.

"Well," said Dave, breaking the tension with a grin, "I account for two! Both my parents are voting Nat."

Manfred, whose parents had been ardent ANC supporters since the seventies, began to laugh. "Yooohhhhh, ma broe. I'm so *embarrassed* for you! That's *kak* embarrassing!"

Perhaps feeling a vague sense of familial esprit de corps, Dave began to make a half-hearted argument about the necessity of an opposition party in government but he abandoned it mid-sentence and trailed off, conceding, "Jaaaa … it *is* embarrassing."

The circle took up the subject and began to embroider it; this one had a mother in the UDF, this one had a sell-out uncle in the TriCameral Parliament, this one had a cousin who had been in solitary, another was still pissed off about having to stay home during the uprisings. Alia was quiet. Up to this moment she had not really considered which party her parents would support. She was pretty sure her mother would vote ANC, but her father was something of a mystery on these issues. He hated the Nats, but he didn't like the ANC's ties to the Communist Party, he was never going to vote for any of the cookie cutter parties that were cropping up, and he had laughed openly at a cousin who was campaigning for the newly minted Muslim Party. Adam felt edgy about anyone who asserted Africanist beliefs (with an eye on the bad news stories from up north) and was offended by the Christian-based movements, so Alia suspected that he might vote DP. She heard herself telling the group that her mother would go with Mandela and her father would go with Helen Suzman.

The jeering began en masse.

"The DP!" they chortled. "The DP?!"

"That's a bladdy joke!"

"White liberals?"

"Give me the Nats any day."

"Nothing worse than a white liberal!"

Alia struggled to speak above the fury of voices. "But don't you think ... don't you think ..." she found herself defending something she didn't believe in, "I really *think*," she was bleating now, and their boy-laughter grew louder, until she shouted, "Surely a liberal white is better than a racist one?"

A silence descended, as though she had taken the whole conversation far too seriously. AJ took a long drag of a cigarette and announced, "Well, you know what my mother always says ... 'Scratch a liberal and you find a Nat.'"

The boys emptied into laughter, backs were slapped, fists were bumped.

"One time, brother!"

"Irie, AJ!"

"Dread-ie, my man!"

Alia's fist was knocked too, to show that it was good-natured. No harm done. No foul. But she couldn't help but wonder if she had blown it badly with Nick.

A silence flew overhead. Manfred filled it by rolling a skinny joint – the last of the baggie – and passing it around with the same ceremony as a peace pipe which, in a sense, it was. The door opened and a song by Black Box drifted up. Manfred began to dance, moving his arms and legs as though he was balancing on a gliding skateboard. "De de de DE, de de de dede dedededeDE," he chanted while Dave clapped and whistled and punctuated each move with an "Aweh", and then transformed the lyrics, "Jou ma en pa is Ninja Turtles! *ow!* Mandela skop vir Buthelezi! *ow!*"

They had formed a circle around Manfred, Alia feeling a laugh taking shape on her face and rising through the windless, empty cavities of her skull, when Mikhail burst in on them, flinging the heavy door open, his face smarting at the fat clouds of smoke, his eyes squinting at the sun.

"We going now," he growled at Alia. "Shaheen is downstairs. Jasus, man! You are kak geroek! You just better not get me into trouble with your parents."

Alia waved him away, even as the first trace of paranoia skittered through her. Mikhail shook his head at all of them, turned heel in disgust and left.

She wandered down the staircase followed by Nick and they found themselves alone between the noise of the club and the goings-on on the roof deck. Alia stood with one foot arranged to accommodate a rusted hole in the step. Nick stood one step above her, so that they could pretend that he was taller. The moment unfolded in a mixture of gloomy yellow light, the burnt smell of rust, and some thin traces of marijuana. They leaned in, as if by mutual design, for a kiss. It was the first for Alia, the fourth for Nick. Neither said anything afterwards. She placed her head against his elevated chest, took a deep breath as if to store up his boy-smell, and said, "I'll call you," before walking away.

Her triumph would last all the way down the stairs and

into the noise of the club until a series of questions slammed up against her mind: Should I have said I'd call? Was that stupid? Will he call me? Should I have kissed him? What if I did it wrong? How do I get hold of him?

Her internal interrogation was matched only by Mikhail's external one. "Where were you? Have you gone mad in your head? Did you even know those boys? Do you know what people think of girls who smoke?! And he's *Christian*. I mus' jus' tell your father and then you'll see!"

"See what?" said Alia but her stomach began to stutter and curdle under his threats all the same.

Mikhail stood with his hands on his hips and Alia thought suddenly, though she had never noticed it before, that he was a bit like a pigeon, all puffed chest and strutting. She blinked, adjusting her eyes to the strobes and flashing lights (which were admittedly somehow brighter and a little more animated), gathering herself, and then said with deliberate imperiousness, "Actually, I think I am ready to go. You?"

Mikhail gave her a cold hard look and stalked off to find Farouk.

Shaheen drove home sedately; it was almost magriep and he was, underneath it all, a respectful boy. Farouk spoke enthusiastically about his school's upcoming cricket team tryouts, while Mikhail alternated between shaking his head ruefully at Alia and telling Farouk that his school was populated entirely by untalented homosexuals. Alia did not come to Farouk's defence, nor did she ask Shaheen to turn up the music to drown out the talking. Instead, she watched the hills of her neighbourhood rise up as if for the first time: something she could not yet name had shifted, changed, been made anew.

4

Saturday, 9 January 1993

A kitchen, early evening. In it, a mother and daughter, preparing a meal. It was a lesson for them both. For the girl it was how to make her favourite dish, for the woman it was how to hold herself still against the fast-moving shifts in her child's mood. Now curious, now helpful and full of moments from the not-so-long-ago past, now surly and sighing, resentful of even the smallest task, critical of the state of her mother's spice cupboard, annoyed at where the rice was kept. Zarina tried to remember if it had been this way with her own mother. But the elegant, shadowy figure that had moved though her girlhood in a haze of cigarette smoke, peppermint lozenges and migraines had seldom been in the kitchen. And if she was, it only was to fill up on the idea of food. She would walk into the unfamiliar room, lift the lid on a pot the housekeeper was watching, take a long lingering gulp of the flavoured air and declare herself full enough for the next week.

"Mom? *Mom?*"

Her daughter was calling her back to this pot.

"Honestly," Nasreen continued, "it's a wonder you don't burn the food, you are *such* a daydreamer."

Zarina wondered when her daughter had found this new voice laden with sarcasm, filled with wisdom. Nasreen did not have to be on familiar ground to take a stance. It could be anywhere. Now in the kitchen among the spices she could not name, last week in the city centre when they had been caught in one of the mass marches, the last demonstrations against a dying regime. Zarina, timid, a little frightened by the crowds, had gripped her child's arm. Nasreen had shaken her hand off impatiently, saying that her fear was rooted in an unarticulated terror of black people. When did this start, thought Zarina. Was it this summer? Or was it the summer before?

The onions, long past translucence, were beginning to brown. She shook the heavy-bottomed orange pot against the flames, moving the oil around more freely, and began to spoon in her spices, hands and mouth working together – "First the jeera and mustard seeds, wait until they darken and pop" – while her mind kept edging down another path. When had she and this child broken apart? Had their closeness only been out of necessity? Did all children cling to their parents and then run from the village screaming for liberation the moment they could? This child of hers, perfectly formed, her body in delicate, precise proportions, her movements small and deft. Her other child (still too young to run?) was a long, lanky thing made up of rectangles and flailing limbs. She heard her now, feet pounding up the stairs to the front door, the inevitable almost-trip, the soft moan, "Oh shit," and the bungle with the keys. Alia always crashed into the house, walking blindly into the hallway table, tripping over the carpet-fringe, falling off a perfectly still couch. Her body was almost always covered in bruises that Zarina had had to explain away to concerned teachers for years.

Alia walked towards the kitchen, relieved to be home. Here was what she knew. The smell of mutton curry cooking, the last light before the athaan. Here it all was. Despite the day's events, it had not changed, it had not disappeared. The world had remained. When she was little, her mother seemed to her to be a magician of sorts, someone who conjured food from nowhere, who cast spice into pots like so many spells, a woman who could manage fire. Unlike Nasreen, she didn't want to learn these secrets. This was part of her mother's mystery, the same mystery that meant Zarina would smile while she cleaned her house, that she sniffed at fresh laundry with deep satisfaction, that she stood like a vigilant general between the clean surfaces of her house and the world's armies of dust.

Alia stood in the doorway of the kitchen, slightly mesmerised by a bowl of tangerines. Had they always been so ... *orangey*?

Her mother and sister turned to her.

"Did you have a nice time?" asked Zarina. "What did you watch?"

Alia waited a fraction too long, forgetting the lie that had secured the afternoon at the club. Nasreen, in a rare gesture of rescue, mimed a microphone reminding Alia of the movie they had seen the week before.

"The Commitments!" Alia shouted, pitching her voice too high, backing up her lie by trotting out an absurd Irish accent. "Sure, it was a grand flick."

Her mother laughed. She was like this, never casual with her children's jokes; they were always funny, their observations always new.

"Come here and taste for me, Alia," she said, holding up the spoon. "My nose is blocked. Is there enough salt?"

Alia pursed her lips over a turmeric potato, and the taste of it, its warm comfort, made her lean into her mother's shoulder. She was almost taller than her now. Just a few months ago, mother and daughter had locked easily against each other, child into parent. Now limbs had to be readjusted, new angles had to be found. Zarina took this part of parenting seriously too; hugs, kisses, touched faces were all in daily supply. She gave them even when they were unwanted, unasked for, and in this unusual moment of being sought out and needed, she pulled the girl tight towards her. She breathed into the brown curls and then snapped back. "Have you been smoking?"

Alia's stomach flipped over. Her cheeks flooded with guilt and her breath became shallow until she realised that her mother meant cigarettes, not dagga. Immediately she went on the defensive. "It wasn't me! It was people *around* me!"

Zarina adopted a tough pose, hand on hip, all business. "You better be telling the truth. You just wait till your father gets home."

Nasreen shrugged, coming to her aid: "I don't see what the big deal is, Dad used to smoke."

By the time Adam walked in, hot and tired from a day of weekend work at his fabric shop, the Dawoods had taken on a collective bad mood. Everyone brought a sort of soured gloom to the table. Zarina didn't mention the word "tobacco", but Adam's nose circled with the disgust and jealousy of an ex-smoker when he kissed Alia hello. She rallied once again. "It wasn't me! It was people—"

"Around you," he completed in an echo. "Yes, I'm sure."

To drive her point home, Alia's voice rose in self-justifying registers. "I *hate* smoking. I hate the way it stays in your hair and your clothes, that *smell*."

Nasreen gave her one of her coded looks: too much ... keep it simple. But Alia was long gone. She had moved from just attacking smokers to the Surgeon General's warning. "It's so self-destructive! What kind of person intentionally goes about killing herself? And it's not like the government actually help the situation, with their deals and ..." She stopped. She had no data to back up her feeling but she was one of those people who tended to believe their own cant. If she was mid-tirade, she would continue, perhaps unsure of her own logic, edged along by a deep sense of what was just, until both she and the point became unassailable. The weed further jeopardised any possibility of coherence, so she just abandoned one thread and picked up another. "I mean, we should be *campaigning* ... or *organising* ... or something ..." She petered out, a little deflated.

But Adam had lost interest, he was panicked about an upcoming strike and enraged at Nasreen's support of it. "Strikes only ever mean another broken shop window, my girlie, another afternoon hiding behind the register, of wondering if everyone would make it home on the trains okay." Letting out one of her customary sighs, Nasreen finished her meal, pushed back against the chair and said, "I'm going to my room."

Her mother called after her, "It's your turn to do the dishes," but her daughter's defiant back, the disdainful shrug of a delicate shoulder without turning around said no. Adam seldom interfered with the domestic but tonight everything felt out of hand; Alia's smoking, Nasreen's saunter. He could raise his voice to a pitch faster than most, and he used that skill now, while scraping emphatically at his plate. "Nasreen, you get back here this minute and help your mother!"

Nasreen turned around. "Can't," she said with a tight smile of triumph. "I've got to prepare for school. So much homework from the holidays."

Adam raised both hands to acknowledge her victory and send her on her way. The remaining Dawoods sat at the table, each wrapped in a different form of silence: Alia still slightly stoned and skittish, internally replaying her afternoon with Nick frame by frame, Adam grim, Zarina distracted, dishing up more rice, eating the curry no one had thanked her for making. No one bothered to make conversation. Alia was flipping the meaty tastiness of the mutton over in her mouth and considering relaunching her anti-smoking diatribe, when the doorbell rang.

"Oh *God*" Adam moaned. "Who could be coming here now? At this hour, this is outrageous, it's *supper*time."

"It's probably Taatie," said Zarina.

Taatie was the neighborhood's homeless beggar and madman. He raced up the Walmer Estate hills armed with a stick, a haversack and a stream of muttered observations. He was always specific about what he asked for, be it food or money: he'd been known to return the extra orange or offer you change. ("Just the apple is fine. Here's a twenty cent back, I mos only asked for a three rand.") Alia leapt out of her chair. An encounter with Taatie was always welcome, somewhere between comedy and prophecy. She swung the door open, saw who it was, and launched herself into the visitor's arms.

"Uncle Waleed!" she shouted and began to call to her father. "Dad! Daddy! Daaaad, Uncle Wa*leed* is here!"

She clung to Waleed's arm, leading him into the kitchen where her parents stood.

"We thought it was Taatie," Adam laughed.

"Jesus, is he still alive?" said Waleed, not bothering to say hello either.

Zarina was already heating food for him. "You staying for supper. No, no, it's not a question. I've made you a plate already. Don't be silly, it's no trouble."

Adam talked over her. "Of course he is staying. How often do we get to see you? You *must* stay. Nasreen is here tonight too. Not with her friends for once. Nas*reen*! Your Uncle Waleed is here! Come down!"

Always less impressed than others, Nasreen sauntered in. "Hello," she said to him coolly, "haven't seen you in a while."

To which Waleed, who responded well to those who snubbed him, replied enthusiastically, "Yes! I was wondering how you all were! Thought I would come by."

Alia spoke in and over her parents, vying for Waleed's attention. The last remnants of the weed were gone, the adrenalin brought about by her uncle's visit had seen to that. She talked incessantly about her school, dancing a clumsy line between caricature and admiration. Waleed ran a thin finger continuously over a snake-like scar on his left hand, the result of a small but awful encounter with a policeman in the eighties in his own playground. He had not yet learned how to indulge this child. Everything about her screamed their difference: the clipped ends of her words, the swallowed vowels, the easy way she spoke to her parents, the casual references to things like hockey and tennis and art class and piano lessons, the endless anecdotes about Debating Society and swimming galas, the way she looked to him for approval when she chattered about her friends Sophie's and Katie's tennis-courted homes in Bishopscourt. He felt his skin crawl. Alia carried on blithely, for once not noticing Nasreen's glares, assuming her kicks under the table were not deliberate.

Zarina fussed about Waleed. He was her cadre in her skirmishes with her mother-in-law, rolling his eyes gamely at whatever came out of the older woman's mouth. She fried up extra papir and searched through her pantry for his favourite pickle. She asked about his thesis (still going) and about his white Christian girlfriend, Anna (still going). Adam was mostly quiet and Waleed knew he was trying to work out the purpose of the visit: he usually only came by when he needed something, a small loan, or someone to accompany him on a visit to their mother.

The two men were unalike. There were physical similarities; the same thin, high-bridged nose with the slight bump that gave it an uneven profile, the same eyes, hooded and dark beneath deep brows, and the same residual internal scars from a "difficult childhood". But in adulthood they had chosen to wear those scars quite differently. Adam had chosen the safety of the world of commerce where, except for laws around ownership of property and business, he was a free agent. Waleed had chosen the realm of agonised imaginings and his doctoral thesis, *How political trauma limits creative output*, now six years in the writing, was both his revenge and his uneasy obsession. For Waleed, it was personal. He felt his life and his work had been royally fucked by apartheid; he was convinced that the conclusion of the research was dependent on the end of the system.

Nasreen watched her uncle closely, not saying very much. Her admiration and love was always offered at a slight distance. He turned to her in the midst of one of Alia's interminable stories and said, "What standard are you in again?"

"Nine," she answered, a little warily.

Waleed assumed an expression of interest but he felt as though he was mimicking something he had once seen on a sitcom: concerned uncle, reluctant niece.

"So just one more year until Matric?"

"Yes."

He pressed on. "And that's when the pressure really begins, hey?"

Nasreen shrugged and Zarina leapt into the little pocket of quiet that gathered. When they were not alone, the Dawoods were no good with awkward silences.

"You would think it would only begin in Matric, but honestly, they work these kids *so* hard. You should see the homework they have. I think it's completely over the top." She gave her daughter's shoulder a supportive squeeze and Nasreen squirmed with embarrassment. Waleed smiled, somewhere between kindness and envy.

"Have you decided what you want to do after school?"

She glanced at her father. "Well, I'd like to start out with a BA, and then just see how things go."

"Which we think is a great idea," Zarina interjected with a beam. "UCT, obviously."

"She might even get there before you finish!" Adam alone cackled at his own joke.

"And then, I don't know," Nasreen continued, "I'll see from there. Maybe psychology, maybe law."

"Maybe nothing?" Waleed had said it with a grin, but Adam gave him a censorious glance and said with a forced laugh, "Hah! None of that. Don't go putting ideas into her head."

They were intended innocently enough, but Waleed's questions, like all lines of enquiry in this family, had rolled around the room gathering the moss of history. The adults at the table turned their minds in unspoken unison to 1985, when Waleed had had a brief foray into law school. Adam had approved. "Fantastic! You can handle all my legal stuff. Always keep it in the family." But law school was short-lived. Waleed had found the lectures tedious and the coldness of law's (only rarely) resistant language repellent. He longed for the furious rants of struggle writers and artists, not these attempts at careful, measured reasoning from strategic men. ("It's pathetic," he said after a lecture on constitutional law, "any attempt to work within the system fails before it begins.") His dropping out had been the source of a bitter fight between him and his brother. "I've never *heard* of anything so selfish. I would have given anything to go to university. I didn't even have the option. Had to go straight to work, didn't I? Straight into peddling whatever I could to put *you* through!"

Waleed had stalked off in a cold fury, while his brother remained simmering in a hot one. Neither man was good at reconciliation, for which those twin virtues of flexibility and culpability are essential. They did not speak for several months and by the time they did, Waleed had registered for an Arts degree and would skulk round their mother's house smoking rollies and quoting Hegel.

The meal finished, the girls trailed upstairs reluctantly, Zarina went to make a phone call, and the brothers nibbled at the last bits of papir. They sat in an asymmetrical silence, Waleed feeling the first pocket of peace in a day full of unexpected stresses. "Actually," he began as though answering Adam's unspoken question, "I just came up from Rashaad's place."

"The Jacobses? Coronation Street?"

"Ja. His mommy sends her salaams."

Adam nodded and offered reciprocal greetings. "You heard what happened to their cousin, hey? Hell, but that was now something."

"Which cousin?" Waleed felt himself being lured into a dramatic narrative that had nothing to do with him. It was why he relished his visits to his old world and why he kept them so brief.

"Boeta Amien, up in Joburg. He was hijacked in broad bladdy daylight. Now-now, the other day."

"Huh." Waleed inspected a piece of hard papir that had not been fully fried up.

"That's all you have to say?" Adam shook his head as though Waleed's one-syllabic answer put him in alliance with the crime and its perpetrators.

"Is he okay?"

"I suppose so. I mean, they took his car off him. At gunpoint no less. Probably some of your lot."

Leaning back in his chair, arms locked behind his head, Waleed offered his brother a bemused face. "Writers?"

Adam looked at him irritably until Waleed said, "How are things at the shop?"

"The same. There may be a strike next week."

Waleed reached for more coffee and wondered if Adam had said this to bait him – a bait which, after a brief struggle, Waleed took. "Damn those troublemakers wanting a living wage."

"Oh for fucksake. Here we go again. How many times must I tell you? No one who works for me wants to strike. Every one of them makes a decent living. It's the unions again!"

"Okay. *Relax*, ek sê!" Waleed scowled into his cup.

"Mass action. Hah! Mass-bladdy-*in*action. Nothing gets done. No one gets paid. Nobody eats." Adam wagged a finger at Waleed who in turn had tilted his head towards the ceiling, declaring at once his disagreement and disinterest. They held those poses, Waleed gazing upwards, Adam frozen mid-gesture, until Waleed broke the small silence, saying, "I went to the District today." He said it casually, tilting his face to avoid looking directly at Adam.

"Why?"

"I don't know – I go sometimes."

"Oh." Adam rapped at the table as if to announce the subject was closed. "Do you want some decent coffee? I have this new French press thing."

"Ja. Okay."

He unpacked the press and filled the kettle with water, and with his back still turned, said, "Don't mention to Zarina that you went, it upsets her still." He held the freshly ground beans up to Waleed's nose. "Smell that! I found a man from Mozambique in town … imports this … says this is the only stuff he'll drink."

~

Alia sat at her desk scribbling furiously in her journal. To her, Waleed's visits were rare but treasured, a reason for celebration and excitement. Her parents never visited his Observatory house and Alia was not allowed to take taxis so she'd long ago decided that her uncle's life was one of bohemian splendour. Not for him the slavish devotion to bonds and the acquisition of *things*. He stood apart, someone who had forged a different, better path. One day, she would introduce him to Nick.

What a day! Soooo much to write about. Can't think where to begin. Nick, Uncle Waleed. Family first ... family takes precedence I guess ...

"*Family takes precedence* ... over what? Who, pray tell, is Nick?"

Nasreen had snuck up behind Alia.

"You cow!" said Alia, huddling over her book, glaring at her sister. "You're the one who always goes on and on about privacy and your *space* and ..."

She was working herself up into happy self-righteousness when Nasreen interrupted. "Oh, relax," she said, flinging herself on the bed. "I've done enough for you today ... covered for you about HAL's and the whole smoking thing. Besides, I'm not really interested in your personal life."

"You're not?" said Alia, awash with disappointment.

"Nope ... I just wanted to check something with you."

"What?" asked Alia, full of a thrill she could not name. Nasreen never sought her out.

"You know when Uncle Waleed stayed here?"

"Which time?" Alia began to pack away her journal, making a show of secrecy.

"Years ago, ages and ages," said Nasreen, ignoring the performance, "when he was here for a long time."

"When that boy was here?"

"Yes. Do you know why he left?"

Alia was gripped by a sudden panic. She felt her breath shorten and her stomach lunge into her coccyx. "No," she answered her sister, lying to her for perhaps only the third time in her life, "do you?"

"Yes."

Nasreen looked at the ceiling and then swung up an arm to swipe at the unstable bookshelves above Alia's pillows.

"Jesus, aren't you afraid these things will kill you in your sleep?"

Alia shrugged, as though her ability to sleep through imminent death were a virtue.

"Do you remember when Waleed took us fishing ... for sand sharks in Hout Bay?"

Alia did remember. Flat on their stomachs on the hot cement of the pier, legs in the air like upside-down tables, dangling thin curling fishing gut with tiny hooks into the pull and froth of the shallow part of the ocean. Beneath the water the sand sharks black and flat, moving between thick woven ropes and columns of light. Alia had caught one, so had Nasreen, both times they were exultant, triumphant, tugging at the gut while the fish had flipped and bled, both times Waleed had unhooked the creatures and gently, gently sent them back into the water. Later, when the sun was setting and the sea was beginning to darken and cool, he had heated their hands and stomachs with hot chips, shown them how to douse them with vinegar and learn to love the sour acid taste of it.

Then Alia did something she hadn't done in years. She took off her beetle-crushers, climbed onto the bed, curled herself into a half-moon and put her head in Nasreen's lap. The older girl let her and began, almost unconsciously, to stroke her sister's hair, smoothing out a few soft damp curls that had gathered at her forehead. They stayed like that for a few minutes, until they both separated, as if by invisible command.

8 May 1986

Waleed and Adam are engaged in one of their not-speaking stand-offs. Adam will not forgive Waleed for leaving law school and expects Zarina to join him in condemnation. But Zarina is torn between loyalty and self-preservation because Adam is a useless ally when visiting Fozia.

It is Waleed, full of rebellious charm even in a domestic setting, who offers his sister-in-law social refuge, a silent, sly camaraderie.

But all is thrown into chaos, all solidarity is suspended, when Waleed decides to get dreadlocks. It is not an easy task. His hair, straight and thick, is a reluctant accomplice. He perseveres, taking his instructions from a combination of newly discovered identity politics and the seductive cool of a collection of Bob Marley LP covers. Waleed tweaks and teases, dips his head into buckets of salt water and rubs the slowly clumping strands together with beeswax. At first there is resistance. The careful corkscrews unwind and the wax falls onto his shoulders in discarded crumbs. He carries an afro-pick with him wherever he goes and works his scalp whenever he can, coaxing and coercing it into obedience. When he is at home he hides his head under a nubby woollen beanie, letting the follicles toil away with all the secrecy of a scientist in an atomic lab. One morning he wakes up, reaches for his head, feels the hair wrapped around itself in tiny miniature locks and he knows that it is his Einstein poster moment. He strolls from his bedroom to bathroom and bumps into his mother along the way. Fozia opens a Munch mouth. Waleed performs a little two-step victory shuffle in response; her silent scream can only mean that his hair is a success.

When she recovers her voice, Fozia immediately begins to call her family. She starts with Adam and works her way steadily through four sisters, two brothers and an army of cousins. She opens each conversation with the shrieking sentence, "You will not *believe* what this child of mine has done this time! He has become a filthy Rasta!" Sometimes she has to explain what a Rasta is and these explanations stop her short. She knows nothing of the gentle art of rolling a joint, the rhythmic nodding of one's head in agreement with a beat, the understanding that "Jah" is the name of God not the Afrikaans word for "yes", and so in fury she bellows down the phone, "It means he has become a bladdy good-for-nothing skollie! That's what it blessed well means. My son, the univarsty-high-an'-mighty-I-can-quote-Shakespeare is a bladdy skollie." She stops herself from saying what they all know anyway: that Rasta is code for black, that Waleed has gone native, that he doesn't know how good he has it, that there are people out there who would *kill* for his hair, that his ingratitude is insufferable, it's insulting, it's just wrong. Wrong.

When she runs out of blood relatives she begins to talk over her fence to whichever neighbour will listen. She even confides her woes to her Christian neighbour, Mrs May Erensen, because she knows, though each woman privately thinks the other will burn in the everlasting flames of hell, that *this* is a subject upon which they can agree. In floral house-dresses that clash with their gardens the women accept support from the walls and each other. They touch their own heads as if to protect the hair on it, hair that has only ever been straightened or swirled or scarved.

May blinks repeatedly as Fozia speaks, widening her eyes a little more each time to indicate her growing horror. She has always been slightly jealous of Fozia. Her own sons dropped out of high school and now spend their days drunk in dingy bars listening to easy jazz covers, while Fozia, a loyal but not particularly sensitive friend, wastes no opportunity to brag about Adam's financial success or Waleed's academic prowess. The crisis of Waleed's hair gives May a certain tight satisfaction, and she milks each moment with precision.

"You know, hey, Fozy, I now don't know much about this Rasta nonsense, but what I do know is that they all smoke a lotta dagga and you know it's a hop, skip an' a jump to buttons."

Though the day is hot, Fozia feels her bones chill. She has always been susceptible to a dramatically timed sentence, her own or someone else's: hair can be cut; drugs are harder to get rid of. She runs inside to phone Zarina, cloaked in a new panic. "Waleed is becoming a button kop," she chokes. "I don't know how far along he is, but I know it's just a matter of time, just a hop, skip and a jump before he is stealing my copper pots and melting them down."

When all Zarina returns with is a collection of non-committal sounds, Fozia's terms become concrete. "I am telling you, and I am telling Adam: I don't want him *near* the girls. This child needs to be stopped and admitting it is the first step. That's what Mrs Erenson says and she should know, her boys are all drunks. Don't you let him in the house."

"Mama, Waleed is just being young. He's just experimenting."

"With what? Experimenting with bladdy *what*? With *drugs*? If his father was alive he would give him such a bladdy klap."

"No, Mama, I mean he's finding himself ..."

"Now listen, I don't know what you talking about. I mos didn't go to *univarsity* ... I'm probably just too stupid to understand what you saying."

"I just mean Waleed is finding out who he is, and maybe this is part of it."

"What you mean who he is? He is a Dawood, he is my son and he is a Muslim. Finish and *kla*. You want to tell me now it's not enough to be my child or his father's child, or Allah's child?"

In Zarina's silence, Fozia reads a triumph of logic and strategy. One down! She has spent most of the day in tears, but feels, suddenly, an impish grin spread across her mouth. "Okay, but anyway, thanks for listening, hey? I have to go now. Tell Adam he must come see me tomorrow."

~

That night Waleed returns to a house that is curiously still. His mother is not in the kitchen cooking, but sitting in the dark, smoking a cigarette, listening to Cole Porter.

"Good choice," he says to her by way of greeting. "Nothing like a little Cole in the evening."

Fozia doesn't answer him immediately. She exhales and studies the tip of glowing coal for a long moment.

"I've been sitting here, trying to work out what you think you are doing. Why you are doing it. And I can only think of one thing."

"Oh?" Waleed is intrigued. It is unlike his mother to offer analysis. He considers it an olive branch. Gratefully, he reaches for it.

"You are doing it to hurt me. You are trying to get me back for wanting you to be a lawyer. For wanting the best for you." Fozia begins to rock herself slightly like a woman in mourning. "You give and give and *give* as a mother and you ask for just a few things in return: that they don't steal from you or kill you in your sleep. When your father died, he thought he was leaving me in good hands. I can almost see that man turning in his grave." She looks into the distance as though she is summoning her husband to return. Waleed has to resist following her gaze, for a moment imagining his father Abe, transparent, weary even in death, arriving to mediate, yet again, between mother and son. He chooses derision instead.

"Oh, for God's sake."

Fozia's head jerks up and she raises a hand that both testifies and admonishes, as though the combination of his locks and blasphemy are too much for her to bear, but Waleed beats her to the righteous finish line.

"That really is the limit, Mommy ... talking about Daddy in that way? You must either say you sorry or I am leaving this house."

Waleed thinks he has played it beautifully: he can have his hair and style it too. He has delivered the perfect ultimatum. His mother hates to be alone; her days revolve around taking care of him. ("Your clothing is done." "What do you want to eat tonight?" "I put new sheets on the bed.")

But he hasn't counted on her social panic and he hears the full weight of it in her voice now ragged from tears and smoke.

"Leave! Then just *leave*. I don't know how I am going to show my face to anyone anyway."

Shocked, Waleed looks at his mother: in all their arguments, and there have been many over the years – bunking madressa, facing expulsion because of his refusal to attend woodwork ("I won't be turned into a handyman for white people"), marching down to Caledon Square to demand the release of one of his imprisoned high-school teachers, the endless stream of visible and invisible Christian girls – she has never told him to leave, she has never thrown him out.

Waleed stalks towards his bedroom. Fozia unable, even now, to let him from her sight, follows. He scoops the clothing that his mother has carefully washed and ironed, talking as he packs. "Ja. You *say* you won't be able to show your face and then there'll be some crisis, some scandal. Some poor unmarried girl who gets pregnant, or someone will lose their job, or be found out as a gambler, or an adulterer, and Mama will be lured to the garden wall again."

He knows it is his cheeriness that strikes her as the most

disrespectful thing. Passion, anger, hurt, tears, shouting, all these would have been more permissible, less offensive. But Waleed has begun to inhabit the upbeat disregard of a diffident Englishman who is bidding a formal farewell to his landlady. To this Fozia is unequal, and as she charges after her son down the dim corridor towards the front door, she flings out her final accusation, perhaps the most damning. "Don't you bladdy come keep yourself *white* with me!"

"Surely, Mama, you mean quite the opposite," says Waleed as he pointedly twirls his strongest dreadlock, fixes his headphones over his ears, and gently shuts the door on his mother's stricken face.

~

Waleed and Adam have not spoken since he left law school but there are moments that only a sibling will ever understand. Regardless of their own bickering and arguments and divergent world views, Adam knows Waleed, Waleed knows Adam, and they both know their mother.

When Waleed rings the doorbell, Adam, fresh from a phone call from an inconsolable Fozia, opens it without a word, takes the duffel bag from his brother's shoulder and leads him into the spare room that has already been made up for him. "We had a suspicion you would be here in the next few days," he says wryly.

Waleed throws himself on the bed and lights a rollie. "She's mad. She is absolutely mad. She said some terrible things to me."

"Yes, well," Adam shifts from one foot to the other, "you know how she gets."

Waleed shuts his eyes as if he is very tired. "She even said" – and here he allows for a slow chuckle – "She even said, I mustn't keep myself white."

When Zarina appears in the doorway, the men are still laughing and repeating "keep myself white".

"Oh, Waleed, I think your hairstyle is fantastic. Very mod."

"Don't be ridiculous, Zina, the hairstyle is a joke. It's not even his own, and it looks bladdy dirty."

"Well, *I* like it. And what do you mean it's not his own? It's on his head so of course it's his own."

From behind a wisp of smoke Waleed rewards Zarina with a comradely wink while Adam goes in search of the girls to tell them about their new house guest.

~

In the weeks ahead, Waleed comes and goes as he pleases, occupying that peculiar space of freedom that is one of the advantages of living in an older sibling's house. He is relieved of his usual duties and pretences: he doesn't need to lie about making salaat, or have to play his reggae records softly or hide eating meat outside of the house. Waleed's visit grants Alia and Nasreen a sense of holiday: the ordinary is shot through with the celebratory. It isn't that he spends a great deal of time with them, but his youth and his energy disseminate a sort of independent magic; their parents feel lighter, younger. Their mother laughs more and their father's bad moods recede in depth and frequency. Adam appears to have forgiven Waleed for leaving law school and indulges the steady pile of banned literature that his brother presses on him. Suppertime lasts longer, there are late-night discussions in the lounge: the girls are shooed to bed but they sit, unseen, arms wrapped around their legs, at the top of the staircase, listening in, fleetingly close to adult conversation, not understanding any of it, but absorbing the laughter, watching in wonder as their father allows Waleed to borrow his precious jazz records, stunned when they see him roll and smoke the occasional cigarette. Even Waleed and Fozia seem to reach a truce; he always wears a beanie when he occasionally visits her and she pretends that it is a modern-day fez, telling the neighbours that her son is embracing an ascetic branch of Islam. When Waleed pins up his UDF flyers and a poster of Che on the wall in the spare room, the girls are elated. They think it means he is staying for good.

5

Monday, 11 January 1993

"And so, it is with great sadness that at the end of this term, I will bid you all, not goodbye, but au revoir ... 'til we meet again."

Mr Gresham lifted his rectangular smile towards the assembly of girls and three hundred of them looked back. They ranged in age from five years old (impatient and sweet in turned-down white socks) to seventeen (legs encased in regulation stockings, faces full of learned expressions of interest). Mr Gresham had been speaking for perhaps forty-five minutes: an inordinately long time, even by his standards. But this was his farewell performance and he was speechifying towards a legacy. The pleasure and engagement of his audience was fleeting, but the reproduction of the full text in the school magazine was forever. He sat down, swishing his academic robes with great effect; it would have looked slightly camp had he not been so utterly asexual.

Dutifully, the students of St Michaels applauded while Mr Gresham lifted a puffy, dry palm as if to say *Please. No, really. Seventeen years of service here has been the mere fulfilment of a pleasurable duty.*

Alia staccatoed her clap into a sarcastic beat. She was sitting next to the new girl (very pretty, maybe Xhosa, completely unreadable) who stared ahead pretending not to notice Alia's cynical rhythm. Gresham, Alia thought, looked a little like a large grey bat. His suit, an ugly merging of brown and grey, was the same colour as his thinning hair, and his ears sprouted out from his head as if they were tuning in for a high-pitched signal. Alia loathed this man and she often cited his external ugliness as proof of his morally defective insides. Across the hall she spied Nasreen flicking through her hymnbook, not bothering to participate in the applause. It was Nasreen who had told her about how Gresham had made their father wait for three long and humiliating hours outside his office before he'd let him put in an application for them. It was Nasreen who had given her the little titbit she now whispered to the new girl. "You know he's an ex-Rhodesian? Used to go to South-West too. Got on his horse to hunt SWAPO during the war. Shot them on sight. But he's on his way out. I heard from my mother that he's been asked to leave because he can't move-with-the-times. I'm Alia, by the way."

"I'm Lizzie."

"Lizzie? Like Elizabeth."

"No, like Lizzie. L-I-Z-Z-I-E."

"Quiet, you two." Angela James, a tiny rail-thin girl who had begun campaigning to be head-girl since she was eleven, shot them both a look. Alia narrowed her eyes at Angela. They fought regularly, sometimes bitterly, sometimes with a sort of weary indifference, but it was a spat about last year's referendum that really tipped them into full-scale war. For months St Michaels, like the rest of the country, had talked of little else. On the day the results came in, the girls were ushered en masse up to the Viewing Room to watch the television broadcast. Nasreen had sat in the back row, deriding the whole process as nothing more than a farce, an attempt to pander to white hysteria, maintaining that a change was coming whether they liked it or not and that this was just to make them feel as if they were still in control. She was asked to be quiet. Alia had watched as Nasreen first raised an eyebrow at the teacher and then proceeded to doodle with supreme disinterest on her exam pad. Perhaps it was this that prompted Alia's response to Angela, which seemed to come unbidden and unexpected.

The results had come through slowly: Cape Town, Durban, Pretoria, Northern Transvaal ... sixty-eight per cent of people affirmed. The rest did not. A victory then.

"Well," Angela had said briskly, "I think you should all be very grateful for that."

"Fuck you."

Alia thought she had said it in her head and hoped, when she realised she had not, that she had at least said it softly. But as Nasreen told her later, she had shouted it loudly enough for the gardeners, who had been watching the results through the window, to hear too. She was given detention for three days.

Alia made a mental note to tell Lizzie about what had happened. She had already made all sorts of assumptions that the other girl would be in her corner on this one.

Gresham announced they would sing the Our Father. Three hundred heads bent in obedience as the hall filled up with devotion. Alia arched back to see if Angela's eyes were shut in prayer. The other girl was not above reporting people to Gresham if they broke the silence rule in assembly, but Alia was in a daring mood.

"So where are you from?" she asked Lizzie.

"Cape Town." Lizzie broke off from singing to answer Alia, her tone only a little puzzled.

"Oh, okay ... it's just that most of the—" here Alia fumbled and quickly reached for one of her mother's phrases – "It's just that most of the girls who board are usually from up-country."

This was an outrageous lie and Alia began to blush, but

Lizzie didn't seem to notice, going on to say, "Why do you think I am a boarder?"

"I just—"

"I'm from Gugulethu."

"*Are* you?" breathed Alia, impressed.

"Alia," Angela hissed, "if you keep this up, I'm going to report you."

But Alia had fallen silent of her own volition. She had not met anyone since Zonnebloem who lived in the townships. A horrible memory surfaced: she saw herself, seven years old in that school's playground, her legs nimbly darting in and out of the two lines of pantyhose that wrapped around two other girls' legs, chanting a call-response playground song towards a crescendo as she jumped.

> I called you!
> I didn't hear!
> I CALLED you!
> I didn't HEAR!
> Where's my money?
> In my shoe!
> Take it out!
> And that's for you!
> Who's your black servant?!
> YOU!

Whoever was pointed at, singled out as the servant, would shriek and throw her hands to her face, denying and protecting herself all at once. The children's voices seemed to close in and Alia's cheeks turned shame-red. Assembly ended and the girls began to file neatly out of the hall.

"Jaaaaa ... Guguleeethuuuu," said Lizzie, drawing out each syllable, "but in the good part, Malunga Park." She began to giggle and mimic a ghetto accent. "It's like the bleck Bevarlee Heels."

"Do your neighbours give you a hard time about coming here?"

"Sure. But what are we supposed to do? My parents are taking their orders from the top."

It was not the first time Alia had been given this as a reason for private schooling: some of St Michaels black students were the daughters of high-ranking ANC members, exactly the people of her father's and uncle's arguments. Alia remembered Zarina returning home from a PTA meeting one afternoon and telling Adam in low, scandalised tones about how Mrs Lekoto had said that by sending their children to these schools they were being prepared, no, *groomed*, to take over when the change came. They themselves, Mrs Lekoto went on, had all been missionary school educated, they knew the true, long-term dangers of Bantu Education. "And the other children," Zarina had ventured hesitantly, feeling out of her depth, "the ones who are dying at the schools?"

Well, that was another matter entirely, Mrs Lekoto had answered, a delicate shrug matching her dismissive tone. "The poor are always with us. For now, this is what we can do, we have priorities. After all," reaching for another cup of tea, "we are not Communists."

Lizzie and Alia walked up the little path between the school hall and the red-brick, ivy-clung chapel towards the tall main building. In the summer the insides were wonderfully cool, and in the winter, bitterly cold. Capetonian architects had remained loyal to eighteenth-century European travelogues about African winters at the expense of their own experiences: *It does not get cold in Africa!* Plummeting winter temperatures, heavy rains and occasional floods aside. No heating would be put in, no concessions to a fluctuating climate. Besides, a little cold never hurt anyone. It was good for the girls, the school board had decided. "I myself," said Mrs Hugo-Churchill, the school's chair, "I myself used to *name* my chilblains."

Hundreds of girls were moving through the corridors; black shoes on maroon tiles. Alia was walking in step with Lizzie.

"What's it like in Gugs? Does the army still go in?"

"Not so much anymore. There are patrols and that kind of crap. But not like it used to be."

"Have you ever been to HAL's?"

"To what?"

"HAL's. It's this club in Woodstock."

"Oh, ja, it's that coloured place? No. Never been."

Alia jolted. "I mean, I don't know, I never would have called it that. And there were black people there too." She shut off the memory of those black kids dancing at the edge of the floor, cordoned off by things said and unsaid.

"But it's for coloureds, right?" Lizzie bagged a desk next to Alia's and began unpacking her books.

Alia knew how she would react to a white person saying this, but this was uncharted territory. When she thought about it, she supposed Lizzie was right. Anyone could go, in theory. But mostly coloureds went. So what did that mean? Still, she thought, she should react in some way, not least of which because that word was sitting on her tongue like a clump of dirt.

"I just don't like that word."

Lizzie, puzzled, furrowed her forehead a little. "Why? What's wrong with it?"

"It's not a term I relate to." Alia found the relief, once again, in Zarina's words.

Lizzie nodded. "Oh, okay. But what would you like me to call you?"

This conversation was not going anywhere Alia was expecting. She reached towards Waleed's teachings about Biko and blackness and offered them up to Lizzie, but the other girl dismissed the man and the movement with an easy shrug, telling Alia that it was not the same thing, she had a clan and a country and a knowingness that went back thousands of years and, for her, *that's* what being black was about.

"But in the Struggle—" Alia was flailing.

"In the *Struggle*. Ja, but that's the Struggle."

"I suppose."

"Jeez. I feel like I've been a bitch. I'm really just interested, because I never know with coloureds, like which way they are going to go."

"Can you please stop using that word? It's actually really offensive."

"Okay, so but what should I call you?"

"Alia."

"Come on, man. You know what I mean."

"Well, my family is mostly from the Cape—"

"So, you mixed?"

"Mixed what? Is your whole family from the same village, for a thousand years?"

"No."

"I should hope not. That would mean some serious inbreeding."

"Ja, but—"

"Well then, same thing. Just my people are from villages further apart from one another." Alia arrived at this thought with a very small sense of victory that turned from tiny to hollow when Lizzie said soothingly, "Okay. Sure man."

Their class teacher, an enthusiastic, well-meaning young woman who had not yet begun to hate her pupils, arrived and began to take register. Between the rhythm of shouted surnames and affirmation, the girls began to tell each other about their holidays, of trips to Europe and Plettenberg Bay.

Alia zoned out somewhere between jealousy and boredom. Lizzie was tapping her on the shoulder. She handed her a piece of paper.

Listen, the note read, *I'm sorry if I hurt your feelings. I didn't mean anything by it. Hope we can be friends?* Alia shrugged an "I guess so". She was more wounded than she knew how to say. And she couldn't really explain why.

~

A classroom. Early afternoon. The most unneutral of spaces in this unsettled land. Fifteen plaited and ponytailed heads bent over desks in a large airy room where the wooden windows ushered in streams of light and thin gusts of dust and pollen. Earlier that day they had dissected a paper frog; now they were dissecting a poem by a young man who had died in the trenches of World War One. Their teacher, Mr Jameson, perched himself on the desk, one short leg angled against the other, his face tight and pink, and began to read. It was a perfect piece of writing, generous, emotional, deep in breath, sure of pace, full of the ache and imagery of the fallen in the fields of France and the senselessness of war. But Alia would not allow herself to sink into it at all, arranging her face into stony scorn. As the poem ended (Mr Jameson always took a moment after this one; it was rumoured that he had spent two years on the Angolan border), Alia's hand shot up, signing her indignation before she spoke. "Why are we learning about this? This man is not even from our country. What does he have to do with us? Why do we learn about European wars? We have wars of our own and we certainly have enough people who've died in them. Why don't we learn our own poets?"

It came out just as she had rehearsed it. It contained all the parts of one of Waleed's arguments that she had heard and understood. What she didn't know, couldn't know, was that he would have been horrified by what she took from him, because he, like Jameson, had taken this poet up, held him close, loved him across time and geography.

Mr Jameson looked up at Alia, who was sending off waves of self-righteousness. Eyes had been rolling for some time and he picked the nearest and most furious roller. "Angela," he said gratefully, "what are your thoughts?"

"What I would like to know," said Angela, primly placing her eraser in her pencil case, "is what Alia is proposing as an alternative ... I often think that *people*," and here she paused meaningfully and allowed herself the slight, internal smile of the public speaker who knows she is about to win her audience over, "people," she continued, "like to *ask* for change," an appreciative murmur rippled through the room, "without really having any *idea* about what the alternative would be."

Alia was almost out of her seat by now, but Mr Jameson, skilled in diplomacy, waved his arm at Lizzie as if to say, *Let's give the new girl a chance.*

Lizzie looked down for a moment, then brought her head up and said slowly, "I like the poem. It's beautiful, right? No doubt. But it's hard for me," here she stumbled a little, "I just think, and I said this at my old school as well—" Her voice trailed off. The girls leaned in close. Mr Jameson began to gather himself, ready to interject. "I don't want us *not* to read this poem," Lizzie continued, "but it would be good to read other things as well. We have poets who write about wars. I want two things, or three things, not one thing."

Alia was not expecting this. She was ready to back an argument about swapping one for the other. Mr Jameson looked relieved, too relieved, as though Lizzie had been talking about much more than just a poem. Angela broke into the gathering silence with a snap. "Well, maybe your poets aren't good enough. Have you ever thought of that?"

Alia threw up her hands and slammed them down again on the desk. Mr Jameson rallied a little. "I, um, I don't think that's where we want to go with this ... you ... er, may want to think about what it means ... what you just said ... though I don't think you meant it."

Lizzie reached into her book bag, rummaging through it with one hand, while she signed with the other that she had something more to contribute. She drew out a small thin book, curly paged, well thumbed, and flicked purposefully through it. Settling on a page, she cast a leaden look to all, cleared her throat and, alive to the drama of the moment, began to read.

> So
> child of the song, sing don't cry
> with song and dance we defied death
> remember
> like
> the heavens are blue because they are
> empty
> and
> beware, my brother, of park benches
> sitting there
> is the last thing a fighter must do.

Lizzie held the moment, drew it out like a long-released sigh, eventually announcing, "Mongane Wally Serote, 1975, New York City, exile."

Alia fell in love for the second time that week.

6

Tuesday, 26th January 1993

The room was filled with oblong blocks of morning light, temporary patterns made by venetian blinds. At the doorway a very small, very faded Persian rug, at the window a bed crumpled by two seemingly sleeping figures. Between the rusting burglar bars flew the last of summer's mosquitoes, one of the abiding irritations of a long, hot season. At some point in the night Waleed had flung the sheets to where they lay tangled in a puddle of thick ribbons around his feet. His left arm was cast across his face in an ineffectual attempt to ward off the bright and early sun, his eyes shut against exhaustion. But he was awake, balefully awake, and cursing the antagonistic buzz and drone near his ears and the itchiness he was certain would follow.

It was the ninth anniversary of his father's death, and this year, like every year since that day, would be marked by the ritual of prayers as remembrance. He had been at his mother's the night before, dutifully helping her to make pies until three in the morning, unpacking the trellis tables stacked up in the garage, inspecting the white sheets that would be laid out on the floor for their guests to sit on. Tonight his childhood home would be full of family and neighbours and food and invocation. Tonight he would wear a koffeya and lock his arms around folded knees while he rocked and swayed and recited in unison with other men.

Next to him lay Anna, blissfully immune to the warring insects, cupped beneath his arm and locked against his body. Anna was twenty-three, liked Moroccan food, was committed to building her vinyl collection despite the recent onslaught of CDs, hoped to finish her Masters thesis this year, worried a little about how her belly was beginning to plump no matter how much she jogged and loved the man lying next to her. She was also white. Christian by birth, secular humanist by choice. And so today, like all days that involved Waleed's old world, she would say goodbye and pretend not to mind very much when he returned morose, miserable and full of front-door-slamming guilt. Today she would send his family greetings and condolences she knew they would never receive. These undelivered messages would be tucked away in an ever-growing pile of small slights, unreasonable requests and large omissions, until they could be called upon in an argument.

Sometimes, at their frequent and much envied dinner parties, when Waleed was buoyed up by good wine and the success of his staggeringly accurate impersonations of the absent and the uninvited (a genetic gift and social fallback; both Alia and Adam were similarly inclined), he would collapse his shoulders into his mother's slouch and moan, "Ag, well at least we know he's not a moffie. But now that he's with this Kriste girl, he is just so *thin*, like a piece of paper, because you know, nè, they don't cook because they *can't* cook."

Anna's part in this was to beg for the performance and then laugh when the mimicry reached its apex. She was usually loudest when it was pitched at her expense: this, she decided, would sanction the hilarity, make everyone comfortable. She would toss back wine, refill everyone's glass and enthusiastically suggest a toast to Waleed's skill, all the while being secretly devastated. Later, when the guests had gone and all that was left were dirty dishes and a couple's post-party post-mortem, she would pick a fight, always trivial, always irrelevant, always resulting in a tearful "But *why* does she hate me? I haven't done anything. She doesn't even *know* me."

Waleed, who seldom defended his mother's prejudices, would find himself spouting phrases like "the burden of whiteness". They had met through their mutual supervisor, Derek Reed, and Waleed had fallen early into the trap of relating to Anna as he did to all white academics, as slightly hostile and actively theorising the personal.

On this morning, Anna woke with the familiar dread that comes when you know an argument with a lover is inevitable. She reminded herself of the day's sorrow, the anniversary of loss, and the old grief that still gripped Waleed. She looked at his face and trailed her gaze over its still-boyish prettiness and then (*God help me, I am still not over this yet, there must be something wrong with me*), she let herself just stare at all that brown skin. Anna knew what she was doing when she did this; she was (ironically? inevitably?) writing a thesis on the way black bodies were fetishised in literature. "Feel free to use me as a part of your research," had been Waleed's pick-up line. Yes, it had all been funny then. A flirtation. A *lark*. Months later in the midst of a terrible fight, Waleed, who wielded other people's insecurities as a weapon, had cast the thesis upon her as an indictment and accused her of doing exactly what he had once playfully suggested. Anna had wept at this, terrified that it was true.

At twenty-three, she had missed the era when whites were welcomed to the debate, when the academics who turned their attention to the marginal and the wounded were rewarded not just with inclusion but with gratitude. The fifties were over. So were the sixties. It was the beginning of the nineties and the terrible eighties were still in every room. Anna would have an anxiety attack every time she went to a conference. Inexorably, eyes would roll and she would have to defend her position before she even began. She was small-boned and pretty with shiny reddish-blonde hair that did her no good in these environments. She didn't have the strident boldness of some liberal white South Africans with their bead-wearing, left-leaning, unapologetic professions of being "African". Neither did she have the steely indifference of their conservative counterparts. ("We voted Yes in the referendum – what more do they want?") Anna, in all her delicate, transparent guilt, was chum for everyone with even a bit of residual anger: she was soft and open to the horrors of the country she was raised in. And she had got there herself. No one in her family saw things the way she did. She had a hungry need to pay penance, to help repair things.

But her relationship with Waleed, she told herself, wasn't a part of all that: the problems between them had far more to do with the differences between men and women than they ever had to do with race. Perhaps, they could only have known that in a different country.

She slipped out from the bed and padded towards the kitchen. Here were his LPs stacked in piles against the wall of the lounge collecting dust and admiration from guests, here the poster of James Baldwin, his furrow almost popping off the page, that blazing intelligence holding everyone accountable. There were Waleed's books, spirited from the study to the lounge, arranged to look scattered, but in reality carefully curated to present a certain self, a self that placed Neruda next to Fanon and leaned them both against Coetzee. Anna read all the books Waleed pressed on her hungrily, eagerly, the way that only those in love will. She searched each text for clues about herself, about him, wanting to find a version of their life together in every character, hoping that if she read quickly she would know him faster, know him completely. In turn, Waleed studied her old photograph albums and went into strange and unexpected fits of jealousy when he saw her smiling shyly next to a pimply tow-haired youth at her matric dance, or, equally, felt surges of sorrow when he found evidence of her lonely childhood punctuated as it was by sporadic attempts at playing family: the photos of half-term gatherings, the disinterested older brother, the thin, anxious mother, the morose, over-worked father.

Anna made her way to the kitchen where a small breakfast nook was crowded with unopened bills and a cluster of photos of parties past were stuck on the fridge. The one of a five-year-old Waleed posing as a voorloper always elicited a chuckle from her. Behind that, the kitchen window was crowded over by a thick-leaved, bright-petalled bougainvillea bush.

She put the kettle on and reached for the ground coffee beans. At the back of the cupboard was a miniature tin of Ricoffy. She remembered when she had first seen it and the pleasure of teasing Waleed about it, *him*, the known coffee connoisseur.

"It's my mother's," he had answered with mock defensiveness. "She doesn't go for the whole coffee beans things ... she's suspicious of it ... maintains that chicory is far superior."

They had laughed then, Anna delighted by Fozia's working-class toughness. *Chicory! So funny! So real!* She thought it was adorable, endearing, but her lover's mother would seem less and less so as the months passed.

"Got you! You fucker!" Waleed was waging war against the mosquitoes in the bedroom.

She began to clear a space on the narrow counter and, in doing so, remembered her first night in this house. Waleed's seduction had begun with food. He had heard about her love of all things Moroccan, invited her over and devoted a day to slow roasting a lamb tagine, letting the house fill with the smell of flesh and herbs, finding at Balmoral Fruit Supply the Cape's last pomegranate, scattering rubies of fruit on the couscous. He had declared that they would spend an evening in the Maghreb "That crescent of countries," he intoned, trailing a finger from her cheek to her throat, "curving between the Middle-East and the north of Africa." He played Um Kulthum in the background, lit an incense stick, and heated the coals on the hookah pipe packed tight with orange-infused tobacco and a little crumbled hash.

She was a nice middle-class girl who had gone to school in Rondebosch, who up to three years earlier had lived with her parents. She didn't stand a chance. They got as far as wine, but not as far as dinner. Waleed had lifted her onto the countertop and they had fucked right there, the low windows of the old house letting in the still light of dusk, bright purple petals shivering against the sill.

They announced their exclusivity a week later, her parents anxious and outraged – "Racist," she said – her university friends jubilant, their supervisor amused. Waleed and Anna, together. Privately, she thought, *in spite of things*, privately he thought, *because of them*. The truth was that these two would have loved each other regardless of circumstances, but as the poet had prophesied, "you can enter history, you cannot leave it." And that history ensured that Waleed was ashamed of Anna. Just a little. Enough to make her feel like she wanted to die every time she saw herself refracted through the eyes he borrowed from his mother.

He walked in now, fresh from a triumphant battle with mosquitoes, gently pushing her away from the business of making coffee, grumpy, as always in the morning, searching for a bit of quiet, almost annoyed to find another person in his space.

The previous week she had come back from the Oriental Plaza laden with thin silk scarves and spices bought wholesale, pretending to Waleed that the scarves were strictly ornamental, but they both knew that she had bought the thick cotton black one just in case she was invited to tonight's prayers, just in case she was welcomed into that circle of women who gathered in the kitchen preparing plates draped with doilies and foodstuffs sprinkled with dustings of parsley.

"Did you get him?"

Waleed showed her the paper; there, on the front page was De Klerk's cheek now decorated with a large smear of flattened black-purple insect and human blood.

"Look at that. That's *my* blood. Look at my arm! That bastard had a field day. Why are you so immune?" He made for the bathroom and began scratching around aggressively in the small cabinet next to the sink, calling out to her, "You could be sleeping under a net for all the difference it makes to you."

"I'm tougher. All those years of being forced to go camping in the veld." Anna stifled a yawn and looked hopefully at the filter. "Coffee's almost done," she shouted.

Waleed came charging into the kitchen, taking up a protective position in front of the machine. "Not yet." He held out the tube of ointment as if he was making an offering, not a request. "I'm serious. Why do they go for only me when you're lying right there? There's just no justice in the world."

"You speak the truth," intoned Anna playfully while she dutifully dabbed at the angry-looking red blotches. And then, "Are you going to mosque first?" She looked down after she asked it. The question, with its semi-antagonistic tone, seemed to have come from out of nowhere.

Waleed registered the inquiry oddly, shaking the tin of beans, not his head. "No."

"So just supper then," she pressed on.

"Nope," said Waleed. "Going to stay the night probably."

"So we'll see each other tomorrow night?"

"I'm going to the meeting at Woodstock Town Hall. Hani is speaking. Come, if you like."

Anna sat down on the patch of floor between couch and coffee table, folding her legs deftly beneath her bottom and reaching for the Indian print cushions studded with tiny mirrors (another Plaza purchase) to prop up her back. The meeting could be wonderful. It could be terrible. To walk into that room with Waleed, to listen to Hani, the communist, the soldier, the talker, the man who was travelling the length of the country speaking in halls, in churches, at schools and rallies, the man whom the weary factions in the townships listened to when he asked them for a little more time. ("A little more, comrades, just a little.") The man who offered Anna something of a life-raft because he wasn't interested, he said again and again, in an easy collapse into race. What he wanted was what she wanted: roofs, clean water, schools, hospitals, for everyone, not for a handful, what was just, what was just. To listen to the man who, Waleed kept insisting, was more important than Mandela ("Sacrilege," she had responded, only half teasing).

To see Waleed in that room, in among the flags and the songs, the comrades and the handshakes, to see him surrounded by the props by which she had learned to love him, learned to be in awe of him. Yes, she would go. Perhaps this, somehow, would make up for tonight. For Fozia.

Anna tilted her head, angling for the sun to find her face. "It's a beautiful day for a zikr. Is your mom going to have one every year?" She said the foreign word hesitantly.

Waleed grunted, remaining non-committal. Was it worse, she wondered, when she tried to show him just how *down* she was with everything he was? "Zarina will be there, right? And the girls? Don't make that *face*. From the sounds of things they adore you and you're just so *oblivious*. You be careful about that, even adoration runs out eventually." She stopped. Embarrassed, she looked searchingly into her coffee cup as if there were a future cast in it. Waleed was smiling. She threw a cushion at him.

"Stop it!" she laughed. "I am a verbal person. I sort things out in my head by talking."

Waleed sipped his coffee, frowned and added a bit more brown sugar. "I sort things out in my head by talking," he repeated mockingly, shaking his head despairingly and making his way to the couch. "The converse of which, of course, is actual introspection. Which some might say, is the mark of adulthood."

Placing two hands on the bar counter as if to steady herself, she said levelly, "Take that back."

Mystified, he looked up. "What?"

"What you said just now. About introspection and adulthood."

"It was a joke." He tucked himself deeper into a cushion and tried to draw her attention to a headline article about how the factional in-fighting between the ANC and Inkatha was being fuelled by the "Third Force". "Have you seen this? Bladdy Buthelezi falling for their tricks again, stirring up rubbish ..."

"What?"

"This Third Force thing." He was smiling pleasantly now. "Rashaad says it's one hundred per cent true and I wouldn't put anything past those bastards."

Anna crouched down in front of him, alive suddenly to what the moment needed. "Waleed," a deep in-breath, a clasp at his hands, an attempt to push air through angst, "I know today is really painful— "

Waleed began to twist on the couch, narrowing his eyes,

head flung back, legs drawn towards his chest. "I wonder if you said it because you're trying to deflect—"

Waleed groaned, unfurling himself. "Please not this again. It's nine in the morning. I've had *five* hours' sleep. I really don't need to be psychoanalysed today of all days—"

"It's *not* psychoanalysis—"

"Oh *God*, Anna." Waleed put the blood-stained paper down wearily. "What exactly is the problem here? You're cross that you didn't make the guest list for something? I didn't go to Christmas lunch at your parents."

"You were invited. You chose not to go."

"So, let me get this straight," he addressed himself to an article on the third page – another fucking compromise at the negotiating table – "I'm supposed to feel better than you do, because *your* parents are more adept at handling their racism socially than my mother is at managing hers?"

"That is such bull—"

"Anna!"

"Waleeeed!"

He began to smile mischievously. "I promise to bring you a plate of barakat, okay? This is clearly really about missing out on the food, isn't it?"

But Anna refused to be tricked or charmed out of her outrage. "You and your mother can keep her greasy, psychic poison. I'm just glad she's not my parent."

This first bit was thrown in purely for malice. Anna loved Fozia's cooking: the little piles of golden pastries that Waleed would bring home were the source of jubilant welcome, particularly on nights of munchies and movies. They would sit and eat this food and she would wonder, while she licked away at the cream of the last éclair, how a woman whose food she loved so could in turn hate her, unknown and unseen.

His eyebrows were knitted, face taut with anger. He was

preparing to throw some mud. "At least my mother had the decency to keep me at home. From the sounds of it, boarding school was a great way to get rid of the unwanted."

He said this, eyes still on the paper, as though he was uninterested, bored even. Anna leapt back as if she had been slapped, her eyes filled with tears and she ran to the bedroom and began throwing clothes in a canvas tote bag. This happened several times a month.

Waleed stood in the doorway, contrite now. "I was kidding ... You need to be able to take it if you can dish it. Hey. Come on." He reached for the bag, felt her shoulder go slack at his touch and made the mistake of letting out a soft laugh. He was shocked when Anna aimed a strong elbow into his stomach.

"Jesus fucking Christ," he wheezed and grabbed her wrist.

They stood, like a version of the child's game Statue: her hand inches from his face, fingers in a claw as if still trying to get a scratch in; he holding her arm in a grip, the vein running from elbow to wrist pulsing a little from the effort. Anna breathing heavily, shocked by her own violence, Waleed less so. He had grown up, he told her, in a house where arguments took different forms: slaps, hidings, tears, fighting, always followed by grand reunions. But to Anna, whose parents had raised her remotely ("by decree" she used to say), whose adolescence had been negotiated through dorm matrons and teachers' reports, these dense theatrical demonstrations were foreign and depleting.

"I promise you are not missing out on anything. All these events are the same. It's just eating and gossip and the same people. Zarina said she would trade places with you any day."

At this, Anna made a small sound somewhere between a groan and a laugh. She let herself be led back to the unmade bed where they would refuse again the many-layered logic of their parents' disapproval.

~

Afterwards they lay, as they always did, he flat on his back rubbing at his chin as if he had a beard, she curled towards him, one leg hiked in a half square over his torso, her face turned to his neck.

"Are you going to write today?"

The question could have come from either of them, but this time it was Waleed who said it. Anna understood what this cost him. She was on track with her thesis, knocking off chapters at a pace that astonished her supervisor and her boyfriend. It was as though her fear of being judged made her read everything rapidly, made her write up as though the devil was on her back. That she was having terrible misgivings about the actual research had not affected the speed or scholarship. Conversely, Waleed had spent most of the year in a horrendous mixture of panic and jealousy that meant a string of cancelled supervision meetings and a complete inability to bring himself to read the bundles of paper she deliberately left lying about in the very obvious hope that he would pick them up.

"I have a meeting with Derek tomorrow. Do you want me to tell him anything?"

"God no!" he cut her off. "Don't say a word about me. I'm just hoping I'll sort of fade from his memory."

"That's realistic," she pronounced and then, after a small pause, "We're both probably going to be in his bad books for a while. I'm actually thinking of changing focus."

"Why would you do that?"

"I'm just tired of … ag … you know what I'm talking about, I complain about this endlessly." She shrugged, pretending an indifference she did not feel.

Anna had hit a wall in her research, partly because her interest had begun to fade – *So, black bodies are fetishised in literature, after ten thousand words that's a given, and then what? How much longer can I drag that out?* – partly because she was beginning to see herself through other people's eyes. It was starting to feel intellectually sordid. Besides, her reading had taken her somewhere new, and that somewhere was Rosa Luxemburg.

"I should get going." Waleed hauled himself up, turning to look at her, and placed a soft kiss on each of her cheeks.

"You're going to write something brilliant. You know that, don't you?"

"Define 'brilliant'."

"Something that helps us all through the mess of this place."

He leapt from the bed as though he was suddenly aware of the time. She heard him charge through his small home and turn on the shower and, knowing she could be heard, called out, "I mean that, you know! Something that contributes ... something that helps things along!"

Waleed reappeared in the doorway in a pre-shower towel, grabbed his deodorant and offered her a grin. "I'm a writer, not a social worker."

7

SATURDAY, 6 FEBRUARY 1993

Nick and Alia were now "going out", which was an odd phrase, Alia reflected, because their relationship was really about "staying in": they spent most of their time together on the telephone. When they did go out, they usually met up in town at Greenmarket Square. The square's cobbled streets had once known vegetable carts and the bare feet of just-auctioned slaves; today it was hemmed by history: a Gothic-style church appropriately clocked and spired, a pale yellow, cream-trimmed Dutch colonial townhouse and several tall art deco office blocks. Inside, it was all plastic crates of dog-eared books, jumbled displays of old-women jewellery, stalls of Congolese drums and long-necked wooden figurines, hangers of badly cut, garishly bright floral halter-neck and baby-doll dresses, rows of oversized, greenish, wrought-iron candlesticks, several stoned stall owners, the occasional street musician. At the corner of Greenmarket and Burg streets, a coffee shop, modelled diligently after its Parisian parent, checked tablecloths, basket-woven chairs and compulsively smoking patrons; further up, a recently opened Italian restaurant owned by brothers known for vicious tempers and a penchant for beating up the homeless.

Today, Alia was to meet Nick on the wide, grey-white steps of the South African Natural History Museum. Neither had been since junior school, but the museum was free and it promised to be shaded and cool. February in Cape Town was an unforgiving month. In the city, the heat fell from above, sank into the buildings and ground, then rose again from the tar, keeping the weather trapped and churning. It did not occur to Nick or Alia to spend the day at the beach: for reasons neither of them could put into words, the alcoves of the Atlantic seaboard, despite being open since 1990, were still, somehow, out of bounds.

Alia made her way towards the Company's Gardens from the bus depot, past the Golden Acre Shopping Centre and up Adderley Street, weaving her way through a city temporarily animated by the throngs of Saturday shoppers. In just a few minutes, she would be with Nick, and they would pick up the conversation that had ended the night before in a drawn-out series of farewells, final stories, just-remembered details. With Nick, the hours always passed in a haze of ceaseless talk, traded ideas, exchanged books, the recitation of reams and reams of hip-hop lyrics (Nick had *flow*, Alia had told Lizzie), shared cigarettes, complaints about parents, teachers, prefects and siblings, arguments about the country, derision about classmates, plots for long bouts of overseas travel coupled with declarations that they would *never* leave the country, and beneath it all, a thin but continuous stream of relief that they had found each other. There were few silent moments between: there was so much to say, so much to talk about, every goodbye regretful, every hello euphoric, every conversation a chance to find out more about the other, to announce a new reading of an old topic, to be heard, to be heard.

Alia walked past the bronze-brown, domed-roofed planetarium – rumoured to have once been a synagogue – and found Nick sitting on the steps. Dressed in loose-fitting cargo shorts that fell below his knees, a baggy navy-blue

T-shirt, white cotton socks tugged up towards his calves, box-fresh sneakers with tongues that splayed thick and puffy over the laces, the ever-present Malcolm X cap. Next to him, an open knapsack, a half-drunk bottle of Coke, in his hands a book. Alia ran a hand through hair damp and sticky from the hot walk and tugged at the hem of her summery dress in an effort to hide knees she was suddenly convinced were chubby, ill-shaped.

"Hey."

Nick looked up, smiling, squinting at her outline against the bright sun.

~

Thirty minutes later they emerged, exhausted, from the gloom of the museum, having spent that time in the uncomfortable and depressing company of the Bushman diorama.

In the dark, dimly lit passageway was a series of tall glass display boxes and in those boxes were grass huts and in those grass huts, like some terrifying Matryoshka doll, were clay models of brown men and women, their privates covered by beads and leather. Next to the hut a woven basket and a narrow, leafless tree. A model woman lay on her side, her eyes protected by the reach of the hut's shadow. A model man squinted as he rubbed a stick into the earth. Everything was lit to a warm glow, the dusty brown of the bodies and the dirt washed yellow by a thin imitation of the Karoo sun. There were arrows and ostrich eggs, thorn bushes and large boulders, no detail was left unspoken. No detail except for this: that the casts were made long after the beginning of the end. That those who stood static and timeless in the transparent cages of the museum had left home long, long before, had been dressed in trousers and shirts and had been made to wear hats and smash away at bricks in the prison quarry and then asked to stand while a plaster cast was made of them. No detail except this: that their bodies were divided up into arms and legs and penises and buttocks and skulls and bellies, and that when they had died some of those parts were pickled and placed in glass jars and labelled:

> Item: a Hottentot male brain
> Item: a Hottentot female femur
> Item: a Hottentot vagina

Just down the hall, a collection of rocks and African taxidermy. And in a back room that would only be discovered in the decade ahead, hundreds of human skeletons, the quickly boxed remains of bodies dug up fresh from burial in the early 1900s, the flesh boiled off them until just the bones remained, then kept there to be measured, scraped, or sent off to Europe, bound for museums with marble halls and bronze balustrades.

Nick hovered in front of one figure longer than others. It was of a warrior, bows and arrows resting in a dried bark bag on his back, his head tilted to the side as though he was listening, waiting for something. Eventually, the boy looked around and gave a low, bitter laugh. "My family and other animals."

"I can't believe they still have them up here," said Alia, trying to lock eyes with a man hunched over a calabash.

"Can't you? I can. First to die, last to be cared about."

They walked upstairs and passed through the rows of wood-trimmed glass cabinets full of stuffed birds posed angrily in mid-flight, ready to peck their way through the glass and sink their beaks into the curators' eyes. They examined the old instruments of science, the measuring scales, the preserved pots of ink with their labels thin and yellow. Nick tapped at the cabinets without saying anything, a morse code Alia could not decipher.

He was given to occasional though intense bouts of silence and Alia was often uncertain how to respond to them. She usually chose chattering as a way to move in and around them.

"Come let's go to the Art Gallery. It will be so much less miserable than this."

"Maybe later." Nick walked off before turning to ask, "You coming?"

Outside, at the larger of the two ponds, they fed Simba crisps to the fish, watched water arc and spurt through the stone fountain, screwed their un-sunglassed eyes against the intense brightness of the sun, while Nick threaded his thoughts together. "When I look in those glass cages, I see my family. And you don't. Do you?"

Alia shook her head. She didn't. She thought of her mother's mother, Catherine, and her collection of Royal Family plates, her Italian arias, her constant references to her own mother's Irish family. She would never see herself or her history in the glass cabinet and so neither could her granddaughter. Alia knew too that Fozia, protected by her recipes and her prayers, would have refused any association, been horrified by it.

"Well, I do," Nick continued, scattering the remaining crisps in one movement across the water, making the fish flip about in dizzy, ecstatic circles. "I promise you, I see my whole family. And I have all these questions, but I just end up hitting a wall. I swear my grandmother's mouth clamps shut if I ask her anything." Nick pressed his lips together as though they were being forcibly glued and widened his eyes in a cartoonish warning. Once Alia supplied the hoped-for laugh, he continued, "Seriously, haven't you noticed? You can't ask anyone from Cape Town about their family more than four generations back. You just get these vague answers. Either no one knows anything, or else everyone knows everything but they just not saying."

"Ja. Ja. Everyone in Cape Town's got an Irish grandmother," said Alia.

"I even remember once my grandmother telling me I was being rude asking her where her family came from. Can you believe that shit? I sometimes wonder if it's easier for Muslims—"

"*Sooo* much easier for us to live in this Calvanist nightmare—"

"No, listen. I mean it. Because you people—"

"*You* people?"

"Just *listen* man. You people can always do that Malay thing. Or call on that Indian history—"

"So?"

"*So*. It means that you still have something to hold on to – even if it's not true. It means you … I don't know … you know who you are, or something—"

"Oh *please*—"

"Ag. Anyway." He drew out a cigarette and smoked in silence for a moment before asking, "Do your parents give you a hard time about me being Christian?"

"No, they don't really get fazed by that stuff. But Uncle Waleed's girlfriend is Christian, well, *atheist*, and my Mama is absolutely furious about it. You should hear her go on, you'd think the world had ended."

Nick exhaled and nodded knowingly into the smoke. There was something about the way in which he seemed to understand this that prompted a realisation in Alia.

"What about your parents? What have they said about me?"

Nick looked down and then into the middle distance. "Not … *thrilled*," he said eventually.

Alia was temporarily speechless and, beyond that, faintly outraged that *any* parent was not delighted at the prospect of her being with their son. "What do you mean, 'not thrilled'?" she said. "What did they say?"

"It's really not worth repeating."

"Then I'm going to head home—"

"*Fine*. Here's a random example: last night, the *athaan* is going at the mosque down the street and my father starts to complain about it being too loud, interfering with his music …"

"Charming."

"Wait, it gets worse. So then he starts to sing along with the man, but he changes the words." Here Nick began to whine in the rhythms and cadence of the call to prayer, replacing the Arabic with Afrikaans words. "Vanaaaaaaaand, stiel-onse-'n-kaaaaaaar." *Toniiiiiiiight, we're-going-to-steal-a-caaaaaar*.

A middle-aged woman in a pale blue and cream maid's uniform (skirt, apron, doek), pushing a white baby in an expensive-looking pram, threw him a quizzical look. Noticing, Nick cut the impersonation short.

Alia burst out laughing but Nick flicked his cigarette into a nearby bin with a frown. "It's not funny, Alia."

"It's a *little* funny."

Nick grinned. "What is it about South Africans that makes them think it's okay to laugh about fucked-up shit?"

Alia shrugged and looked around her. "It's the dark side of the rainbow. It's so hot today. I can't sit here anymore."

"Where d'you want to go?" Nick had turned his attention to the uniformed maid who had taken the child – a little boy – out of his pram and was walking him over to a shaded area on the lawn.

"Ice-suckers," said Alia, following his gaze, "and then the gallery."

The child took two, three eager steps and then fell to his knees. Anxious, loving, the woman rushed towards him.

"Did you have a nanny?" asked Nick.

"Sort of. We had a sleep-in maid and she took care of us

when my parents were working late, but not like that, with that insane uniform and stuff. You?"

Again the child fell and this time began to howl. Again the woman picked him up, rocked him and then began to twirl rapidly, so that his little legs flew out from the centrifugal force of her spin, while he shrieked and she beamed. Alia knew what was wrong with the scene. She also struggled not to see what was right with it. She tugged Nick to his feet and they walked over to the ice-cream cart, leaving behind the fish, the maid, the toddler, and the memory of the trapped Bushmen.

8

Sunday, 7 February 1993

Alia woke to a room full of sun and a house full of movement. Across the landing Nasreen's eyes were shut against the drone and heat of the hairdryer. Downstairs Zarina was preparing breakfast, cracking eggs and slamming cupboard doors with a little more energy than was required. It was a demonstration of annoyance; her daughters were *still* in their rooms, her husband was *still* in the shower. It was all wrong. Sunday morning at the Dawoods were usually days of lazy beginnings, of warmish koesisters and cups of strong, sugary Nescafé. Alia lay in bed, the thin summer duvet kicked down around her ankles, her head a little hazy, the now familiar taste of nicotine lingering in her mouth dry and ashy, trying to work out why her family seemed so oddly industrious.

She heard another door meet its frame and willed herself out of bed, determined to ferret out the root of the anti-Sunday behaviour. She left her bedroom just as her father, immaculate in a superbly cut grey suit, his step light and buoyant, emerged from his own. "Why aren't you dressed?" he asked.

She looked at the hallway clock. "Why are *you* dressed? It's barely ten o'clock."

"I'm going to your cousin's Nikha," Adam answered smugly.

Alia suddenly remembered and regretted the agenda for

the day ahead. The frenzy of activity was explained. It was her cousin Tasneem's wedding and, like all family get-togethers, it promised to be a day of uneasy compromises, extra grooming and warped time. Eids, weddings, naming ceremonies, funerals all followed a consistent pattern. The morning would be framed by two bitter disagreements: the first about attendance and duty, the second about appropriate dress. The afternoon would be spent in a stupor of boredom and fitful gossip. Once Nasreen and Alia were suitably, though resentfully, garbed and safely ensconced in the designated hall, lounge, or garden, they would cling stubbornly to a childhood fantasy that every adult had, in a collective conspiracy, set their watches back by two hours. Alia fared worse at these events than her sister. She seemed fated either to miss something in the getting ready process (chipped nails, laddered stockings) or to be subjected to a catastrophe in the course of the day. She flinched, recalling a spray of samoosa oil on a new top last Eid.

"I didn't get new *shoes*," she moaned. "Mom said we would go this week ... but we didn't get to it ... what am I going to *wear*?"

"Your sister," Adam said, ignoring Alia's growing crisis and allowing a note of pride to creep into his voice, "has been up since seven doing her hair ... She is going to look fantastic." He stopped, noticing how this daughter's face had assumed a tragic arrangement. "What's the matter?"

"I don't have any *shoes*," Alia repeated mournfully.

"So borrow something from your sister."

"She's got smaller feet than me." Said as though it were an admission of failure.

"Surely you've got another pair?"

"I suppose." Alia thought of her beetle-crushers and wondered how well they would twin with the floral two-piece she had bought.

"Hey! You better opskud! You girls are not going to Tasneem's house first?"

Alia tugged at her pyjamas. "I don't know ... I don't know what's going on ... I'll be done in a bit, I just need to shower."

"Mind you do! It's going to be a big affair. So please, none of your 'grunge'."

Adam loved picking up slang of all kinds: generational, cultural, national, and then using it on the group he assumed generated it. It meant he dropped Yiddish phrases to his Jewish customers ("You wanna twalk to me about a ragmonise cut? We don't sew from just any shmatta in this shop"), spoke Malay-Afrikaans to his family ("Ek het gehoer dat Boeta Kaatjie het geamalingil"), elongated his jaw and propped his tongue up on air when he was taking orders for a posh Englishman ("I say! Indeed!"), and borrowed rude-boy phrases when they were not ("Go on, my son!"). The results were often mixed. Sometimes people nodded with laughter and recognition, sometimes they were slightly bewildered. Sometimes it was important that the other person got it, sometimes it wasn't. Adam, a natural shape-shifter, did it because he could. Other places found new homes in his mouth and head. Zarina would beg him to stop, warning that he was wading dangerously close to racial caricaturing, but Adam insisted that because he did it to everyone, her concern was misplaced, no, *paranoid*.

His word missed today. His youngest daughter looked at him wonderingly,

"*Grunge?*" she repeated, letting the word contain the full weight of her disdain.

"You know what I mean! None of your Spanish plonk! None of your tat! Try not to look like a nogschlepper."

Adam bounded down the stairs, full of the energy that comes from being good-looking and well dressed. He lived for these kinds of gatherings, the hosts of Mercedes-Benzes and BMWs parked in the mosque's lot, the men leaning against their vehicles in a not-so-casual announcement of ownership, the ritualised handshaking, the careful sizing up of each other's suits, the shifting preference between crocheted koffeyas or the classic box fez. Wedding ceremonies at mosques had an air both exclusive and celebratory. The bride-to-be was seldom there and if she was, she was ensconced somewhere behind a curtain in a partition reserved for women. This part of the day belonged to men and their sons. It was a place to solidify business deals, to talk politics and to swap gossip out of earshot of censorious wives or protected daughters.

At this wedding, the bride was breaking slightly with her family's traditions and would be at the mosque. "I'm *going* to be there!" Tasneem had fumed. "I don't want Daddy signing the contract without me there to see it! What if I am sitting on the toilet when it happens?" The bride's father had yielded only because his wife, in a stunning about-face, had championed her daughter's cause, declaring, "Of course she is going to be there, and I am going to be with her."

Sometimes, when a country is full of the talk of freedom all day, every day, its effects are felt in the most unexpected places.

Alia fumbled after her father towards the kitchen, her eyes still full of sleep. Adam was tucking into his breakfast and elatedly recounting the wedding rumours. "Abdullah told me that this man spent *seventy-five thousand* on this function. I mean, can you imagine that?" He turned to Alia. "You're not going to cost me that much, are you?" She giggled and he drew her onto his lap, continuing, "No ways! This one is going to do the sensible thing and elope ... Seventy-five thousand rand! It's outrageous! They could have bought a home. They could have bought *two* cars."

Nasreen walked in looking like a teenage Annie Hall,

hair in a tight coif, body in baggy trousers and shirt. Alia wondered if this meant that Nasreen's much coveted pale-blue chiffon dress was free to borrow. She was about to suggest just this when Nasreen launched eagerly into contributing to Adam's wedding rant.

"They did buy a house ... Uncle Ismail bought it for them two weeks ago, and Tasneem told me her dress is made from imported silk. *Italian*. And that the whole thing is beaded ... top to bottom ... even the inside of the hem!"

"Good God!" answered Adam, almost crowing with delight, pushing Alia towards her own chair. "Why would Miley do that? He *owns* a fabric shop ... he didn't tell me about an Italian contact. But then, you can't put a price on overseas. Even if the fabric is poor quality, people go nuts for an import."

Zarina was beating eggs with one eye on the clock.

Alia watched as Zarina tipped the eggs into the hot pan, allowing them to coagulate before working them over with a rapid spatula.

"Mom?"

"Mmm?"

"I need to ask you something."

"Adam, say now if you want anything else to eat so you can get to mosque. Alia, you're not even showered yet so I'm going to give you your eggs now and *no*, Nasreen, I don't want you to read this as a preferential gesture. It's just practical." *It's ten now*, Zarina thought, *Nasreen and Adam are done, if Alia showers straight after breakfast, it will give me about thirty minutes to get done ... Is there time to colour my hair? No, no, probably not. Dammit, I should have done it last night.*

Nasreen moved towards the toaster and began popping slices of white bread into the orange-glowing rack. Zarina talked to herself while she shook the pan back and forth.

"Can someone please tell me why people *insist* on having weddings on a Sunday? It throws the whole week out. The entire morning gets taken up and then, before you know it, it's afternoon and no time to prepare anything."

"Mom!"

"*What*?"

"I don't have shoes."

"What do you mean you don't have shoes? We went shopping for you last week. We spent four hours in Cavendish, four hours in which you complained about everything you tried on. You got your whole outfit."

"But we didn't get shoes."

"So just wear another pair."

"I don't think I can wear my beetle-crushers."

"No, you are certainly not wearing those things ... borrow something of Nasreen's."

"Her shoes don't fit me."

"You can wear my navy pumps, they will go nicely."

"They *won't*."

"Well, they will just have to."

Adam had tuned into the conversation and looked pained. It was important to him that his daughters were well turned out for community events. He had strong and unwavering feelings about the relationship between success and presentation. "Why does the child not have the right shoes, Zarina?" he asked in a wounded voice.

"Because," Zarina said, matching his wounded tone with a flinty one, "the *child* had tennis, swimming, volleyball, debating, drama and a school social this week after school, and I had to take her to and from each of those things."

Adam knew when to back down and he also knew that when it came to ferrying their children from one self-improving activity to another, Zarina occupied a moral high ground he had no interest in contesting.

Zarina looked at her family and made a mental note of the culinary tyranny she was being subjected to and then, perhaps even willingly, pushed on regardless, her jaw set.

"Nasreen, how do you want your eggs?" Nasreen sat next to her father, waiting expectantly.

"What?"

"Don't 'what' me. Soft? Runny? With onion? *Speak*, child."

"*Whatever*. I don't care."

"Fine, you get what I give you."

"No, wait – soft, *soft*, mother dearest, please!" Nasreen turned to her father and guided their mutual attention back to the wedding. "Don't you think it's a bit much, Dad?" she said winningly. "The house *and* the cars *and* the hem?"

"Of course it's a bit much!" said Adam, delighted both with the new morsel Nasreen had gifted him with, and the opportunity to turn away from Zarina's resentful cooking and Alia's footwear crisis. "The whole thing is a bit much! Over a thousand guests! A football team for a retinue! Crayfish curry for everyone! Seven hajis to carry her off … a bruid's *huis*, never mind a bruid's kamer! Bregat Slamse! What happened to the days of a humble bredie? A close gathering at the father's home?"

Adam, whose own wedding had been far closer to Tasneem's than the fictional one to which he was declaring allegiance, was playing to his daughters who in turn rewarded him with their complete attention. They laughed as he reeled them in with each exclamation, and just as their laughter was reaching a crescendo, Adam, as he did so often, abruptly changed tack, drawing his mouth into a serious line, which made him look both censorious and conscience stricken. "And why shouldn't he? That man works so hard for his money. I happen to know for a fact that he is up and at that factory by six-thirty every morning, and he's had a helluva year with those bladdy unions. He can do what he likes with his own money. Where else are you supposed to find your joy? It's his only daughter ..." He warmed to this theme, looking at his two children with reproach. "Yes, if you have only the one, you can have a big thing like that."

The girls' laughter dropped into silence before Alia said, "But Tasneem *has* got sisters. Imtiaaz and Zainab and Shakirah."

Adam flicked a dismissive hand her way; he didn't always remember the names or numbers of his family's or friends' children. "You know what I mean. There are big age gaps between all of them. Plenty of time to recover from one to the other." He stood up. "See you all later. I'm off."

Nasreen rose with him. Alia noticed for the first time that her sister was carrying a fez in her left hand. "I'm coming with you," Nasreen said.

"What about your eggs?" Her mother held a plate towards her.

"This may prove more important than breakfast," Nasreen said, assuming an air of grand significance, of sacrifice.

"Suit yourself," said Zarina, managing to pack away pots, brush away crumbs and flick on the kettle in a single movement. "Don't come crying to me when you feel sick later."

"Hurry up then," answered her father, searching for his keys. "Be quick about it. You lucky the women are going to this one or you would be stuck. I still have to fetch my mother."

"No, you don't," said Zarina, head in the fridge. "She called to say she's got one of her headaches. She's not coming." She closed the fridge door, touched Alia's shoulders to remind her to sit up straight and continued, this time addressing in a just-audible mutter the dishcloths she'd begun folding, "Though I'm pretty sure she'd get herself out of bed if it was for her side of the family."

Adam threw his wife a reproachful look before turning to Nasreen. "Where's your scarf?"

Nasreen hesitated before saying, "I'm not going to sit with the women. I want to sit with you." And she put the fez on as if to punctuate her sentence. It fitted her perfectly, her head disappearing into a boyish dome where the hat sat against her clipped hair.

Adam did not bother to respond. He simply walked towards the door.

Nasreen trailed him in rapid steps. "Dad, I'm serious. I want to sit with you ... *please*. The whole point is that men are not supposed to be in mosque and get ... aroused."

Adam flinched at the word. Trying to sound clinical, Nasreen pressed on. "They're not supposed to get aroused, but here's the thing, right? If I dress like a boy then no one will know! And they won't think anything if I sit next to them! And we can sit together." Her eyes were shining and she began to turn around, letting the full meaning of her boyish shirt and baggy trousers set in.

Alia watched her father groping towards words that refused to come. Nasreen stood very still as if her immobility itself was an argument, as if the rootedness of her feet – clad, Alia noticed, in a pair of really cool burgundy brogues. *When did she get those?* – would persuade him of her seriousness.

It was Zarina who cut through the gathering tension. "Adam, go ... just go or you are going to be late. Nasreen, please don't be foolish. This is not some crazy version of *Yentl*. You can go and sit with the women if you want to, and that's that."

Nasreen had been counting on a dramatic face-off. She had not anticipated Zarina's briskness. She watched her plan disintegrate in front of her and collapsed into a rage of disappointment. "I don't *want* to sit with the women," she growled. "They get stuck in the fucking basement."

"Language," Zarina snapped.

Adam remained silent. The sight of his daughter in what he was beginning to think of as drag had shocked the power of speech from him. But Nasreen had heard the clarion call to battle and pushed on heroically. "We're in the basement. The BASEMENT!" she called after her mother, who was now halfway up the stairs, her hands racing through her hair as if she was trying to shortcut having to style it. "Behind a curtain!" Nasreen chased after Zarina, taking the steps two at a time while Adam took the opportunity to head off. Nasreen turned heel and began to pursue him. "We can't see the imam, or the mimbar or anything!"

"Oh, for God's sake," muttered Zarina as she turned on the landing.

When Adam reached the front door, the familiarity of the leaving ritual – *keys, koffeya, shut the balcony door* – allowed him to recover his voice and authority all in one breath. "I'll be home in an hour," he announced and then directed commands at the daughter in front of him (still glowering, aflame with righteousness) and the one in the kitchen (trying to balance the need to eat with the desire to listen in). "When I get back here, I expect you both to be dressed appropriately."

Nasreen made a show of acknowledging defeat. She heaved a deep sigh and went to join her sister, all the while shaking her head from side to side like someone whose worst suspicions about the world had just been confirmed.

"I didn't do anything!" Alia bellowed after her father.

"Well, you're not dressed yet, are you? Not even showered. That's just as bad." Adam's voice unsteady, he occupied himself with the business of leaving, hoping he would not burst out laughing before he exited the house. He *still* couldn't find his keys. He began scratching through the collection of Turkish bowls that sat plump, blue-green and trimmed with dull silver on the entrance hall table.

"Ziiiinaaa!" he called out in a panic.

"*What*?" came the long-suffering answer.

"I can't find my bladdy *keys* again."

"Ask the girls to help you – I'm in the *shower*."

Adam darted into the kitchen.

"Nalia!" (He often combined their names when he was in a hurry, not from affection, but from carelessness.) Both daughters stared at him frozen faced; they had made a pact not to respond to the amalgam. Nasreen began to make a show of looking round the room and under the table.

"Who is this Nalia?" she asked Alia curiously. "Any idea where she might be?"

"I can't think," Alia answered on cue.

"I mean *Nalia, Alia, Nasreen, man*." Adam rushed energetically through the small room, lifting envelopes and cereal boxes up and down as though the keys were hiding in the least likely places. "Where the hell are my keys? I know one of you must have taken them."

"Why would we have *your* car keys? We can't even drive."

Adam looked pained. He was genuinely panicked. He hated arriving late at mosque, he regularly railed against others who did, especially for a Nikha. *The height of rudeness*, he would complain if someone arrived midway through the ceremony.

Just then, Zarina reappeared, keys in hand, hair dripping, already dressed. *How did she do that*, wondered Alia, *it's been barely seven minutes*.

"Here they are." Her husband reached for them, grateful. "You left them upstairs in your jeans." She turned to the girls to assess how far from done they were. Nasreen made a show of ignoring her eggs and sulkily poured cereal into a bowl, allowing a few crispy grains to fall onto the table, while Alia took up her now cold breakfast with a special effort: this was not the time to draw attention to her usual wastefulness. Zarina shot Nasreen a warning look. "This isn't over. I don't know what you are thinking, pulling a time-wasting stunt like this. Adam, wait there, I want to talk to you." She followed her husband to the door as though something had only just occurred to her.

In the kitchen, Alia laboured heroically through a piece of cold toast. "Why did you do that?" she asked Nasreen curiously. "You must have known there was no *way* Dad would go along with it."

Nasreen chewed for several moments, staring at Alia before answering. "Pushing boundaries. That's the only way to change things. You ask for more than they'll give, but as much as you deserve. Have you learned nothing from this country?"

Not for the first time, Alia looked at her sister with something approaching reverence.

Adam and Zarina were talking in loud whispers at the front door. Alia was about to say something when Nasreen raised her hand irritably; she wanted to listen in properly. Their father was protesting that he was going to be late as Zarina talked in a low urgent tone. "... may be more serious than we think ... adolescence ... *prime time* ... What if we are ignoring some warning signs? An *all-girls school*? There was even a parents' teachers meeting about it last term ... it's all the fashion now ... *lesbianism* is rife there ... and if it is so, we will just have to find a way to deal with it, to really *accept* it—"

Alia looked down at her plate and focused intently on re-buttering her toast, while Nasreen scooped up the last splash of milk from her bowl, an amused cat-like smile playing around her mouth.

~

The Good Hope Centre sat between the beginning of the city and on the frayed edge of what had once been District Six. It was an oddly shaped building with a rounded roof that, from a distance, looked as though it met the pavement at a shingled tip. It gave the impression that its other half existed in a curved symmetry beneath the ground. It looked, said Alia as they pulled up, like a sub-standard UFO.

"What I don't understand," said Zarina as she climbed out of the car, breathing deeply at the fresh air after the strong, sickly smell of leather seats, "what I have never understood, is how the government could build this monstrosity but tear down all those beautiful Victorians. I mean, where is the logic to that?"

Adam was pointing his hand towards his car to activate the new alarm; it was the latest in vehicle accoutrements and he always felt a small thrill of pride when it announced that he could afford both the car and its protection. He waved the girls out of the Mercedes like a conductor, sweeping his arm in strong stretches. "Come on! Come on! You *both* look very nice, by the way."

They didn't. It was a lie, though a very kind one. Nasreen did. She had capitulated entirely, abandoned her previous costume and was now wearing (to Alia's envy) the pale-blue chiffon dress, the soft material patterned by abstract blossoms. The cloth fell in transparent lines over a darker blue slip and she held herself with a practised grace that marked all her movements and spoke to years of dedicated afternoons at the ballet bar. But her expression, pinched and self-righteous (she had not expected to win the mosque argument, but she was furious at how quickly it had been dismissed), clashed with the girlish demureness of the outfit. Later, people would murmur, "That Dawood girl has her parents' features, but her grandmother's attitude. If looks could kill, hey? If-looks-could-*kill* ..."

Alia, on the other hand, was a catastrophe. It wasn't her fault. It was not for lack of trying, or for lack of preparation. She had thought this through for weeks, she had strategised against this day, she had a mental image of what the moment *should* have been, but the best laid plans and so forth. Her first mistake was the colour, a muddled burnt sienna that sounded wonderful in description but did nothing for the yellowish undertone of her skin. The second was the style: knee-length culottes and a matching buttoned-up top. In an attempt to be chic and grown-up she had gravitated towards something that a conservative forty-year-old might wear. Zarina had very gently tried to dissuade her from buying it but Alia had been determined. She had a fixed image of how she wanted to look and she pursued it, with dismal results. The crochet lace at the collar did not help and neither did her mother's sensible navy pumps. *It was the shoes*, she had thought when she looked in the full-length bathroom mirror, *wasn't it?*

She only grasped the full meaning of her failure an hour earlier when she had left the comfort of her room, met Nasreen and seen herself reflected in her sister's eyes. The worst was that Nasreen tried to be nice about it, which made Alia realise she must look irredeemable. It was difficult for her. She had been an exceptionally pretty child, all huge delightful eyes, boundless energy, shiny hair and round cheeks. But adolescence had been cruel, distorting her prettiness, making a mockery of her toddling years, leaving Alia bewildered, spending hours in front of the mirror, searching for traces of her old adorable self. It was a phase that marked the end of vanity and ushered in vanity's dark twin, self-doubt.

The Dawoods walked up the wide shallow steps of the centre, the women holding their skirts down against a mischievous breeze, Adam stopping to greet old friends. These were the moments in which the taciturn man of the working week made an abrupt exit and a creature charmed and energised by social interaction emerged. His wife and daughters hovered a few steps behind him, the girls on standby in case they were ushered forward for an introduction. Zarina pulled an impatient face, using a tissue to ward off any wind-born pollen that could spark her allergies. Adam was giddy with excitement. There were almost too many people to talk to. He felt torn – filled with all this new information about the bride's new house and the dress hem and agonising about whom to tell first. He zeroed in on Mustapha Ebrahim, a chubby man who had always been slightly in awe of him, and Taariq Dickenson, a childhood friend who was also second cousin to the groom.

"So have you heard?" he said as an opening. "Your cousin has landed with his bum in the clarified ghee. A bladdy *house*, never mind a backroom."

Taariq inclined his head as if to indicate that his new uncle-in-law was a generous man, but that his cousin was worth it. It was the perfect response.

Adam was on the cusp of sharing the details of Tasneem's dress, when Zarina pulled him up short. "Adam, we have to get a move on," and then by way of explanation to Mustapha and Taariq, "my parents are waiting for us inside."

"Hey!" said Taariq as Adam made his apologies. "Is Waleed coming? I got him now-now the other day in Observatory and he said he might come down."

"I don't know if he was invited," said Adam. "We're here with Zina's side."

"I guess it's not really his thing, hey?" said Mustapha, worried that what he was saying could be offensive.

"Not his thing at all," replied Adam gaily, "never was! I'll see you chaps later. I have to go and greet Mr and Mrs H."

Adam returned to his family.

"Why do you always have to do that?" said Zarina crossly. "We don't even know if we are supposed to know about the house."

But Adam refused to feel guilty. "Trust me, Miley wants *everyone* to know about that house. I'm doing him a favour. It looks better if I tell people than if he goes about boasting. Christ Almighty, is the whole community here? Everyone from Gujerat and the Archipelago?"

The Dawoods had stopped on the lip of the main hall, a cavernous, poorly ventilated room. Every inch had been accounted for, with fabric, gifts, tables, food or people. There must have been close to eight hundred guests already, with table settings for a few hundred more.

Tasneem (née Hassan) Mukherjee's wedding was clearly a major social event, though it stood to reason: the bride and groom's families were vast, and in addition, at least twenty people from every clan (from the Abrahamses to the Zakirs) were there.

The families of this world were huge and scattered. Adam found himself thinking of his own relatives. There had been a time when the Dawoods had lived in just a few places, and he had grown up knowing only a tight urban grid from Niall Street in the District to Coventry Road in Woodstock, but with the removals had come new places and new names: the Dawoods from Lansdowne, Mitchell's Plain, Fairways (the coloured Constantia), Bridgetown, Bonteheuwel, Manenberg. They were all there and so were the others: the Isaacs, the Williamses, the Gools, and the Behardiens, the Samies, the Shamsodiens, the Essops, the Effendies, the Masoets, the Jamals, the Kaders and the Kahns, the Adamses, the

Jaffers, the Safodiens, the Frederickses, the Hartleys, the Jeppies and the Jacobses.

The hall had been festooned with flowers and draped with hundreds, perhaps thousands of metres of gold and cream voile, the material fitted round chairs, hung at a drop from the tall walls and gathered in bunches at the windows. Each table had been covered with three layers of cloth of varying sizes to create a pattern. As Alia walked in she saw one man lean towards another and heard him say, "You see this voile? It's bladdy *ten rand* a metre in the shop. This must have cost him an arm and a leg." "But you forgetting," answered the friend, "they in the *textile* business ..."

Tables were never assigned. Guests arrived as soon as they could and gravitated towards those people they knew. Accordingly, Adam made a beeline for some friends, and Zarina spotted her friend Shehnaz and waved as she walked towards her. The girls trailed their mother and stopped in front of Shehnaz, who was sunk in conversation with another woman. Shehnaz, a rangy, vivacious woman in her late thirties, lifted her eyes hopefully towards Zarina, shorthand that she needed to be rescued. She made a show of lifting, billowing and replacing a large black-fringed Spanish shawl about her shoulders as though at any moment she would have to either leave or dance. Some of the tassels caught on the chair where the leg met the seat and Shehnaz gave the freeing of the material her full and unnecessary focus.

"So we looking round, looking round," the woman was saying to Shehnaz, bearing down to help liberate the scarf. "We down for just the week and the boy is here from Texas ... in *engineering*, no less ... You look around for me too, hey? Don't be shy about coming to talk to Auntie Marrel!"

Auntie Marrel, amply bosomed, with a thin laugh that

streamed like a ribbon through all her sentences, was clutching Shehnaz's hand as though she was trying to extract a promise from her.

Zarina leaned past the older woman to kiss her friend. She had a fundamental distrust of people who referred to themselves in the third person. "Sorry, sorry," she excused herself, "I just haven't seen Shehnaz in so long."

Shehnaz grabbed her chance and began to gabble. "Oh, Zina, you remember my Auntie Marrel? She's Uncle Amien's sister, from the people up in Transvaal? Well, her cousin's nephew is here from Texas … amazing, hey? Texas! He's an engineer, and they looking for introductions to a nice girl."

Marrel snapped her head towards Zarina, her smile full and beaming. "Salam Wailakom," she said in a high, nasally voice that didn't match her round face and eyes. "I remember *you*. I haven't seen you in a long time, hey? But what I do know is you have two girls." She said this delightedly, joyously, as if she had been holding Zarina in her thoughts for the last decade and had been waiting for just this moment of reconnection. Zarina nodded cautiously and Marrel pushed on, her face a mask of innocence. "How old are they now?"

"Oh, far, *far* too young, Auntie," Zarina shot back. "Fourteen and sixteen."

Marrel cast a beady eye on Nasreen and Alia, who had both unconsciously moved closer to their mother. Zarina, equally instinctively, had positioned herself between them and Marrel.

"Mmm," Marrel, undeterred, began to size them up. "Very. Nice. Girls," she pronounced with finality.

Alia offered a smile. She always responded to praise with some display of gratitude; it was hard-wired in her. Nasreen, on the other hand, let outrage gather on her face and she began to channel her mosque-anger towards the old woman.

Marrel mistook the intensity of Nasreen's gaze for interest and she cupped her chin approvingly. "Don't worry! Auntie Marrel doesn't think sixteen is so young. Auntie Marrel had had her *third child* by the time she was sixteen. Zina, you listen close: now more than ever, you want to make sure they meet the right boys. These new people are going to blow the country wide open – make it fine for anyone to marry anyone. And then you have dogs and cats in the same stable."

Nasreen jerked her face away, while Zarina offered her daughter an apologetic grimace.

Marrel looked bewildered and sought to make amends. "And both very pretty, hey? And so *light* of complexion."

Nasreen took a deep breath, preparing to respond, but the old lady cut her off by reaching in front of Shehnaz towards the table's primary decoration, two white interlinked fake porcelain hands that met at the wrist and clasped a pink net bag of Jordan almonds.

"Shehnaz, are you going to take these?" she asked, her own hands already around the ornamental ones.

"Er, no, Auntie."

"Okay then," said Marrel, opening her vast handbag, making quick work of depositing the party favour. As she did, Alia caught a glimpse of the purse's contents and was treated to the bizarre sight of several ceramic hands nestling in the dark, reaching up towards the light. "I want to take some home for my daughters ... they very nice, hey?" Here she gestured unashamedly at the pale fingers and slender palms. "I haven't seen ones like this before. It's now really something you can put in your house. If you see any more, let me know."

And with that she trundled off, working her way past each table, stopping either to peddle her own merchandise – *An engineer! Texas!* – or to collect the wedding's.

With Auntie Marrel's departure, Zarina began to hurl accusations. "The absolute nerve of her! What are we – still in the village? Bartering our girls off? These *people*—"

"Oh, relax," answered Shehnaz, reaching for the bowl of chevra, "it's not like she's doing any real harm. The woman's just doing what she thinks is right." She stopped and opened her arms and offered her cheek to the girls. "Kisses!" she demanded and they supplied. "Sorry about that, lovelies! Pay no attention to the quest for child brides." She turned to Zarina. "Where's Adam?"

Zarina sighed into her seat. "Off talking to his friends. Are my parents here?"

"Naturally," said Shehnaz, munching on the salty-sweet pale gold snack flecked with iridescent green and red. "By the time I got here their table was already full. Everyone clamoured for it the moment they sat down."

Zarina's parents, Ebrahim and Catherine, had met at the Drill Hall and made eyes at each other while around them swirled a discussion about Lenin's "What is to be done?" Ebrahim, Indian and Muslim, had just joined the Unity Movement, and Catherine, coloured and Catholic, had just joined the Eon Group. They were both exactly daring enough not to demand that the other convert, but neither had ever fully shed their respective faiths to become full agnostics. It had something to do with fear and something to do with old loyalties and love. Catherine incorporated a few Islamic rituals in her life: she stayed away from pork, poured water on herself after she went to the toilet, hid her vodka bottles in among her shoes at the back of her cupboard, and gave her children Muslim names. She celebrated Eid, but smoked through the Fast, kept a mostly halaal house, but insisted on a full Christmas lunch.

"No, nobody has mentioned the fire yet." Shehnaz was answering Zarina's question. "It's subject non grata."

"But they're all here, aren't they," said Zarina, "both sides?"

"Both sides," confirmed Shehnaz gleefully. "An invisible line has been drawn down the hall. Can't you feel it? I swear it's almost palpable. Oh! I forgot to tell you! Uncle Sammy is back. And he's here, at the wedding."

"Really?" Zarina turned excitedly to her daughters. "You girls are in for a special treat. Uncle Sammy is one of your grandfather's closest friends and he's been in exile in London for almost thirty years."

Nasreen refused to be impressed. She was always slightly unnerved by talk of her mother's childhood. She didn't like to think of her as having had a life before them. "How do you know he's so great if you haven't seen him in thirty years?" She did some rapid calculations. "That means you haven't seen him since you were twelve or something. How do you even remember him after all this time?"

Zarina offered Nasreen her profile and began to talk about her daughters in front of them, a tactic that enraged both girls but proved curiously effective in getting their tongues under control. "You see this?" she said to Shehnaz. "You see what I have to deal with? It's always something. Just go and find your grandparents."

Nasreen and Alia got up dutifully. Something happened to them in these environments, making them obey their parents blindly. They always felt slightly foreign and rudderless. The weight of tradition would lean heavily on them and they would feel cloaked in difference, their accents, mannerisms, and frame of reference all serving as a deep and wide boundary between them and the others in the hall.

"Come on," said Nasreen and she began to walk towards their grandparents. As they walked the girls became increasingly conscious of eyes trained towards them. They were related to almost everyone there through immediate or distant but always intricate bonds of marriage or blood, and there was little doubt that every adult there felt a sense of claim on them. Walking the full diagonal of this hall was not unlike running the social gauntlet of a medieval court. Alia's shoulders curved around her heart and she tucked her chin into her chest so that her body began to take on the lank stoop of a Walmer Estate tree. She cursed the navy pumps which, along with their ugliness, had also granted her an additional two inches. Nasreen floated ahead in a trail of confident chiffon. At the end of their journey lay the oasis of their grandparents, and the particular blend of respect and envy the Hassans generated.

Nasreen and Alia worshipped their grandparents as if they embodied the gendered principals of two alternating gods: he, authoritarian, successful, bright; she, beautiful, sophisticated, wonderfully social. There was just one seat open at their table and Nasreen grabbed it, saying as she sat down, "I'm older." Alia hovered behind her, hands touching the cream voile that masked the chair's aluminum frame, like someone posing for a turn of the century family portrait.

Their grandmother was talking to an agitated Auntie Waarda, one of the victims of the fire, and their grandfather was laughing with a man they presumed to be the once-exiled Uncle Sammy. The girls knew better than to think the Hassans senior would open a space in the conversation for them. For all their social rebellions the couple was conservative about child-rearing; they were fond of all their progeny, but they had not made a successful transition to modern day grandparenting, nor did they wish to.

~

As she watched her two daughters walk off, Zarina leaned in to Shenaz. "*Naz* ... I must talk to you about something. What do you know about the first signs of," she dropped her voice to an agonised whisper, "*lesbianism*?"

Shehnaz, who at this point had commandeered the chevra,

began to choke on a mouthful of the toasted rice. "What?" she coughed.

"We think," Zarina continued, "we *think*, Nasreen may have been trying to tell us something."

She etched out the morning's fight.

"You're quite right," Shehnaz shot back. "She's trying to tell you she sees through it. All of it ... this whole hoo-hah."

"So you don't think? You don't think – oh, thank *goodness* ... you don't think?"

Shehnaz stared at her coldly, while Zarina beamed, glossing over a twinge of conscience at the relief she felt.

"I don't know what you so relieved about, Zina," said Shehnaz. "This is just the tip of the iceberg. It took me well into my twenties before I realised how chronically unfair all this shit is."

"Hah!" said Zarina happily. The future was a long way off and hopefully all Nasreen's major rebellions would take place overseas. The two women glanced as one around the hall, lost for a moment in the flamingo menagerie of pastels and sequins and craned necks. Zarina broke through their reverie and steered the conversation back to her. It was so rare for her to have this sort of attention. "We got their school fees bill last week," she said gloomily and reached into her tiny clutch for a mint, popping one in her mouth and offering another to her friend.

"I just hope it's worth it," said Shehnaz, accepting the sweet.

"It's not like we have any options."

~

Having laid exclusive claim to the chair by placing her bag on the seat, Nasreen got up and motioned Alia forward to greet their grandfather. Ebrahim smiled at them and reached out to hold their hands, absently, as if they were toddlers, while continuing to listen to what his friend was saying.

"It's going to be a place for people to talk, to come forward and tell their stories, and we want the perpetrators there, too."

The girls struggled to place his accent; it had traces of a Capetonian origin but was shot through with the rounded vowels and even rhythms of the English.

Ebrahim's forehead furrowed. "It sounds like a trial, Sammy," he said.

"No," answered Uncle Sammy, tugging at his cravat, "that's just it. It's not supposed to be some sort of Nuremberg. It's not a forum for doling out punishment. We just want to hear the truth. That's all."

"Well," said Ebrahim, reaching for the water jug, looking at its contents a little regretfully before shrugging apologetically and pouring his friend a glass of tepid Oros, "*that* is something I look forward to."

A white-haired, dark-skinned man, who Alia recognised vaguely as one of the Muslim Council elders, was sitting at the table too. His cheeks drooped into his jowls and hung in flabby half-moons over his jaw; together with his doleful eyes, they made him look like a disconsolate basset hound. He was gobbling his way through a silver-gold sweetmeat, the tassel of his fez swinging close to a spittle-laced lower lip, when he leaned across the table and, with unexpected venom, addressed Uncle Sammy. "This country is going to the dogs. The *dogs*! Everybody knows you can't trust the Africans. You can't even *smile* at the kaffirs because they will steal the teeth straight out of your mouth. We would be better off under the Nats. You mark my words. They just a bunch of skollies, of communists. That Mandela at least wears a suit, he's respectable, but those other ones, they just terrorists and that's that. And they try to trick you with sweet names! They think if they called Honey or Sugar or I don't know what, you won't think about who they really are. Like when this girl who worked for us was called Precious or Patience or something, and then she stole the money right out of my wife's jewellery box. Tell them, Diji! Sê vir hulle! She just took that money!"

"Is waar," affirmed Diji glumly, reaching a satin clad arm out, making a play for the last samoosa.

Ebrahim and Sammy turned to each other, a grinning, wicked delight passing over and through their wrinkles. Alia saw her grandfather at twelve, at twenty, laughing with this same friend. Eventually, Ebrahim stopped. "Did you mean Hani? Hani! Not," he began to laugh again, "Honey."

The man raised a glass to his vinegary, trembling lips, saying between darting sips, "One way or the other they all killers. You mark my words. And you, Shamiel," he turned to Sammy, "you the *worst*. Because you always choose the Africans over your own."

Sammy didn't bother responding. He merely turned to Ebrahim. "People still think like this? I would have thought this sort had died off already."

"My friend," said Ebrahim, pausing to sneer at the elder, "you have come back to a place both new and rotten." He had long since dropped his granddaughters' hands and started guiltily when he realised they were still standing there, in need of some sort of directive. "Sammy," he announced largely, rising to his familial duty, "these are my grandchildren. This is Nasreen. And this is Alia. Zarina's girls."

Sammy nodded and smiled but offered none of the usual platitudes. He didn't comment on the miracle of Zarina being old enough, thirty years after his departure, to have children of her own, he didn't congratulate his friend on the girls' decorous smiles, he didn't ask them how they liked school. Instead, he let his gaze roam the hall in a half-circle before saying to Ebrahim, "You don't know what it's like to be back. I felt half dead every day I was there, and now that I'm here ..." He shook his head free of whatever was stuck in his mouth and Ebrahim placed a hand on his shoulder in a gesture of intimate, awkward consolation. The girls drifted back to Catherine.

"But you are all safe and that's what matters," their grandmother was saying. "They put it out just in time?" Catherine patted the woman's hand as if that was the end of it.

But Waarda shook her head, refusing to be comforted. "We have been saying for years, for *years* that that tree was a health hazard. Did they listen? No, they did not! And now we all sit with the damage."

The combination of Waarda's rhetoric and rage was hard to break through, but Catherine managed it by breathing out her cigarette smoke and turning towards the other end of the hall, a clear signal that she was bored. "Look how nicely they've done it," she said waving towards the stage.

Waarda, sensing that she had wrung the last bit of interest from Catherine, bade her farewell and went off in search of a new audience. Alia sank into the empty chair and followed her grandmother's smoky gesture towards the other end of the hall. There it was, the centrepiece of any Cape Muslim wedding: the stage. Once the bride had made her entrance she would march past the thousand guests and take her place, along with her husband, three bridesmaids, their attendant best men and the mini-bride and groom on its elevated dais. They would stand for a moment and then proceed to sit. And sit. For about an hour. With a marked and disciplined stillness. They would do nothing but sit, giving the guests a chance to look at the bride's dress, the bridesmaids' outfits, the best men's suits, and the curious phenomenon of the toddling bride and groom, those hapless children dressed in corresponding mini-outfits.

This stage had been designed around the central theme of the cream and gold drapery, but at least six palm fronds had been added as a decorative touch. In the centre of the stage were three-foot tall chairs that looked suspiciously like the thrones used in the previous year's Christmas pantomime at the Baxter Theatre. They were high-backed, plush, red velvet, and trimmed with thick gold brocade. To the couple's left and right were three hard-backed wooden chairs, and in the centre, three Moroccan striped leather poufs for the little ones.

The soft, nondescript but vaguely Eastern background music was shut off abruptly and a solemn voice came over the PA system. "*As*Salamwalaikom! Ladies and gentlemen, brothers and sisters, it is my *great* privilege to announce to you that the bride is about to proceed in her commencement into the hall. She will be here momentarily, Insh'Allah, and we must say Mash'Allah that Allah'Tallah have granted this young couple *plenty* of barakat, because we have only just heard that they have received a wonderful gift from her parents." A drum roll of a pause followed. "A brand new Mercedes-Benz!"

A gasping sigh rippled through the audience, deep nods of approval were exchanged by the elder people, tight and jealous expressions by the younger ones.

Alia felt Nasreen jab her in the ribs.

"Hello? Stop daydreaming. Tasneem just walked in. Look!"

The appearance of their cousin afforded both the girls' cynicism and boredom a brief but pronounced hiatus. The rumours of heavy Swarovski crystal beadwork on imported Italian silk had been greatly exaggerated, but Tasneem, an average looking young woman, was one of those people intended for the wedding day, if not for marriage. She had accepted all its conventional magic and had allowed herself to be touched by something, its sense of occasion, the permission to be lovely, a shift into the other-worldliness that celebrities sometimes assume under the spotlight. She was everything bridal: lovely, manicured, cream and serene. She negotiated the almost thousand pairs of eyes trained towards her as though aware of them, but also indifferent, grateful for their presence, but only really interested in her husband, glad to see whoever she made eye contact with, but not giving anyone preferential treatment. It was a flawless performance. Her husband Shafiek stood beside her, pristine in a Fabiani suit, his thinning black hair gelled into an ambitious flock-of-seagulls quiff.

The bride and her retinue took their seats. Tasneem's three sisters were all bridesmaids, so the tableau had a repetitive, genetic weirdness to it.

"Look at the Christian table," said Nasreen. "God, they look miserable."

The Christian Table was an assembly of people who miserably collected together, despite the open seating, with nothing to bind them, apart from their shared faith. It was always populated by unscarved women and bewildered-looking men. The women always tried, and generally failed, to wear appropriately modest outfits. Their dresses or blouses would be cut from the same cloth as their Muslim counterparts but they always exposed a little cleavage or defiantly flashed a shoulder. The men would blend in slightly better (a suit is a suit is a suit) but they were conspicuous by their actual presence at the table. Muslim men seldom sat still at weddings. It was the one time they did not expect to have food brought to them. Only older men in weakened health sat at tables, men who were grey and holding court and complaining about indigestion. Boys in their teens who were peripherally connected to the wedding party could sometimes be found out in the parking lot sitting in cars pumping beats in a subdued version of the gathering outside of HAL's, but every other able-bodied man would be seen pacing up and down, shouting orders at the cooks, bringing food in on huge platters, coaching the photographer into co-coordinating group shots, instructing the videographer about whom to focus on, helping the dressmaker field questions about bridal fabric, or decorating cars with thick shiny ribbons that stretched from door to emblem. Girls between the ages of thirteen and twenty-two did lots of getting up and walking around. It was a key way to show off your outfit and demonstrate that you had good use of all your limbs, a not especially radical version of the animal kingdom's mating ritual, although it meant that half the seats in the hall were perpetually empty.

The Christian table on the other hand was always full. It was usually made up of several aunties who were either neighbours or from a branch of a family who had "turned". Occasionally there would be a young white couple, colleagues of the groom, a fellow accountant and his wife, who would sit grinning and puzzled for most of the day. The wife would begin the afternoon with interested nods and stop-start attempts at chatter and would generally leave with a renewed gratitude for alcohol as a social lubricant.

"Hi," said a voice in Alia's ear.

She turned around and gave a start. "Oh my God! What are *you* doing here?"

"Celebrating." The boy gave a wide smile. "Don't look so shocked, I'm not *stalking* you. I'm Nick," he said, holding his hand out to Nasreen.

"Hi," Nasreen nodded and did a quick scan of his suit. Her father's daughter, she took just a few moments to conclude that it was not his, but probably borrowed.

Alia could barely contain her delight, or her shock. "But what are you *doing* here? How did you get in?"

"Well, it's not like it's a club – you don't have to have your name on the list."

"Are you gate-crashing?" Alia was thrilled at the thought.

"No, man. My dad's in business with Uncle Ismail."

"Ohhhh." Alia felt the Capetonian circle describe itself in its inevitable closeness. "So is *mine*. That's amazing! Isn't that amazing, Nasreen?"

"It is ... *amazing*."

Alia and Nick were too ensconced in their private miracle to notice her sarcasm.

"Where are you sitting?" asked Alia.

Nick pointed towards the Christian Table, saying, "I'm over there, with my parents. That's my mom." He singled out a woman in a severe black wrap dress who was dividing her time between talking to Auntie May and looking at her watch. Alia knew, without asking, that no introductions would be forthcoming.

"So, when does the dancing start?" said Nick. When Nasreen deadpanned him, he responded with an apologetic chuckle, "I was just going outside for a smoke. You guys want to come with?"

Alia started out of her chair but stopped when her sister touched her hand and said, "You can't."

Her obedience was instinctive but her understanding was not. "Why?" she asked. "It's not like I'm going to light up in front of the entire hall."

"You can't walk out together," said Nasreen, staring levelly at them both. Nick's forehead furrowed. Alia could barely look at him.

"You could meet up," continued Nasreen soothingly. "Nick, you go outside and she'll meet you in the front."

"Ok*ay*." Nick made a show of being puzzled, knitting his eyebrows together and drawing out the last part of the word.

He shrugged himself into a dark jacket he had been holding over one arm in an expansive gesture and looked around the hall, feeling suddenly both the eyes and their masked pretence of indifference and he remembered his mother's warning when he had first told her about Alia. "You watch out, those people think they better than everyone else, and in no time they will be trying to convert you."

"So, I'll get you outside," he said to Alia. "Farouk is here, too. I'm going to hang with him."

"Okay, I'll see you now-now."

Alia watched Nick walk down the length of the hall, his body full of the cocky saunter she had first seen in the club.

"Jesus, you are pathetic at this." Nasreen's words jolted her out of her reverie.

"What?"

"*What*? What are you thinking? Are you crazy? Everyone will see you."

"Ja, well … sorry I don't have your gifts of subterfuge."

"Survival," corrected her sister.

Alia reached sulkily for a cold samoosa. "Anyway, I have bigger problems."

"Like what?"

"Like *this*." She cast a despairing hand over what she was wearing. "I forgot about this. He only saw the top half, how am I going to explain this" – she touched the floral knee-length culottes – "or this?" She tapped her heavy leather pumps to the floor. "I look like a freak." She was close to tears.

"But your face looks pretty," said Nasreen, offering what Alia thought was cold comfort. "Hey! He's no great shakes himself. He looks like he borrowed one of his father's old suits."

"No, he doesn't," said Alia, now completely in the thrall of her own misery. "He looks great."

"Okay, well, I have an idea. Get up."

Alia scraped herself out of the cream swathed chair.

"Where do you think you are going?" asked Catherine in a tone that warned against lying.

"To the bathroom, Granny," answered Nasreen.

"Mind you back in ten minutes. Your grandfather wants to introduce you properly to Uncle Sammy."

"We've been sitting here the whole time."

Catherine pursed her lips and looked away. Her granddaughters' extraordinary capacity to feel equal to the adults in their lives was an abiding source of deep irritation for her. She blamed her daughter's hippie-like enthusiasm for their feelings and her son-in-law's crazed indulgence of their every whim.

~

The mirrors around the bathroom were crowded three-deep with women reapplying lipstick and mascara (mouths parted, eyebrows arched) and the stalls held at least two people at a time: giggling pairs of teenagers, mothers guiding toddlers – *Sit nicely there, come, stop playing, there's people waiting outside* – everyone making way for the old auntie who limped in complaining loudly about the late food, her bad legs, terrible bladder, that there were no stinja jugs. Two of Tasneem's bridesmaid sisters were there, too, dividing their time between puffing at a shared cigarette and driving in hairpins to secure their up-styles. One reached down to massage swollen feet. "Oh my word, I am in serious *pain* here."

From the doorway a male voice called out, "Gigi! Ilhaam! Are you in here? Come quick, they want to take some photos."

Ilhaam rifled through her tiny clutch and pulled out a small bottle of perfume. She sprayed herself and Gigi liberally, gave her mouth a quick rinse in a useless attempt to rid it of a nicotine smell and pushed her sore feet resolutely back into her ill-fitting shoes.

"Do you think they like being up on that stage?" said Alia as she watched the women hobbling off in a glimmering flurry of embellished satin.

"Christ, no," said Nasreen. "Who wants to spend their day looking out onto a room of unexamined lives? Okay. Come here."

Then Nasreen did a lovely thing for her sister. She swapped outfits. She took on the horrible awkwardness of Alia's bad choices and replaced them with the elegance of her own. Only Alia's shoes remained, but their ugly clumpiness was a little diminished by the new ensemble. She'd rescued herself from her sister's original outfit by not tucking the shirt in, flicking the lace collar under the shoulders so that it was hidden from view, unbuttoning the front so that it looked like a jacket and rolling up the sleeves to break down the stuffy feel.

"How did you do that?" asked Alia.

Nasreen gave her newly woven French plait a pat before herding her sister out the door.

"Won't he notice?" Alia was seized by a new terror that Nick would see what she had done and brand it as an exercise in vanity, second cousin to superficiality and therefore in close kinship with all the things they professed to despise.

"Doubtful," said Nasreen authoritatively. "I'm going to stand by the door, you've got five minutes. Go say hi and then we have to go back. And don't *smoke*."

Alia marched down the corridor between the hall and the centre's main entrance. Her heels clacked on the linoleum floor, each step taking her further from the assembly of scarves and sequins and closer to the freedom of nicotine and a snatched conversation. Small groups of paisley-tied, metallic-suited boys and men dotted the building's concrete slabs, around their shoes bits of confetti caught in the swirl of a light city wind and pigeons who'd confused the paper with crumbs. Alia searched for Nick, knowing she couldn't stand there indefinitely. At some point an uncle, a cousin, or a self-appointed morality guardian was going to look up, see her, and take it upon himself either to shepherd her back inside or complain to her parents in scandalised and concerned tones that she was behaving badly, ruining her reputation, pouring shame on her family's name, pulling the skin off their collective face. Alia shivered very slightly. The day was darkening and the thin chiffon felt even thinner outside. She saw Farouk first.

"Howzit?" he smiled, appearing next to her. "I thought maybe we should stand round the back?"

"Cool. I have literally three minutes. Where is he?"

"Just here."

Farouk guided her to a small staircase to the left of the entrance. Nick was standing in a scattered puddle of sunlight, puffing away at a cigarette.

"Hi." Alia smiled shyly.

"You look nice," Nick said, handing his cigarette over to Farouk, who stood considerately to the side.

"It's my sister's actually," said Alia, and then, "Sorry about all this subterfuge."

"Ja, it's kind of weird. I don't really understand. Who, exactly, are we hiding from?"

"My family."

"But your parents *know* me. It's not like I'm some random stranger."

"Oh, it's not my parents, more like my extended family."

"What, your cousins? But I *know* Tasneem."

Alia was wordless with the effort of making excuse and logic work in concert. She had no idea how to describe the people she was concerned about. There was reason to what Nick was saying, reason she longed to attach herself to. He *had* met her parents; he *did* know her cousin.

"I guess when *we* say family, we mean everyone." She gestured vaguely towards to hall.

"That's a lot of people to worry about."

"Ja," said Alia, and then, with a weary sense of defeat, "I have to go back in, my sister's waiting for me."

"Kiss me first." Nick threw the sentence down like a challenge.

"What? Are you crazy? I can't kiss you here."

"It's a *wedding*!" He spread his arms wide as if to take in the day and invoke the moments that had led its starring couple to this point. "What better place for a kiss than a wedding?"

In the background, Farouk let out a small chuckle and shook his head. Nick reached forward and picked Alia up, spinning her in a circle as if they were folk dancing. She was still almost an inch taller than him so he struggled a little with the effort, but he kept grinning up at her and her face now softened through the movement. She felt herself breaking into laughter and he deposited her back on the ground, both of them giggling.

"Alia, *Alia*." Farouk said her name with urgency. She looked at him and saw that he had tossed his cigarette away and was waving his hand to disperse the smoke. He lifted his eyes towards the top of the stairs. She followed his gaze and saw that she had been in full view of her father's cousins, men who had warned Adam for years that he was parenting his daughters with too little Koran and too much freedom.

"Oh shit, oh *shit*," she whispered to Farouk. "Did they see? Did they?"

Farouk nodded and then tried to ameliorate her panic. "Don't worry, it's nothing. Plus, I was here."

"Fuck."

"Chill, man, I think it will be okay – it was nothing."

"They saw you pick me up," said Alia accusingly.

"*Ja*. And?"

"*And*. Now I'll be in trouble."

"That's ridiculous."

"This is all your fault," said Alia, furious and anxious. "I *told* you not to pick me up."

"Oh my God. You people are nuts, you know that?"

Farouk had found his way to Alia's side where they now stood in unconscious solidarity. Alia glowered at Nick, who was moving his head with ostentatious slowness between them, a travelling, uncomprehending gaze that affirmed their alliance. Alia looked up to gauge how many of her uncles were still on the balcony, only to find that they were gone, had scattered like crows to spread their news and disapproval.

"Great," she said, noting their absence and knowing what it meant. "I am in for a world of pain."

Nick's bewilderment had eased but had been replaced with anger. "You people are living in the Dark Ages, man, this is some Stone Age shit."

"Look who's talking. You won't even introduce me to your mother!"

"Ja, but she knows I'm talking to you, and it's no big deal at all. It's not like she's going to issue some kind of *edict* about it."

Alia gave him a hard look, turned heel and stalked off, walking as furiously as she could in chiffon, a material that softens everything. When she got to the top of the stairs, she stopped, spun round and spat out a cruelty. "At least *we* know who we are."

When Nick looked up at her, his shock and hurt obvious, Alia scowled back, allowing herself a little smile of triumph. Her poisonous little blow had hit right where she intended.

Nasreen had gone back to her seat and Alia walked the length of the hall alone, her gloating carrying her easily back to her family. It was only when she saw her once-Christian grandmother that she began to feel queasy and guilt-ridden.

She got back to her seat, sighing deeply, and began to make a detailed study of her hands. She noticed that she had applied her nail polish unevenly; there were thick ridges and globs on some nails and missed sections on others. So that, too, had gone badly.

"Why all the groaning? What happened out there?"

Alia began to tell Nasreen, describing the twirl (lovely while it lasted), sketching a slightly mendacious version of her conversation with Nick, glossing over the way in which she had spat out her final words, pretending she had said them kindly, interestedly, not viciously, cruelly. Nasreen saw right through her.

"You said *what*?" She ended in a question mark but her shocked face made it more of a statement.

"I just said ... I didn't mean to make it a whole *thing*, it just came out before I could help it. And I was freaked by the uncles, okay?"

Nasreen shook her head. "I don't know, man. Your mouth ... you really need to watch yourself."

Alia felt her stomach shoot through with panic. And then a greater feeling of shame hit her. She scrambled to avoid it.

"Maybe he's really sensitive about *everything*."

"He's not sensitive. You're the asshole."

Catherine's head whipped round at the expletive. "I don't know what's going on over there, and I don't know *why* you have changed outfits – I've still got no explanation from Nasreen – but," she said, not bothering to lean in, instead tilting her head back as though she was issuing statements through the length of her nose, "I'm warning you both, keep this up and we are going to have words."

"I hate that phrase," Nasreen whispered to Alia, "'going to have words.' What the fuck does that mean? How? Are 'words' on the menu for today's lunch?"

"I *know*," answered Alia, shooting her grandmother a dark look. "It's totally pathetic. And who is *she*," this almost pejorative use of pronoun felt at least as daring as cursing, "who is *she* to tell us? She's not our mother."

There is nothing like being disciplined by an adult to realign sibling allegiances. Nasreen and Alia were on the same team again, and there was relief in that.

"Why are these events always so stressful?" said Alia morosely, putting her head in her hands, holding the pose for a moment before peeking up at Nasreen through her fingers.

"Samoosas and mind games," replied her sister cryptically. "Samoosas and mind games."

11 June 1986

Waleed's father left him two things: his mechanic toolbox with each wrench, screwdriver and hammer laid in perfect polished order, and a pale-blue '68 Mercedes Benz. The car had been the old man's most triumphant purchase, something he had saved and worked towards since his days as a teenage apprentice. Abe Dawood had bought the automobile in 1972 off a rich customer who had grown annoyed and impatient with its deterioration. Every hour he spent restoring that car was an hour full of small satisfactions. He worked until the wheels spun with new hubcaps, all the dings were tapped out and the scratches were invisible. It gave the old man unnamed pleasure to lie beneath the vehicle as patiently as a lover and coax from the car all its secrets and failures. He spent his Sundays in a haze of devotional activity, polishing down its wide-eyed lights and hefty silver bumpers until it was ready for a slow cruising drive around the Peninsula.

When this first started, Fozia was furious. She would hold up lunch and make the boys wait, sometimes for hours, until their father ambled in serene and Zen-like, looking vaguely at the dark wood table with its lace overlay, smart crockery and full-bowled Sunday abundance, and finally ask his sons to pick the day's destination. In the end, his wife learned to set down a tray of tea and sandwiches next to his triangled legs and preside over the lunch table by herself. What she lost in the familiar was made up for in the new. Whatever it was that Abe was doing under that car on a Sunday seemed to be just enough to take him through his working week.

The car became a part of the Dawood present and later, their past. Any family photos from between '72 and '83 were posed in front of that Merc: Adam, lanky and glowering into the sun; Waleed doing scrappy impersonations of gangsters; Fozia frowning, dishcloth in hand, impatient to get back to her stove. Later, there were ones of the girls perched on top of their grandfather's bonnet in their Eid outfits, the old man smiling from a slight distance as though he could not believe a photograph could contain both his joys at once.

Waleed used to spend the hours after Sunday lunch sitting with his father while he restored the car, asking questions, passing tools. The old man mistook his son's longing to spend time with him for an interest in cars and so when he died he left the huge pale blue conversation piece to his youngest boy.

Waleed never drives the car, but he visits the garage instead of his father's grave. He sits in that dark musty box of a room, poking around, occasionally polishing the car and vacuuming its insides.

When he announces that he is coming to collect it, Fozia is surprised.

~

Alia and Nasreen are playing hopscotch in the driveway when Waleed drives into view. Alia is mid-hop, one leg tucked towards her chest, the other trembling slightly while she balances, when she sees her grandfather's car. Her heart slams with fright and, agape, she gestures wordlessly at Nasreen, who looks, sees, mirrors her sister's thought and then just as rapidly does away with it, saying chidingly, protectively, "It's not Papa, silly! It's Uncle Waleed."

Waleed pulls cautiously onto the pavement. He has only been away a few hours but the girls sense that some rhythm has been broken. He climbs out of the car and lets them hang on him as he gamely skips through their square chalk outline on his way to the stairs, asking, "Is your mommy home?"

To which Alia, hurrying behind him, says, "She's in the kitchen, I'll show you," as if he is a visitor.

Zarina is not in the kitchen. She is sitting at the dining-room table, surrounded by a pile of paperwork, crying, just a little.

"Zina? What's the matter?"

Zarina jerks her head up, embarrassed when she sees him, and then cross when she notices Alia. She does not cry in front of her children. Alia looks at her mother curiously; the vulnerable red-veined eyes make her seem a stranger. Zarina reaches for a tissue. "It's nothing, it's allergies," she says, with a warning nod to Alia, and then in a lower voice to Waleed, "just these, here ..." she passes her hand over the files, "I can't read any more of these goddam affidavits. Some poor woman asking when her child is going to be released, they've had him for months now. No one wants to be the one to tell her there isn't a hope in hell."

Had him where, thinks Alia. *Who is "he"*?

She looks between her mother and her uncle, ears straining to hear the unspoken. Zarina blows her nose and fakes a sneeze before moving her voice hurriedly into controlled sharpness. "Alia, where is your sister?"

"Outside."

"Why aren't you with her? Go and *play*. You only have a little bit of time left. Supper in half an hour ... go on ... I'll come out in a bit and challenge the winner!" The last bit, brightly, falsely, as much for the child as for herself.

Alia runs out as Waleed leans in over Zarina's shoulder, looking at the reports without actually reading them. "You okay?"

"Sure. Who am I to complain? My kids are playing hopscotch."

"Still."

His eyes trail absently across the manila envelopes.

"Waleed."

"What?"

"These are *private*."

"Oh, ja. Sorry, I just …" He doesn't know if it is worth saying that it isn't the detail he is interested in, the names of the jailed, it is more the idea of them, reduced to a couple of forms, gathered on this dining room table like some kind of installation.

"Did I hear a car in the driveway?"

Waleed raises the finger from which a key-ring swings. "You did. I fetched my dad's car."

"Well, that's new." Zarina breaks into a smile, relieved to have an excuse to do so. "You finally tired of the bus?"

"No. Actually," Waleed treads carefully, "you seem upset so this may not be the best time to tell you, but a couple of us are going to Crossroads tonight."

"Why?"

"The army is going to raze the shacks again."

Zarina gives a small shudder before nodding over to the clouds gathering low and banked on the horizon. "It's going to rain tonight, you know. They can be so cruel."

"Jaaaa …" Waleed lets his voice taper off.

Zarina understands. "Oh, no. No! You're not going to try and stop them?"

It is a question longing for a mixture of reassurance and denial but Waleed merely rolls his neck as if to stretch out a crick. "You are absolutely crazy," she hisses, abruptly shifting tone as though suddenly aware that the conversation carried weight and danger.

Waleed sits down and then gets up again, unable to find his place. "Rashaad is going with, taking his camera, and Yusuf and Georgie."

"I suppose this was Yusuf's idea."

"Well, he told us about it happening, he knew first, if that's what you mean."

"What am I going to tell your mother if something happens to you?"

"Zina." He tries to fill those two syllables with everything he can.

She throws up her hands as if she hears it all. Waleed thinks he is speaking reasonably. "If we need to get away fast, we can. That car is a *beast*, man. It's probably bladdy bullet proof, knowing the old man."

Zarina laughs in spite of herself.

"Seriously though," he goes on, "I won't be able to sleep tonight knowing what they are doing. It's not sentimental. I'm just – I won't *sleep*. Couldn't. Not when I know."

Zarina nods. "I'll make some soup and sandwiches, get some thermoses together."

She doesn't tell Adam where Waleed is going, only that the extra food is for some people who have just been evicted. He is barely listening as she chats through her explanation, and packs two large cardboard boxes full of flasks and bread. Adam is packing a box of his own, though one filled with different contents and different intentions.

"Just got a new shipment in," he says, beaming. "Look at this jacket – this lining is *magnificent*. I'm going to be home late tonight, going to Omar straight after I do my last pickup. Hey! Did you see my dad's car outside?"

"Yes," says Zarina, tightening her focus on covering the sandwiches in cling-wrap, hiding a sudden and acute prick of conscience.

"I think Waleed's going out with his friends in it. I saw them outside – Georgie, Yusuf, all of them. Be good for him, he's been ... ag, I dunno, *moody* or something lately. But it's been good to have him stay here, don't you think, Zina?" He kisses her goodbye and hurries out before she can reply. She hears him hoot his horn at his brother as he pulls away, a greeting that is both a farewell and, in sonic terms, an affectionate hug. She calls to Waleed from the balcony to help her with the boxes.

~

"Hello, Rashaad, Georgie … Hi, *Yusuf*." Zarina throws out her greetings and hoists a box towards them cheerfully, as if she is distributing a picnic hamper. She inflects Yusuf's name with the emphasis of an accusation. The men, barely nineteen, barely twenty, sit in the car, letting it fill with their sense of purpose. Rashaad fiddles with his camera, looks briefly up at Zarina and flashes her a charming grin in greeting. Georgie leaps up to help her, while Waleed revs the engine to check if it needs petrol. There is an air of excitement, of holiday, as if the evening is an adventure waiting to unfold. Only Yusuf, tucked in a tight corner despite the leather spaciousness of the vehicle, is serious, scribbling notes in a book, looks tense.

"Do you boys actually know where you are going?" asks Zarina, choosing a matronly role.

Rashaad and Georgie are play-fighting over who called shotgun and don't answer her. Yusuf puts down his notebook, pushes at his round Lennon spectacles and says with a self-conscious seriousness that matches his glasses, "I do, Zina."

Zarina fights an impulse to take Yusuf aside and bombard him with questions. She has heard from various people that he is *involved* and she wants to say, *Tell me things are getting better. Say we are going to win. Please make sure Waleed doesn't get hurt.*

Yusuf offers her a half-mocking smile as if in answer. Zarina looks at the four of them. She has known them since they were in nursery school, scrubbed, dimpled and earnest.

Twelve years their senior, she will always feel like the adult. *Four-year-olds on a mercy mission*, she thinks, *the world has gone mad*.

Then, after much tapping at the petrol gauge, Waleed announces that they have half a tank. As the large blue car pulls cautiously out of the driveway, Zarina suddenly feels as though her father-in-law is about to appear and demand that the boys pose next to it for a photo before they leave.

~

When he was little, Waleed used to plan the moment in his future when, armed only with a backpack, his grandfather's knobkierrie and a pair of Onyx binoculars, he would bid farewell to an assembled group of family and friends and set forth by foot on a journey that would take him from the District (first left at Adderley Street then *straight*) to the Pyramids. A boy who loved maps, he would trace his fingers and eyes over his school geography book, murmuring the names and matching them with history: Huguenot Tunnel, Du Toit's Kloof Pass, Hex River Pass, Three Sisters, Warmbad, Pietersburg, the ever mysterious Tropic of Capricorn, and finally, Rhodesia. Where the N1 ended, at the border, he would speak his own route, he would pick the names he loved best, let them sit on his tongue and in his head. Lusaka, Tanzania, Morogoro, the plains of Atbara and Wada Haifa, Alexandria, Cairo, until finally he was in front of the Sphinx. It would take him *months*, maybe *years*, he would tell his friends.

But Waleed is not on that road now. He is not on the road that will take him out of the country, but on the one that will take him into it. As he rounds Hospital Bend, he secures his own and his friends' fate. They will not end this journey smoking shisha in a café with turbanned men; instead, they drive that bleak road into the country's deepest shames, its secrets, its deceits.

And Waleed drives the car with regret. What he wants is to sit tucked against a backseat window, face turned to the glass, letting the blurred landscape find and lose its own shape. Behind him, Yusuf, folding, unfolding, refolding a small piece of paper, as if his hands have found a replacement rosary. Georgie and Rashaad, still not properly reconciled after the shotgun argument, are fighting about what to play, Heron or Springsteen, Fassie or Fela. Georgie makes an impassioned plea for Heron, citing "What's the Word from Johannesburg" as the perfect backing track for their mission, while Rashaad insists that Springsteen's credibility has gone through the roof after "I ain't gonna play Sun City". Fassie's "Weekend Special" is judged too jolly and the Fela tape is badly stretched. They eventually settle on Genesis, which no one is happy about and which prompts Rashaad to rage about religion, a rant which takes him from the Ayatollah Khomeini ("I don't care if he's a *poet*, Waleed, or a Marxist, the man is kak dangerous, ma broe. He'd hold the whole bladdy world to hostage if he could. I don't trust anyone with a beard, on principle. Except for *Fidel* and even then it's touch and go. And Khomeini's poetry is kak versin. My uncle is this tablikie fool and he's been forcing me to read some of it. Rumi he is *not*, ek sê!") to Israel ("It's taatie this idea that God is some sort of cosmic real estate agent parcelling off land to some people he likes better than others. It's like, 'Check here, ouens, my *book* says this house, this garden, this car is mine so just kindly step aside and if you don't I'll just ma' back up this book with this gun.' Check here *naai*, man! It's *kak* unfair!").

Rashaad is like a wind-up doll. He can be counted on to spin and spit for whole paragraphs once he starts.

Georgie begins to double over with laughter. "Chant it, brother, *chant* it!" he shouts.

Yusuf looks up from his folding and catches Waleed's eye

in the rear-view mirror, communicating his annoyance. It had been Waleed's idea to invite the other two and he is beginning to feel acutely embarrassed and responsible.

"I'm speaking the *truth*, that's what I'm doing," Rashaad is saying.

"Hell, yes, you are," Georgie replies on cue.

"Look, just shut up." Waleed is a little shocked at how loudly he says it.

Georgie responds by pushing the Genesis tape out, shoving Bob Marley in, and singing defiantly along to "And *Georgie* will make the fire light."

Waleed's insides are strung tight. The free-floating anxiety he always feels has found tangible focus. He is scared. He has always harboured a deep fear of physical violence, avoided fights at school, shrunk back when he got a beating from either of his parents. When he is alone, he calls himself a coward. His psychic skin is so thin it is almost translucent. Waleed pretends to the world to have walls that in truth have no foundations. When he hears about the suffering of strangers, his pores open and he lets sadness seep into him. He does not, cannot, differentiate between himself and others, at least when the others are unknown to him. It is what makes him a good writer, but means that there are no still points in his body, that he spins like mad, rocked by stories that are seldom his own. In the quiet moments, the dark ones, he tells himself that there is something parasitical about this, to feel so deeply for the unfamiliar, but to struggle so mightily to connect with his own family. When Yusuf had told him about the demolitions, he had felt a heartache he could not name. He'd rushed to the immediate, always accessible image of the wrecking ball in the District and the women gathered around it, wondering if it were just that. He offered the image, the dreadful symmetry of it, hesitantly to Yusuf who snorted in response, "You can't even begin to compare – they moved us out to actual places, let us pack up our shit and go. You think they do the same thing for the Africans? Please, man. They point and shoot and don't give a fuck what's in their way."

Yusuf, as always, had met his observation with a radical's derision, had dragged him in front of a mirror and showed him a reflection full of inadequacies and cowardice. "No point in being brave on paper," he had said before to Waleed in a sneering reference to the coded anger of his writing, "and chicken shit in real life."

They drive past the curved grey ugliness of the power stations, past the sandy plains of the Cape Flats where the schools have spent the winter in a haze of boycotts and teargas, moving further and further into the deterioration, where houses eventually stop being made of bricks, roofs of shingle, roads of tar, until eventually the materials are all scrap metal and cardboard, muddy, filthy streets, streams of water run thick with faeces and Coke cans, children playing in thin, fraying jerseys, weak and wheezy against the gathering cold, women standing with heads wrapped in fabric and worry, men bleary-eyed from booze and depression. And through it all, a blue Mercedes Benz with four boys armed with thermoses of soup and a tray of sandwiches. Waleed has never felt more useless.

"Left just here," says Yusuf, guiding him, consulting a hand-drawn map, "and then another right here."

People come out of their shacks to stare, their faces blank, suspicious, grateful, hostile, surprised, amused, furious, sometimes all those things at once. At Yusuf's signal Waleed stops the car. Georgie and Rashaad have grown quiet. None of them except Yusuf has been so deep into a township before and the poverty of it shocks them. Crossroads. Waleed cannot think of a more appropriate name. Rashaad has started taking pictures, already using his lens as a hiding place. Georgie, the most gregarious of the quartet, finds a child to engage with, high-fiving him, doing a hackneyed magician's trick with a coin.

A slightly chubby black man, about their age, wearing a UDF T-shirt walks towards them, waving. "Yusuf," he calls out. "Howzit, wena?"

"Sharp, sharp," answers Yusuf, taking his hand and introducing him to the others as Tsepho, "our contact".

Tsepho smiles at Waleed. "Thank you for coming."

"I haven't done anything," answers Waleed, embarrassed because he is fighting an impulse to get back into the car and drive as far away as fast as possible.

"You're here," says Tsepho. "It's a start." He turns to Yusuf. "They scheduled to come in about half an hour but sometimes they come early, especially if they think, you know – if intelligence has been leaked." Here he looks carefully, almost accusingly, at the boys. "Someone may have seen your car come in, impimpis everywhere these days ..."

Waleed tries hard to swallow his building panic.

"They usually try and clear about three hundred people a night, the target is sixty thousand apparently."

Yusuf removes his glasses as though preparing for a fight. "What must we do?"

"Just stand here. Just watch for now. That way they less likely to do anything to you." Tsepho gives a small grin. "Get a little Gandhi with them."

Georgie walks up, bearing the food. "We brought some soup and stuff."

"That's great, thank you." Tsepho turns to an older woman who is sitting on a makeshift stoep watching them, switching to Xhosa, "Mama, will you take this food to the centre?" and then back to them, "She'll make sure it all gets distributed okay."

"Can we just make sure we get the thermoses back?"

Waleed regrets it the moment he says it, and begins to stutter, something he hasn't done since childhood. "It's just th-that ... my s-sister-in-law borrowed them from her neighbours and she asked me to make sure ..."

The others stare at him.

"You'll get the flasks back," says Tsepho gravely, his eyes laughing.

~

Waleed is talking quietly to a woman about Zarina's age. She is showing him where she fetches her water every morning, when the shrill warning moan of a plastic whistle bites through her words. Her body tightens and her face drains. She calls her daughter away from her friends – teenagers, all comparing sjambok-welts – and picks up a blanket to strap her baby to her back. Her husband disappears into their shack and emerges holding an old man's cane, an insignificant defence, a gesture more than anything else. Tsepho and Yusuf begin to run back towards the car.

"Get in! Get in!" Tsepho shouts at the boys.

"What? Why?" Georgie is sharing a chocolate with a child. The little boy is laughing and hanging onto his leg.

"Get in the fucking car, Georgie!" Yusuf's voice flies far from its usual controlled registers.

Waleed obeys him, mostly because the woman lays a hand on his shoulder and pushes him towards the vehicle. Along with Rashaad and Georgie, he scrambles onto the backseat, reacting blindly to a surrounding panic he knows nothing about. He leans in to say something to Yusuf, but his friend has already started the engine and Waleed is flung back as the car begins to move. Tsepho is halfway out the passenger seat window, gesturing wildly at families gathered in ragged circles outside their small shacks. He shouts "Hamba! Hamba!" and points towards the centre. Some of them begin to run in the instructed direction, others watch as Tsepho disappears in a spin of wheels and attendant dust, their faces indecipherable. The car takes off down the narrow uncertain roads of the township, Yusuf following Tsepho's commands with mute concentration. Waleed turns around and looks through the back window. Through a swirl of dirt and sand he can make out a group of men advancing towards the centre, carrying pangas, hammers, guns, axes. Their heads are wrapped in strips of white fabric, something between a bandage and a bandana.

The car is filled with tension. Waleed says to Yusuf in a low voice, "You're in my seat ... you going to tell us what's going on?"

"Witdoeke," answers Tsepho, as if that explains everything.

"I thought that was just propaganda," says Rashaad quietly.

"Can someone tell me what the *fuck* is going on?" demands Georgie.

Rashaad fits the lens back on his camera, describes the witdoeke as a bunch of township thugs. That they roam about scaring the crap out of everyone, getting money from them, mafia style. "They have this leader ... Nxgobongwena," he finishes.

"Nxgobong*wana*," Tsepho corrects him, "and that's only half the story. They not ordinary thieves, man, they paid by the government."

"Ja, right! *Sure*." Rashaad becomes defensive, he doesn't like being wrong, and likes it still less when he is shown up in front of other people. "What good would that do? I mean, I hate the bastards, but even that's a bit much."

Tsepho looks at him pityingly and, not bothering to turn round, just directs his words through the rear-view mirror. He explains with painstaking slowness, designed as much to instruct as to expose his listener, that Bongwana's men are paid to terrorise everyone, to create scenes of mad chaos that cloak the real reasons for army incursions into the townships. That way, the government can tell the foreign press they were subduing an outbreak of violence, that they *had* to demolish houses because they found bombs or weapons, or any other lie they want. "Everyone knows about it."

"I didn't," offers Georgie, caught somewhere between loyalty to Rashaad and wanting to learn more.

But Tsepho has lost the will to teach. "So," he says, "I guess we don't live in the same country."

Yusuf snorts, at once showing his solidarity with Tsepho and distancing himself from Georgie, whose cheeks are flame red, his eyes downcast. Waleed grimaces out the window while Rashaad fiddles with his camera, muttering under his breath about a bit of sand that has gotten in under the lens. The backseat holds the three boys in various poses of impotence.

The car takes a final turn and leaves the township just as the Casspirs drive in. Young men peek out of Casspirs, their R4s ready to discharge. Beside them sit some witdoeke. One is drinking a can of beer and grinning at a crowd of screaming, running women. Rashaad pulls out his camera and just as quickly Tsepho smacks it down, "Are you *mad*? Do you want to get us all killed? *Jesus Christ*, it's like fucking amateur hour in this car."

Rashaad reaches around the passenger seat headrest, grabs the other man's ear and says, "Touch my camera again and I will rip your fucking fingers off."

Their faces are almost touching. Rashaad is speaking into Tsepho's neck as if they are lovers. Yusuf keeps his eyes on the road. They are back on the N2 and he needs no further directions back to town. Ahead of them lies the mountain, solid and comforting. It is Georgie who breaks through the moment's weird intimacy saying, "*Relax*, ek sê."

No music is played on the return journey. The quiet is punctuated only when Yusuf and Tsepho make arrangements for Tsepho to stay the night in a safe house. Rashaad, Georgie and Waleed sit in the back like silent, guilty children. Waleed reflects that he has, after all, been granted his wish; he has the backseat and the chance to stare at the landscape. But the trip has not been a success. He has not saved anyone or anything. He has not stopped a single home from being demolished. He does not know where that woman has gone, or if her thin husband with the old-man cane had been any kind of defence, or if their crotchety baby is still on her mother's back. He will probably never know either. His head is swirling with a maelstrom of conspiracy theories. He has always believed in government secrecy and evil – that was not a problem or a stretch for him –but it has been seeing the effects in real time that has shaken him up. It is one thing to sit with friends and chatter with grand and stoned reverence about Martin and Malcolm and Patrice's sacrifices; it is another to think about black men in white bandanas taking Judas coins and wielding knobkierries and pangas at four-year-old girls and old men too slow to move. He asks Yusuf to stop the car so he can vomit.

Waleed stands on the dark thin highway and retches while his friends look the other way, as if they are giving him the space to weep in private.

Inside the car Georgie summons the courage to blurt out what he, and perhaps they all, have been thinking. "How can they do that, man? To their own people? What kind of people do that?" Here Tsepho turns to him, offers him a cigarette and says, "Think of it this way: one thousand witdoeke, one million comrades. The odds are in our favour."

Georgie takes the smoke, looking unconvinced.

His ears near his knees, Waleed listens to the exchange. Tsepho's comment annoys him. It sounds like the exit line of a bad TV show, something McGyver or The Face would say if this were the closing beat of a scene. The *least* Tsepho can do, thinks Waleed, heaving again, is give them something real to hold on to.

~

Adam is visiting his cousin Omar in Athlone, enjoying an afternoon of tea and sales talk, attempting to coax him into buying a new jacket – *Beautifully lined! Look at that craftsmanship!* – when a teenage boy, a neighbour, bursts in the front door, sweating and gasping.

"Uncle! Uncle! They shooting there by the mosque!"

Adam feels his mouth go dry. "Which one?" he asks, his voice coming like a thin zephyr from the back of his throat while his ears begin to thump red with blood.

"St Athans Street, Uncle, and they shot someone! They killed him right there outside the masjid."

"My father!" Omar makes for the door, gesturing at Adam to follow him, talking while he struggles into his jacket. "My dad went there today ... said there was a meeting ... about the kids that were shot in the street a few days ago ... Oh, Jesus. I *told* him not to go!"

The men and boy run out the house with Omar shouting questions. "Do you know who they killed? Was he young or old?"

"He was young," the boy says. "He was someone from my madressa, Uncle Amien's son. He was trying to stop them from going inside the mosque."

Adam glances at his cousin and sees horror and relief work across his face; it is a terrible thing to feel reassured when the dead are not yours.

They turn the corner, breathless and terrified, and there, laid out with all the distorted reality of a nightmare, is St Athans Street. The mosque is surrounded by Casspirs and soldiers and everywhere are the signs of a street battle, pools of darkening blood, torn bits of clothing abandoned mid-struggle, small fires from lit tyres, a coterie of photographers and newsmen in flak jackets. A crowd has formed in front of the gates so that from certain angles all that is visible is a pale cream minaret floating above a collection of heads. A group of mourners has already gathered around the dead boy's body, having wrapped him in cloth and lifted him onto the shoulders of weeping men who circle the building with elephant-like fury. It is a world full of screams and also quiet. Every so often a woman emits a high-pitched wail, or a man turns towards the army trucks to throw curses and rocks. Clusters of schoolchildren sit on the pavement, held in check by three moustached soldiers. From the loudspeaker wails the voice of the sheik, asking for calm, denouncing the government, declaring that the army's actions are unlawful.

Adam stretches his neck and feels himself rise onto his toes as though he can listen to the man's voice more carefully if he is just a little closer to it, that those additional inches will allow him to work out what is happening inside the mosque. The longer he strains and listens, the more surreal things become.

Here is an army.

Here is a body.

Here is a mosque, a crowd, and a loudspeaker.

He fixes his stare on the minaret and sees a shower of sparks before hearing the sheik's voice explode into the sound of shrapnel against metal. One of the soldiers has shot the loudspeaker down. The crowd stands, their necks tilted, their chins angled towards the clouds, and they watch as the sheik's voice transforms, as if by some strange alchemy, into a waterfall of light and fire. The soldiers point their guns as one towards the speaker. The entrance to the building is blocked off, no one has been able to get in or out for almost an hour.

Omar is in a panic, asking if anyone had seen his father, while Adam tries to piece together the afternoon's events. The crowd is full of the story, there are dozens of different versions, but each shares the same spine. "The sheik had called a meeting," people tell him, "because of those children, the ones who were shot now-now the other day, in the street. You know, man, when the soldiers came out of that box, there by Thornton Road? And so Sheik now said it was enough, too many people were dead, too many kids were missing, enough with this bladdy curfew. Enough."

"It was just a meeting."

Just a meeting.

They are allowed to meet in a mosque.

Aren't they?

Someone begins to demand that the gates to the mosque be opened. "This is our place!" he keeps shouting at the soldiers, "our place!" A group of young men stand, their shoulders touching, their arms linking tightly, trying to stop the tanks from inching closer towards the building.

Adam and Omar wait, two more bodies in a crowd on the verge of a riot. They hear the rest of it. That the army killed a boy who tried to stop them going inside.

"They just shot him then and there, like he was nothing, like he was an animal, you understand?"

An animal.

"And then," Omar asks, "did they get inside?"

"Not straightaway," a woman answers, and then tells them how someone climbed onto the roof of the mosque and also shot off a gun, like he was firing back. "At the boere. Can you imagine? Then Sheik heard about the dead boy and came outside, tried to talk to the army, but the boere had said if you don't get back inside we'll kill you right where you stand. Right there."

"They said that to Sheik ... can you believe it?"

"These people have no respect for anyone."

"And then, to top it all off, the soldiers went inside the mosque."

"They did *what?*" Adam and Omar are shocked at this.

They went inside. Right inside.

This piece of information gives Adam a vertiginous feeling. He begins to exhibit all the symptoms that characterise extreme panic; his palms grow clammy, his voice hoarse. He looks up and inadvertently makes eye contact with one of the soldiers, a boy of eighteen, nineteen. He thinks, *I am a reasonable man. I have a business. I am an adult. I am a father. I am a husband. This boy is less than half my age. He is a child.* The soldier catches his eye and trains his gun on him in response. "You want to say something?" he says. His voice is shrill, still slightly high, as though it has only just broken, not yet settled into manhood. Adam drops his gaze and feels his body flood with shame.

In June, the weather always contradicts itself. The day had begun full of bright sun and chilly winds; Zarina had mentioned something about rain when he left the house, but here in this street, in this moment, as the heat of his panic attack recedes, Adam realises that now he feels nothing, neither hot, nor cold, neither clammy nor dry. He looks to the sky, trying to check for signs of rain, but can read nothing. He registers the thick and gathering clouds, he knows that dusk will fall in just a little while, that the shadows will lengthen, that night will close on all these things, the blood, the torn cloth, the screaming women, the cries about a secret killing box that has been dumped in the middle of the street. He knows these things, but he also doesn't quite believe them. A part of him is convinced that the day will not end. Not ever. That he will be trapped here, on this street, waiting outside this mosque, with the detritus of war all around him, forever. *This is what it feels like*, he thinks without thinking, *this is what it feels like, to wait for the end*.

There is some movement in front. The doors have been opened. First comes a row of soldiers, their expressions a little dazed, and after them a slow trickle of men and boys, their feet still bare, their hands above their heads, their faces inscrutable. They are being herded into the crowd. No arrests are being made. Omar sees his father and rushes towards him. He catches the old man in an embarrassed hug and he and Adam begin to usher him home.

Omar's father is quiet at first. He says nothing until he is sitting down, a hot cup of tea in one hand, strong cigarette in the other. "Something happened in that mosque," he says, "what, I don't know. But when the boere came in, I don't know how, but everything just went very still and very slow, like things were being stretched out. Like there was time but there also wasn't. And Sheik, he just closed his eyes and he prayed, and even when they started shooting, he didn't stop praying, and he didn't open his eyes, not once. And there was one boy, it was like he was bosbefok in there, just shooting and shooting, the whole wall was sprayed with bullets, at what and at whom, I don't know. But he touched no one, he hit no one."

Adam hears the story once, twice, three times, but feels none of his uncle's exultation, latches onto none of the old man's beliefs that God had protected them. He has always been suspicious of this kind of thinking, it was what drove him to despair as a child, this easy collapse into the mystical, the inexplicable. *It's God's will. There is a curse on this house. So and so has to go to Boeta so and so to have it lifted.*

He ignores his uncle's logic, steps away from the insistence on supernatural salvation and instead follows the links of his own thoughts with burgeoning dread. *If they are invading mosques and churches it means they have stopped pretending. They don't care anymore how they look to the outside world or to us. No more placatory gestures. The gloves are off. Things could not be worse. My children could die here.*

This last thought reanimates his anxiety, only worse this time, far worse. His throat thickens somewhere between grief and nausea, his bowels feel loose, his eyes strain as he tries to stop the wall in front of him from dissolving. He knows it is an exaggerated thought, an indulgent thought, that for the most part the kids in coloured schools don't get killed, that that horror is reserved for black parents in townships, that at worst the girls could get beaten, or teargassed, and even then, only when they are in high school. There will be a few years for things to calm down. Surely the boycotts will have stopped by then? *It would not be death*, he thinks, as he kisses his uncle goodbye, *to even think such a thing!* But his legs and hands shake for most of the journey back to Walmer Estate.

When he gets home Adam does two things. He rinses his mouth on a loop for minutes as if he is washing away the day and then he sits his wife down.

"We need to make a plan," he says. "We need to change the girls' school."

9

Wednesday, 4 March 1993

"I guess the *real* question here, Waleed, is if you are planning to finish on time?"

Waleed cast his eyes to the high ceiling, where an ugly wooden fan with long flat blades was doing its whirring work, and pursed his lips as though he was suppressing a wild laugh. His supervisor, an affable man who wore his rumpled beige jacket and Marxist past with equal lightness, struggled to see the joke.

"The thing is," the older man pressed on a little apologetically, "you need to finish on time or your funding is going to run out. And I can assure you," earnestly, body leaning across desk, "that there is *no way* you want to be in a position of writing up without funding. You're already stretched with your work at the ... the—"

"Bookshop," Waleed supplied, bringing his head down and meeting Derek's eye.

"Yes, yes, of course, the bookshop," Derek nodded approvingly. He was, as he had told Waleed in the past, a *firm* believer in the maxim that to encourage, to *actively reinforce*, was a central pillar of learning. What he didn't believe (to his detriment, the cynical might say) was that the encouraging nods made some students underestimate him and think he was easily satisfied with nothing much at all.

Waleed began to make a study of his hands. He liked and

respected Derek. He had been grateful that the one lecturer with whom he had felt a kinship during his undergraduate years had also shepherded him through his Masters and agreed to take him through his PhD. He felt now, with good reason, as though he was letting him down and he knew that Derek, for his part, needed Waleed to do well. He needed all the impassioned arguments he had made to his colleagues about the development of young black academics to pay off. He needed to justify the rousing letters he had written to funding bodies in support of Waleed's research. It was not something he would ever say out loud, but they both knew that if Waleed drifted, as he was wont to do, into a haze of non-productivity, he would jeopardise the chances of all those other would-be scholars of colour, their dashed hopes and failed applications the result of nothing more than the most tenuous and imagined link of guilt by association. Waleed winced as he thought of what this said about labour, race and capital.

Derek picked up Waleed's latest offering, a half-written chapter replete with spelling errors, scrappy research and under-developed trajectories, and gingerly turned it over, making a genuine effort to focus on the encouraging marks and comments he had scrawled in the margins.

"You *know* I think that your central argument, the premise, as it were, about the negative impact that apartheid has had on the imaginative dimensions of black literary production, is really strong. I think it's tremendously rich ... and what you've written here is really heartfelt." Both men gave a slight intellectual shudder when he said that. "No, *no*, I really mean it. It's *heartfelt*, it just lacks the necessary theorising." Derek said the last word with regret, and Waleed heard it with embarrassment. It is the word that separates out the academy from the rest of the world, the word that creates a distinction between real research and a dinner party rant. Waleed nodded, his mind in agreement, his body pulling opposite. Of *course* it lacked theory. He knew his arguments were full of intellectual holes, that part of what he had submitted read more like a diary of his feelings and grievances than a chapter.

"The thing is, Derek …"

Derek perched forward eagerly. For a moment Waleed was convinced he was smoking a pipe and that his jacket was corduroy and patched with leather. "Yes, Waleed?"

"I'm just not sure if *theory* is really my thing."

"Ah," said Derek, appearing deflated.

"I just don't know if *politically* I can stomach the idea of theorising around people's stories. People who won't ever be able to compre*hend* what I've written …" When Waleed was feeling impassioned, he landed hard on the ends of words, giving his sentences the inverse rhythm of a revivalist preacher.

Derek nodded and Waleed understood that he had just out-manoeuvred his supervisor. He had just invoked that which is sacrosanct to those who believe in the holy nexus of politics, research and wider impact: he was talking about accessibility.

"Well, certainly," said Derek carefully, tightly, "that's something to be thought about. The idea of *who* has access and *who* doesn't is not a trivial question by any means. But perhaps," his smile widened, "you could find ways to actually write towards that, to make it a part of the debate, so to speak, as opposed to a means of ending it?"

"You're saying that I should theorise around a lack of access?"

"Absolutely!" Derek added a vigorous nod to the wide smile, and began to suggest how, properly guided, this thesis might actually lend itself to the interdisciplinary; someone in education, or even sociology might find it interesting! He was not, he continued, one of those purist English academics who found the idea of cross-departmental pollination distasteful, an act of "intellectual miscegenation", he had sneered at a recent postcolonial conference – a phrase that had got him a few nods and laughs – in fact he *prided* himself on regularly reaching across the aisle, insisting on a *democracy of methodology*.

"Have you spoken to Anna about this?"

Waleed's head jerked up, his eyes alight with such unexpected venom that both men began to talk at once.

"I really don't know why you would bring my girlfriend into this—"

"I didn't mean to pry, I only meant—"

They stopped, equally abashed, Derek wearing his embarrassment on his flushed cheeks, Waleed in an agitated squirming. Eventually Derek said, "I only meant it might be useful to talk to someone in your peer group about this. I, for one, find it extremely useful to talk to my partner."

Waleed sat in a corrective quiet, somewhere between old indignation and new flattery. Derek's wife *(partner)* Hanelie Anthonissen was, like him, a celebrated academic. She was also a novelist who had written three inspired sagas about Afrikaner identity, from the trek to the camps to parliament. She had, in these stories, humanised the inhuman, placed her people within the flow of their own history, and asked those of Waleed's generation to understand, if not to forgive. Together Derek and Hanelie cut a wide and commanding swathe through the nascent literary scene of just-pre-post-apartheid Cape Town, she, with her collection of shawls, ags and angst and refusal to accede to the oft-believed trope that Afrikaners were any worse than white English speakers, he with his full, thick head of silver hair and the still-imposing frame of a man who had come of age playing cricket.

Waleed allowed himself to preen just a little by association but then collapsed back under the weight of the unwritten work.

"I've heard Anna has shifted her research focus?"

Waleed nodded and confirmed what Derek already knew, that Anna had left African Studies and was now ensconced in the relative safety of the History Department churning out chapter after chapter on Rosa Luxemburg's influence on the Unity Movement. She had, Waleed explained awkwardly, found her niche. Derek looked at Waleed's pained expression and wondered how much of this was political and how much was the fairly banal stuff of student research anxiety. He gave a deep internal sigh; no one tells you how to prepare emotionally for the academic world, no one sits you down and explains that the competitive, sometimes bloodthirsty dynamic of the seminar room will crawl into your sleeping hours and hold you hostage during your writing ones. That a few months in, under the pressures of an Honours year (somewhere, some student had picked up and propagated the global notion that in order for a lecturer to notice you, you had to decimate your peers) your psyche splits inexorably, inevitably, in two; there is a part of your brain that wants to do the work, but there is another more powerful part that sets up enemy camp, occupies your thoughts and destroys even embryonic ideas. That you sit down already hating what you've not yet written, already convinced of the hatred of whoever reads it. Waleed was still talking, blithely unaware that Derek had not been listening.

"And I think that's really what it boils down to."

Derek hazarded an accurate but regretful guess. "The politics of access?"

"Correct."

"I think it may be useful for you to consider this through a different lens."

Waleed frowned, but raised his palms, as if to invite the other man to speak freely.

"Perhaps you should think a little about who it is you think would be served by your text. Who might benefit? And also who is this 'they' that you keep referring to?" On "they" he pulled out Waleed's (and every humanities scholar who had come of age in the late 1980s) preferred means of demonstrating that there are no stable categories: invisible air quotes.

"Surely, by allowing space within these ... *rarefied halls*," he said this last phrase in a way that indicated he believed exactly the opposite, thus successfully eliciting a smile from his student, "you give weight to the struggles of these writers."

Waleed made a show of rubbing at his face, pushing his fingers back into his hair, saying nothing through the hands he parted and peeked through like an old theatre curtain.

After a few minutes, perhaps weary of Waleed's harried righteousness, Derek began to enact a little routine of his own. He pulled out a pouch of Drum tobacco and, though there were no anti-smoking laws, asked Waleed conspiratorially to close the door. As his student obliged, he rolled one for him, telling him that the feminist professor in the office next door had just spent a semester at Berkeley and had returned with a barrage of new bumper stickers (had Waleed seen the latest one stuck up on her door? FEMINISM IS THE RADICAL NOTION THAT WOMEN ARE PEOPLE) and an annoying habit of attempting to curtail tobacco-induced pleasure. She told people it was part of a larger social movement which insisted that people take responsibility for each other. "The thing I want to know is," Derek said, while Waleed cackled on cue, "where was *she* in the eighties when all this talk would have meant something?"

The diversion had worked: Derek, skilled in manipulation through his own years in the UDF, had created a bond between himself and Waleed. They spent the next thirty minutes in a pleasantly smoky-hazy room, talking around and about the country, avoiding as if by mutual design any direct reference to the thesis. As the hour drew to a close Derek, with apparently tremendous reluctance, told Waleed he had another meeting, and Waleed heard himself promising both to follow up with Professors Ridley and Van Schoor (Education and Sociology respectively), and to deliver a revised chapter in the next few weeks. It was a good way to conclude things; Waleed was at least temporarily cleansed of his privileged agonising, and Derek felt an almost physical relief at having something positive to report back at the next staff meeting.

They stood in the oak-panelled corridor making plans to meet for a drink later in the week, each man feeling that warmth for the other that only comes after a fair fight. Waleed was patting himself down, looking for his tobacco when Derek said, "Before I forget, I've put your name forward for some tutoring. Nothing too onerous, just some Honours coursework. There are a couple of interesting students from Joburg. I don't know why, but they just seem to *get* this country and its dynamics better than the Cape Town kids. Not surprising, is it? This is hardly an African city."

Waleed felt his face give a small, entirely involuntary, flinch. He was always amazed at how frequently people said this to him, stated it as fact, and how ritually they expected him to agree. *What did that even mean, an African city? Why? Because Joburg was soundtracked by the* maquamba beat? *There was nothing un-African about Cape Town.* He felt the old sentences begin to take shape, the old argument begin to coalesce. *This city and all its fucked-up divisions and casual cruelties was the way it was because of slavery and colonialism and you don't get more African than that.*

"Waleed?" Derek was looking at him quizzically. "So you'll take the job?"

"Ja. Thanks. Thank you."

"Where did you go just now? Something I said?"

"What? No, no, sorry. I'm just … I was just going through some stuff I have to do later." What was the point of explaining? He was likely to agree with Derek on another occasion. It all depended on his mood and how many ways the city had revealed her history on any given day.

The men were beginning once again to issue their goodbyes when they heard the clatter of plastic heels against the stone floor. Bearing down towards them, course outlines under her arm, was Rukaya, the department's secretary, looking sour and fatigued. Derek flashed her a wide grin, coupled with a hearty salutation. He always made a point of acknowledging the administrative staff, both as a gesture of egalitarianism and because he routinely got paper jammed in the photocopier and needed Rukaya or someone else equal to the task to rescue him.

"Prof, we just heard there's some kids organising a protest on University Avenue. They going to shut down the afternoon's classes."

"Really?" Derek could not hide a grin, despite Rukaya's obvious disapproval. "What are they protesting?"

"I don't know. But I just hope this doesn't hit public transport. I have to get home for magriep. I don't have time for all their shenanigans on the train. Everyone is a bladdy communist till graduation."

"How's the fast going?" asked Derek, while Waleed hoped that the uncomfortable image of this woman waiting indefinitely on a train platform would subside.

"Fine, thank you, Prof." She said this stoically, eyes a little unfocused, lips betraying the thin breaks and cracks of dehydration.

"Listen, let me give you a lift home. No, don't say no. It's no hassle."

Waleed said goodbye and left them to their arrangement, knowing that Derek's offer would take him just twenty minutes out of his way, knowing that Rukaya's gratitude for this small kindness would elevate Derek to the heroic. He walked down the avenue, towards the Greek-Roman building, saw the students, a scattered assembly, noted their placards, felt their urgency, their fervour, saw, too, himself at their age, nineteen – *just seven years ago* – but knew that it was just different, different. He looked at a group of boys, joking, talking, punching their fists in the air, and saw in them Rashaad, his camera broken around his feet, his hands bloody from a baton; saw Yusuf, dragged away, feet tripping over a potholed pavement, hauled into a police van, kept out of sight and light for weeks.

He would walk home. He would not bother with trains or taxis today.

10

Wednesday, 24 March 1993

That year summer ended on the twenty-third of February. Not because of the weather, but because of the fast. Ramadaan meant an abrupt cessation to all those long days spent in the sweltering sun, eating sugary granadilla ice-suckers, waiting for sausages to braai, turning over lazily in the cooling water of a pool, standing on corners smoking illicit cigarettes with friends. Those things made a quick exit and a new rhythm of austerity was ushered in. Mornings were divided into four parts. Waking. Eating. Sleeping. Waking Again. Afternoons changed meaning; sun and heat were no longer welcome and every upward quiver of the thermometer, however infinitesimal, was met with a grimace and a sigh. Evenings were suddenly devoid of television or trips to the newly opened Waterfront. Phone calls to boys were absolutely off limits.

"It's like being grounded by God for a month," a moribund Alia told Nick.

She was in a waspish mood. The fast filled her with deep and abiding resentment: in her mind it put an end to everything joyous and replaced it with a series of trials-by-deprivation that she felt she could do without. And this year, because it both fell at the height of summer *and* she could not see Nick for four weeks, she felt doubly robbed. Alia was not very good at fasting. She would wake up filled with conviction, but the resolve and resilience she had built up between supper and breakfast would fray by mid-morning, and crumble entirely with Pavlovian regularity at the chimes of the first break bell. The dread of compulsory sports practice would drive her to the tuck-shop where she would buy a roll and eat it, without a modicum of irony, behind the chapel wall.

"Will I only see you when the month is out?"

Their moodiness had become a shared thing. They had grown closer in the last month, in part because Alia had had to do what the youngest members of families are seldom called upon to do: apologise and be accountable. The casual cruelty of her behaviour at the wedding, her subsequent attempts to trip past it, brazen her way through, pretend it was all forgotten; none of these tactics held any sway with Nick. He carried his hurt in brusque answers and broken coffee-dates until eventually Alia admitted that the comment had been designed to sting, to wound, but that she had felt regret almost as soon as the words left her mouth. To this confession, Nick offered complete absolution: he didn't believe in grudges, he preferred calm at almost any cost.

"I really can't believe the Fast hit in February this year." Alia said the last part with great bitterness.

"It's not a hurricane ... it didn't *hit*. It's a lunar calendar."

From the bottom of the staircase came Zarina's voice, thin and dehydrated, telling Alia to hang up, that they were about to leave, that Fozia was expecting them and that it really wouldn't do to be late.

Zarina was tired. She'd woken the girls up at three that morning, the night still close, the air still warmed from day-before heat. She had roused them with a gentle hug, her own face swallowed by an apologetic yawn. Adam had refused, as always, to actually get up: he drank a cup of tea and then collapsed his exhausted, work-heavy head on the pillow, going without anything until the evening.

Alia, Nasreen and Zarina had sat, staring uneasily at the kitchen table heavy with eggs, fried spice-beef, sugary tea and juice, unsure of how to consume anything at this hour. Zarina made them each drink two glasses of water, with an eye on the predicted spike in temperature and an afternoon of tennis practice. Nasreen ate silently, one eye on the buttery toast, the other on the clock. It was an odd meal. It had elements of a feast but it was geared towards abstinence. They knew they were having breakfast but it was dark night outside; they were three ordinarily very chatty people but all efforts to make conversation tapered off into bewildered quiet. The three of them sat in a disassociated triangle, staring off into space, the fried food heavy in their stomachs, their bodies confused by a mixture of the hour, the jolt of caffeine and sugar-high from the tea, and the torpor of oil and bread.

When the others went back to bed Alia walked through the unlit rooms, her thin frame and cotton shift making her seem like a ghost from another century. She stole onto the balcony and felt the soft hot air drop like a folded garment onto her shoulders and arms. She leaned against the long, low wall, the same place from which she had watched the Hassans' fire, and looked out past the city into the dark still waters of the bay, into that expanse of watery blackness broken only by the ships that had docked in the harbour and the tall cranes that bent towards them. Down the street she saw each lit house signalling the same faith and action. The road seemed to hum with a muted glow from the black tar and the dimmed streetlights, and in that perfect stillness, in that thick dark of predawn, lights winked at kitchen windows and behind the blinds and shutters were families, gathered at countless tables, full of odd combinations of irritable weariness and quiet determination, hoping to get through the day ahead with control and thoughtfulness. It was an in-between time. A time when the world belonged to no one. Alia was alone, secluded in the shadow of her balcony, but all around her she could feel people, the people of her street, preparing with faith and purpose for the day in the best way they knew how. She knew the hour that their heads rose from their pillows, the way they groped through the dark towards the light switch, she knew the way their eyes would adjust to the lamplight, the order with which they washed their bodies in preparation for prayer. She knew how many times their knees would touch their muslahs and how many ways their mouths would praise God. It was the only time in her life when other people's lives were not a mystery. In these hours, in this month, people she'd mocked and glared at suspiciously throughout the rest of year became, by some unnamed alchemy, as close to her through thought and intention as her own family.

When the Bilal's voice came, it signalled the moment's end, the no-man's-land annexed, the lights switched off, the street crawled back into the last hour of sleep before the day belonging to the West would begin.

~

Zarina hustled the girls up the small cement path that took them to their grandmother's front door, swung wide open in anticipation of their arrival. Inside, in a configuration that had not altered in almost thirty years, were three of the original Dawoods: Adam in the lounge presiding over the plates of dates and daltjies, Fozia in the kitchen ladling out six bowls of thin vegetable soup, and with her Waleed, standing on the maroon polished stoep that sat in a small, square at the top of a short flight of stairs connecting house and back yard. His body was draped at a dangerous angle over the low wall, while he leaned and strained his left ear towards the first notes of the athaan. Behind him, three things: a sky full of swollen pink and peach clouds, three rows of old woman washing, moving with jubilant, unfamiliar lightness in the quick breeze, and a group of pigeons assembled expectantly on a telephone wire as though they, too, were waiting for a sign.

~

Fozia decided that *this* year, *this* Eid, they would all have to come to her, the whole family, no questions asked. She had spent the last three years eating Zarina's food and although (despite her best efforts) she couldn't fault her daughter-in-law's skill as a cook, she was convinced that Zarina's slavish devotion to the recipes of *Indian Delights* was somehow intended as a slight. Cape Malay dishes, she complained to May next door, were conspicuous in their absence.

Fozia had been up late the night before, and again early this morning. Not that either of her granddaughters had offered to help her, *oh no*, she was in it alone. Where were they? Drying their hair probably, and reading. They should be with her now, learning how to make this; flaky pastry and fillings didn't just magically appear, no matter what their parents taught them. They certainly weren't going to learn in their mother's kitchen. Fozia gave the top of each dome a quick twist to indicate that they were chicken pies. Would Zarina eat these, with all her airs and graces under the pretence of concern? *Mama we need to be careful about cholesterol, lots of heart attacks in our family, from both sides*. "Well," she wanted to say, glancing at her husband's photo (dead at fifty-three), "there are two kinds of heart failures, and not having pies on Labarang Eid could certainly lead to one of them."

Fozia checked her apron to see that the money she had set aside for the girls' Eid present was still there. Fifty rand each. It was a massive amount of money by any standards. Adam was bound to get upset with her for "squandering her pension" but she planned to ignore him and just make sure she gave it to the girls first thing. Let *him* tell them himself if he wants to confiscate their present. And then there was poor Waleed, who had been so good and come round the night before but then had scurried back to that *loose girl*, as if she, his own mother, did not know it. But they had had a good night of it, rolling out the pastry together, smoking and talking. She had had him to herself.

This day, this hour, Waleed was saintly, the loved child who had come through all his rebellions and tantrums onto the other side, and was still here, in the kitchen with the butter and the flour. Last month when Adam had bought her a new portable radio, no one had understood her better, no one had had such a considerate son, no one had been more blessed. But you can't tell a radio about your problems with your neighbours, you can't tell a radio to pass you the salt or to fetch the semolina, so Adam's gift had revealed its purchase impulse: a stand-in for company, a way to stave off an old woman's loneliness.

Against her better instincts Fozia had developed a tendency to talk to the radio; she shouted her irritations about the provisional government – "Don't you blessed well give him the time of day, Mr Ramaphosa ... although Roelf Meyer seems okay ... ja ... maybe talk to him ..." She also corrected recipes to the empty air: "I think you will find that a pinch of white pepper will bring that whole stew together." She listened avidly to Astrology Hour (a most un-Islamic activity) and became ruthless about forging friendships with people based on their birthdays. "I'm not saying that there is not room for us all, but I can tell you straight, Nasreen, that child you dragged in here last week is a Scorpio, and that is just now asking for trouble with a Sagittarius such as yourself."

As if sensing his waning status as favourite, Adam had come to greet his mother straight after Eid mosque. It was a well-timed visit because Fozia was in the midst of one of her violent surges of resentment towards her daughter-in-law. There was, she had conceded to May, no rhyme or reason to this. The feeling would arrive uninvited and would remain for an indefinite period, sometimes a few hours, occasionally a few weeks. Fozia had never thought to connect a rise in loneliness with a spike in bitterness; she only knew that it made everything, but *everything* the other woman did a source of annoyance, a wellspring of displeasure. Fozia would have been horrified if anyone had told her she was in competition with her daughter-in-law but when she answered the door and saw that Adam had not gone directly home to Zarina but had come to her and that this meant she would also get to feed him first, she positively preened with delight.

"Samoosa?" she had asked, holding up one of several doily-decorated plates. Adam accepted and then looked approvingly around the room.

"The table looks fantastic, Mommy."

"Yes, well, I thought it would be nice to have some of our people's food for a change."

Her son made an indecipherable sound, piling his plate, while Fozia continued relentlessly. "Not that I'm saying Zarina's food isn't very tasty—"

"Mmm ..." Adam offered some focused chewing as a response.

"So what time are they getting here?" Fozia settled into an armchair, tucking her substantial bottom into its deep seat so that her feet rose a little off the ground.

"Who?"

"Who? The cat's mother! The *girls*," and then as an afterthought, "and Zarina. Unless she's working today."

Adam leaned back in his chair. So it was going to be like this today. With what he thought was remarkable restraint, he asked, "Why would Zarina be working today?"

"I don't know. Isn't she always by the office?"

Fozia heard herself pass off a lying statement as though it was fact. She knew Zarina only worked as a paralegal part-time. Further, she knew that Jakoet, Zarina's boss, was Muslim, and would never dream of opening his office on Eid. She could not account for her question and she could not account for her statement. Both seemed to have arrived unbidden but fully formed and ready to be delivered. But (and here she catalogued the complaints as recited to May), she didn't understand why her daughter-in-law *insisted* on staying in her job. Her son made good money, so why couldn't she just be satisfied with that? Spend the time with her children. These years, the ones between now and when they would be grown-ups and gone, were nothing. They lasted a breath, and then they were over. If *she* had had the choice, she would have quit that factory with its predawn hours and icy winters. She would have given anything to be at home when Adam came back from school; she would have been able to watch Waleed more closely.

Why all these thoughts now? Lately, she'd been feeling so much regret.

Fozia looked over at her eldest son who was inspecting a small but deep scratch on the coffee table. "When did this happen?" he asked, tracing an accusing finger over the mark. Adam hated to see any of his father's pieces damaged.

"The Williams boy did it. He came round to help me with the light bulbs. They fused and I couldn't reach them."

"The *Williams* boy?"

"From Park Road. Why?"

"Why didn't you just ask me or Waleed to help you? Why you bothering other people?"

"I'm not bothering anyone! I paid him."

"But, Mommy, you shouldn't." Adam stopped, trying to manage the charge of frustration that was coursing through him. "Why must you waste your money? Just ask one of us to do it."

"You not always available, are you?" The sentence was muttered under her breath. "Anyway," she steered the conversation back to his family, "I'm still waiting to hear. What time they coming?"

"At one," and then, responding to the look of consternation that crossed his mother's face, "you said at one. But I can tell them to come earlier? They'd be happy to—"

"No, no. I don't want to put anyone out … far be it from me … I'm just going to make some tea. No, sit. You just sit ma', and answer for me in case the children come … there's one rand coins there by the door, in the brass bowl."

"Mommy, you can't give them all one rand! That's outrageous! You'll have a line around the block if word gets out."

"Ag, shush, man, don't be such a Scrooge. What can a one rand buy anyone these days? Listen! There's a knock. They here already. I'm going to put the kettle on, you get that for me."

Adam, always biddable in his mother's house, went and answered the door to a group of six children all in their Eid best who responded to his festive greeting with a resounding "Slamat for Labarang, Uncle." The front four, he decided, using a racialised coding indecipherable to anyone not South African, were definitely Muslim, the back two possibly Christian and in it for free sweets and money. These two mouthed the words uncertainly, trying their best not to draw attention to their awkwardly perched koffeyas. Adam scratched through Fozia's bowl of coins, searching unsuccessfully for smaller ones. He looked at the children with growing irritation; probably none of them even knew his mother. He cursed their opportunism. He dug into his own pocket and fished out a few twenty and fifty-cent pieces and doled them out to three disappointed girls and three angry boys. The youngest, a sight to behold in a flouncing crimson velvet dress and matching bag trimmed with crocheted lace, clutched her money with one hand and pulled her bobby socks up with the other, eventually saying bravely, "Is Auntie Fozia home?"

"She's busy." Adam was wise to their ways. He had been a champion Eid cash collector in his day, going from door to door leaving no bell unrung, no hand unshaken. It was how he had financed his comic collection and lorded it over the other boys at school.

His mother's voice floated down the hallway. "Who's there, Adam?" and the children replied as one in a relieved cry, "It's *us*, Auntie Fozia!"

Fozia bustled through, greeting everyone with a kiss, telling them all how smart they looked, pretending she didn't know that the two at the back were in fact Christian – *May's nephews* – and handed out one rand coins to each of them while Adam looked on with disapproval. As the children bade their goodbyes the youngest girl triumphantly twirled her mass of ringlets at Adam and then bounced down the stairs with the jaunt of the victorious. The other kids clattered down the steps in a gaggle of whoops and yohs; they had made out like bandits, more than a rand each!

"Daylight robbery," pronounced Adam as he shut the door.

"What? Ag, don't be silly. Listen," Fozia was suddenly urgent, "I want to talk to you about Waleed."

"Why? What's he done now?"

Waleed. Of course. Adam realised that this was why she had wanted the girls and Zarina to arrive a little later.

"Nothing ... no, that's not true, just nothing new ... Oh, Adam, I'm so worried about him."

"You're always worried about Waleed. You think it's your life purpose."

Fozia pretended she didn't hear and began to keen very gently. "What do you know about this girl?"

"Her name's Anna, Mommy. You know that. And she doesn't live with him, she has her own place."

"I don't need to know her name. Because she won't be around for very long. These girls come and these girls go and they only ever have one thing on their minds. Jy ken mos vir daai mense."

"What people?" Adam found himself in a curious position; whenever he was alone with his mother he was the most progressive person in the room. "Zarina and I have met her and we really like her."

"Did he bring her into your house? Did you introduce her to the girls?" asked Fozia, her outrage moving her bottom to the front of the chair, letting her feet touch the floor.

"What? *No*! We went out for dinner. But she's welcome anytime—"

"Where did you go for supper?"

"Mommy, it was *months* ago, I don't remember. Why?"

Fozia pursed her lips and tilted her head as if the world's answers were to be found on the plastered cornices of her still intact Victorian ceiling. *Why could neither of her children just live a simple life? Why was everything made into a saga? Why must people ask for trouble and then pretend they don't know what the trouble is or how it got there? And just when exactly was she going to be able to stop explaining how the world worked? You would think they would know by now. Especially this son, Mr Big Deal, who only wants to give out twenty cents to small children on Labarang Eid.*

She brought her head back, her neck cricked uncomfortably with the effort.

"You should be careful where you go, you don't want people seeing you eating in a haraam place."

"Anyone who sees us in a restaurant is doing the same thing." Adam said this flippantly, in no mood for a lecture, the sermon at mosque had been enough.

"You want to be smart now, but I know a man, he used to go to the races and watch his horse run and he always had a lemonade but people would think God knows what because they served it to him in a glass for liquor and his reputation was ruined after that."

"We didn't go to the racecourse."

"Small mercies. So she's not been around the girls?"

"Not yet, but she's intelligent, she's a decent person, she works hard—"

So what? Smart her son could find anywhere! Didn't he go to university? There must be smart Muslim girls all over the place. And decent is as decent does. There is nothing decent about living in sin like they do.

"I don't like her!"

"You've never even met her."

"It's illegal. It's dangerous."

"Mommy knows those laws have been over for years."

"How would you feel if your girls came home with a Kriste boy?"

Adam was silent. Since Zarina had told him about Alia and Nick, he had been grappling with a combination of rage and helplessness.

"When I think of those greasy porky lips on my child ..." Fozia twisted this way and that on the chair, torturing herself with the image of Waleed and Anna embracing over a plate of gammon while a mounted hog's head leered from the wall. Adam grimaced at the thought – *Pork, how could anyone? Why would anyone?* –and then responded to his mother as a man of the world, widely travelled, cosmopolitan.

"She doesn't eat pork," he said.

"How do you know?"

"She's become a vegetarian."

Fozia took in this bit of information as though it confirmed the worst. "You certainly very cosy."

"You know what?" said Adam as if something had only just occurred to him, as if it was not the result of long and strategic consultation with Zarina. "Mommy, you should ask her to come to lunch today! She would really enjoy this. She's very interested in the *culture*."

Adam used the word a little suspiciously; it was Zarina's preferred angle, she was convinced Fozia would respond to it. Adam watched his mother for any sign of her wavering. Nothing. He decided to pull his trump card. "Apparently," he said, "she is a huge fan of Mommy's cooking. Waleed says she goes mad with excitement anytime he brings a plate home. So imagine how she would be if she saw this table today."

But Fozia's reactions were never easily predicted; instead of gratitude she felt outrage. Not only was this woman stealing her son, she was also stealing the food that she, *his mother*, had prepared for him and him alone. She was taking it straight out of his mouth. She drew herself up grandly and strode over to Adam, standing directly in front of him, blocking the sun, lighting herself in outline. As a girl Fozia had spent one summer as the apprentice seamstress for the Eon Group and in addition to mastering a French knot, she had learned to hit her light without fail. "In *this* house? In your *father's* house? On *Labarang Eid?* Now I have heard it all! If your brother so much as tries to bring that jintoe within an *inch* of my house ..."

With great deliberation Adam brought two fingers towards his nose and pinched its bridge. His eyes screwed tight, he said, "I shouldn't have to tell Mommy that Waleed always does precisely what Waleed wants to do."

Shaking her head, Fozia offered him a samoosa and Adam acceped, caught somewhere in a swirling maternal matrix of comfort, resignation and helplessness.

19 June 1986

It is late. Later even than the midnight knock. Waleed is standing in the thin alleyway between his brother's house and the neighbour's wall. He taps his feet on the cement strip wild with cracks and obstinate weeds. It is a sharp winter's night and his breath is hot and visible. He hunches further into his jacket and blows onto his hands to warm them. He is alert: ears pricked, waiting for the signal. When it comes, a low soft whistle, so soft it could have been nothing, just a thin reedy sigh of the wind, his heart beats rapidly (loudly, he panics) in response. He purses his lips and whistles back. He counts to ten then steps out from the shelter of the wall's long shadow. Two figures come towards him, eyes peering out beneath close-cropped beanies and thick scarves. The one is familiar. Yusuf. The other, thin and lissome, the form of a delicate woman. Reaching for Yusuf's hand, Waleed says, "Is this him? Come on, everyone in the house is asleep."

Yusuf casts an arm around his companion's flimsy shoulders. "Yes, this is Firoze."

Not a woman then, just a small, frail man. Yusuf is still talking. "He just needs two nights. That's all."

Waleed motions them both towards the steel-trimmed sliding door that leads into his bedroom. In it burns a small reading lamp. Angled towards the floor, it gives off just enough light to see features if not expressions. Waleed takes Firoze's jacket and sees him properly for the first time. Shocked, he says to Yusuf, "Can I just talk to you? In the kitchen?" Without waiting for a response he turns and makes his way through the house. Yusuf, in an inversion of their usual dynamic, follows him.

"Are you *mad*?" Waleed is so angry his voice rises to speaking level. Yusuf quiets him with an admonishing grimace and a frantic gesture, his body and face an orchestra of alarm. Waleed continues, softer now, "He's a *child*. He can't be more than fourteen. Are you totally befok?"

"He's fifteen." Yusuf's voice is steady but he looks searchingly at Waleed. "And he wants to go. Apart from anything else, if he doesn't, they will find him and he will go to jail." The last four words bleed into each other. "If he's lucky, it will be solitary. But most likely it will be torture." Unwanted images and sounds gather close, walls smeared with shit and blood, bodies twitching and convulsing with the force of electricity, soap-slip deaths and falls down staircase shafts. Waleed tries to shake his head free of them as Yusuf continues, "I didn't think I would have to *explain* this to you."

Waleed pats at his pockets, searching for his pouch of tobacco. He finds it and pulls out the rolling papers but can't still his hands.

"Jesus, Waleed. Pull yourself together. You shouldn't have offered to help if you were going to be like this. I had to vouch for you. You're not even in the Party. I've taken a serious risk trusting you."

"What do you mean 'risk'? I've known you for *twenty years*, man." Waleed forces a laugh and looks from left to right as if he is greeting his angels at the end of salaat or searching for support from an invisible audience. He is alive to the seriousness of the moment, present in it, but another part of him is absorbed in the archness of Yusuf's language. He wonders how long his friend has been speaking like this. And if he has always drawn himself up to full height and looked so ... *pompous* when he did. Waleed watches Yusuf's face, the quick shaping of his mouth in speech, the way his hands twitch as if they want to be used – as a boy, he had been gestural to a fault – and how now he holds them stiffly at his side, as though he is – *Could it be?* – standing to attention. Yusuf is speaking and Waleed feels suddenly as if his voice is coming from a long way off, as if he is listening to a recording of something made in a secret cell, where words like "discipline" and phrases like "isolate him" have replaced words like "friendship" and memories like "We were once six years old together. We picked green figs together from Mrs Williams' tree."

"A *serious* risk, man. For myself, never mind for the boy. Now will you help or not?"

Waleed hesitates. The experience at Crossroads had changed him. Afterwards he had approached Yusuf and said, "I need to do more. Just tell me what. I will do anything." And Yusuf, after weeks of questioning him closely and then further weeks of absolutely no contact, had finally given him a time and an address. Giddy and eager at that first secret meeting, full and satisfied, his mouth stretched wide with talk, his head weighed down with new ideas. He didn't realise that his moment of heroism would take the form of a thin boy-child with large eyes ringed heavily from sleepless, frightened nights, as he flees like a homeless ghost from house to house.

"Waleed? This is real, hey. No time for thinking."

Waleed gives him a mute nod, his tongue lies flat and useless in his mouth. In his silence, acquiescence.

"I'll be back for him in two days. Until then, not a word to anyone. Not a fucking word."

Upstairs a door creaks open, the sound of feet on the landing. Both men stiffen, their bodies taut with terror.

"Who's that?" asks Yusuf.

Waleed makes his way from the kitchen, past the lounge, grateful for the carpet that muffles his steps. A bathroom light has been switched on and it casts a thin illuminating rectangle that zigzags down the staircase. The sound of running water. The door opens. It is Alia, her hair in a damp, tangled mess that evidences a restless sleep. Her flannel pyjamas catch around her ankles. She walks back to her bedroom with the unsteady gait of a child ready to tumble into bed and dreaming. Relieved, Waleed returns to Yusuf and tells him everything is fine.

In the bedroom they find Firoze sitting on the edge of a chair, a movement away from running. Yusuf rests a hand on the boy's shoulder. Waleed cannot tell if it's meant to comfort him or to hold him in place. Yusuf catches Firoze's eye and smiles into and past his worry. "Comrade, I'll fetch you in forty-eight hours. You'll be in Angola in a week. So rest all you can, it's a long journey."

~

For the first two days Firoze is safe, stowed away in the Dawoods' basement. But on the third day Waleed gets word that the escape plan has been delayed. Somewhere, someone has got caught and the boy will now need to stay a week. The trapdoor beneath the spare bed should have made things easy for Waleed, but he is unskilled at subterfuge. He leaves a trail of tell-tale signs: there are extra dirty plates, favourite coffee mugs go missing, furtive, loud whispers are overheard, there are failed attempts at hushed phone calls, a general air of mystery, until eventually, after a rapid transition from inkling via disbelief to realisation, Adam and Zarina confront him. They are furious. There is, naturally, no question of turning the boy over to the police. Zarina sets to work, feeding him soup and finding valerian root to calm his nerves; Adam sources extra blankets and gives him a gas lamp to stave off the cold, damp black of the cellar. This child, so fearless in the face of the soldiers' boots and batons, fears the dark and has spent both nights weeping.

After a night of sleeplessness and arguing, Zarina and Adam move Firoze into the spare room and make Waleed sleep on the couch in the lounge. Zarina lends her full support to Firoze. "It will be okay, not long now, not long now," she soothes, and directs all her anger at Waleed. "Do we know this boy's family? Has someone bothered to tell his mother?" she spits. After that she stops speaking to Waleed.

Adam, appalled, behaves simply as though Waleed does not exist. They tell the girls that Firoze is a cousin in bad trouble with his parents, and, for reasons they can't explain ("Just because. Because we say so"), they are not to say a word to anyone about it. They say it with such ceremony, with such solemnity and panic, that Nasreen and Alia spend the next few days seized by a terror they cannot name. Alia comes down with a terrible sore throat that means she can't speak anyway. Nasreen, overcome with curiosity, tries to talk to Firoze through the door of the spare room. When Zarina catches her, she gives her a series of smacks so hard and sharp that both adult and child are shocked into silence and then tears.

Waleed does not fare any better. His generalised anxiety builds towards such a crescendo that he cannot eat or sleep. His fretful eyes and mournful expression elicit no sympathy from his brother and sister-in-law, and the silence that cloaks the house affords him a great deal of time to think about Firoze and what his future might hold. Waleed is an imaginative creature and a mixture of deep guilt and horror means that it is a line of thought he cannot always bear. He pictures jungles and Firoze's slender build in oversized military fatigues, he hears the insistent rhythm of a training song and sees bowls of thin rations and watery beer. He layers the imagery with stories of ambush, of comrades sitting together, quietly planning a free future, sucking on cigarettes, dreaming of home, and then being gunned down by enraged SADF generals who have found their hiding place. He agonises, wondering if anyone has told Firoze any of this, has sat him down and explained: *You will probably never see your mother again. You may well be on the run for the rest of your life. And the rest of your life might only be a few months.* Zarina's silent treatment, Firoze's huge eyes and extended stay, Adam's fury, the girls' anxious curiosity and finally his own troubled convictions lead him in an endless circle of panic and remorse. Should he say something to Firoze? Dissuade him about going? And then? If he was picked up by the police, he would be tortured. Maybe killed. This way he had a fighting chance ... and what was the point of complicated arguments about ethics now? All this child (and he *is* a child, *he is*, Waleed tells himself sometimes furiously, sometimes tearfully), all this child *has is* his convictions. He poses these questions and then refutes them, becoming the lawyer his brother had always wanted him to be. He allows the questions to take the place of action. It is exhausting enough living in his own head, never mind the world, so he avoids the spare room and thus Firoze, and when he does have to see him, he is cautious. He creeps along the party line, and allows himself a guilty relief when the boy does the same.

His mind returns insistently to that first meeting. A night's subterfuge behind him: *Turn left at the alley, meet so and so at the corner, knock on the door three times*; a night's consolations ahead of him: *Comrades, reassurances*.

He admits to himself now that he had been thrilled to hear of this one's banning, that one's sentence, had been awed by the way they spoke the names of the hidden, the imprisoned, the known, the fearless, with such familiarity. But, quietly, secretly, he had also been besieged by questions. What if he didn't agree with everything? What if he worried endlessly about child-soldiers? What if the ideology (and it was good, it was moral, it was just), what if it wasn't always the compass you could shake to find the right direction? He had looked around the room and wondered if anyone else was plagued by these doubts. They all seemed so steady, certain, sincere. *Perhaps there is no space for irony or doubt in a revolution,* he thought.

Tonight those feelings gather close, those questions will not retreat. He hears, too, Fozia's voice in his head. (Would she ever just leave him alone?) *If you lie, I will wash your mouth out with soap and water.* Fozia, who Waleed still believes sees more clearly than anyone, had told him, *Ag, you believe anything.* His own mother thinks he is gullible. What would she make of that room? Of those men and women? *Better to have joined, to have tried,* he tells himself, *than to have done nothing.*

Yusuf had said, "This is no time for thinking."

~

The endless week passes and the boy eventually leaves as he came, blurred by the dark and a too-big coat. It is only after Waleed bids him goodbye, wishes him luck, and thanks him for taking up something he himself will never have the courage to do, that he realises the child has few of his anxieties. That whatever panic he has been feeling has miraculously dissipated in the light movement, that once the plan has been put back in place, he is replete with readiness, with an eagerness to fight and to win. Waleed searches his face for signs that it is the allure of adventure the boy is seeking, and he sees that, yes, that is there, but more than that, he is fuelled by purpose and commitment and faith, a sense of honour. And perhaps even an understanding that the fiction of childhood can only be sustained in certain contexts. This is what Waleed sees. He tells himself to take that alone from their farewell and tuck the fear away.

Later in Adam's study, he looks at his brother encouragingly, as if the other man just needs to take a few steps before they are on the same page, but Adam turns away, refusing Waleed's expression, letting his eye catch instead the pile of banned magazines – all linocuts and slogans – his brother has been trying to get him to read. He picks up the first few and brandishes them as though they were all part of the same argument.

"Do you have any idea the danger you put us in? Of what could have been done to me, or to Zarina, or the girls? I *told* you what happened at the mosque last month! These people have gone mad! We could have lost everything ... I could have gone to jail."

Waleed waits a second, and then says quietly, "You already in jail."

Adam leaps towards his brother, closing in on him, his words merging somewhere between menace, righteousness and contempt. "Don't you give me that. Jesus. I don't have time for that. 'Already in jail.' What absolute rub*bish*."

Waleed reaches for Yusuf's words, gratefully finding relief and sense in them. "That boy is making sacrifices so that *you* and your girls and your wife can be free. The least Zina could have done was offer him some legal advice ... but no! Nothing! I am getting the silent treatment."

"Zina could have offered legal advice?" Adam repeats Waleed's words with wonderment.

"Yes! Yes! She could have!" Waleed hears his voice climb to the thin and high octaves of hysteria. He realises he is sounding ridiculous, but he keeps on, worrying away at an unwinnable point, ignoring the actual issue, a family trait that makes resolving arguments almost impossible.

"Now you listen here," Adam drops his voice low, "I don't believe in sending children to do a man's job. It's immoral and you know it. I don't send my kids to work everyday. I send them to school. There are other ways to end this."

Waleed shrinks back a little when Adam's voice shifts, a reflex action born of years of older brother bullying. But there are certain things he had held back from saying for weeks and he says them now.

"Yes," and then with the slyness of an aunt delivering a barb and a cup of tea at the same time, "and what school, exactly, would that be?"

"What?"

"Don't play innocent with me. I know what you and Zarina have up your sleeves. Mommy told me all about it. You going to send the girls to some whitey school." Waleed throws whitey out of his mouth like it is a piece of dry dirt.

Adam waves the accusation away impatiently. "It's not *white*, Waleed. It's private."

"Same thing."

"This from a man who peddles words for a living ... you really can't tell the difference between the two? No wonder you broke."

Later, when Waleed mulls over and parses apart the argument, this will be the thing that causes him the most resentment.

"What are you teaching those girls if you send them there? They are safe in that clean white world while other schools are burning?"

"Oh, for God's sake."

"*Adam*," as if speaking to the willfully deaf, "Papa would have been horrified. Mommy's pretending she's okay with it, but you know what everyone is going to say."

Adam drops into his desk chair. "Well, what do you propose I do?" The question, sitting at a junction between weary resignation and hopelessness, invites Waleed into the world of the problem. "Should I send them out to die while your glorious leaders' children are safe in Swaziland and London?"

Waleed offers Adam a different silence this time, furtive

and unsure. He tucks his neck into his chest and makes a study of his feet, holds the pose for a moment and then retreats to the couch and puts his head in his hands. Adam lets all this movement about the room pass without comment. In their family, Waleed is known for his baroque body language. Once he'd lain down in the middle of a fight and placed blankets and cushions over his face to block out the argument; another time he had poured cold milk over his brother's head as an alternative to punching him.

Adam reorganises his already pristine work area, tapping papers into place, shifting his office supplies into ninety-degree angles. Eventually, with nothing left to rearrange, he rests in his own familiar attitude, his chin on the tips of his steepled fingers. Waleed raises his head and trains his stare at Adam, who in return removes his fingers from his chin.

The younger man gets up. "I'll leave today. Thanks for letting me stay."

"And?"

"And what? I'm not going to apologise. I didn't do anything wrong. If anything—"

"Yes, all right." Adam is more tired than irritable as he cuts him off. "I know what you *think* you were doing."

Waleed shrugs and makes for the door as Alia darts away from it – *Had she been there all the time?* – running in a six-year-old blur down the corridor. He strolls to his bedroom, his niece trailing him, an insistent, persistent shadow. She stands in the doorway watching him pack, making a small sound when he takes down his posters.

"Are you coming back?" she asks.

"Hey, listen, I want to tell you something." He calls her over. He is kneeling as he packs, so they are the same height. "When you go to that new school—"

"What new school?"

"Alia," Waleed looks up and sees his brother, "leave Uncle Waleed alone, let him finish packing."

Adam and Waleed do not look at each other while Alia finds her place tucked beneath her father's arm.

Waleed leaves later that day, destined once again for the forgiveness and welcome of Fozia's house. The brothers have come to the finite point of an argument that will sit, still and thick, inside both of them for years to come. Whenever they recount the story of the fight (still plagued by the need for secrecy, Adam to Zarina, Waleed to Yusuf) they will feel their beliefs cemented. Each retelling will, as if by emotional surgery, remove the nuance of the argument, take out the awkward, pained moments in the study, gloss over the unanswered questions. Waleed will paint it in broad strokes, casting every accusation he can against his brother and Zarina – *sell-outs, privileged, self-serving* – and yet will feel a modicum of unspoken relief every time he imagines his nieces sitting in the bright calmness of a safe classroom, staring wide-eyed and fearless into the possibility of a different sort of future.

11

Saturday, 10 April 1993

Working in a bookshop was not a job anyone in Waleed's family had ever had. He could not recall a single such place in either the District of his childhood or the Woodstock of his adolescence. Libraries, yes. There had been weekly Saturday morning trips to the library at the City Hall, first with his mother, who would hesitate at the doorway before nudging him to walk ahead of her. They would spend the next thirty minutes apart: she would wait outside while Waleed inspected the sparsely stocked children's section. Later, Adam was tasked with accompanying him. Waleed would hold onto his older brother's hand and watch in awe as he sauntered into the tall grey-brown building, greeted the security guard by name and leaned over the loans desk to shamelessly flirt his way out of having to paying a fine. Adam, thought Waleed, as he walked to work, would have made terrible enemies had he actually gone to university, because he always kept books long past their due date. It was as if he believed that the intensity of his attachment made him the rightful owner. When he did eventually return a book he loved, sometimes months later, he would do so with tremendous reluctance: he would hand it over to the librarian, flinch as she stamped it and give a slight shudder when she tossed it in the shallow wooden box at her feet. Or at least that was how Waleed remembered it. Once he'd returned a book, Adam would never borrow it again; instead, he would add its title to an ever-growing list of things that he vowed he would one day buy.

Waleed had thought that working in a bookshop would mean certain things: that along with his life at university, his friends, his relationship with Anna (always, he recited this catalogue to confirm to himself that he had left), he had moved further and further away from the place he'd once called home. He had thought that in spending his hours surrounded by books in a place unlikely to be frequented by most of the people of his past – with their immediate needs, their scramble to survive, their petty gossip, the way they just went on and on making miserable, predictable choices, *marriage, babies, houses* – that he had created another boundary between then and now. What Waleed had not expected was for Adam to feature so prominently. Though his brother rarely visited him at work – Adam preferred the large, exclusive stores that had recently begun springing up in shopping malls – it was him Waleed thought of whenever he walked into that small, sometimes chaotic room, with its low ceilings and its unopened packages on the sales room floor. It was Adam his mind turned to when he took stock at the end of a long day, when he replaced and reordered the un-alphabetised mess made by the customers. He wondered once if he would have felt his brother as closely in a library, and he decided not. It was the bookshop itself, sitting at that nexus between literature and commerce that summoned Adam. In this, they were one. Books in Cape Town were never easily found, or cheaply bought. To own them, to have them about with such fantastic abundance, was to make a public proclamation of one's love for literature. And yet Waleed knew, too, that it was not merely about love, it was also about acquisition and possession, about writing his name in his book, declaring it his, refusing, on principle, to loan it to anyone. It was about the very particular mix of exhilaration and selfishness brought about by private property.

He placed his mug of coffee next to the till and began to count out the cash float. It was the Saturday morning of Easter Weekend, the only day in four that the shop would trade. He had not yet opened the doors; the blinds were still down, blocking out a thin autumn sun. Outside, between slight wisps of wind, came the sound of a crazed homeless man shouting abuse at his dog. Waleed cracked an eye and looked out onto Rondebosch's still quiet main road: fewer taxis and pedestrians than Woodstock, more than Constantia.

Waleed rolled up the blinds and opened the shop doors, knowing that this first hour, at least, would be his. There would be no familiar faces from the university, no gaggles of undergraduate girls with their crushes and projections, no women standing in the tiny fantasy fiction section searching for something that could break the impossible silence between them and their teenage sons.

Waleed had expected to loathe the menial tasks involved in this job. Instead, he found that he enjoyed stacking the shelves, signing for deliveries, creating order. There was something about the low stakes, almost non-existent pressure of it all that made this one of the gentlest spaces he had known.

The tutoring work, on the other hand, had fulfilled all his worst expectations and invented some new ones. He could not contain his aggravation towards most of his students and every time he walked into that ivy-clung building, he was reminded again and again of his long overdue chapters. The thesis, despite the easily delivered assurances to Derek a few months before, had not been touched. Instead, he had devoted his time to writing a little collection of interlocking short stories, knowing that short stories, unlike novels, poetry, or theatre, had little currency in the country: they were not the stuff of audience and export. But this was what had come to him, this was what woke him up and led him to his desk, and Waleed, uncertain about so many other things in his life, was always sure about his writing. He had started with a small memory, one in which he woke up in a sudden fit, damp with the sweat, alive with panic.

After the move from the District, Waleed had begun to have nightmares. He would wake up shouting, calling for his mother, telling her the roof had been blown off, the ground had given way, their house was nothing but dust and rubble, rubble and dust.

Fozia did everything she could, she rocked, she soothed, she told him again and again that the roof was not going anywhere, the ground was solid, *look*, she stamped her feet as proof, she gave him hot milk, she put him in her own bed, she left the light on in his bedroom. And still the dreams. Still the horror. Sleepless herself, walking through the day in a haze of exhaustion usually reserved for new mothers, she turned to her sisters and they all agreed that though the move had been difficult, things were not so bad as all that, it must be something else. Perhaps it was a doekoem? A curse? The child should be taken to Gadija. She would put him right in no time. And so Waleed found himself one morning, scrubbed clean by his mother, stuffed into a formal shirt and pants, on a chair in a small outhouse in the BoKaap while a tall woman with startled eyes and a continuous bruise in the centre of her forehead – the mark of someone who had been praying the requisite five times a day for years and years – asked him an array of strange questions.

Did he ever hear pigeons walking on the roof at night?
Did he see shapes in the dark?
Did he always leave the toilet on his right foot?

Waleed nodded yes to the pigeons. There was a flock he watched every morning from his window. They perched on the slack-bell wires of the telephone pole outside his house, leaving as one to trace their geometries against sky and cloud. Yes to the shapes in the dark. All kinds. Lumbering giants, small goblins, the tokolosh of the weekly char's stories, the shadow of the uncle he knew had died in his room. He saw them all, he knew them all. Yes to leaving the toilet on his right foot, though this last declaration was a lie. Gadija had nodded deeply and then told Fozia in low tones that it was certainly a curse, that the djinn were scratching on the roof every night, that the child could *see*, that he was being woken by them. She would do what she could, Gadija promised Fozia, but it was almost certain that this child would spend his life seeing things: it just was that way for some people. Waleed stopped watching the pigeons after that. The birds were not to be trusted. Neither was the dark.

He began the story there, in among the agir-bitti incense and the crumbling, burning frankincense, with the image of his mother's worried mouth set in a flat line and the sound of Gadija's mumbled prayers as she massaged his neck with oil that she promised was special, was blessed.

It was a start, he thought, looking over the work. It was a beginning. He tried to focus on the smell of that moment, the heat of it, the sound of the praying and the hushed conversation between the two women and not, explicitly not, on the questions that came thick and fast while he wrote. How would his mother feel about it? Did it make his people look primitive and superstitious? Was it betrayal? Was it love?

"I've brought you elevenses."

Waleed looked up. He had not even noticed that someone had walked in. It was Anna, holding out a homemade sandwich wrapped in opaque wax paper. Around her neck a thin Indian silk scarf, around her wrists rows of glittering bangles. She had, just the week before, told Waleed about plans for a nose-ring.

"This I don't deserve." He reached up his hands to cup her face, covering it with a dozen kisses. Sometimes, he thought, it was so easy to love.

"How's it going?"

"Quiet. Which is great. I've been thinking over the stories."

"Excellent." Anna stationed herself on a tall wooden stool that acted as both seat and boundary between customers and staff. "The one about the curse?"

"Yes."

"I still can't wrap my head around it," she said, inspecting the greeting cards displayed on a rotatable wire wheel.

Anna reached into her bag to pull out a naartjie, early to the season. Waleed felt a twinge of guilt. Telling Anna that story, sketching out how he had felt freakish, alone, somehow responsible, had furnished her with yet another example, another confirmation, that Fozia was a monster. And perhaps more than that, that he came from a world that was irrational and backward.

"Do you think what I'm doing is wrong?"

"This is how it goes, right?" said Anna carefully. "People write what they know."

"Ja. *But*—"

"Worrying about what your mom is going to think is probably not a good thing to have in your head when you are writing."

"You *cold*, man."

Anna peeled off the naartjie's skin, leaving an orangey peel snaked on the countertop, and then turned her attention to removing the feathery rind, so that each segment was individually plump and smooth.

Anna considered the fruit. "Your intentions are honourable."

"As my mother would say, 'The road to hell ...'"

"Look," Anna silenced him by popping several more naartjie segments in his mouth, "people are just going to have to *deal*. And they will. It will be fine. Half of them will probably be ecstatic about it. Can you imagine those preening aunties," here she launched into an impersonation of one such woman, loud, all knowing, full of unconscious insight and poetry, "That was *me*, nè. He was now writing my own life."

Anna had never actually met or spoken to any of these women; her voice and her pose were filtered through Waleed's many performances.

He stopped her irritably. "Don't do that. It's just—" He let a grimace do the rest of the remonstrative work.

"Sorry." But she remained buoyant. "I'm just saying, don't censor yourself. We've had enough of that here."

Waleed began to rearrange the shop's collection of literary gimmicks. In the midst of placing a made-in-China Lady Windermere's fan next to a plastic Proust's madeleine, he asked, "What if I were writing about you?"

Anna picked up the fan, spread out its wooden blades, raised them just beneath her eyes and asked, mock coquettishly, "Are you?"

"What if I were?"

She shifted back into a teasing humour. "It all depends. If you are describing someone of rare intelligence—"

"Well, quite—"

A woman and her sulking eleven-year-old daughter walked into the shop, bringing Anna and Waleed's exchange to an end. Other customers began to arrive, drifters, hoverers, taking up positions in the room's tight corners, shifting their weight from foot to foot, hunching over the merchandise at ground level, speaking in the hushed tones people always assume in a bookshop, granting it, as if by general consensus, the quiet reverence of a church or a court of law.

Anna went outside to have a cigarette. Waleed watched her from the window, watched how wisps of hair escaped her messy bun and were made light by the sun and a gust of wind, how she offered nervous smiles to strangers, trying, even in this moment of solitary smoking, to be nice, to be liked. *How differently they occupied space.* She, a woman in this country, trained to be afraid of men (any men), of dark corners, of dead ends. He, a brown man, the source of some of that fear, the reason white women crossed the street or clutched their handbags close to their bodies. *That* had started happening when he was around twelve. He wondered if all that fear of violence directed at him, more than a decade of it, if it had somehow made him violent: just last week he had got into an elevator, a woman had surreptitiously clasped her hand over her watch and he had felt an urge, both new and total, to punch either her or the wall. He picked up his notebook, remembering another detail: Gadija had told his mother that she'd made a terrible mistake naming him Waleed, that there were too many "Ws" in his family, too many angles that didn't meet up. It could only lead to terrible misunderstandings.

"Waleed! Waleed!" It was Anna, her voice midway between laughter and panic.

"What?"

"*Derek*."

"Oh, *fuck*. Where?"

"Quite far down the street. He went into the stationery shop but he gave me this tentative wave. I think he's coming in here after."

Waleed's eyes darted about, seeking escape routes. "You mind the shop for me. I'm going to duck out."

"What? *No.* I'm not doing that! I wouldn't know what to do."

"It's easy. You could do it with your eyes closed. Nobody's going to buy anything anyway. They never do. Come on. Help a brother out."

"You're out of your mind. How long are you going for? What if Matthew comes back?"

Matthew, Waleed's affable if absent-minded boss, sometimes made unexpected appearances mid-shift.

"He'll probably think he hired you himself. *Please*, An."

"Just relax. You're panicking."

"Of course I'm panicking. Oh, God." Waleed began to pace around the tiny area behind the counter, making a show of his entrapment. The smattering of browsers looked up, a few bemused, others irritated. "I owe him three chapters. *Three*. I haven't even done one."

"Relax." There was something about Anna's flat command that stopped Waleed's flailing. It was the voice, Waleed suspected, of a prefect, or someone who had gone through the jolly rigours of boarding school. "He's not your parent. He's your supervisor. He can't punish you because you haven't written something."

"Easy for some." The reality of Anna's steadily growing thesis cast its usual shadow.

"Hello, Waleed."

Tall and broad-shouldered enough to dwarf the small doorway, Professor Derek Reed offered his greetings.

"Howzit, Derek." Waleed bounced up and down in his chair and reached out an ever-so-slightly trembling hand. Derek grasped it with enough firmness to steady it and when the shake was over Waleed surreptitiously nursed what he was convinced was an internally bruised knuckle. Derek, he thought crossly, never seemed to know his own strength.

"Hi, Anna."

"Hi, Prof."

"Do you work here too now?" Derek asked her, glancing uncomfortably at Waleed, who was just about managing to produce a blank expression.

"Nope. Just making a nuisance of myself."

"That's nice." Derek began to move further inside the shop, gesturing vaguely, unknowingly towards the toilet as if that was where he was bound.

Waleed nodded and signed back, both men undone by each other's awkwardness. Derek turned as though remembering something and called out to Anna, "I actually had dinner with your supervisor last night. She was very pleased, said you are doing such vital work. If you want another reader just let me know."

Anna blushed slightly and tilted her head, suggesting both supplication and encouragement, while Waleed tried to stop his face assuming a scowl.

"Jesus. He fucking hates me, doesn't he?" Waleed said in a low whisper to Anna, who was absorbed in an endless exercise of transferring one set of bangles to the other arm and then back again. She looked up at him, incredulous, three thin turquoise-blue circles dangling from long, biro-stained fingers.

"Waleed. It's Easter Saturday. He doesn't want to talk about work. He's come here to buy a book. It's probably one of the highlights of his week. He's not chasing you down."

"I'm not saying that!" Again, customers looked his way. Derek, focusing intently on a coffee table book about Cape mountain trails, appeared not to have heard.

"Then what are you saying?"

Waleed's voice dropped back to a discreet murmur. "Just that it's hard to face him, considering everything—"

"Considering what?"

"The *funding*, man. It's like being a cheat. Taking money and not doing the job."

"You're not his employee."

"But—"

"Listen to me. You'll get the work done. And you'll get it done in your own time. And it will be good. But. You. Are. Not. His. Employee." Anna laid out those six words with finality.

Anna rubbed away at the biro stains on her fingertips and asked Waleed with studied casualness if he'd had a chance to look over the thesis chapter she'd left him. He was explaining why he hadn't had the time when Derek returned, a book about hiking trails under one arm. "This is excellent," he announced, taking out his money. "Did you order this one?"

Waleed shook his head and began to ring up the purchase. "Nah. I'm a child of the city. We didn't go walkabout."

"Well," Derek chuckled as he took his change.

Anna asked to look at the book. She paged through it, exclaiming at the photographs (the drama of the Cape vista, the expanse of water, the caves, the sun, both rising and setting), reminisced about childhood walks and school excursions. Waleed did not participate. The conversation had turned away from him in ways they could not understand.

Though his parents had known the rocks and shrubs of the Cape mountains, had walked its pathways, called its vegetation by names old and affectionate, had sat with impunity on every beach, it had been different for him, different even for Adam. After the removals, there had been fewer opportunities to gather up far-flung family members for mid-week hikes, and anyway, those routes had become uncharted territories. There were no guarantees that a loved path would still be open to everyone, that you wouldn't arrive, with satchels full of fruit and rotis and water, women in sunhats, children in shorts, men with cameras, only to be told *Not here. Not now. Leave. Pay the fine*. How to explain to them, he thought almost dreamily, that today everyone behaved as though it had always been *just so*. As though it had always been 1993 and that this moment, in which he could sit in this chair and sell these books, hadn't extracted its price.

Anna was laughing, recounting the hysterical terrors of her classmates on a camping trip down the Orange River; Derek offered a story of his own about being separated from his group for several long hours in the Cango Caves. They turned expectantly, encouragingly, to Waleed.

"Actually," he said, unable to censor himself, "we didn't do too many hikes. I spent most of Standard Eight and Nine boycotting, and my teachers didn't seem all that interested in organising away-days or group hikes."

Both Anna and Derek's cheeks grew red with embarrassment, one of the few downsides, Waleed thought now, to being white. He leaned back in his chair, knowing that he had drained the atmosphere of all its warmth and he felt no satisfaction in having done so. He huddled into his suede jacket as if the emotional chill was real. Derek leaned in to inspect the greeting cards. He picked up the Wilde-themed fan, remarked over its cleverness and then claimed that he was late to meet a friend at a coffee shop.

Anna watched the older man with a measure of pity. She kept faith with him while he raced down the street, passed the coffee shop of his alleged rendezvous, hopped into his car, and sped off. "Well, at least you found a way to stop him from asking about your research."

"Right. I always mobilise my oppression for my own ends."

"Oh, come *on*. The man was pretending to like *this*." She held up the fan as if it were Exhibit A. When Waleed didn't answer her, she told him she was leaving to meet Megan, her American housemate, for lunch.

Megan, a researcher doing fieldwork in South Africa, had been a source of both mirth and derision for Waleed. He gave a doleful shake of the head.

"You should give her a chance," said Anna. "She's doing some good work."

"She's an *anthropologist*. She's nothing more than a cultural bounty hunter."

"*God*. You're just angry with the world today."

"Ja, ja. Angry black man."

Anna gave him a small, apologetic smile and traced a finger around his mouth before leaning in to kiss it. Waleed kissed her back. He felt like a bully, and not for the first time, filled with a sense of bewilderment at how difficult, how *impossible*, things were.

She left the shop and Waleed watched as she made her way towards the station, arms swinging, her bangles a flash of colour and glint against her black jeans. He settled back into the chair and picked up a book, tried to focus, but found himself distracted both by the steady trickle and smatter of customers and by the worry that engulfed him daily: the endless negotiations, the seeming stalemate, the blinking mirage that was the election date, the *fucking disregard* the Nats seemed to have for just how much they were all conceding.

A figure rushed through the door and Waleed, attune to the dangers of sudden movement in this city, thought it signalled that first moment – always unexpected, horribly desperate – of a robbery. He reached for the only thing of weight and steel close by, the stapler. But no, it was Anna. She had only just stopped running, hair in sheaves around her face, breath hard, shallow, panicked, eyes full of streaming wind.

"What's wrong? What's happened?" Waleed leapt from his chair.

"It's Hani," she answered hoarsely, as though to say it at a normal volume would bring it into the realm of the real, the irrevocable. "He's been shot." And then in a wail that came up from her belly and through her throat, "He's dead."

12

Monday, 12 April 1993

It had been raining for three days. Rain without end and out of season. April was usually a month reserved for coolly indifferent nights and mild afternoons, but today it felt as though they were days deep in the toughest weeks of July when all the doors of the city, whether of wood or corrugated iron, remained shut against the cold. There had been a time when Nasreen had loved the Cape winter, had longed for the way it demanded that her family collect in one place, draw the circle close, light the consoling fires. An early memory of her first hail, white and clear, falling, then melting on the maroon-painted cement of Fozia's stoep and of herself transfixed by the wonder of it. Her grandmother was smoking in the lounge, on the stove something good and hot was cooking. Uncle Waleed was playing a record. Her parents were reading. Alia was asleep on the couch, her toddling legs and arms splayed free. The circle was drawn. The fire lit. Everyone was safe. Then Nasreen heard her grandmother say to Waleed, "Listen to that hail. Poor people going to be soaked to the bone. This is not a night I would wish on my worst enemy."

And with that, the hail became something menacing and cruel, something to be feared and fled from.

Today was such a day. The rain fell in full sheets, filling the dams, saving farms from drought and washing away homes in the townships. Always, in this place, it was a choice between two things, salvation or loss.

The week had begun with an assassination that had touched off protests all across the country. From Boksburg to Bonteheuwel, from Soweto to Midrand, the streets had been full of men and women lifting weapons, imaginary and real, dancing on the border between anguish and war. There had been placards and fury, threatening chants and open weeping; there had been violent suspicion, ongoing hunger, no voting day set, conspiracy theories everywhere, all that trust, all that talk, gone, evaporated, nothing. A man had been loved and now he was dead and people were angry. For almost a year Nasreen had become used to seeing Chris Hani on television, his round face, his khaki camouflage, his worried eyes. She'd watched him on podiums framed by large banners or standing in a circle of young men who pulled their berets at smart angles, offering salutes and toyi-toyi as a greeting.

She had watched the news, seen the ease with which he walked through the crowds and felt the weight of all his concessions when he had agreed to lay down his arms. "Not like he had much choice," Adam had insisted, but Nasreen wasn't sure about that. The way she saw it, for months and months he had supported the hammering out of an agreement with men who had spent all their days and many of their nights ensuring that he would never vote, men who said that all he wanted was to take white wealth and put it into the hands of black criminals, that he was masterminding a bloodbath, that he was too stupid to govern, that he was too clever for his own good, that he craved white women, that he hated white men, that his sexual appetite was insatiable, that he was a filthy communist, that if they'd ever caught him, back then, back in those days when he was on the run, they would have tortured all these thoughts out of him, that all he understood was violence anyway, that he was a coward, that he was a dangerous Africanist, that he was an inconsequential African.

He knew all these things, Nasreen told herself, he understood the depth of their old cruelties, the weight and smell of their snatched privilege, but he still put down his weapon and sat down with them.

"Peaceful transition, my foot," Zarina had said when the dreadful news was announced (a humiliating ending, a death in a driveway, a killing after freedom). "What kind of peace is this?"

Nasreen thought of him on that Easter afternoon. She imagined him getting out of his car, holding his groceries and newspapers, a little heavy-footed from observing a long week of slow arguments and grudging compromises, thinking, perhaps, about his wife who was away visiting family, or about the supper his daughter was preparing, or reaching further back, as adults always do, turning his mind to the long journey from Sabalela to Dawn Park. Or maybe, she told herself, he was thinking of nothing, nothing at all. She wondered if it had taken a moment for him to understand that he had been shot. She conjured it: how he turned to face the hired Polish gunman who flew by in a filmic blur and shot him once in the chest, three times in the head. She saw how his white trainers pointed towards the car, how around his head blood bloomed like flowers. How in the doorway, his daughter, like her, fifteen, sixteen, raised a hand to her mouth that did not stop her from screaming, a scream heard first throughout the neighbourhood, and then by the alchemy of grief and rage throughout the country. She saw Oliver Tambo arrive, a red handkerchief in his pocket, struck quiet with grief and shock, and his wife Adelaide collapse into Walter Sisulu's arms. She heard the chant go up: "Hamba, Hamba Kahle Umkhonto, khonto we Siswe."

There was a question Nasreen could not stop asking. She wanted to know, once he realised what was happening, if he regretted sanctioning those hours at that table; she wanted to know if, during those last moments, he hated them, as she did now. She was convinced he must have, even as she hoped he didn't.

Tuesday, 13 April 1993

Nasreen and Alia were at school, waiting for their mother to fetch them. The hard-as-nails games teacher had reluctantly cancelled hockey practice, conceding that a field of churning mud and water might be too dangerous for twenty girls to pound up and down on shoving a fast-spinning leather ball between them. Nasreen lined up with the other daygirls to use the public phone, grateful and happy for the cancellation even as Alia stood dramatically trembling and chattering her teeth, an action designed as much for the amusement of her peers as it was to elicit her mother's pity. It worked. Though Zarina was in the middle of processing a deposition for Jakoet, she felt a tug of guilt at asking her children to wait in this weather.

But an hour later the girls were still standing beneath one of St Michaels' oversized wooden doors. Alia scowled out angrily, all beetling eyebrows and clenched jaw – *Late again! so unfair!* – at the oak-lined sweeping driveway, taking tremendous satisfaction in how awful she felt. She began to catalogue her discomforts to Nasreen, reaching for the poetic even as she moaned. Her blazer was wet on her back, her stockings were clinging to her legs like sticky bandages, her hair was plastered into limp clumps dampened by rain and sweat, her mouth dry from the unripe orange she had just eaten. She was starving! Everything felt sour! It was as though her entire body had suddenly curdled!

In the middle of this litany Alia sneezed violently and looked at Nasreen in utter astonishment as though this was the first time she had ever experienced the beginnings of a cold. In Zarina's absence, it fell to Nasreen to search for a tissue and to offer her sister her own scarf. Alia accepted both and huddled on the bench, asking plaintively and feebly how much longer Zarina would be.

"Oh, for God's sake, Dramaticus," said Nasreen, whose first year of Latin had changed the way in which she nicknamed people, "she said she'd be here as soon as possible. She's *working*."

Alia nodded and looked stoically into the middle distance, torturing her nose with a scrap of toilet paper.

Eventually Zarina arrived, armed with sympathy and a flask of hot chocolate, both of which her daughters gulped down in rapid sips. "Sorry I'm late, you poor things," she said. "It's barbaric even to have considered you playing in this weather."

Zarina always matched her children's distress with hyperbolic outrage; it was a trait that ensured they felt understood, treasured and important, and convinced their teachers that the Dawood girls were coddled and indulged beyond measure.

Nasreen, now in the front seat, jerked at a sticky seatbelt and responded morosely, "It's character-building apparently. What made the Empire great."

This was no ordinary complaint; it was part of a strategy. Nasreen had a couple of memoranda she had been trying to push for the last few months and changing schools was one of them. She felt genuinely suffocated at St Michaels. She had never been a fan of the school – her conscience had been tormented by its wealth and privilege and inordinately high fees. Recently, all the things she had once thought of as harmless ritual, as charming tradition – the giving of badges, the demands of servitude that matriculants made on standard sixes, the operatic school song – had begun to strike her as being part of a much larger, longer problem. And she wanted no part in it. She begged her parents to let her spend her last year of high school elsewhere. They refused. Nasreen registered their refusal, regrouped and launched a campaign based on a symmetrical combination of resignation and resistance. She knew she was fighting a losing battle (the failed mosque debacle was never far from her mind), but she positioned it as a loss that would result in a won war. Her tactic was to make disparaging comments whenever she could. Continuous, relentless passive aggression, she told herself, would eventually wear away at her parents' resolve.

Her mother had ignored the first comment and so she offered another.

"Nice place. *Educational*. Really great. You'll have to pay huge fees and doctor's bills because of the flu we are all doomed to catch. Just look at Alia," she reached back to touch a solicitous hand to her sister's forehead, "she feels as if she's about to catch her death."

Alia coughed obligingly, offering threadlike wheezy gasps at first and then working her way towards someone in the last stages of consumption.

Nasreen clucked sympathetically, handing her another piece of toiletpaper and glaring at Zarina at the same time.

"Okay, enough. That's enough, Alia." Zarina's impatience carried the unspoken threat of a later discipline. Alia reined in her comic rasping and Nasreen busied herself with resetting her wristwatch while sighing deeply, a sound her sister read as a criticism that their parents had not yet replaced her faulty timepiece and Zarina recognised as the wordless lament of adolescence, that dreadful time when everything, even the inanimate, conspires against you. Nasreen burrowed back into the car seat. Her mother's all-powerful hold on her might have begun to thin, but essentially it remained in place; certain words, certain tones even, held her to a ransom she could not name. Old phrases, sentences from childhood still carried so much psychic weight:

Okay, I said that's enough.
You just wait till your father gets home.

I'm warning you.

Zarina hummed along in a waning voice to a radio jingle and then made a conciliatory offering. "The great thing about sport is that you get to meet so many new people. You really widen your social circle. A lot of people would absolutely kill for the chances you get. And the *facilities*? My word, the places you kids get to play …" She shook her head in wonder as if imagining all the various and verdant venues for their matches and training. "So I don't want to hear you two complaining about it again." Zarina sat up in her seat, feeling that she had done quite well; she had nipped her daughters' whining in the bud and delivered a valuable life lesson to boot.

"Yes," Nasreen paused and gathered herself, ready to deliver her winning blow, "it is truly amazing what money can buy. It's just incredible how diverse people are at Cape Town private schools. Really, the *range* of people. "

Zarina shrugged, pretending an indifference she did not feel. Privately she registered the impossible narrowness of her daughters' experience, but did anyone, she argued with herself, did anyone in this bladdy country escape from that? She looked over at Nasreen, caught Alia's eye in the rear-view mirror and said, "Okay. But how about we try and be grateful for what we all have right now?"

A difficult silence spread over the car's three occupants. There were so many ways to be wrong and right. Zarina fiddled with the dial, trying to find a news-free station, and Alia focused intently on her hot chocolate. The weather had caused a traffic jam and their car idled to a long stillness. The silence grew, as did the tension, until Zarina said, "No one's going to riot in this weather."

Nasreen looked at the rain on the window. The car suddenly felt quite flimsy. She glanced back at her younger sister, staring, as always, out the window, and sensed that she knew what Alia did not, what she would not tell her, that the country had taken a bad tilt, that it was dangerously off course, that it could all be okay or it could all go spectacularly wrong.

~

Once home, Nasreen raced upstairs to the phone. There was going to be a memorial service for Hani at St George's Cathedral the next day and somehow she had to get down there. Perhaps Emma would go with her. Her mind became very clear; there was a strategy in place. She passed her mother in the corridor, felt a pinch of guilt and then assured herself that it was not really deceit, it was not really bunking if it was politically motivated.

She was midway through attempting to convince a very reluctant Emma to accompany her to the memorial when Alia announced her presence by standing in the doorway.

"I'm. On. The. Phone."

"I know," answered Alia, sitting down.

Nasreen put her mouth close to the receiver. "Just hold on, Emma," she said, and then let out a high-pitched bellow: "Mooooooooommmmmmm! Can you please tell Alia to respect my privacy?"

Zarina, at the dining-room table leafing her way through the last of Jakoet's paperwork for the day, pretended to be deaf.

"Were you just listening in? My God, it's like living with the CIA."

"I'm just here to watch TV," lied Alia, settling onto the couch. "It's a free country."

"No, Alia," corrected Nasreen, "it's *not*." She turned back to the phone. "Sorry, Ems. Come to the cathedral. *Please*. They won't expel us. Okay ... ja. I see your point ... but. Fine. I'll go alone." She said goodbye, hung up and glared at the phone as if it were responsible for her friend's wariness. Why was everyone so *timid*?

"Are you going to the memorial?"

Nasreen grabbed the remote control from Alia and flicked the television on, settling on an afternoon soap that dealt in high fashion and inferred incest. One of Fozia's pithy sayings flitted through her thoughts: *When days are dark, friends are few. Too bladdy right.*

Alia was repeating her question.

"I'm trying to watch this."

"Why won't Emma go with you?"

"One, she's scared, which is fair enough. And two, if she gets caught, she won't make head-girl."

"That's terrible."

"To each her own." Nasreen fought to remain neutral, to relax her face, which had grown pinched and hard.

"You don't feel that way at all – that's not how you sounded on the phone just now!"

"Well, *Jesus*, Alia, what do you want me to say? It's obvious what her priorities are—"

"Is it because she's white?"

Nasreen took a moment to consider this, her heart chafing against the question. Emma had been the first person to offer her friendship in those first few difficult months at St Michaels when everything, from her accent to her address, had screamed her difference. Emma stayed over on weekends, ate and loved Zarina's cooking, laughed at Adam's retold jokes, indulged Alia's constant interruptions, and had passionately defended the armed struggle in a tense and argumentative history class the week before. *But maybe, maybe, not coming to the memorial was about her being white.* Nasreen searched her memory, trying to recall instances that would simultaneously confirm and refute this. She chose eventually to shrug in response. There was no way of knowing.

Alia was making an annoyingly intent study of her profile. "You can't go alone," she announced with finality. And then, "I'm coming with you."

13

Wednesday, 14 April 1993

The day of the memorial returned the weather to its season. It was bright, rainless and cloudless. The morning sun hung high and sharp yellow against a thin early sky. There was a promise of heat again, a promise and a threat that seemed to shrug off a week of wet days, discount the first signs of winter, and raise, dangerously, the blood, the temperature, of everyone in the city.

Nasreen and Alia were hiding, crouched, in a damp patch of overgrown grass that rose up between the groundsmen's toolshed and the spiked wooden gate that separated St Michaels from the world. Alia heard something.

"What's that?"

The high-pitched chatter of children's voices began to gain in volume.

Nasreen lifted herself a few inches. "It's the Sub BS. They're going to the Art Block."

Alia gave a short, soldier-like nod. The day's defiance, the careful planning, the hushed conversations, had made her feel that she was one breath away from saluting Nasreen and inventing a secret code. From behind the grass she watched a pony- and pig-tailed swarm of little girls move from one activity to another. She hunched forward, inadvertently stepping with her full weight on Nasreen's foot.

"Oww! Watch it!"

"I barely touched you!"

The girls placed cautious hands between the spikes and hoisted themselves over the fence. As their feet touched the pavement they felt a light giddiness.

"We are free," announced Alia with solemnity.

They broke into their pre-agreed two-block run, putting an initial distance between themselves and the school, stopping panting and laughing, outside a row of ladylike Victorian cottages. Alia twisted her neck round to inspect her skirt. "Oh shit. Look, it's all wet from the grass."

"Don't worry, it'll dry in a minute."

Alia nodded at Nasreen gravely, the marked skirt suddenly a sacrifice in the service of the greater good. They stood for a moment close to the base of an old oak, whose stronger roots had ruffled and hilled and broken through the surface of the pavement. Nasreen leaned against the looped decorative railings that stood between the cottages' small front gardens and the street, staring wonderingly out at the world before her. It was a street she knew well, but on this morning, its smells and sounds seemed entirely new, as though the rules that she had just broken, smashed through, disregarded, made the street and all its contents, made the day and all its possible futures, entirely hers.

~

They walked the rest of the way at a normal pace, crossing the small two-lane highway between the Mount Nelson Hotel and the exit to the Company's Gardens. The avenue opened in a straight, oak-lined path before them, leaves full and wet from the previous night's rain. Between every four or so trees were wooden benches and large tin rubbish bins and between those bins and benches darted anxious acorn-clutching squirrels. It was not quite nine o'clock. The Gardens were still empty, just groundsmen raking the damp soil and newly arrived German tourists in safari gear with heavy cameras slung about their necks.

In the distance as through a stereoscope, Nasreen could see the avenue's entrance with its miniature arrangement of peanut sellers, fruit vendors and ageing white hippie landscape painters. As they passed Parliament, Nasreen spared a withering thought for the statue of Rhodes who leaned forward, arm extended in a Nazi-style salute, pointing vaguely to the north, above an inscription that read "Yonder is your hinterland", and she blew a mocking kiss to Queen Victoria, stout and stone, sceptre in hand.

They reached the entrance and Alia bought a bag of peanuts, letting her fingers work off the papery brown skins, scattering a few to hopeful squirrels. Nasreen stood beneath the semi-reclining figure of Smuts looking for some sort of sign about what to do and where to go.

The girls were now living out that unhappy axiom, better to travel than to arrive. They had no particular plan. Instead, guided by St Michaels, they had assumed that once they arrived, there would be people to greet them, hand them the appropriate ribbons, badges, order of service, and that would be that.

Alia walked over to the paintings propped up against wooden crates and pretended to admire a lurid sunset scene of streaked orange sky and turquoise water. Though a small pool of sun had now broken through the leaves, a flower seller and her small son huddled further into their cardigans. Alia smiled at the painter who looked back without interest and fiddled with her lanky, greasy plait.

She wandered over to the grey slate steps of the cathedral and motioned at her sister to join her, but Nasreen paused at the Gardens' entrance, a still point between three buildings – the Slave Lodge, the Houses of Parliament and the cathedral. She thought of a recurring childhood nightmare. In it, her family's home was built on a Khoisan burial ground. The bones of the ancient, the long gone, were deep in the ground beneath them. Far below the garage the souls were in a restless fury, angry, so angry that people were walking on their heads. *This part of the city*, she thought, *the oldest, the strangest, the bloodiest.*

This city, where bones spoke, where every home was an ossuary, where spirits were trapped in the twilight.

~

The girls ran lightly up the shallow granite steps towards the cathedral's thick wooden door. It was just a little ajar, enough to let them know it was open but not yet ready for the day. Nasreen pushed at it gently, then with more force so that it swung open, and ushered her sister inside with an authority she did not feel. They stood hesitantly at the entrance, allowing themselves to be dwarfed and awed by the high Gothic vault whose crisscrossed ribs made a long clean sweep of stone from floor to ceiling. Alia felt the smallness the design asked her to, but behind that, she recognised another feeling, one of longing and not belonging. She turned to face the windows, where light stuck to the glass and spilled out on the white stone floor, decorating it with bits of darting ethereal colour: fish shadows in a pond.

The cathedral was still almost empty and the girls tried to lighten their steps, move cautiously, do nothing to disrupt the quiet of the building. The caretakers and priests were unpacking chairs. Nasreen felt her body filling with a sense of hushed wonder, partly from the miracle of the echoing emptiness, but also because within the building's grandness and its conscience she intuited the history of her city, and parrellel to that wonder, a small thrum of guilt: she was not supposed to feel anything in these places, except perhaps scepticism. The imam at their madressa had regularly railed against the deification of Jesus and the iconography of Mary and, though Nasreen always felt unnerved by the images of a man's body in the final stages of protracted torture, she often thought that the woman with her blue scarf and her pretty eyes could, but for her stone stillness, have been any one of her many aunts.

She crept ahead of her sister towards the south transept's rose window. At its centre, Jesus, and around him a radiating circle of saints and seraphim. It was a window that she loved instantly, a love she shared now with Alia, who in a few weeks would show it to Nick, aggressively insisting that he find it extraordinary. Nasreen noticed a bronze plaque and she leaned in to read it. A surge of disappointment flooded through her. "I don't believe this," she said in a disgusted voice. "It's a memorial to George VI. Why does *everything* in this city have to be dedicated to some dead white guy?"

Nasreen was used to seeing the streets of Cape Town dotted with the bronze statues of men, rearing on horseback or galloping into fountains, mounted on granite blocks, but it was difficult to think of this window as belonging, along with everything else, to them. She added sadness to her disappointment, and fought to find something to say that would cancel out the dedication. Eventually, defiantly, she said, "I think it looks like something out of a mosque."

Alia nodded vigorously. "Me, too. If you squint you can't really tell that there are all those figures. You just see the patterns and it looks like something out of the Ottoman Empire, or the Raj maybe."

"That's probably where they got the idea."

The two girls stood, heads tilted up towards the stained glass, eyes avoiding the brass plaque. They didn't have anything to base their thesis on, but they had imbibed – and applied here – their grandfather Ebrahim's belief that everything of excellence that Europe produced, from mathematics to masonry, from philosophy to food, had its origins in the East.

~

Alia and Nasreen watched as the men moved between the pews, counting out hymnbooks, cleaning wax off wooden holders, carrying in simple bunches of white flowers. There was something festive in the preparation. The flowers, the candles, the counting of the seats, all so much like a wedding, until they saw one of the priests stop in the business of duty to kneel on one of the taut maroon leather cushions, his head unbowed, staring fixedly, challengingly, at the altar, his mouth clamped shut. A caretaker, movements fast and fussy, called out softly, "The programmes are late ... Father? The programmes are late."

The kneeling priest did not answer him, continuing instead to stare at the altar. The caretaker turned away, warned off, as the girls were, by a silence none of them could name. The man heaved himself up and began to count out the cushions. The sisters settled eventually on two hard seats behind a pillar, purchasing some refuge in the shadows.

The church began to fill up and, as it did, Nasreen and Alia shrank further and further into the archway, as if it were a shelter in which they could make their navy blazers a little less crisp, could make everything about them announce a little less privilege.

There were other schoolchildren there, too. But they all wore their ties at skewed angles, shrugging off their jackets as a concession to the growing heat of the crowded building. The girls sported bangles, the boys earrings, all unthinkable adornments at St Michaels. Nasreen wondered if rolling up the sleeves on her blazer would help. She had just begun to fold back the thick material when she saw a familiar figure that made her heart and stomach skitter in concert. "Look," she said to Alia, "there's Uncle Waleed."

Alia looked up. Neither of the girls had seen him since Eid, a tense affair that had forced everyone into comfort eating and then, later, resentful fullness. Waleed had been in a foul mood all morning and had picked a bickering argument with his mother about her not having invited Anna to lunch. Adam had been first dismissive and then angry, Zarina had attempted to negotiate between them, and Waleed had eventually left the house after slamming his glass down hard and sloshing juice all over Fozia's good tablecloth. Adam had shouted that he had no respect for other people's things, that if he insisted on breaking all the rules, what did he expect their mother to do? Fozia had run after Waleed, begging him to stay a little longer, but Waleed had shaken her off a little more roughly than he intended, which meant that Zarina only just about managed to stop her husband from landing a punch on his brother, while the girls looked on, mouths agape, minds aghast. Somehow this segued into Waleed announcing that he expected nothing less than violence from a greedy capitalist before turning on his nieces, taking in their carefully planned ensembles and blow-dried hair and intoning in a prophet's voice, "I weep for the future." When everyone except Waleed was back inside, a wailing Fozia had blamed Adam for having been too hard on his brother, and Adam, full of injury, had gathered up his family and taken them to Zarina's parents, which he knew would wound Fozia deeply. It had not been a good day. The girls had ended it by lying fully clothed on the floor in Nasreen's room, eating leftover daltjies, unable to work up the energy or interest to go to the Waterfront for the biannual showing off of new Eid outfits and fathers' cars.

Waleed was standing with a group of men and women, all similarly dressed in jeans, cargo flak jackets and t-shirts, their heads a collective of unkempt styles, deliberately careless, messy. Nasreen tucked a flyaway bit of fringe behind her ear while her uncle and his friends stood near the doors, welcoming people. Waleed was listening intently to a man who had an expensive-looking camera slung around his neck. He was telling Waleed a story, expression tense, eyes rimmed with sleeplessness, hands gripped tightly to his camera. Waleed was shaking his head in sympathy and Nasreen almost believed she could hear him across the now packed church saying his familiar phrase, "This country, man. This *fucking* country."

"Should we go and say hello?" she asked her sister.

Alia didn't respond immediately; she and Nasreen smiled at each other hesitantly, shyly. Here was the man they had loved, seen and unseen, for years. They lurched forward, wanting to talk to him, but held back by something no one in their family had dared name yet. The latest fight had exposed too many things, things that for years their parents had cloaked in a protective device of half-truths and halting explanations. At all the tense Eids and birthdays, at the infrequent visits, they had always been told that Waleed's moods were personal, his grumpiness his own. They had not known, not understood, that any of it was connected to something larger. They had almost seen him last week, but not quite. On a visit to their grandmother, they were convinced they'd seen him sneak down the alleyway. Nonsense, their grandmother had said, but it was true. He had made his exit the minute he heard their voices.

When she looked at him now, Nasreen saw for the first time her father, younger, freer. Without Adam there, the resemblance assumed a new strength. The two men were composed of the same elements, the nose, the mouth, the angle of the jaw, but they carried and remade their worlds so differently. Here was Waleed in his dusty suede jacket and his hair coaxed into a curly halo, and somehow through him, her father too, in his silk suits, his exact grooming.

Nasreen glanced at her watch. "I think we should say hello." She offered this to Alia, waiting for her to object. The boldness was in the suggestion; executing it was a different matter. But Nasreen was desperate to talk to Waleed and so the girls began to move towards him. Close in height, their steps matched, the shoulder pads of their blazers meeting in a straight line. They stood in front of Waleed, waiting, but he did not recognise the uniformed teenagers. Instead, he was listening closely to what Rashaad, the photographer, was saying.

"I don't know why this one got to me the way it did, but it did, ma broe. It *got* me, somewhere I wasn't expecting. And to see Sexwale crying. And Ma Adelaide, that was fucking *hard*, man. She just let off this wail. And it tore right through me. Sisulu was holding her and then the chant went up. When they put the flag on his body, right there in the driveway, I soema felt like they were laying a wreath on the whole bladdy process."

Waleed shook his head, murmuring so that the girls could only hear fragments of what he was saying. They crept closer slowly, still unseen. This man had been there. Right there. Had seen the blood and the white trainers. They kept silent, wanting to hear more, to listen to Waleed's responses. It seemed precious, fleeting, this chance to hear what those in that inner circle felt, knew.

"I still can't believe this has happened." Rashaad passed a weary hand over his eyes and then cradled his forehead as though taking his own temperature. "I just can't associate Chris with death."

Waleed looked down at his shoes and said something about never having actually talked to him, just having met him once, briefly, at a meeting in Woodstock a few months before. Rashaad lifted his camera, squinting an eye, obscuring much of his own face, taking the measure of the room. He moved slightly away from the large glass doors, making room for a group of elderly women, all dressed in the impeccable blue and white uniform of the Church of Zion. "This is going to start late."

Alia touched him, briefly, just below his elbow, "Uncle Waleed?"

"Jesus," he exhaled in a whistle through his teeth, "do your parents know you here?"

"No," answered Nasreen, "and please don't tell them."

Waleed grunted in response, committing to nothing.

"Where's Anna?" asked Alia, though neither of them had ever met her.

Waleed looked almost touched. "She's not in town. She's up in Joburg at Wits doing some research. She's staying for the funeral in Soweto."

"Are we going to get to meet her?"

"Alia!" Nasreen turned on her with warning eyes. "Uncle Waleed doesn't have to talk to you about his private life."

Waleed nodded gravely, then turned to Alia, saying that she could meet Anna anytime she wanted, that his door was always open, that she knew where he was. It seemed to give Waleed great satisfaction to announce he had an open house policy. The girls knew, as was wont in their family, that he was sending a coded message back to their parents and the message was *I am welcoming. I am not the problem*.

Rashaad was talking to a woman standing next to him. One of the memorial organisers, she was speaking in a rapid, frenzied way, telling him that if he wanted pictures he'd better get himself outside *now*, that the cars were about to arrive. She shot this advice out as though issuing a command, all the while grabbing at her left shoulder with her right hand and massaging it with a grimace. Nasreen, emboldened by the way Waleed seemed to be accepted by everyone, joked, "Aren't they always late?"

It was something she'd always heard those in the know say about political meetings and she offered it as though she too were a part of things. The woman turned to her now, seeing her for the first time. She swooped her eyes up and down, took in the uniform, the blazer trimmed with rows of rectangular and shield-shaped badges as if Nasreen were a highly decorated officer, the clipped accent, and spat out, "Sorry, but are you even in this conversation? Because I don't remember asking you to join it."

Waleed shook his head. "Lee-Anne, Lee-*Anne*, come on, man, this is my niece."

"Well, then you should teach her to watch what she is saying—"

"Ag, relax, ek sê," said Waleed dismissively. "You being oversensitive."

"Is this a joke to you?"

Nasreen, without realising it, had positioned herself behind Waleed, shielding Alia. She glanced at her sister, trying to reassure her by playing her embarrassment off as amusement. Lee-Anne caught the look and snapped, "Listen here, am I a bladdy *joke* to you? Is something funny? You find this place *funny*? Maybe you should think about *where* you are. And then maybe you should think about *who* you are."

Nasreen's mouth opened, in an effort to form a response, but nothing took shape or sound. Waleed had been trying, unsuccessfully, to cut Lee-Anne off for several sentences. He raised his voice over and through hers. "Okay, Lee-Anne, that's enough. They didn't come here for that, and I don't think you did either."

Lee-Anne was almost foaming at the mouth; if she had swayed just a little people might have thought she was drunk. "I don't know why you came, but I didn't a fuck come here or go through what I went through so that some laaitie in a white uniform could make jokes about my leaders."

She stalked off and Waleed was left with two nieces who were now struggling not to cry. He patted Nasreen absently on the arm. "It's okay. Don't take it so personally. Lee-Anne is just—"

Alia hunched into herself. "What's her problem?"

"Fucked if I know," said Waleed, and then started as though he remembered his surroundings and his responsibilities; he was in a church, these were his nieces. "Listen, don't worry about it. She's been having a hard time lately. She has to have an operation next week. Something was done to her a while back when she was in solitary."

Nasreen's eyes widened at the inference of torture and Alia, too, was a little shaken. Until that moment she had thought everyone vaguely or closely related to The Struggle (even in her head, an always capitalised phrase) was somehow blessed with extraordinary gifts of conduct, that every single activist generated waves of compassion, that all their macro-struggles mirrored their micro ones. She didn't know where she had got this idea, it had taken root somewhere between *Star Wars* and a smuggled copy of *I Write What I Like*, but it was a persistent, determined notion which had taken up residence in her busy little brain for years now. She felt a sudden fury at having to let go of this idea. But Nasreen took the blow. She believed at some level she deserved it, and would go on deserving it until she paid in full for wearing that uniform.

Waleed draped a theatrical arm over his elder niece's shoulder. "Chin up!" he said in an English accent.

Nasreen forced a small laugh, though she was on the verge of full-scale melancholy.

Waleed gave her a gentle push. "You two should get moving, the service is going to start. I have to manage the crowd and it's better if you not right by the door, you never know what's going to happen."

The girls retreated to a far corner. Waleed registered their position, promising himself (and Fozia, who had taken up residence in his head) that he would check in on them every few minutes. Sometimes he was uncertain about how to deal with all their affection; it felt misplaced. Not insincere, just as though it was being given to the wrong person. He walked over to Rashaad, who was standing in the doorway, ready to capture those first images. He sketched out his nieces' encounter with Lee-Anne. "She just went bosbefok on them, ma broe," he said, clapping once, to punctuate, letting his hands frame his face like parenthesis.

Rashaad listened absently, refilling his reel. "Why didn't you just tell her to fuck off? She mus' try talk to my family like that. I would have fucking klapped her one." He jerked his neck violently towards Lee-Anne when he said the last bit.

"Can't," answered Waleed. "I'd be punching above my weight." He registered the unfairness of the comment and amended it. "Figuratively, I mean."

But Rashaad laughed; gallows humour had cemented and re-cemented this friendship for over twenty years. He began to focus his lens, shooting off the first reel and a truism as he did. "Ja, I suppose if you go around trying to protect people from every bit of anger everyone has in this fucked-up place, you not gonna have much time for anything else. Anyone who has kids in this country is mad in their head."

There was something to be said, Waleed reflected, about the right outfit. Lee-Anne always got it exactly right. She always managed to make her hair and her eyebrows and her unmanicured toes into a larger part of her unkempt indignation, her ungroomed self-righteousness. Of course one had to respect Lee-Anne. Everyone did. Quite rightly too. There was a lot to be said, and even more to be gained, by her unflinching, intractable stance on everything, her fury about the negotiations, her need to ferret out everyone who was hopping on the reconciliation bandwagon, her tireless (huh *authoritarian*) work for the Cultural Desk. But he also had to wonder whether she still felt as she had all those years ago at that first meeting, when he had gone, lightly and eagerly, to share his thoughts, if he were still *just* a writer, an artist, if he was perpetually to be prescribed the title of *featherweight*, if he was still forbidden to talk because he had "no mandate". It was different for Rashaad. His work was considered vital. He shot frame after frame, his images went out into the world and jostled Europe and America's conscience, he documented facts, lives. Waleed merely interpreted them. Of course he had no mandate. Of course he sounded bourgeois. He had made a role-defining mistake in the mid-eighties, arguing passionately in front of an entire meeting of activists that an artist's first loyalty must be to art not to politics, that critique was as important as solidarity, that a mandate was a form of dictatorship, that he would have written against the system anyway – anyone with a brain and a heart would – but he didn't need to be *told* that. Lee-Anne had sneered then and she had never stopped.

Enough. He shouldn't think like this. She was upset. They all were. The country was teetering on the edge of an abyss and they all knew it.

All those awful years.

And now this.

They had been almost there, almost, and now in its place, the old future: *warring, febrile, dark, clogged with blood.*

There was some movement ahead, a flurry of doors being opened for men in suits accompanying men in robes.

"Here comes the Arch," said Rashaad, consumed as always by the opportunity to document. Waleed shook off the despondency of his last thought and watched the famous priest enter. His hair was not yet grey; that would only come later, years later, when he would preside over the nation's catalogue of horrors. Today his face was etched in hard lines, some for anger, some for grief. His mouth was a firm rectangle. His eyes were no-sleep-obsidian. This man, who beamed from the pulpit even while he lamented and raged, who told people to clap and cheer in God's house, to make a noise, stomp feet, who kissed his hands and waved them when he offered a blessing. He walked, gripping the gold mitre, his feet heavy, his eyes fixed, like the priest's earlier, on the high altar ahead, and the cross in the middle of it. Behind him walked an imam and two priests. They sang as they walked, each note pushing towards a steadiness, a sureness that no one felt. The air inside the cathedral had turned sour from all the bodies. Everything felt damp and musty. The mood was full of mournful anger, but it was tempered by the building itself, the pageantry of its prayer, the rules of its rituals.

But the cathedral was not the country. It was not even the city. Beyond its walls was a larger, much angrier congregation. Waleed looked out the glass doors, knowing with sudden certainty that behind them, fury was gathering.

~

Nasreen walked outside, Alia, as ever, her close shadow. A glaring sun made Nasreen blink back against the sky. She had not eaten for hours; her hunger and the disorientating brightness after the dim, tight-packed safety of the service made her feel dazed and unfocused. They had been singing the same song over and over for what felt like hours: "Senzenina? Senzenina? What have we done? What have we done?" A tall man in a suit had taken her hand and lifted it up and they, along with the rest of the congregation, had waved and swayed and sang that same question. Her shoulder ached a little from the pull and stretch. In the midst of the singing there had been crying and shouting and then, without warning, the service had been brought to a halt. They were told that something had gone wrong, something had happened to the mourners who were coming in on the trains, that it was best to leave. It was best to leave *now*. People had begun to heave and rush and push towards the glass and wood doors; she found herself now, on the steps she and Alia had run up that morning. Her ears were full of a whirring dullness and so at first she did not understand that the faint outline of a repetitive beat was coming from the outside. There was something unsettlingly familiar about it. Then she recognised the staccato chant of unseen marchers, and with them the first bars of the soundtrack of a riot: the slam of thousands of feet against pavement, the screech of police vans, the sirens, the incantations. Tja! Tja-*tja*! Tja! Tja-*tja*!

She knew then that the city had turned in on itself, heaved, roared, broken loose. Tja! Tja-tja! The marchers were coming closer. Nasreen inhaled the fear tunnelling through the city. Lee-Anne bolted past her, her face alive with alarm. Then she turned back, shouting, 'Get inside! *Please*. Your uncle is looking for you!"

The cathedral kept emptying, men, women and children spilling out onto its stone steps. There was jostling and pushing, everyone trying to listen for the marchers, to gauge where they were, to know the reach of their anger. Nasreen grabbed Alia's hand, telling her to stay close. She felt a sharp jab in her back.

"You two!"

It was Waleed, wearing a harried expression, hurriedly

working a peace monitor's armband up his elbow and over his bicep. "Listen, you go straight back to school. There's people coming. I can't walk you up, I've got to go and talk to those boys there," he pointed at a group of youths standing on the opposite street corner. "Just head straight up Company Avenue. You'll be okay. I'll call you later to check in." He hugged them towards him briefly and crossed the crowded street, weaving, darting.

Alia stretched out to grab Waleed's arm, but he was already beyond reach, she was snatching at air. She looked to her left up the wide incline of Wale Street and tugged wordlessly at Nasreen to look too. The marchers. Heading down the hill, rows and rows and rows of arms and legs, limbs gangling, limbs fat, long, stubby, young, old, bare shoulders, clenched fists, covered ankles, shoals of bobbing heads, above them banners, a flash and splash of bright T-shirts, jeans torn down to a loose tonguing flap, the swish of hippie skirts, intricate shwe-shwe, the chequered rebellion of intifada scarves, camouflage berets, bodies, bodies, moving as one, no *I* only *we*. Tja-tja! A loose-limbed man with an oversized Adam's apple and a fraying cream shirt that clung to frail shoulders placed himself in front of the first row of a thirty-wide phalanx of toyi-toyiers. He began to charge up and down in a straight line as though confined to an invisible corridor, lifting his knees, miming an AK-47, turning, snapping, curving, a peacock, a tiger.

"U*left*. U*right*. U*left*. U*right*. U*left*. U*right*.Tja-tja."

Nasreen grabbed Alia's other hand, gripping it with a pale-knuckled panic that matched her now-grinding jaw.

Another row and another and another, and with each bit of ground gained, more bodies emerged from side streets. Tja! Tja-tja! Tja! Tja-tja!

Suddenly, a merging. The cathedral mourners became one with the marchers, the girls, caught between bodies, were propelled forward, their school shoes a part of the thousand slamming feet. They were on the street now, inescapably on the street, the safe steps of the church an unreachable few metres away. In front of them, a woman, head in a tight doek, large feet peeking from a floor-length print skirt, tilted her face continuously from sky to ground. She screamed and cried, waved a testifying hand, from her mouth a torrent of Xhosa. Two men charged through everyone, racing, racing, arms above their heads, in their hands rifles, dark skin against gun metal. Careless, furious, they pushed Alia out of their way, knocking her first into a stumble and then a fall. She tumbled, knees first, getting the gravelled scraping of childhood. Nasreen bent to help her up, and for a moment they were both crouched, seeing only shoes, shoes, bare feet, shoes, bare feet bloodied, toes, sandals, shoes, shoes trammel past. A girl, perhaps their age, stopped in front of them, her calves smeared with fading bruises, her shorts letting them see three cigarette burns walking a trail to her crotch. She turned to scream shrilly into the crowd, "*Faz*lin! Ja*nine*! Pasop! Die boere kom! Hulle kom nou-nou!"

Someone had dropped a banner and the red material lay like a draped wound on the tar. Carried high on the air, the discordant song of a siren, the desperate snatched efforts to keep a marching chant going, the knowing certainty that teargas was coming, that bullets were not far behind.

Alia remembered a faraway day: the pole, the mad wind, the fear of being blown up the mountain, swept into a cave, taken from everything she knew. A still point now, the world seemed to freeze tight. She curved herself, wrapped her arms around her knees, tried to make herself as small as possible, wondered if it was possible to stay just there, very still, until everything was over.

It was Nasreen who shook their bodies free of that stasis,

pulled Alia up, pushed to the edge of the crowd, to a thinning, a small opening at the entrance to the Gardens. In the distance, the trace and smell of teargas. The flower seller was still there; she and her small son tugged carnations, roses, baby's breath and freesias from their plastic buckets and wrapped the stems with damp newspaper. The woman threw pained glances at her boy and her produce while Nasreen pulled her school scarf free, dunked it into an empty bucket and brought the soaking, dripping thing up to Alia's nose and mouth.

"What are you doing!?" Alia smacked the wet acrylic away from her face and stared incredulously at Nasreen, who was looking at the scarf in a bewildered way that suggested she didn't know either.

The flower seller grabbed her buckets and her child and ran. The girls stood beneath the entrance sign while around them the crowd splintered and shook and split into three chaotic currents: through St George's Mall, down towards Adderley Street, and over the tight lawns and manicured flowerbeds of the Gardens.

"Can you see Uncle Waleed?" Alia touched a tissue to her bloody knee. The move from steps to entrance had lasted just a few short minutes. It was possible, she told Nasreen, that he was still across the street. Nasreen scrambled onto a park bench and looked over the streaming, bobbing heads. There, beneath the Board of Executors sign, was their uncle. He seemed to be pleading with a group of about ten black and coloured teenagers, not much older than her. One of them was deftly waving a bicycle chain as though training for a Karate Kid audition, another was tossing a rock from hand to hand, ball-like. Waleed was waving his hands, flattening his palms against the makeshift weapons, as though he was trying to calm them. One boy moved close to Waleed's face and began to shout into it, then he turned heel and flipped his hand as if to say "Voetsek." Lee-Anne was there, too, standing just behind Waleed, hands on her hips, neck strained forward, staring up at the tall boys through a fringe that fell hard on thick eyebrows. Waleed was talking, talking, gabbling in a way that Nasreen knew meant he was nervous, but whatever he was saying seemed to be working. He was drawing the boys in.

"Hey! What's going on? Can you see?"

"He's talking to those boys," Nasreen answered her sister. "I think he's trying to stop things getting worse. Let's give him a minute."

Nasreen watched as the boys began to nod in agreement. The bicycle chain was tied around a telephone pole, the rock was dropped. The others, though weaponless, had looked ready, charged for battle, but they began to soften their postures. For a moment the circle stood, shoulders dropped, as though a tiredness had enveloped them. And then a police car turned the corner at a screech, the driver gearing down as though intending to take it at an angle. The two men in the car laughed uproariously when they missed Waleed and the boys by inches. Waleed darted away from the vehicle, tripping, falling, hitting the pavement with a thud. Lee-Anne bent to help him, one hand hooked into the curve of his elbow, the other throwing a furious, swearing gesture at the car. One of the boys returned, shouting, and set about dismantling the chain from the pole, handing the rock back to his friend, making easy work of telling the others to reignite their fury. Waleed tried to take the rock by force and the boy lost his temper, punching the older man full force in the stomach. Nasreen felt her own stomach drop somewhere around her pelvis. She screamed and pitched herself into the crowd and towards her uncle. Alia followed her and soon they were both standing over Waleed, crying out, close to hysteria, asking him if he was all right.

Waleed pulled himself off the ground, angrily waving his arm at their concern. "What the HELL are you still doing here? I told you to GO BACK TO SCHOOL!"

Alia began to cry, and Rashaad, who had been firing off frames of his friend getting beat up, rallied round and ushered them into the relative calm of a doorway. He propped Waleed up against a wall and offered him a smoke, "You okay, brother?" Waleed nodded.

Rashaad turned to the girls. "Don't worry, man, your uncle's been through a lot worse."

It was difficult to know what shocked them more, the beating or Rashaad's casual response to it. Waleed was holding himself so that he didn't knock into anyone, trying to appear sturdier than he was. The rock boy was gone. Waleed heaved himself up, and stood, painfully searching for the child, looking up and over the crowd, seeing only the tops of heads like so many buoys, unmoored and floating. He turned to Lee-Anne, angrily demanding to know why she had let them get away. She offered no retort, no explanation; she just cast her eyes over and around the still teeming crowds, flinching when they all heard a shop window being smashed. At the sound Waleed began to walk, saying he had to find the boys. He turned briefly to reissue his instruction to his nieces. Rashaad followed, his hands clasping protectively around his camera. The girls stood on the corner, their uncle lost to them once again.

"Come. I'll walk you up the Avenue."

It was Lee-Anne. Nasreen shook her head, refusing, hating the debt she might accrue, but the older woman had already placed a hand on Alia's shoulder and was guiding her through the crowd and across the road, cloaking both girls in a protection they did not understand.

~

Zarina sat in the lounge watching television, lips pursed, cheeks sucked in against her gums, body perched on the chair's edge. Adam stood fidgeting in the doorway, as though the metres-long distance could put some space between him and what he was seeing. For both of them, the news had only ever been a daily violence thermometer. They were used to seeing people hurt, burnt, broken, angry. They had learned, long ago, the script of survival and staying:

Things are bad.
They could be worse.
Let's wait and see.

"It's an absolute train wreck," said Adam glumly, taking in the coverage of town. "Do you want a cup of tea?"

Zarina removed an anxious thumb from between her teeth. "Please."

The television panned over screaming, jeering teenagers who shoved at each other to be in the frame, all the while swearing at the cameraman and what lay beyond. A boy crashed a furious foot through an already smashed shop window. Adam shook his head in disgust. "And these, *these* are the people that are going to rule? God help us."

Zarina waved a dismissive hand at him. "Ag, man, don't take too much notice of that. They always focus on the worst of it. What I'd like to know," primly, "is where their parents are."

"In jail. Or drunk."

She tut-tutted in response.

"I make no apologies for stating the truth. I refuse to tip-toe. Enough's enough. That child smashes some poor bastard's window. Who's going to pay for that? Certainly not *him*. Does he think Mandela is going to thank him for doing that?"

"Well, this is what happens. Maybe now they'll stop pushing the election date back."

"He should get such a bladdy smack for that! Look, *look* there at all the damage they've done. It's *criminal*. What if those people don't have insurance?" Adam always levelled these kinds of practical questions at Zarina as though her fairly mild connections between injustice and anger had meant that she had swathed herself in an anarchist's flag and had begun serenading him with the "Internationale". From the kitchen he heard the high whistle of a boiling kettle. "How many sugars?"

"We've been married nearly twenty years. I've never changed how many sugars I take in my tea. Not once. Or is it so rare that you actually make *me* tea instead of the other way round?"

"Zarina. *Please*."

She held his gaze.

"One and a bit?" he said.

"One and a bit," she confirmed.

Adam disappeared into the kitchen while Zarina relayed to him the reporter's comments. "They're replaying Mandela's address again."

She looked at the screen, only just conscious that she was holding her breath. It had been three years, but it was still a shock to see him, still a surprise to see that *face*, to see what everyone had longed for, what had been guarded and hidden for all those years.

Adam came back, holding her tea. He, too, became slightly hushed whenever he saw this man. Eventually he said, "Hell, but he was now really robbed of his time."

Zarina moved her head in agreement. She took her tea, tasted it, and got up with an aggrieved sigh to add more milk.

"It's these kids we have to worry about," Adam muttered as she passed him.

"What?" she called out, opening the fridge.

"These *kids*. The ones causing a ruckus in town. In ten

years' time, you mark my words, not much will have changed and they will be baying for blood."

Zarina returned to the irresistible lure of bad news coverage, her tea appropriately milky and sweet. There was something slightly sinister, addictive even, about watching the imagery of her smashed-up city, looking at the disaster that was smoking just a few kilometres away. It was the thrill not to be named.

"I don't want you talking like that in front of the girls, no point in making them anxious—"

"They wouldn't believe me anyway. I've never seen children so starry-eyed about revolution. They'll probably come home and say all this looting is a good thing."

"Sjoe. But you are in a mood today."

"You disagree?"

He was just spoiling for a fight and Zarina made a mental promise to herself not to take the bait. She set down her tea and turned to a pile of waiting laundry instead. She grabbed at everyone in her family's clothing except her own, rolling her husband's socks into rapid little balls. It was a warning, a small stack of woollen grenades.

"When you take everything from a person, and you've been taking things from him for years and years and carrying on like it's normal, you can't just get away with a promise that you going give it back – it doesn't mean you going to. And just because you say you sorry, doesn't mean you are."

Zarina shook her head and the sock folding reached new speed. "Of course it *means* something. How can you say that? That's how we keep a civil world. It's basic. It's what we need to move on."

She was searching for the words Uncle Sammy had given her the week before. "It's about *humanising* things. Apologies are important."

"Okay. *So*. If all we get out of being kicked out the

District is a 'sorry', you are going to just leave it? The next time you pretend you just by chance took a route around it, I'll remind you that the Nats said 'sorry', so you better be over it."

Zarina began to busy herself with tearing open a packet of shortbread. She was suddenly quite shy. Even in this moment they could not be entirely honest with each other. It was Adam who struggled with the District, not her. She had found ways of carrying on years ago.

"I've been over that for a long time, Adam," she said, not unkindly. "Don't worry about it."

In the background the television was narrating the fruits of some of that history; the volume had been turned down, but there was nothing to be done about the visuals. It was all there, the burning country. In Technicolor. Adam's response came in a clipped and neat voice; he followed the links of the logic and in doing so swept a wide path through her.

"Well, that's very nice for you. Maybe it's easier when you get moved to Walmer Estate. Much tougher when you some poor bastard out in Ocean View."

Zarina went to fetch the ironing board. "I don't know what you want me to tell you. I say I'm okay with the move and you tell me it's because we were moved here. You're not even making sense. You're just trying to make me feel guilty."

"Guilty?" he scoffed, twisting his head to yell back at her. "Don't be ridiculous. The only ones who should feel guilty are the bladdy Nats!"

Zarina re-entered the room, armed with the stuff of domestic righteousness. She began to make a virtue out of unpacking Adam's clothing first; shaking his shirts out, grimacing with the effort of finding the right angle at which to place iron to cloth.

"Zarina, why in God's name are you doing that *now*? Patricia is coming in tomorrow."

"So you say now and when there are no fresh shirts for you tomorrow, there'll be a big fuss." She brought the heat to bear against her husband's clothing, and began to direct her comments to the middle of the room, addressing an imaginary crowd. "You know, I am really getting sick of people thinking that everything is going to come right overnight—"

"That's just it!" Adam began to slap a hand against the arm of his leather seat as though Zarina had finally understood him. "*Here* is what I am saying. Suffering is one thing, recovery is something else altogether. 'I'm sorry' is a nothing. People want like a … like a *reversal* … for … a … a *wrong to be righted*. Yes! That's what I'm trying to say."

"Well, exactly."

"But how is that supposed to happen? It won't, you know. Not in the way people will want it to. Feel grateful, Zina, not guilty, that your family had money. It's much easier to move on when you are not hungry. You mark my words …" He turned to the television, dragging her eyes with his to a tyre burning in the road, matching image with prophecy.

"Oh, my God!"

"What? *What*?"

"It's already five. I'm late to fetch the girls."

"Oh, they'll be fine, man – probably better that you're a bit late … avoid all this nonsense. Do you want me to come with you?"

"No. You stay. In case they call. Say I'm on my way."

~

Zina drove past the old library, its dignified dome caked with bird shit. Past the Parade, which had changed even in her memory from a place of fruit sellers and speeches to stall after stall of knock-off Chinese goods and masala steak sandwiches. Though the crowds were gone, their remnants were everywhere: smashed shop windows, bits of torn clothing, broken beer bottles, small fires that were not worth putting out, the last of the riot police in their bullet-proof jackets, and finally, the memorial organisers, walking as if in a daze, picking up the glass, comforting weeping shopkeepers, looking at everything as though it was an entirely different kind of funeral.

Zarina was used to moving through her city and living three or four memories at once – Zarina at four, at twelve, at seventeen, as a new mother – and in those memories the smell and feel of this place were always on her skin, in her bones. Nothing was neutral, there was always something attached to it, clinging to it, triggering, pulling, insisting, asking her to look, telling her not to forget. She'd tried explaining this once to Adam, but he had shaken his head and insisted that she was going to exhaust herself, that it sounded like she was living several lives at once, all stacked up on her, weighing her down, bottoming her out. Waleed had understood, a little. He had told her it was the same for him, to walk through the city was to walk with ghosts. As Zarina drove, she saw a girl, perhaps eleven years old, walking. There was something about her straight-shouldered purpose, her eyes fixed on the horizon, that made her see herself at that age, walking home, terrified.

Zarina's father had dabbled in politics. Not very much and not all the time, but enough to court attention, to get him on a watch list. He had attended meetings, defended some political prisoners, given them a final home-cooked meal before the journey into exile, hid one or two in his basement, taken food parcels round to their families. And that was why a policeman would wait for Zarina outside her school and would follow her, matching her scurry with the leisurely roll of his car wheels. His was a snail's pace and with a snail's way he left a trail of haunting slime. "We've got him," he would say to her. "We've got him and he's not coming back home … not ever … You tell your mother. And then who's going to take care of you? Your bladdy coolie-loving mother, or your commie-loving father?"

As she turned the corner towards the cathedral she saw a familiar figure, head tilted towards the ground, smoking, walking with the painful limped gait of the injured. She slammed her foot on the brake and did a U-turn. She stopped and leaned across the empty passenger seat and stuck her head out as far as it could go.

Waleed turned and held his hand in a cradling gesture beneath his heart while he shuffled towards her.

"What's wrong with you?" asked Zarina in a panic. "Are you hurt?"

Waleed waved away her questions and said, "Have you picked up the girls yet?"

"What? Why do you ask? Why?"

Waleed no longer cared if he had made earlier promises of secrecy. "They were here earlier," he sighed. "They bunked school to come down."

Zarina's chest flooded with a numbing panic. She accidentaly took her foot off the clutch and the car lurched forward. She sat, shocked, fingers still on the wheel, temporarily beyond speech. "Where are they?"

"At school, at *school*." Waleed was getting irritable. He thought he might have cracked a rib. "They're fine, man. They went back up the hill," he added, allowing himself a laugh.

Zarina's eyes narrowed but Waleed was grimacing, already paying for the pun.

"Get in the car," she said. "It's ridiculous standing here – you're obviously hurt. Let me see. Take a breath. Why so shallow? I think you've bruised your rib. It's not cracked.

You can take that disappointed look off your face and get in the car. You're coming with me."

"I can't. I have to wait for Rashaad."

"Rashaad will have to do the waiting. Get in. *Now.*"

~

Alia had arrived back at St Michaels on a rebellious high. Back and safe behind the high walls and the gentle playing fields, she could begin to start the inevitable process of embroidering and embellishment. *I was right there! There was blood and everything!* In those seductive thirty minutes when everyone gathered around her, Alia could practically feel the thrums of envy and awe emanating from the other girls. Even Lizzie had granted her a temporary respect, until she reasserted herself saying, "Well, *obviously* there was a riot, what did you expect? If you knew anything about the man, you'd have known how upset people would be."

Lizzie's corrective speech, combined with their mother's sudden arrival, brought Alia's newfound political credibility to an unceremonious halt. Zarina pulled up in her boxy green car, jerking the handbrake so violently the girls heard it squawk from where they were standing. She got out of the car in a series of short, sharp moves, the sunglasses on her face doing nothing to camouflage her anger.

"Get in," she hissed at her daughters.

Uncharacteristically quiet and suddenly meek, Nasreen obeyed immediately, but Alia, trying to harness some of the leftover defiance of the day, made an elaborate show of picking up her bag and saying goodbye to her friends.

"Alia!" barked Zarina. *"Today."*

At Alia's request, Lizzie came with her. Zarina had a soft spot for her and, sneakily, Alia hoped this would blunt her mother's fury.

"Afternoon, Mrs Dawood."

"Hi, Lizzie. Were you part of this insanity?"

"No, Mrs D, my mom said specially not to go."

"Did she?" Zarina's eyes narrowed and once again she looked out on the landscape of her own failures, populated by undisciplined children and disrespected parents.

"Thanks a lot," Alia mumbled, opening the car door.

"What exactly was it your mother said, Lizzie?" asked Zarina, placing herself at the apex of a newly formed triangle, with her daughter and Lizzie forming the base.

Lizzie's fingers crept nervously into the overly long arms of her blazer. "She ... um ..." here she pulled a regretful face at Alia, "she said it would be an unpredictable day. You know, it was *Hani*. Not nobody."

Zarina nodded vigorously. "Did you hear that?" she asked her youngest child. "Even Lizzie's mom said not to go."

"So what if Mrs Ndlovu said that? It's not like Lizzie and I agree on everything."

"We're leaving," said Zarina, walking away.

"Sorry," said Lizzie, turning to Alia, conscience-stricken. "Did I make it worse?"

"Of *course* you made it worse."

"Your mom asked me a question. I didn't want to lie to her."

"So you pulled an impimpi."

Lizzie's eyes widened. "Sometimes I wonder if you understand what you're saying." She turned slightly, gesturing at the scowling man in the car, "Is that your uncle?"

Midway through rolling a cigarette, Waleed looked up, scowling, and Alia read on his face the scene before him: clusters of teenage girls, all plaited, uniformed, mild and decorous. The question was writ large on his expression: how on *earth* had he ended up *here* on the day of Hani's memorial?

"You not smoking that in my car," Alia felt a rush of gratitude that Zarina's anger was being directed elsewhere, while Waleed's distress became more animated.

"But I—"

"Waleed. *No.*"

He unwound his window and interrupted the girls. "Alia, can you get a move on?"

"I'm coming. This is my friend Lizzie."

Waleed gave her a weary nod and then reached out to shake Lizzie's hand, embarrassing both girls when he locked it back and forth in a comrade's shake.

Alia and Nasreen confined themselves to opposite ends of the car, their recent alliance lying in a tattered heap in the space in-between. Alia turned her face from her family, staring out of the car window, waiting for her view to transition from city to harbour, looking at how the small street fed into the highway, how the vista opened up over the District and the playing fields of her old school, leading inevitably to the grey expanse of the harbour waters, the white foam galloping on the peak of the waves. It was then that she began to realise that what she felt was not guilt or remorse, but rather quiet triumph and jubilation. She had stepped from a place of hearing into a place of seeing.

~

"Could you just drop me at home? It's been a helluva day."

Zarina ignored her brother-in-law and turned up towards Walmer Estate.

"*Zina,*" he groaned.

"Waleed, I am really not in the mood to discuss anything with you right now. I'm still waiting to get to the bottom of all of this."

"Well what about the hospital? I need to get examined!"

"You'll be fine," came the merciless answer as she pulled into the driveway. "A bruised rib is not a concussion."

Zarina exited the car issuing orders at the others to follow her. They did.

"Adam!" Zarina's voice tore through the house, commanding her husband to rush down the stairs, his feet stamping loudly on each step.

"What? Has something happened? What took you so long?" He turned into the hallway as he said this and stopped short, while Zarina placed her handbag on the thin-legged teak table, her back to his three round-shouldered, guilty looking relatives.

"What are you doing here?" he asked Waleed and then in a panic, "Is Mommy okay?"

"I don't know, and she's fine," Waleed scowled back.

"They were at the memorial," Zarina announced without looking at her daughters.

"*What?*" Adam exploded. It was a response Zarina had wanted and immediately regretted seeking. "Just what the bladdy hell is going on here?"

The girls and Waleed began to shout as one.

"We had a right to go!"

"I *told* Alia not to come with me!"

"Look, I don't even know why I'm here. I'm leaving."

Adam raised his arms – a cross between benediction and surrender – in a feeble bid to quiet his family while Zarina rounded on Waleed, pointing a violent finger in his face. "You're not going anywhere, you've got a lot to answer for."

"What? I don't even … Zina, you *crazy* if you think I've got anything to do with them having been there. In fact I resent this whole little kangaroo court you people have going here."

"Watch yourself! Don't you talk to my wife like that!"

"Look, man, I'm not involved in your weird parenting dynamics. I don't know what Dr Spock shit you have going on. They here, they safe and I actually need to rest. In case you haven't noticed, I need bandages, I've got a cracked rib here, man."

"Oh, my God. Are you okay?"

"I'm fine. I just want to go home."

Waleed turned to go and Adam held the door open for him as sanction, offering to drive him down to Observatory. He had almost made his escape when Zarina, still furious, yelled, "He saw them at the service and he didn't have the common *decency* to walk them back to school when everything went to hell and gone."

Adam closed the door, turned incredulously towards his brother and then towards his wife. "He did what?" he said quietly.

"You heard me."

Adam faced his brother. "You're not going anywhere. You and I are going to have some words."

"Is this some kind of joke? I'm leaving. I don't have time for this shit."

Waleed yanked the door open and Adam took advantage of his diminished state and shoved it closed again. "You've got some explaining to do. You staying right here."

"Or what?"

"Or I'll tell Mommy."

This elicited a high-pitched but mirthless laugh from Waleed. "You'll what? I'm not *five* anymore, Adam. Every time I come here you people seem to be in some kind of crisis." He shook his head but then strode ahead of them into the living room, took a seat and made himself comfortable on the couch piled with brocade cushions. "Well, come on," he called out, "Let's have those *words* you're so keen on. I'm only staying so that you don't upset Mommy. Let's have it. I invite you to catalogue my faults for today."

Adam and Zarina looked at each other and then followed him into the room, where they remained standing, glowering down at him. Alia and Nasreen followed, a forgotten, perhaps unwanted tail. "Get the bag of frozen peas, Alia," Zarina ordered.

"Where are they?"

"*Where are they?* Where would *frozen* peas be? Sometimes I wonder what that school is teaching you."

"Is it true?" Adam pointed an accusing biblical finger at the end of a long arm towards his brother.

"Is what true? What the hell is all this drama about?"

"You are something else, Waleed," said Zarina, leaning against a cabinet as though she had neither the energy to sit nor the capacity to hold herself up.

"You just left them to it? Just to hell with them? This is really the pits, Waleed ... even for you." Adam said this as Zarina chimed in.

"After everything we've done for you—"

"Wait a minute. Now just wait a bladdy minute!" Waleed looked as though he could not believe what he was hearing. "Are you fucking kidding me? I had a *job* to do! I was trying to stop the whole city from exploding. I couldn't be responsible for your kids."

"There. You see!" Adam turned triumphantly to Zarina. "Why did I expect anything less?" She looked almost tearful in response, and Adam began directing his tirade at Waleed. "So you care about strangers, about these *hooligans* before us? We your *family*."

"That's not fair. Uncle Waleed was just—" Alia had returned, armed with the peas, but stopped as her father whipped his head round.

"Alia, you stay out of this," said Adam.

"Then why are you making me stand here?"

Zarina flung her arms out as if to take in the ridiculousness of her child's statement, and began to talk, making the swiping, definitive, drive-a-point-home gestures of a politician. "So you can see for once the repercussions of your actions. So you kids stop thinking you can move through the world without any consequences. Look what you've done!"

With that, she grabbed the bag of peas from her youngest and stalked towards Waleed. "Here, put that on the bruise."

"This is such bullshit," murmured Nasreen.

"What did you say? What did you just say to your mother?" Adam approached Nasreen, a fierce look on his face. She shrank back a little, glancing at her uncle and then pressed on.

"How can you shout at Uncle Waleed one minute and blame us for going the next?"

"We haven't gotten started on you! You wait your turn! Just what the hell were you doing there in the first place?"

"We went to mourn Hani."

Adam gave a bitter laugh. "*Mourn Hani?* Now I've heard it all. You didn't even know who he was until a few weeks ago."

"And whose fault is that?" Nasreen said this quietly, just a decibel less and her parents could have pretended not to have heard her.

Zarina sensed there was something behind the statement that she might regret uncovering but she followed up anyway, her own voice full of hostility and curiosity. "And just what do you mean by that?"

"We didn't know about him because you didn't tell us. Because you don't take a stand." Nasreen began to weep uncontrollably, the intensity of the day, the confrontation with her parents, her disappointment in all the adults in her life catching up with her. "You don't do anything!" her voice broke in the middle of her words. "It's … *shameful*. At least Uncle Waleed is out there, he's doing something. He hid that boy here. He was doing the *right* thing, and you people punished him for it."

Waleed, shocked, finally said, "Nasreen, take it easy."

"No! I won't! You people all think we don't care. That we don't know. And you're no better," she took aim at Waleed. "You think we just spoilt. You were embarrassed by us today. Don't think we're so stupid we couldn't see that."

"That's not true," Waleed lied, re-angling the peas.

"It is! And you people," she brought Adam and Zarina back into equation with a cry, "you're all safe here in your big house and other people are *dying*. Somebody important to this country died. He *died*. Somebody *shot* him."

"Oh, Nasreen," said Zarina, her own voice suddenly breaking, "please try and calm down, sweetheart."

"We are all aware," said Adam icily, "about the week's events."

"No, you're not!" continued a defiant, enraged Nasreen. "Not really. Or you would have been there. It wouldn't have been up to Uncle Waleed to have taken care of us, because you would have been there." She shook with tears and rage and turned to Zarina. "You *should* have been there."

Zarina looked as if someone had walked up to her and very deliberately spat in her face. She gazed at her daughter in a daze, shocked by her intensity, overwhelmed by her blurry, incandescent fury, recognising in it her own rage somehow encrypted in another body.

"You don't know the first thing about this, man." Adam had found his voice. "I'm sorry he is dead. It's a tragedy. But do you even know who you are so sorry for? This man was a communist."

"So is Uncle Sammy."

"Who?"

"Uncle Sammy."

Adam continued to look blankly at his daughter until Zarina pulled herself up and snapped irritably, "*Uncle Sammy*, man, my father's friend." And to Nasreen, "And what's that got to do with anything?"

"Only that Dad's being stupid, there's nothing wrong with being a com—"

"Listen," said Adam quickly, "Uncle Sammy is something else, he's a District Six communist. That's something totally different."

"Oh, my God." Waleed let out a barking laugh. "Now I've really heard it all. This is ludicrous. What kind of equivocating is this? A 'District Six communist'? Are you trying to say he's not black?"

"You be quiet," Adam said, not taking his eyes off his daughter.

"Zarina, are you going to let him fill your child's mind with this nonsense?"

Zarina shook her head as if she was trying to clear away the last vestiges of sleep. "What your father is trying to say is that Uncle Sammy is from a different era. He didn't advocate violence."

"Oh, now come on!" Waleed blanched a little, touching his rib for effect. "I've heard some historical revisionism in my time but this is now really the limit—"

"You could try and remember, Waleed, that I actually know this man, okay? He's *my* father's friend. This was all a little before your time."

Waleed leaned back to offer his rib a kinder angle. "Far be it from me to stop you trading on your old man's actions from forty years ago."

"Well, so what?" said Nasreen.

The three adults looked at her. For a moment it seemed they had forgotten all about the girls.

Adam took a seat. "What are you talking about now, Nasreen?" he said wearily.

"What's wrong with being a communist? What's wrong with wanting everyone to have a chance?" Waleed nodded in agreement and with that nod, Nasreen turned to Adam. "You're so selfish," she said to her father. "You don't care about anyone but your own."

Then she left the room, jerking her head towards Alia to follow her. As the two girls made for the staircase, Adam charged after them in a burst of rage and energy. "You're both grounded! That's it. Indefinitely. No phone calls, no going out, *nothing*."

Their voices rose with Alia shouting above Nasreen, "But I'm supposed to go to a *play* this week with Nick!"

"That's another thing," Adam said definitively, "*that's* over. You'll tell that Christian boy tonight and that's the last call you'll make to him. I should have put a stop to that nonsense months ago."

Alia draped herself over the railing, shrieking with anger. "No! You can't make me do that. I'll hate you. I promise! I will hate you!"

"I don't care," said Adam, ruthless, cold. "It starts *now*. Go to your rooms."

The girls scurried up the last of the steps with the stumbles of younger children. They parted on the landing, neither, even attempting to slam their doors shut.

"*Adam*." It was Zarina and Waleed, in chorus, looking at him with a single shocked face.

"This is *your* fault, Zarina. I don't know what you've been teaching them all these years but they are totally out of control." He turned to his brother. "I hope you're satisfied. I can barely look at you. I've never been more disappointed in someone in my life. Call yourself a man? What kind of man leaves young girls to a mob? See yourself out. And don't come back here."

He got up and inclined his head to Zarina, who threw Waleed an anxious, regretful look before following her husband out of the room.

24 August 1986

Waleed is dreaming again of Firoze. He will dream of him for years and years, this child he met in a dark alleyway and knew for only a few days. Mostly he sees just Firoze's mouth, soft and full as a girl's, saying something, asking something. Waleed is always hopeful in the dream that he will be able to make out the sentences, but it is only ever dream-noise, unintelligible and teasing, becoming something else as he wakes.

It takes him months to ask Yusuf about Firoze, to say, "Did he make it? Is he still ... around?" And Yusuf replies with that infuriating Sphinx expression – half serious, half mocking – and tells him precisely nothing. Instead, he glances about in an exaggerated fashion, as if Waleed's desperation were an embarrassing indiscretion, the behaviour of an amateur or even an informant.

Their friendship changes after that. It still follows its usual contours; they still play pool and get high together and rage about the government, but between them lies the misery of a complicated betrayal that will never disappear completely.

Waleed never asks for Firoze's last name. Neither do Zarina or Adam. It is as though they all three understand that the dense and tightly woven web that is Cape Town will reveal a known parent, a family, a now empty bed, a table with one less setting. They never speak of it to each other. Zarina and Adam behave as if nothing has happened. When they see Waleed at Fozia's they wear overly bright smiles and speak too fast when she is in the room, but when she is not all three turn from each other. Firoze's story is a part of theirs now and so it becomes inevitable, one day, a month after the frenzy of hiding and escape, that Waleed hears from Fozia about her friend, Layma, who has spent the afternoon, inconsolable, at her kitchen table.

Waleed knows Auntie Layma, remembers her as an unusually thin woman in her late fifties. Like all women of this city and that generation she appears older, her black scarf transforming her into an anachronistic figure, more Troy and Old Testament than Cape Town, 1986; a direct descendant of Andromache, weeping for her lost son.

She told Fozia her story steadily, through tears, her words breaking through rough sobs and unexpected hiccups like someone walking with illogical certainty down a rocky path, deliberately ignoring boulders and scratching shrubs, eyes fixed on the horizon. She had Firoze *late*, she said to Fozia, he was her laatlammetjie. He was her baby. They had heard nothing for so long, maybe a month already, and then suddenly the day before a letter saying he had left the country, he was never coming back. "He is so small," – here her weeping grew deeper, her voice ragged, the tissue she was holding to her bony face ineffectual – "what can he do?" Her arms jutted out of her black robe like the wings of a sparrow. "He is so small, so small. Who would take someone so small? What can he do for them?" And then, bitterness, bewilderment, "Why should he care what happens to the kaffirs? Why must my son bear the brunt of things?"

While Fozia tells Waleed (*Safe! Alive!*), he assembles the information: *Firoze, a month ago, Auntie Layma*, even as his head tries to refuse the details. *Jesus.*

Waleed pictures his mother soothing her friend, rubbing the woman's back, and hears her boiling the kettle, as if cup after cup of sugary tea can wash them all free of this. His mother doesn't ask Layma, as she usually does of people, not to use *that* word.

Waleed finds himself running, straight down the road, right at the corner, banging on Yusuf's door. He rushes past Zubeida, Yusuf's sister, demanding to know where her brother is. "In his room and why you so bladdy rude? Where's the fire?"

She tries to grab his arm. She tells him to take it easy, to leave her brother alone. She tells him, "He hasn't slept since he came back from solitary. Hasn't slept. And when he does, when he does, he wakes up screaming. Do you hear me? Screaming."

But Waleed doesn't listen, can't listen, he charges into his friend's room and finds him on his bed, reading. He swats the book out of Yusuf's hands and says, "His mother. She was beside herself! Crying in *my* mother's kitchen."

"Who?" asks Yusuf, calmly, while Waleed struggles, again, to locate his friend, to find him in this very controlled man, with his Svengali voice and his room full of secrets, the poster demanding the release of child prisoners, the banner with the still-to-dry spray-paint caption: FEEDOM OR DEATH: VICTORY IS CERTAIN.

"Who? *Firoze*, you fucker! Did you know he was from our neighbourhood? He's Auntie Layma's son ... I didn't realise ..." Waleed is moaning now. "I didn't *think*. He's from our neighbourhood. He's one of our boys. He's Auntie LAYMA's boy."

"Of course I know whose son he is." Yusuf places the book carefully under a loose floorboard. "He's my cousin."

Waleed opens his mouth, but like the Firoze of his dreams, the words don't form, just sounds, spluttering.

"Second cousin," Yusuf corrects himself.

"How could you?"

"How *could* I?" Yusuf is genuinely puzzled by Waleed's outrage. "What is it you think we're doing here? I can't keep explaining this to you. Don't you understand, Waleed? Some of us are willing to die for this."

14

Saturday, 31st July 1993

Anna hated rugby. No, she hated all sports. She didn't mind that they happened, out there, in the world, but she failed to understand why her home should be taken over by them and all their grim accompaniments: the ceaseless televisual drone of the commentators, the wasted Saturdays, the interminable post-match analysis. In this she was entirely out of step with her nation. South Africans have always loved sports and worshipped their sportsmen (sportswomen forming a distant second or third interest). Famous rugby players, cricketers and footballers, along with politicians, were the closest approximation the country had to celebrities. Anna had never understood this crazed communal devotion; cricket, rugby, soccer, golf, even diving, racing cars, boxing, anything physical that needed speed and precision. She associated the sound of the commentator with Exeat weekends, those snatched days at half-term when her mother would fetch her from boarding school and two days of enforced family life would ensue. She would be ecstatic on the Friday (she'd escaped the prison and in absentia her parents had grown in her affections). Saturday would inevitably bring a squabble about something and she would begin to feel a little panicked, a little trapped. By Sunday the dull fact of a weekend that had been filled with roast lamb and cloyingly sweet trifle, skittish nerves, the white noise of a crowded stadium, Die Stem, the grunts of the Bokke, all combined to summon a rising nausea.

When she fled that life she believed she had left all its contents behind her, that she had arrived on a new shore happily bereft of her past and open only to new experiences. She was disappointed, even shocked, when she found out that Waleed watched sport. She had no notion of how to reconcile a love of books with a love of the game. "You're not serious?" she had laughed when he called to cancel a movie, citing a much-hyped match. Initially she had thought he was blowing her off, that this was a way of saying he was uninterested. But Waleed merely wanted to shift their plans to the evening, or better yet, for her to come by for the game. "You should come, man. My mom has sent some samoosas. And you know who'll be here. You then met everyone already. Yusuf, Rashaad, Georgie. Just *come*. It will be fun."

She went. She was curious: there was something about watching Waleed do familiar things, whether it was making scrambled eggs or screaming at the television; she thought it contained wonder, she hoped it contained new information.

She'd arrived, beer in hand, at the small house in Observatory. She registered the unmistakable smell of braaied meat. *Check*, she thought, crossing it off her mental list. So he braais when he watches. It may be halaal sausage and it may be laced with coriander and chilli, but it's braai nonetheless. She let herself in. (Waleed, a mutual friend had told her, was always like this, free with his house keys, preferring the kind of trust and transparency it fostered in the moment, forgetting about the invariably hysterical handover scenes that might come later.)

She found his friends in the cramped sitting room at the end of the thin corridor, just as he had said: Yusuf, Rashaad, Georgie – all taut and trained towards the television, joints in one hand, plates of sausage rolls and bowls of crisps before them, a cooler-bag of Heineken at their feet – exhorting the players, "Skop hom! Skop hom! Donner hom! GO, GO, GO GO, BOY! OH, YOU BEAUTY!"

It was all there. Check. Check. *Check*.

But there was something slightly off. Anna stood, swinging her keys, trying to figure out what it was. They glanced up to say hello, offering friendly grins, but stayed fully focused on the screen. She followed their gaze and watched as the men on the screen – rendered tiny, just inches tall, but somehow still oversized – grunted and huffed away in the secrecy of the scrum, moving along the field like a multi-limbed creature from the deep. Yusuf, Rashaad, Georgie were all murmuring now as if they could through sheer collective willpower break the concentration of the opposition and short-circuit their skill.

It was only then that Anna realised that the men, joints, wors, beers in hand, watching the game from a lounge in a small suburb in Cape Town, were supporting the All Blacks.

She saw Waleed through the kitchen window, smoking a joint and tending the fire, and went over to ask him about it. He looked almost confused.

"Well, obviously. Why would we support the Bokke? We always support the All Blacks, since we were kids. We waiting for them to fuck the Bokke up."

It was one of those moments, and their relationship was full of them, when she would glimpse the chasm between their worlds. It had never occurred to her that it was possible to play out a subversive game through rugby. She had thought the only option was to turn away from it, not to love it still, to follow it still.

Today, a year after that first Saturday match, Anna perched precariously on the edge of the sofa, trying and still failing to follow the game. Every once in a while Waleed, or one of the others, would offer a broken explanation and in response Anna would alternate between nodding and staring off into the distance. It was always a disaster, she reflected, when supreme disinterest was forced into contact with ardent worship, it was a situation that could only breed resentment in both parties: it was true of religion and it was true of sport.

"Ma broe! Did you *check* who that was?" Georgie was pointing at the television with manic excitement as the camera panned over the crowd.

"Who? What?" Rashaad, the least interested in the game, was mulling some weed, while Yusuf said quietly, "Yes."

"Yoh! I can't even *believe* this," Georgie hopped from one foot to the other, feet leaping as though the floor was covered in orange coals, "How did *this* fucking bra crawl out of the woodwork?"

With his eyes narrowed and a muscle in his cheek ticking from a clench, Yusuf looked like a sniper getting ready to take a shot.

"What's up with the suspense, ek sê?" said Waleed

"It was *Spielman*, ma broe! Sitting in the box with the bladdy VIPs." Georgie began pacing up and down, his energy somehow doubling his small height. "Yoh! I am finished now. Ouens, now I have seen it all. That bra is getting to sit with the VIPs now? Spielman? *Spielman*?"

Rashaad's weed-cleaning had come to an end: he caught Waleed's gaze and they both glanced nervously over at Yusuf, who had not taken his eyes off the television.

"Sorry, but who is this guy?" It was Anna's question. She tried not to notice the impatient shake of Waleed's head, listening instead to Yusuf's customary deadpan explanation that Oscar Spielman was a teacher, a politician, a sell-out, a poes. A coloured man who had joined the TriCameral parliament in the 1980s, insisting that he was "changing the system from within." A few months into his term, when the schools began to boycott, he'd sent the army in, and when the teargas and the beatings didn't work, he simply closed them all down. Spielman was the man who had ordered Yusuf's first arrest.

The doorbell rang and Anna walked to answer it with a mixture of relief and dread. It was, as she guessed it would be, her American housemate Megan. Anna had invited her in a fit of guilt. She had seen the woman looking morose and lonely on their sagging brown couch and had urged her to join them. She knew at the time that she was giving up the possibility of a relatively peaceful day, and when she saw Megan's pinched, charged face and the way she was clutching a copy of the newspaper *South*, she prepared herself for the worst.

Megan was a tall, dark-haired woman in her early twenties, all mouth and energy and earnest reflection. As she hovered in the doorway, taking in the scene before her, Anna knew that she was trying to assess if there was any possibility in the midst of this assembly of beer and sport for a real conversation. She sat down next to Georgie. "Did you hear about the inquest into what happened in Boipatong?"

"Uh," he grunted, "terrible, hey?"

"Well, *I* think there is definitely a Third Force behind this all. I mean, it would make sense, right?"

Waleed left his chair and turned the volume on the television up. "Half-time is over," he announced.

The hostility between Megan and Waleed had been immediate: they had met at Anna's flat and launched instantly into comparing theoretical positions as if performing one of those ancient, stylised dances of aggression that precedes a battle:

Third Wave feminist with an interest in the developing world researching countries in political transition? Is that longhand for intellectual parasite?

Postmodernism? Still? Seriously?

Later that night, when they had all gathered at a bar, Waleed had turned to Rashaad and Georgie and began to hold forth, loudly, about how The West was beginning to arrive on South African shores: "Here they come, ma broe. Here. They. Come. Just call me "Harry die fucking Strandloper Part Two" watching from the shore. If they not collecting trophies on safari, they gathering up our people's stories and spinning books out of them. Just wait. You'll see. E-ve-ry-thing and e-ve-ry-one here is a *goldmine* for these people."

It had not, Anna reflected now, been a meeting of minds.

"How'd the archives go, Megs? Did you find what you needed?" Anna turned to Waleed. "Megan's been struggling a bit with our resources."

Megan gave Anna a grateful look, was suddenly animated. "It's the *gaps*. The blatant deceit. It's depressing."

"If it's depressing, why you doing it?" Waleed asked coldly, not taking his eyes from the television.

"It's a contribution."

"To what?"

"Um … to *scholarship*? To human *rights*? To women's *voices*?"

The veins on Waleed's neck were beginning to throb noticeably.

"Megan," said Anna, "would you like something to eat?"

"Thanks," Megan hauled herself up, "I don't eat meat."

Waleed groaned and bit so aggressively into a piece of wors that even Georgie looked at him a little reproachfully.

"I can make you a cheese sandwich or something?" said Anna.

The two women stood in the kitchen and Megan watched Anna slice and grate and season. Eventually, hesitantly, she said, "Why are *you* hosting me?"

"Waleed is watching the game."

"And what? You're here in the kitchen?"

Anna fetched herself a cold beer. "I don't like rugby, Megan, I'm not missing out on anything. And Waleed cooks. You know that."

"I'm just saying." Megan absently picked at a curled edge of the Formica countertop. "You guys have one of the highest rape stats in the world. It's gotta come from somewhere. Everything is on a continuum, right? Rugby is like this hyper-masculine space and look how gendered this whole set-up is. So it reinforces all that shit. So there is this line from rape—"

"To *rugby*?"

Megan shrugged as though Anna's reluctance to accept the idea was a part of the problem. Anna closed the fridge door with more force than she intended. Ever since Megan had moved in she felt she had been fluctuating between two poles that were her boyfriend and her housemate, and none of the fluctuating made sense because they were essentially on the same side, weren't they?

"Did I say something wrong?" Megan looked panicked and Anna felt a small, surge of protective tenderness towards her. Just as Anna was terrified of putting a foot wrong in front of Waleed and his friends, Megan would occasionally obsess that she was enacting some obnoxious national stereotype. She offered what she always did in these situations, a sentence that she hoped was an expiation and a salve. "I guess I don't get it. Maybe it's cultural."

"Maybe."

Megan bit into her sandwich and Anna remembered one of their first conversations. Megan had been in the country for a week, reeling, energised, astounded at every turn. Mostly by the women, she kept saying; she just didn't understand South African women. They were all such a mystery: sometimes insanely tough, even militant, especially about race politics, but wilfully blind about gender stuff. For all this talk of "you strike a woman, you strike a rock", in this country, there was more chance of a woman being killed than learning how to read. "Did you know that?" she had asked Anna, her face wide with disbelief. Anna had felt the same unwillingness then as she did now to nod and agree, even as she knew it was true. To say yes to Megan, was to say no to other things.

~

Later that evening an impromptu party was formed, the kind that can only happen in a small town or in a neighbourhood with gardenless houses that sit close to the edge of the street. People began to drop by in twos and threes, their hands bearing six-packs, their conversation full of the details and outcome of the match. These were the members of Waleed's wider circle, people from the university, the bookshop, the various coffee shops and bars he frequented, comrades from a past life of activism, favoured students.

Anyone who cast an eye over the clothing of this assembled group would have been able to deduce a few truths: their collective attire narrated the fifteen-year span between the oldest, who sported the corduroy jacket/beard combination favoured by 1980s trade unionists, to the youngest, a twenty-year-old queer theory acolyte, an art student, all silvery bleached buzz cut and aesthetic androgyny. The others, for the most part, battled out a combination of revivalist 1960s threads (oversized bellbottoms, tight, striped T-shirts and daisy accessories) and *Withnail and I*-inspired overcoats. A very small number were ushering in the embryonic rave scene, everything glittery eyeshadow and second-hand electric blue dresses. Anna herself was wearing her party hat, a floppy black velvet affair with a paisley lining. She scanned the room, hat at a jaunty angle, with a sense of wonder at how Waleed, despite his occasional and unannounced withdrawals from everyone and everything, remained so very popular with so many people. He was often liked and occasionally loved, not just because he was quick and clever and funny, but because he was capable of almost feminine friendships with men; they were not expected to talk about their feelings, but crucially, they were allowed to feel. Women loved him too, he tended to treat them – with the exception of Megan – as equals in both subtle and obvious ways.

The cottage filled up. Georgie assumed control of the music, Waleed scratched through the freezer to find more sausages and make room for beer, Rashaad doubled the speed with which he had been rolling communal joints, breaking only to tell Anna with some satisfaction that Megan, the "kak hyper Americano", had been successfully chilled thanks to large quantities of weed. The easy sounds of a record – spoken word over sampled jazz – played and Anna found herself smashing lumpy cottage cheese into a smooth dip, thinking that this was precisely the life she had always wanted.

Though space was limited the party had instinctively divided itself up into sections; in one corner a passionate re-enactment of the various turning points of the game, in another an argument about who should make room for whom on the English syllabus: Dickens for Brink, Shakespeare for Mda. This discussion was being led by a softly spoken brown-skinned woman, a friend of Waleed's whose head was wrapped in Kente fabric and who kept referring to the group of younger women gathered around her – all similarly attired – as "sistahs".

Anna avoided both groups; she'd had enough of rugby and guessed that her literary suggestion (*Why not have both?*)

would probably be dismissed as wilfully naïve. She also had no wish, once again, to be the only one not referred to as sistah. Instead, she tasked herself with introducing her housemate to everyone. Megan seemed genuinely thrilled, as though she had landed smack bang in the middle of her dream research demographic. In between telling Megan about the subtle differences of everyone's political allegiances (*Yes, she's* ANC *but don't be fooled, went ballistic last week when her maid accidentally put her silk shirt in the laundry and shrank it. Don't bother with him; he doesn't speak to Americans. She's nice. Just don't get her started on the cultural boycott. No, no, he won't vote* ANC *at all, he's Unity Movement*), she found time to whisper about all the room's old love affairs. In a city like Cape Town, where small cliques form with a mixture of tenacious loyalty and conveyer-belt affection, a party is always layered by the ghosts of old relationships and the weary, almost compulsive flirtation that comes with it.

The two women found themselves talking to a feeble-looking man in his early twenties. His dark blond hair was cut in a barley sheath that fell across his left eye. His maroon velvet smoking jacket looked like it had been inherited from a louche ancestor. Anna remembered him vaguely as one of the aesthetes from the English Department and wondered to herself what he was doing there. His name was Ben, he said, he'd been playing pool down the road and had heard there was a party. Did she mind terribly about him barging in like this? He'd hate to leave. He was having such fun. *He hoped*, this last bit said with a timid smile, *that he wasn't lowering the tone*. "Not at all," she'd replied, charmed by his self-deprecation, by his unapologetic Evelyn Waughness, "stay, please."

Anna left them to fetch her cigarettes and found Macbeth's witches: Waleed, Rashaad, and Yusuf standing around the braai muttering about how all of Mandela's recent visits had been to the United States and the United Kingdom while Waleed rolled the sausages, flicking his wrist to dodge the coals and the last, small, still-leaping flames.

"Bargains with the devil," pronounced Rashaad. "We should be careful. The first few days after a revolution are very tender." He rolled the 'r' on the last two words, letting the consonant vibrate and shimmer, a mournful aria against pragmatism and compromise.

Waleed's eyes screwed up against the smoke he had just exhaled, but he took another deep puff before breathing out and saying, "What revolution? This is negotiated *castration*, ma broe." He sampled the crispy-fatty bit of a chop. "Naai, man, Yusuf, you've over-salted again. I mos *told* you that toughens the meat."

"They not going to nationalise the mines, either," said Rashaad. "You watch, ma broe, it's going to be all about a black bourgeoisie." Rashaad drew himself up when he said this last bit: whenever he invoked a struggle phrase he invariably pulled his shoulders back and looked searchingly out into the middle distance. It was a pose he had honed during his years of being the man behind Yusuf, usually on a school stage. Then, almost as an after-thought, "This would not be happening if Hani was alive."

"That's just it. *Fuck*, man." Waleed held both his hands up in front of him, rocking them back and forth, communicating his frustration physically before his words took shape, thrilled, finally, to find someone in his circle who had not been seduced by the ANC. He turned an accusing eye on Yusuf, careful to stay on his right side. Yusuf's left ear-drum had been ruptured by an over-zealous cop during the uprisings at their school; the armed man had beaten the teenage boy until he collapsed onto the playground. His hearing had never quite been the same.

"What's going on up north, ma broe? You then in the inner circle? What's with all the compromises? All this toadying up to the superpowers? Treacherous things are afoot. What's going to happen when the ANC gets two-thirds?"

Yusuf's eyes flattened, the look he offered Waleed seemed simultaneously to warn him against saying more and tempt him to expand. He reached for his cigarettes and then, as though addressing a child, said, "Two-thirds is the best, quickest way to get our people fed and housed and educated. You keep up the good philosophical fight, Waleed. Lekker for some." Yusuf insisted on speaking with deliberate softness, as though he was refusing to let the ever-present cop drive him to a deaf man's shout.

Rashaad threw Waleed the apologetic look of a shamed Brutus before clinking glasses with Yusuf in agreement. But Waleed was unfazed: Rashaad always aligned himself with the most charismatic argument in the room, even if fundamentally he didn't agree with it. Yusuf began to lecture Waleed with his views on the ANC's burgeoning policies both foreign and local; he assured his friend that of course he didn't agree with everything they were doing but that was beside the point, he was throwing his lot in with them because this was not the time to break rank and be critical in front of outsiders, this was the true meaning of political solidarity. To do otherwise would be a fundamental betrayal. It would give the Right too much ammunition.

Anna, on the edge of this discussion, glanced about the room and wondered impatiently just who the Right was supposed to be in this instance. Waleed, she noticed, had sunk into one of his easily reached, moribund states. He'd been made to feel politically lonely in the last few months; one of just a handful of people he knew who would not be voting ANC. Instead, he would throw his lot in with a little-known Marxist intellectual, a vote that would be met with derision from all sides. Waleed's beliefs, Anna reflected, almost sorrowfully, were complicated, but they were his own. He was unflinching about certain things, impossible, intractable, immovable, but principled. And surrounding those principles, an intellectual curiosity, a refusal to toe party lines, the ability to fight furiously with those he loved for things he loved, his politics made up in equal parts joyful hope for what might lie ahead and rage against what lay behind. Within those complications rested a poisoned gift, the capacity to see the fault-lines and failures within success and sacrifice and to mourn them openly. It was this talent for facing disappointment that he had paid for in the past and would be taxed for in the future.

Just last week he had told Anna about Firoze. He had bumped into the boy's father at the corner shop and had come home sick with guilt and resignation. After years of wondering, of nightmares, he had finally learned about the boy's last days. "What happened to him," she had asked, "in the end?" As though it was a story that must have an end.

"Dead," he had told her, pronouncing the word from behind the hand he was using to cradle his forehead. "Killed in an ambush. SADF. Some impimpi gave away their location. At least, that's what his parents were told. After eight years of waiting. There is, of course, no body."

She felt her surge of protectiveness form itself into a sentence. "But, Yusuf, don't you think—"

"No, Anna. No, I don't think. I *do*. That's the point." Yusuf dug a fork angrily into the pasta salad and then bit into a chop, tasting both with a grimace. "There's too much salt on this."

"I told you, ma broe! You always have a heavy hand."

Grateful for the shift in conversation, Anna turned to Waleed. "Ben's here. From the department."

"Oh fuck. No!" he groaned and then, accusingly, "*Why*?"

"*I* don't know. He said he was having a good time."

Waleed dropped his voice and cut a level hand into the air several times: an indication that he was getting serious. The first time Anna met Adam she had noticed the same habit. "Keep an eye on him, will you?" Waleed instructed.

"What do you mean?" she teased.

"I don't trust him."

"You're just jealous of his jacket," Anna said to Waleed.

"That's true."

Waleed narrowed his eyes at Ben who, to his great satisfaction, had been hemmed in by Megan and was propped against the wall looking like a maroon butterfly pinned to a corkboard. "Serve the fucker right if it got stolen. Look at him swanning around in something that would look better on me."

"Actually that cut wouldn't really suit you," said Anna, reaching for her cigarettes.

"Course it wouldn't. It's built for men who've never had to work a day in their lives. Look at that trim little waist."

"You could have a trim little waist, too, if you bothered to exercise," she said, semi-lovingly, her fingers poking into his small beer-bulge.

"I'm genetically encoded to store fat. My ancestors were always on the run or starving, so when we get food we have to keep it. Only the privileged can afford the extravagance of being truly thin."

"Adam's skinny."

"That's different. That's anxiety."

Rashaad interjected, full of dramatic urgency, "I don't know, ma broe, why it is that you feel you need to tolerate these naaiers. Just tell him to get the fuck out."

"Who's this, bra?" said Yusuf disgustedly. "Your *friend*? Jesus."

"He's not my friend. We just work in the same department. You should *see* what he reads. The man is solely responsible for keeping the classics section going. It's like English Literature just stopped at the 19th century"

"Which side does he say he's on?" asked Rashaad, looking entertained.

"He *thinks* he's on the Left, but really he's a conservative, which means at best he's a liberal, the most dangerous of them all."

Yusuf nodded and looked about at the gathering with a slight smile, as though he thought it was full of liberals. A sigh travelled up through Anna's lungs and through her conscience: Waleed's friends' political calibrations were a source of occasional, but acute anxiety for her. She was never sure when she was falling short of truly being on the Left or at which point she was exhibiting what they called BLB (borderline liberal behaviour). She left them, saying she needed to get back to Megan.

~

"*An*. Anna."

It was Rashaad, his arm shyly around the waist of a rather short, exceedingly neat girl.

"This is Melanie. Mel, this is Anna, Waleed's girlfriend."

Anna reached out and shook the other woman's hand, unable to resist feeling giddy about her moniker or to stop herself from swooping her eyes over the beige linen pants, the careful pearl earrings, the other small bits of jewellery (a ring with a spray of diamond shavings, a small gold cross on a thin chain), the cream blouse. Who would have thought Rashaad's tastes could run so conservative?

"Hi. Nice to meet you."

Melanie smiled, answering in a voice so small Anna had to tilt in to hear her over the music.

"I said it's a great party. *Lank* cool," said Melanie.

Anna was momentarily puzzled by the slang and her accent. It sounded like her own, completely white. Melanie looked up at Anna, clearly reading her thoughts, while Rashaad nodded and bopped his head to the beat, oblivious to the unspoken questions and responses that the women were trading. The three of them stood in a grinning circle until the track changed and Rashaad pulled a willing Melanie into the centre of the four-person dance circle that had just formed.

Anna scanned the room for Megan and found that she and Ben had shuffled, as if governed by the same tidal mysteries of an ocean, just one metre to the left. She began to make her way towards them, hearing snatches of conversation as she went.

She returned to find the same election conversation that Waleed and Yusuf had exhausted being played out with new characters. Ben was listening attentively to Megan's steady drawl, a national speech pattern that allowed for the discordance of rapid delivery and a varying, questioning cadence.

"The thing is, what I want to know is how is an opposition going to work, right? Like, obviously the ANC is going to win, so what will that mean for a two-thirds majority? I mean *hello*? That's not a functioning democracy, right?"

Ben's tone was slightly slurred and Anna realised that he was drunker than she had first thought, and possibly giving away more than he imagined.

"That's just what I've been saying," he said eagerly, "but no one will listen. Where will we be without an opposition?"

"I know, right?" said Megan. "I guess it's about finding a way to fortify some party, like the PAC or the Communists?"

Ben gave a small, steady smile. "I don't think we should bother with them."

Anna nodded in a way she hoped would be read as thoughtful and supportive, while casting her mind about desperately, hoping she could come up with an effective way in which to change the course of the conversation. Anna had an instinct about these sorts of interactions; her life had been full of them. She knew, from Ben's lowered voice and his almost imperceptible scan about the room, what was coming, and she hoped she could steer them all away by sheer dint of social grace, from the explosive to the safe: if they focused on soft furnishings and the benefits of drinking Cape tap water and the best walking paths in Newlands Forest, perhaps it would be all right.

Ben did not disappoint. He leaned in to whisper to the two women sorrowfully that he would be voting for the NP; he didn't want to, but he couldn't afford to be sentimental about the election. Let the others have that luxury. He would make the adult choice. The ANC would win anyway, and they needed a party that would keep them on their toes.

Megan's profile pinched immediately into tight disgust and Anna understood now why he leaned in; the three of them were the only white people there.

"You're kidding, right?" Megan's question was delivered flatly, her enthusiasm not just dulled, but absent.

Resting against the wall, Ben assured her that he was not.

Megan was too stunned to respond. She had heard about these sorts of South Africans but it was a surprise to see one up close. She'd been in the country for six months now and, incredibly, had not been able to find a single white person who would admit to having voted for the Nationalists in the past, much less one who openly planned to vote for them in the future.

Anna was speaking, her voice free of its usually gentle contours. "Are you being deliberately stupid? You understand, don't you, that you aren't voting in an effective opposition, you're putting power back into the hands of murderers?"

Ben cast his eyes to the ceiling. "Obviously I understand that. But it's an awful case of needs must."

"So you're not denying what they've done?" It was Megan who said this, her face awash with disappointment.

"Why would I?" answered Ben, "but I also know that they have the expertise to run the country. The roads, the infrastructure—"

"They've made a piece of *shit* infrastructure." Anna was furious. She was back at school fighting with her classmates, back at Christmas lunch arguing with her relatives. In the last year she had been painfully deferential when it came to talking politics with Waleed and his friends – *Who was she to contribute? What did she know? Best to be quiet and learn* – but this was territory she knew, this was a landscape populated by old skirmishes and open warfare and occasional victories. She hissed in an effort to keep her voice down. "It's built on the back of *slave* labour and anyone who knows anything about anything knows how they've run the country into the ground—"

"You're not telling me anything I don't know. *Believe* me. I'm just talking about keeping them there to keep things going."

"Don't *do* that! Don't transform your racism into pragmatisim – it's the worst kind of sophistry." Anna was controlled enough not shout but the intensity of her rage drew people in.

It was Georgie, always a happy, playful drunk, who walked up to them first and cast his arm around her shoulders, offering to top Megan up, taking an automatic dislike to Ben, asking his name again and again, using the old male trick of pretending not to understand – "What did you say? Pen? What kind of name is Pen?"

Though he was drunk, Georgie noticed the strange tension between the three of them, but when he queried it, Anna demurred, and he wandered off. She didn't believe in public lynching.

Ben swirled at his wine as though his glass held a vintage that merited movement and breath. He looked up to offer Anna a grateful smile, transforming her silence into an alliance, a form of wilful protection. Megan chose to make herself peripheral. She suddenly felt horribly out of her depth. Whatever was flowing between Anna and Ben was beyond her and she made the rare decision to be quiet.

Anna shook her head as if to clear it from the gentle fog the wine had dipped it in, and reached for the only sentence that felt right: "Please leave."

"That's not very hospitable."

She looked down and noticed for the first time that her hands were balled and her knuckles were whitened under the strain of her clench. She had, Megan told her later, the whiff of the unpredictable about her; there was something slightly unhinged about the way in which she had fixed her gaze on Ben.

He placed his glass on the bookshelf with ostentatious care, taking a moment to hover in close to Megan and assure her that it gave him no pleasure, none at all, to be right.

A few minutes later Megan and Anna stood on the small stoep as if to make sure that he had really left. They drank tepid beer and watched him saunter down the road, unapologetic, unchanged, the country in his pocket. Megan, still absorbing all, told Anna four things: that the longer she stayed in this country, the less she understood it; that Anna was one of the most surprising people she'd ever met; that she would never criticise her cheese-grating abilities again; and that before Ben opened his mouth, she had considered going home with him. Anna laughed: a performance of a carefree relief that she did not feel.

Later, in the early hours of the next morning, when she

and Waleed were lying in bed talking over the party, she told him about Ben. She almost cried when she did this because she felt implicated by his actions, felt that she would always be part of that story. When he had leaned in to tell her and Megan his decision, it had been a missive from another shore, a command from home. She would only ever be in Waleed's world under sufferance anyway, but it was the only place she wanted to be. At this, Waleed, who had been staring at the ceiling for most of her story, fantasising about punching Ben into a temporary concussion, turned and delicately stroked her face.

15

Saturday, 14 August 1993

If St Michaels was perched in lighthouse splendour on the high slopes of Table Mountain, Canterbury College was its flatly levelled and vast male counterpart spread out over several blocks in the leafy tall-treed suburb of Rondebosch. This suburb, like all southern suburb white neighbourhoods in Cape Town, kept a certain faith with its absent parent England, maintaining through replicated custom and ritual that fragile identity that comes from being a home for a tribe in exile. Dotted along its oak-lined avenues were cheerful women wearing pastel twinsets, ministering to their gardens, watching their sons run mad with the dogs, pouring their daughters into pale satin gowns for cricket club dances. These women were husbanded by men who angled their signet rings left, laughed affably while they tended the weekend braais, tousled their boys' hair, and indulged their daughters' shopping sprees, but could also retreat into old rages and hot tempers, the collective secrets of those dark adolescent years spent guarding the border always just one trigger away.

Though Canterbury College was full of the trappings of maleness (hierarchy, rough sports, and an Old Testament-style angry God) it was tirelessly supported by the boys' mothers, whose bright, occasionally medicinally infused energies and enthusiasms for their sons and the school never seemed to flag. But if there was one thing both the mothers and fathers attended, it was the annual Canterbury versus Simon van der Stel rugby match.

Alia was surprised to find herself at the gates of Canterbury that crisp Saturday morning with her friends Janine and Lizzie, the only ones who would countenance accompanying her to an event that had drawn more scorn from Nasreen than her trip to HAL's. Each girl had her reasons: for Janine, a whippet thin, immaculately groomed girl who dominated the St Michaels sports field, these events, along with school socials and exams, were a natural part of the annual calendar. For Lizzie, it was a chance to see her brother, a Canterbury boarder. For Alia, a now rare opportunity to see Nick, this time under the protective cloak of Lizzie's and Janine's company: the months-long grounding was over, but the ban on seeing Nick was still in place. Zarina had not remembered that Nick was at Canterbury, and though always so permissive of her child's quicksilver allegiances and interests, had expressed bafflement at this newfound interest in school rugby. The rest of Alia's friends had rounded on her, unanimously declaring that it would be a Saturday spent at the mouth of barbarism, but no one had been more puzzled, or had poured more effort into attempting to dissuade her from coming, than Nick.

"I don't understand," he had said. "Why do you want to come?"

"Everyone keeps saying it's going to be fun."

"It *won't*. It will be grim and awful. And it will happen in the absence of everything important."

As Alia walked up the wide and lovely school avenue, the kind suited to a Daimler or a carriage, she herself wasn't altogether certain why she had come. Why did she want to see Nick here? With the uniforms and the prefects and the even more crazed attention to form and discipline than St

Michaels, in this place that mixed privilege with punishment, where students could expect both individual tutelage and a beating from a belligerent housemaster in the same week, where they were told daily that they would inherit the country but were kept far away from its people.

The grounds stretched out before the three girls, the vast fields dotted with occasional buildings, greystone chapels and redbrick dormitories. They called them "Houses", arbitrarily designated living spaces that divided students into lifelong allegiances. And in among the houses and fields and long avenues roamed the boys in their weekend uniform, a slightly relaxed version of what they wore during the week, in a catatonic state of institutionalised boredom.

In the distance, Alia could hear the hum of the already gathered crowd and as she turned the corner a pretty postcard scene of a Surrey village met her. On either side of the field were white wooden stands peopled by young girls in fetching frocks, their hair shiny, their skins lit with the healthy golden glow that comes to those who spend their days in fresh air and sun. Pringle sweaters were tossed around the mothers' shoulders, describing a knotted "v", their wrists and ears decorated with chunky gold jewellery, their heads crowned by puffy foam-lined, fabric covered Alice bands.

"There's Sophie and Abigail," cried Janine, spying friends of hers from another school. "Come on." She moved towards two girls who sat watching the boys warm up, happily discussing the details of the last match with each other. Lizzie went off in search of her brother.

Alia tried surreptitiously to adjust her peach-coloured bodysuit, the material had just crawled into an unpleasant angle. Janine, au fait with all things Canterbury, had advised her on both the outfit and her makeup. "Not too much eyeliner," she had commanded. "It's a day event."

Alia had listened carefully and obeyed. The wedding, and

the trip to HAL's before that, had laid bare her shortcomings around all things public and sartorial. She wondered if, for the rest of her life, she would have to do this; stand in front of someone else and wait for them to reflect her back at herself, let them decide whether she had assumed the correct face with which to greet the world.

Janine slotted easily into Abigail and Sophie's discussion as both girls moved to make room for her and smiled disinterestedly at Alia, who was standing awkwardly to the left of them wondering if they would appreciate her observations about how the whole system was rotten from within. She was about to launch into this as an opening salvo when Janine quickly began to point out people she knew.

Well-mannered to the last, the Canterbury boys waited until all their guests were seated before taking up their own places on the grass. A few prefects with blazers chock full of badges and colours walked up and down the student body shouting the beginnings of a series of exhortations that were designed to sing their school's praises and denigrate their opposition. Across the field the visiting team, an Afrikaans boys' school from one of the far-flung, seldom visited farming districts outside of Cape Town, were doing the same thing.

"Oh, my goodness, they look so brutal, hey?" said Abigail to Sophie, nodding towards the opposition's row of blond mops and shiny faces. "Damon said they practise barefoot."

"Ja," nodded Janine knowingly, while Alia struggled to see what marked the team as different. She continued to stare in a fixed, almost beaky way about her, trying to make sense of the chatter and the opinions, trying to store up things she could repeat later.

Across the field she saw Nick and waved at him to come over. He was in full school uniform, the limped stride of HAL's absent, walking rather (and she shuddered inwardly while she admitted this) with an apparent sense of – *Could it be? – pride* in the place and the outfit. He looked exemplary. He looked like he belonged. He kissed Alia on the cheek and she launched immediately into a satire of what she had just heard. "Apparently you are playing the Barbarians ... this lot have just stopped short of calling them kaalvoet boere ... what is this? Some kind of war re-enactment?"

Nick surprised her by hesitating before answering, "Well, they're fucking scary, man. These boys are hard. Do you know what it's like to play without your boots on? I'm glad it's not me out there!" He ended with an admiring nod towards the home team.

"You seem very interested all of a sudden." Alia was furious. She realised suddenly why she had come – it was not to see Nick in this world; rather it was so that they could both be in it at the same time and so that together they could tear it apart, rip into what made them uncomfortable and angry, disparage all the things that were wrong with it.

"I'm not," returned Nick defensively. "I'm just saying."

It was an inauspicious start.

That first interaction of the day marked the tenor and texture of the hours that would follow. To Alia, Nick appeared transformed and inaccessible, the baggy jeans and Malcolm x cap of town and HAL's, the borrowed suit of the wedding, the clothing that had seemed to gift him with a democracy of movement, was gone. In its place was a straight-shouldered, blazered boy who gave his teachers respectful and helpful answers and called his friends "bru".

Nick seemed popular at the school and perhaps this was the hardest betrayal. Large, bullish boys with wide faces and floppy fringes slapped him on the back and were tickled by what he said. When the prefects shouted his surname to get him to run an errand, he tripped about speedily to do their bidding. She thought about the last few sneaked phone conversations and it seemed now that he had grown progressively more evasive and quiet with each call. When she had asked him what was wrong, he had offered his own father as an excuse, sighing deeply into the receiver, leaving the older man's disciplines to her overactive imagination. Perhaps those evasive sighs were the first sounds of disinterest, the beginning of his ending things. Perhaps he had chosen to disentangle himself from her in the easiest way possible, by engaging a little less enthusiastically, by refusing to laugh at the world with her.

Lizzie was unexpectedly busy: her brother had been at the school since his nursery years and as a result she knew everyone and everyone knew her, so Alia spent a large part of the day drifting between Janine and a friend of Nick's called Charlie Meade. Charlie was a frail mousy-haired boy, who, small for his age, appeared partially submerged by his uniform. He walked through the world in a perpetual haze of bewilderment, giving off waves of tangible loneliness. He seemed to have attached himself to Nick in the hopes that some of the other boy's charisma would rub off on him. Charlie stood next to Alia, occasionally making conversation, but was mainly focused on training his eyes on the game as though the ferocity of his gaze and support could make up for his inability to play. Alia resented spending time with him, realising that the only thing that united them was a deep sense of not belonging, but that Charlie's form of alienation was not like hers. He longed for acceptance. It was palpable. It was painful.

Lunchtime arrived and the boys flocked as one to buy hamburgers from the kiosk – a rare delight in a term filled with overcooked vegetables and tough meat. Charlie chewed his way through his burger with painstaking slowness, favouring, for some inexplicable reason, the left side of his mouth. Alia, full of irritation that she could not channel towards Nick, turned on him and said, "Do you have a tooth loose or something?"

Charlie lifted his head, cattle-like. "No. Why?"

"Because," said Alia, affecting patience, "you're chewing with your left side only."

"Am I?" Charlie's response had a bovine serenity that drove Alia's already fraying nerves towards a shriek below her skin.

"So listen," said Charlie, making a conscious effort to distribute the food evenly in his mouth, "what do you think of Nick's family moving, hey? Such a las, hey?"

Alia had been listening with half an ear, trying to decide whose company she could stomach more easily, Charlie's dullness or Abigail's inanity. But his words and their meaning sunk in eventually.

"Moving? What are you talking about?"

"They're going to Australia." Charlie's brain worked slowly away at realising his indiscretion. "Oh, shit ... sorry, hey? Maybe he wanted to tell you himself. I thought you knew. He's known for ages. Well ... since, like, two weeks ago."

Alia felt a chill that reached in and through her peach bodysuit. When Nick jogged over to them a few minutes later, her rage had reached a silent crescendo and she returned all his questions with an icy stare. Nick took one look at Charlie's guilt-ridden expression and mournful (though persistent) munching on his burger and realised that she had been told about the imminent move.

"I was going to tell you," he said, jumping into the thick of it.

"When?"

Alia folded her arms in front of her chest, giving herself a surreptitious hug that both steadied her and warded him off.

"I don't know," answered Nick, his dodging and weaving of the last two weeks exposed. He looked sheepishly down at his shoes. This normally assured boy, who had just demonstrated how ably he could shift and glide between ghetto-kid and private school role model, was at a loss. He shuffled his well-shined shoes into the still dewy grass. He dug into his pocket. "Do you want some peanuts?" He held up a slightly dusty offering.

"No, I don't want any peanuts," Alia answered furiously, managing, only just, to resist the violent impulse to smack them out of his hand. "When exactly are you leaving?"

Nick glanced over at the players and then at Charlie, who, unable to face his friend, was looking rather miserably into the distance, his jaw clenched.

"We're going at the end of the year."

Alia felt her head go hot, and in her mind's eye she saw herself, cartoon-like, with steam pouring from each ear.

"You mean you're not even staying for the elections?"

The question hung between them, thick and impossible, full of historic accusations and future betrayals. Nick took her arm and began to steer her away from the field, past the mothers with their fixed smiles and tortoise-shell sunglasses, past the fathers who were making grim assessments of Canterbury's three failed attempts at tries. They walked in silence for a little while, until Alia erupted again. "How can you people leave before the elections?"

Nick didn't answer her. Instead, he continued to walk round the back of one of the now-empty Houses, through the low brick archway and down to a circle of drooping willow trees where someone, a hundred years ago, had thoughtfully placed a commemorative bench. He sat down and reached into his jacket pocket and drew out two loose cigarettes. Alia was comforted by them – so *that* hadn't changed – but shook her head when he offered her one. If she breathed too deeply she was afraid she would burst into tears.

"This is my favourite spot in the school," said Nick conversationally.

Alia sat down next to him, staring stonily ahead, unable to leave and unable to keep from asking why. They sat in individual silences; his careful and avoidant, hers resentful and fearful, until eventually Nick said, almost dully, "They just dumped it on me, without any preamble, and said we were going to Brisbane next year."

Alia nodded as though she knew all about Brisbane, but really she knew nothing, not if it was coastal, or inland, not if it was a major or minor city.

"My mom's sister moved there, about twenty years ago – she was involved with some white guy and they couldn't stay here so—"

"Ja." Alia hated the note of indifference in her voice, she'd heard about this aunt before and had pictured the woman saying goodbye to her family and friends and travelling into the ocean and beyond for love; she had felt all the romance of her story, woven as it was with familial and political drama, but right now she didn't want to hear about anyone's story but her own.

"So your parents are just cowards."

Nick's body started in response, even in profile she could see his eyes widen with hurt. Years later she would think of this as a cheap shot, as a way of soothing her own distress as quickly as possible, and in a way of course it was only that, but in another very real way, she believed it. Cowards. Sellouts. Unbelievers.

Nick rolled the tip of his cigarette-coal on the bench, shaping it into a glowing cone. "They're not cowards," he said quietly. "My dad just says he is sick of the violence – he's upset about Hani and—"

"We're all upset about Hani," interrupted Alia. An image of feet running over and through flower beds in the Company's Gardens, of panic, of terror, and behind that, an older memory, of dogs and classrooms.

"Well he's ... he just thinks it's a harbinger of things to come."

"A 'harbinger of things to come'," mocked Alia. "Have you suddenly started working for SABC? You sound like a second-rate newsman."

"Wow. That's not even—"

"Okay, *okay*. I'm sorry. But you don't see what they're doing? Leaving before the election? It's so racist. They might as well vote Nat."

Nick stiffened. He took a breath before launching into a defence. "Don't *talk* about my family in that way. That's not even ... it's not *true*. They stayed the whole time when things were terrible and they didn't go anywhere. Jesus! What's so wrong about wanting to be safe?"

That last sentence, Alia decided, came straight from his mother's mouth. She stood up, eyes blurry and full, reaching for a way to close everything and fit it all into a manageable box. "Well, that's that then." She delivered the words with false brightness, as if she had recovered fully and Nick's presence in her life and his coming absence was nothing. "Thanks for letting me know." She patted his leg before saying, "And by the way, you are one of the fakest people I have ever met."

Nick flung his head back on the bench in disbelief, and then threw up his hands as if to invite her to expand and Alia happily obliged.

"I now understand why you didn't want me to come here today – because you are a big phony. You're *fake*. You talk about how you don't participate in all this crap and here you are, practically *vying* for a prefectship. At least those people over there," she pointed angrily in the direction of the rugby crowd hidden beyond the trees, "at least they *admit* who they are, they don't pretend."

Nick rolled his eyes and began to fidget with his tie, pulling and winding the thin bit over the fat bit.

Alia had set this up as her parting shot but what she was really hoping for was that it would spark some kind of contrition in Nick, or at least prompt some kind of conversation. She stood looking down at him, rooted, waiting. Her hands found her hips and she flooded him with the feelings that were swirling storm-like inside her. It was a pose she had been striking for her father since she was four.

"I'm doing it so that I can stay."

"What?"

"I'm trying to stay."

"Stay?" Alia said the word uncomprehendingly, as though she was repeating a foreign sound.

"Yes. *Stay*." Nick stared ahead, his chin tucked into his throat, resting on his school tie. "Do you think I want to run around and kowtow to these fucking people? I'm trying to get my parents to agree to let me *stay* here. I can't do that without the school's support. Do you think for a moment that I want to leave South Africa? Now? Of all times? *Jesus*. You're so self-involved, Alia. You only think about *yourself* … how *you're* going to feel, how it will hurt *you* that I'm not here. You don't even consider how crap it's going to be for me to leave everyone and everything, just now."

Alia stood still, all her accusations stuck in her mouth like pebbles. She looked this way and that, while Nick scowled at his cigarette, and then she felt a large and wonderful feeling roll over her, a feeling that began to dissolve all the pebbles. She wondered where to begin and started with a very small sentence. "I do."

"Do *what*?" Nick whipped his head sideways.

"I do think about you." And then came the confession, the stones turning to dust, to air and then words. "I think about you all the time. I hardly ever think about myself anymore ... and I think it's because I love you." The last part in a rush, directed at the trees, not the boy. She wondered if it was indecent somehow, if she was not supposed to tell him this, if she was supposed to wait for him to tell her. But the pebbles were nothing now and in their place was an emergent longing that kept its own laws and schedules. Why had he not said anything yet? She turned from a dazed study of an acorn hanging sturdily on a thin dry twig and glowered at him.

"Well, of course you love me," responded Nick crossly, grinding out his cigarette beneath his schoolboy shoes.

"Come again?"

"What else could this all be about?"

"*Listen*," said Alia hotly, full of disbelief that her declaration could be so casually received and passed over, "I don't say that to just anyone."

"I should hope not."

She slammed one balled hand into another. "Are you just going to sit there looking smug? I just told you something important."

"Obviously, I love you too."

"It's not obvious! You've never told me that."

"I thought you *knew*."

"How could I know? You don't tell me anything apparently," she said, dredging the subject of their fight back into the fray.

"I've known for ages."

"Say it."

"I just did." Nick gave her a small smile, the larger version of which was turned inward.

Alia sat next to him and put a soft hand on his face,

offering the moment the seriousness she thought it deserved.

"You must say it," she insisted solemnly.

"I love you."

Alia pulled Nick up by his hands, laying a kiss on his mouth. She ushered him back to the bench so that he could sit and she could lie with her head in his lap, her feet crossed at the ankles, her body warmed by the winter sun. Nick raked his hand through her hair and looked down at her, smiling. "Our faces look weird from this angle, we're upside down, it's all distorted so it looks like your mouth is backwards or something."

She obliged him by pulling her face in different directions. She stopped and assumed what she thought was a pretty expression, appropriate to the moment. A small breeze managed to move the thin branches at the very top of the trees. The sun peered through the leaves in bursts of marbled light. Even her bodysuit was behaving, staying at unobtrusive angles. And following that feeling was another one tumbling through with just as much conviction. That this would not last. He. Was. Leaving.

She thought perhaps it was best to disrupt the scene, to say something that would undo some of the sticky sentimentality that was beginning to gather.

She stretched her arms above her head as though to take in the day and all its pleasures. "It's getting warmer by the minute. It's so nice out today."

Nick stared off at something she couldn't see and all he offered was a noncommittal murmur.

"It *is*. Not even you could debate that."

"Nice for us, but probably not so nice for others."

"Who do you mean?"

"I don't know. I mean I can't say *specifically*. I mean that somewhere, someone is always having a horrible day. Someone's being killed or something terrible is happening to them this very moment, you know? And we *think* it's a good day and maybe *we* are having a good day, but it's not, not really, we just don't know what we're living next to."

"That's a depressing thought," said Alia with a teasing smile. She could see herself stepping into her mother's voice. Isn't this what women must do? They must manage men. Coax them from their gloomy dispositions. But Nick didn't seem to need or want cheering up. He wasn't sad when he offered her this, just a little pensive, looking for a way to integrate a piece of knowledge that he would carry.

"It's depressing because it's true." He took his second cigarette out and lit it. "I know there are good things happening too. But I'm not worried about the good things. I'm glad they're happening. But I don't need to be concerned about them, you know?"

Alia nodded. She understood, but she gave in to the impulse to tease him. "You are sounding positively saintly. It's your Catholicism."

Nick broke into a smile, raised his cigarette to his lips. "Are you getting hot? You want to move into the shade?"

"No, I like it here."

Nick shifted so that Alia's head was angled more comfortably, and then bent down to place a kiss on her forehead. "Do you need to get back to your friends?"

"Mackenzie!" A voice bellowed up from behind the trees.

"Shit! Mr Abbot," said Nick taking a final drag, "hold the smoke?"

"Why?"

"You won't get in trouble."

"Wow, such gallantry."

Two figures came into view, laughing. It was Charlie and another boy, Henry, both of whom had deepened their voices to impersonate the housemaster.

"Abbot's looking for you," announced Henry, smirking at

Alia who was sitting guiltily next to Nick in a position she thought was adult friendly.

"You guys are hilarious. Seriously. You should consider a career in vocal pyrotechnics."

"Too many big words for me, hey, Mackenzie."

"Tell Abbot I'll be there in a minute."

The two boys walked off, with Charlie giving Alia a friendly wave that made her regret the short way she had treated him earlier.

"God, I have to go back," groaned Nick. "He probably wants me to serve half-time oranges. Christ, it's so *humiliating*," and then in response to Alia who was now laughing, "It's not *funny*, could there be a crueler way of dividing up who can and can't play?" He stuck his hands in his pockets, the picture of a boy whose delicate shoulders could never handle the scrum.

"No, man! I was just thinking that's how Farouk knew you, when we first met. At HAL's, remember?

"Oh, ja. *Great*. So all the important moments of our relationship have *this* as their motif."

But Alia felt a delight almost as deep as what held her on the bench. They were already able to look back together. They had accumulated a small collection of memories that belonged to no one but them. They had their own joke and that was everything. Nick took her hand and they walked unseen and unnoticed through the grove of trailing willows.

"Have your parents spoken to Waleed yet?"

"No." She shook her head, feeling a twinge of sadness.

"That's too bad. I'd really like to meet him."

"He'd like you."

"Cool."

"Just don't tell him you're emigrating to Australia."

They traced their steps back, passing the empty Houses and the small archways. Just before they turned the corner that would deliver them back to the crowd and the field, Alia stopped and said, "So if your plan doesn't work – your boarding house plan— "

"Ja?"

"And it turns out," she took a deep breath and pushed the words through, "it turns out you have to go— "

"Ja?"

Nick hung his head, his hands finding his pockets once again. Alia noticed this but still touched his jacket very gently in a way that asked him to look at her and said, "Do you think you'll ever come back?"

"The moment I can, I will."

It was a promise. She understood that. All around the sentence little possibilities gathered.

"Besides, exile is supposed to be good for thinkers."

"Like Nat Nakasa?" Nick didn't say this sarcastically. He was struggling under an oncoming sadness that put him in contact with some of the brooding ache and quiet of the twenty-eight-year old writer who had fallen into the snows and loneliness of New York.

"Nat Nakasa knew he could never go home." She waited a moment before saying, "I'll write to you."

"Hmm?"

"I'll write to you once a week. I'll tell you about everything that's happening. That way when you come home it will be like you've been here all the time, you won't need any explanations or anything. If you go, I mean."

"Okay. Thank you. I'd really like that."

They found themselves back at the game where the cries of half-time victory hung in the air like little celebratory garlands. Nick loped off to bring out the fruit and Alia took her place next to Janine and Lizzie and looked out onto the clearness of the day, marked now by new knowledge, love and a future departure, by the tired happy faces of the boys and by Janine's lovely laugh pealing out at something Sophie had said. She told Lizzie about Nick's leaving and Lizzie placed a consoling hand on Alia's back. Alia took a few seconds to construct an image of herself standing at Cape Town harbour waving a farewell handkerchief, ignoring the knowledge that Nick and his family would travel to Australia by plane.

This was, she thought, the first time she had told someone outside her family that she loved them: she wondered how many people she would say it to in her lifetime; if there was a limit. After a few moments of uncharacteristic silence, Lizzie began to speak, casting prophecies as she pointed out black and coloured Canterbury pupils: "See him? Future pres*ident*. That one, future minister of *Fin*ance. Over there, Future minister of *Cul*ture." Lizzie ended each prediction with a nod and a folding of arms. Alia laughed and found her body relax, as if something had pressed all the right points and somehow kept the future at a firm, unthreatening distance and let her present keep time with itself and with her.

~

Back in Walmer Estate, a gloomy and dark grey northwester had gathered, an unforgiving wind of cold moods and bitter tempers. She took herself to her room, spied a cloud moving with odious thickness over the mountain, promptly flung herself on her bed and wept. This went on for several more minutes and when no one rushed to her side, full of enquiries and concern, she turned the decibel up on the whimpering and yelping, wondering, between hiccups and snot, where *on earth* her mother and sister were.

"What's the matter? Are you sick?"

It was Adam, his face stricken with a panic that both imagined the worst and begged not to be told about it. In one hand a coffee, with a paper towel placed between saucer and cup to catch any spills.

"I'm in the depths of despair," Alia choked.

"Oh." Adam gave his coffee a careful stir.

Alia reached for another tissue and finding the box empty, dragged her sleeve up to her nose. Obligingly, Adam handed her the coffee-speckled towel.

"Your mother's not home." To this, or the tissue, Alia responded with a new deluge of tears. "Alia, calm *down*. You're going to make yourself sick. I'm sure whatever it is, it's not so catastrophic."

"Wh-where's Nasreengg?"

"Also out."

"Hhhhhhe's *leaving*, Dad. He's going to Brisbane."

"Who is?"

"Nick."

"Who?"

"Nick. NICK!" She cast herself, face down, on her pillow.

"Oh, *right*. Nick. Nice boy. Well, sorry to hear that."

"No you're *not*." Alia raised an indignant head, her words still muffled by sobs. "This is completely perfect for you. I'll probably never see him again."

Adam sat down on the edge of the bed, placing his coffee with some care on his daughter's desk while a silence, long and unwieldy, stretched between them, punctuated only by her now soft crying. "I'm sure he'll come back to visit," he said eventually, and then, pensively, "Hell, I wonder if Ismail knows."

"*What*?"

"Uncle Ismail and his father do a lot of business together—"

Alia reached beyond her tears to arrange her face into stony disbelief. She shook her head, sat up, dragged her knees up to her chin and levelled her gaze at her father.

"Ag, man, don't be like that." Adam waved her outrage

away, his large hands making airy motions. "I was just thinking out loud. Here, have some coffee."

"Mom says I shouldn't after five."

"Well," he answered with a confidential wink, "she's not here, is she? Drink up, before it get's cold."

Adam kissed the top of her head, signalling that the conversation was over, and then reached, not entirely awkwardly, to pat her shoulder. "I was thinking," he said as he was walking out, "we should go book shopping. We haven't done that in a while. Would you like that?"

"Ja. Okay."

"Good. Next week then."

Alia turned a red-nosed profile at her father and stared with dramatic intensity at the wall.

"Alia?"

"What?"

"I'm sorry your friend is leaving."

As he left, Adam flicked the light switch on and off several times: as a child, this had been his signal to her that a story was about to begin. She shook her head at the reference and, determined not to be rescued from gloom, dabbed her welling eyes with the paper towel. Adam left the room and she turned her hard stare to the mountain, now almost completely covered in a thick wet greyness, the harbour dull steel.

16 June 1986

A low cement wall runs around the edge of the school declaring at once its borders and its affinities. Inside, a small chapel, an entrance lined by old oaks, a collection of squat eighteenth-century buildings, the dusty rectangle of a tar playground, girls in green uniforms and panama hats, boys in navy blue blazers and grey shorts. Outside, the houses of Walmer Estate and the warren-like streets of Woodstock. At the playground's edge the eerie beginnings of the emptiness of the District. The school had been dreamed up by Sir George Grey, colonist, explorer, learner of new languages, who, fresh from the success of seizing acres and acres of land from the Maori, had turned his attention to the Cape. This school was never intended for Alia. It was not for girl-child descendants of slaves and indentured labourers but rather for the sons of Xhosa chiefs. "Hearts and minds old chap," Grey might have said, "winning hearts and minds ..."

He'd built the school telling those boys' fathers that it would give them a first-rate British education and that its emphasis on carpentry and tailoring would prove most useful in the years to come "for leadership and so forth". In the early mornings of the previous century, kings' sons had sat where Alia did now, learning how to darn trousers and varnish beech chests. And perhaps later in the day during their breaks from lessons, they too had held hands and ran pell-mell down the grass fields that followed the sloping contours of the mountain. Not even Grey's quietest ambitions could have predicted that this school, with its carpentry instead of mathematics, its tailoring in lieu of literature, would light the path for the hated education laws of the 1950s.

Alia has been at this school for almost eight months. It is the end of the bright energetic mornings of nursery school and the beginning of identical outfits, bells, lining up, the pinch of polished black shoes, and the faint but ever present smell of an institution on her hair and clothes. It is the end of scrubbed disinfected toilets and the beginning of dark booths, stolen tissue paper, and walls smeared with shit and graffiti.

It is a long day for any six-year-old with its early morning start and demand for hours of silence and concentration. There is one half an hour break at ten-thirty and then two more hours of lessons. During break Alia plays with her classmates, picking out an activity from a collection of ancient games: five-stones, clapping hands, chanting lyrics, jumps and hops between an old pair of pantyhose, dodging a plastic ball so thin it always skews mid-throw, climbing thick-trunked trees and shaking the branches to dislodge stubborn acorns. But sometimes she drifts across the black gravelled tarmac with its faded white netball lines, through the dry, cool shade of the old Cape oaks towards the wall, and beyond it, the harbour. The District is to her left and Walmer Estate to her right. Across the street is Holy Cross, the Catholic school full of the teeming noise of other girls at break time. If she times it just right before the noise of their break, she can listen for the soft collective hum of the working city.

It is the city she looks to, the city with its sea and its ships that she wants. That expanse of space to her left, that place of field and memory, those hills with their rippling gradients, the roads that still run through it, the patches of cobblestones, the mosque, the church, the school and the emptiness between them – they don't interest her. She has not yet learned to match the nothingness with Zarina's tight face as they drive past and through, with the meandering routes Adam has inherited from his father, with Waleed's furious rants to anyone who will listen, with Fozia's photographs of stoeps and streets and people all packed away in her dressing table. She has heard the name, District Six, but has never thought to call this place, *right here*, this place that begins where her school ends, playground against rubble, by that name. She doesn't understand where it went. She assumes that it had all somehow fallen to pieces, gone to ruin, crumbled like the Rome of her mother's stories, that it took place long ago, in black and white, like Fozia's photographs. She thinks perhaps that this must be what happens, places disappear, they go away, like her grandfather. There are some days when she thinks it must still be there, just in another part of the city: that she could one day turn a corner and find it, and that everyone would rush towards it with a relieved cry, the way you do when something lost turns up unexpectedly. There are other photographs, though, that are even more difficult to talk about. Just last week, she had found a book her uncle had left behind: on the first page, men and women stand around rubbish tins lit with fires waving small books and papers, on the next they lie curling like lopsided starfish, heads against dirt, hands fisted or clawed.

~

Today, Nasreen and Alia set out from home in matching hats and dresses and eventually matching steps. They meet with other little girls on the street corner. An ordinary beginning, a nothing day. But when they walk into the school grounds they feel something is different. People are gathered in groups, the pupils from the boys' school are standing about holding sticks and staging games of mock battle in blue blazers. A cluster of girls stands where the driveway curves and the wall falls in deep dropped steps towards the Teacher's Training College. Alia and Nasreen walk over and gaze down at a small assembly of teenagers holding brown cardboard placards. Alia strains her eyes to sound out the print on the largest poster. "Re-re—l-l-e-a—ee-se," she begins. A girl from Nasreen's class cuts her off from the long process of spelling out the rest of it.

"It says 'Release Nelson Mandela', man."

Alia looks down at her shoes while Nasreen rounds angrily on her classmate. "She's just small! It's not her fault she can't read it yet." And then scornfully tipping her head back, she speaks down the length of her nose. "You probably don't even know who Nelson Mandela is. You probably don't even know *where* he is."

"I know where he is better than *you*."

"Who they?" asks Alia, pointing to the group holding the posters, not knowing who this Nelson is, where he is, or why they are fighting about him.

"They are comrades," answers Nasreen, tossing a plaited head threaded with navy ribbons.

"My daddy says they are just asking for trouble," says a girl with short hair and a spray of freckles, clutching her schoolbag close to her stomach. "My daddy says they just cause problems for everyone."

"Your daddy's talking nonsense," says the girl who has just bullied Alia. She looks down at the small assembly and waves, saying, "My cousin is there. That's him with the purple top on."

The children look down the deep incline of the indented steps and see a long-legged boy in a turtle-neck jersey and a wide grin, his arms moving in wide responsive sweeps. He points to the placard he is holding, punches his fist in the air and shouts up, "Amandla!"

His cousin shouts back excitedly, "A*weth*u!"

When Alia giggles, Nasreen shoots her a warning look and then pulls at her hand to move her out of the way of an incoming car. The jerk is a statement more than anything else, a declaration of authority and responsibility, for the car moves at a crawl, its driver conscious of the children and the unfamiliar gathering.

"It's Imtiaaz and Tasneem." Nasreen recognising the vehicle's occupants, and then commands, "Come."

The girls skip towards the car, over the ground thick with uncollected acorns just as the protesters begin to sing a reedy off-key "We Shall Overcome". In the driver's seat sits their Uncle Ismail, a short man whose naturally gravelly voice has deepened into a growl from years of dedicated smoking. He is puffing at perhaps his fourth cigarette of the day, looking out at the scene before him with an unreadable expression. Imtiaaz is already struggling to raise her haversack onto her diminutive blazered shoulders, while Tasneem, her sister, older by ten years, is not in a school uniform. Instead she is wearing tapered stonewashed jeans, an oversized T-shirt and a banana clip that pushes her bubble-fringe forward. Alia thinks she looks wonderful.

"Salaam, Uncle Ismail," chant the sisters in unison.

"Hello, my girlies." Their uncle removes his cigarette just long enough to greet them and check on his youngest daughter's neatness. "Imtiaaz, you got everything?"

His daughter nods, hopping impatiently from foot to foot, but her father is moving more slowly than usual. "And what have we here?" he says, nodding towards the singing, suddenly very jovial.

"They are comrades," says Nasreen gravely.

"Comrades, eh?'" says Ismail. "Where did you learn that word?"

"From Uncle Waleed," she answers as though expecting the same high five Waleed had offered her when she had said it correctly the week before.

But Ismail doesn't seem to hear her. His eyes are fixed on the singers. "Listen here, I'm going to walk you to class and

I don't want you to come back up here until the end of school, not even in short break, you understand?" He turns to Tasneem, who is leaning against the car in a show of boredom. "You too, Missy. Just because you staying home this week doesn't mean you doing nothing. Come on!"

Tasneem grabs at Alia's hand and marches her towards the gate. Alia almost swoons with delight. Tasneem is eight years older than her and a high-school student. When the Dawood girls visit, their cousin Tasneem's room alone is off limits, with its black and white posters of a pouting Chris Isaak and alphabetised compilation tapes.

"Tasneem?" says Alia.

"What?"

"Why are you not going to school today?"

"It's a boycott."

"Oh." Alia pretends to understand, but then gives up. "But you then a girl."

"No, man!" Her cousin hoots with laughter. "It's a stay-away. We not going to school because of the government."

Alia feels a wave of outrage. "So why can't we stay away?" she says furiously, thinking of all the things she would prefer to be doing. "Why can you do it? That's not fair!"

"You too small," answers Tasneem, tugging at her young charge to hurry her along. "It's not for primary schools. You better make quick, I had Mrs Dean in Sub A and she will shout you out if you late."

"But there's she talking to your daddy."

The girls walk over to Ismail, who appears to be listening carefully to Mrs Dean.

"No," she is saying, "I don't think we need to worry. They've said they won't come into the school, they know the college is separate. They've assured us, and we're not sending the children home. Not a chance. Some of them have come all the way in from the Flats."

Ismail looks uncertainly at his watch. "I have to go, I have to open the shop, but I'll stop by in lunch to check on things." He turns to his older daughter, "Say hello to Mrs Dean."

"Good morning, Mrs Dean."

"Good morning, my girlie, my word, look how big you are what standard are you in now?" Mrs Dean trots out all her faithful questions and observations in one breath.

"Standard Nine, Mrs Dean."

"Standard Nine? And what school are you attending?"

In her own way Mrs Dean is like royalty. She always picks up a question from her respondent's last answer, pushing small talk into an endlessly looped cycle. Tasneem, in return, is biddable but dull.

"I'm at Cressy, Mrs Dean."

"Cressy? That's a good school."

"Yes, Mrs Dean."

"It's stay-away again this week, isn't it?" and here she clucks impatiently and shakes her head at Ismail despairingly.

"Yes, Mrs Dean."

"But you must keep up with your schoolwork, hey? Don't just rest on your laurels because you are at home."

Tasneem nods and with that her eyes fill up. She brushes at them crossly; the tears are unexpected and they embarrass her.

"Why you crying?" says her father, supplying a quick laugh that he hopes will take them through the awkwardness of the moment and into their goodbyes. "You should be happy, *man*. Another whole week off school!"

Tasneem shakes her head and bites at her lip furiously. Her father shuffles about uncomfortably for a beat, shrugs apologetically at Mrs Dean. "She's taking it hard. She's scared she won't pass her exams because of it." He touches

Imtiaaz's hair as a farewell and leads his other daughter up the hill and out of the school grounds. Mrs Dean, Alia, Imtiaaz and Nasreen watch them walk away, the four of them standing in an awkward and unexpected huddle until Mrs Dean says, "What are you just standing there for? Get to class, all of you."

~

Alia's and Nasreen's classrooms are at opposite ends of the school. Alia's is one of a row of four in a cream-walled, green-roofed single storey at the edge of the playground. Nasreen's is all the way at the top of the brick stairs in the main building. At the beginning of each school day they say goodbye, with Alia walking reluctantly, dragging the toes of her shoes so consistently and petulantly on the gravel and grass that Zarina has to ask Sylvia to polish and buff them nightly. Nasreen picks up her pace, looking purposeful, and begins to seek out her friends, but as they turn from one another, she calls out, "I'll come and find you at short break."

"Why?" asks Alia, her stomach skittering just a little. Too many things were different today.

"Just," answers Nasreen and turns back to join the older girls.

Alia joins a tight line of six-year-old girls as they wait to be let inside. Mrs Dean appears in the doorway and ushers them in. The children navigate this next stage quickly, moving towards shared desks, placing their haversacks in a designated corner and standing obediently next to their chairs.

Mrs Dean, too, stands at her desk. Alia knows each of her dresses by heart. There are five of them. They all have the look and feel of another time; they smell faintly of mothballs and lavender oil, both odours pressed weekly into the fabric by an old-fashioned iron. Mrs Dean is old, so old, nearly sixty, but she still sets her coal black and grey hair in rollers and uses a bright red or tangerine lipstick. If it is cold she wears a cardigan and tucks a few tissues up one of the sleeves. Her clothing clings around her curves, ancient and generous. When she lifts an arm to write on the blackboard the skin and dimpled fat falls back from her elbow towards her shoulder. She speaks in a thin accented voice that sounds like an impersonation of someone else. She shouts at the six-year-old girls in her care and cuts their fringes if their hair grows too long. She makes the children line their hands up on their desks and stalks the aisles inspecting their nails. She checks for lice and makes a show of singling out poorer children whose uniforms have not been washed for a few weeks. She delivers smacks if homework is not complete and correct, and she lets her temper fill the room and govern it. She is wearing a brooch today, a silver bird that dips its filigreed beak towards a button on the blue swirls of her dress.

Mrs Dean takes up her place in front of the class, her fat feet made tiny beneath her frame, squashed today into dented cream heels. She draws her cardigan tighter as if to ward off the last of the morning chill and says, "Good morning, children."

As one, the waiting, standing group sing-songs the reply. "Good-morning-Mrs-Dean-and-how-are-you?"

Mrs Dean waits a beat, observing the convention of a real-world conversation before answering, "I am very well thank you and how are you?"

"We-are-very-well-thank-you."

Satisfied, their teacher nods them into their seats. "Sit."

Alia lays out her stationery for the day, a regulation green pencil, a shop-bought eraser, a stone-blue government exercise book and, in pride of place, an *Alice in Wonderland* ruler. The girl behind her throws it a covetous glance and Alia moves it ever so slightly closer to herself in response.

"Take out your *Kathy and Mark* readers, please." Mrs Dean's instruction sends the girls scurrying to their haversacks.

Next to Alia sits Sheila, a slow-learning little girl who cries her way through most lessons, partly from frustration, partly from the fear of a beating. Mrs Dean's smacks and hits cling to the girls even when she is not doling them out; they flinch as one when she passes them in one of her ceremonious strides up and down the aisles.

Alia hears Sheila's breathing begin to gather in speed as she looks up to see Mrs Dean eyeing them both, sussing out whether to praise or castigate.

"Ooh," says the class, sounding out their collective way through Kathy and Mark's excitement.

"Ooh!" Mrs Dean reads along with them, her eyes roving back and forth between page and class, between keeping pace and keeping order. Alia knows the rhythm of this class. She knows that if she refuses to watch the clock, if she can get through all the oohing and the false starts and half sentences, that eventually they will get to short break and that after that, maybe art class, or knitting. She tries to stay still even when Mrs Dean is writing something on the board. Nasreen told her once that Mrs Dean had eyes at the back of her head. Alia searched for the additional pair during her first week of school and concluded, regretfully, that they must be hidden by her hair, in which case they were no good anyway.

Alia looks up from her reader and sees Mrs Williams from the classroom next door standing at the blackboard. She is younger than Mrs Dean, with a sweetness about her that remains despite the overcrowded classrooms and the winter cold that creeps through the broken windows, giving half her pupils hacking coughs and the other half streaming noses. She walks toward Mrs Dean and the girls scramble out of their chairs to greet her.

"Good morning, girls."

"Good-morning-Mrs-Williams-and-how-are-you?"

"I am very well girls and how are you?"

"We-are-very-well-thank-you."

"Good." She smiles out at them, almost expectantly, as though it was *them* not her who had broken the order of things by walking into their lessons.

"Mrs Williams?"

Mrs Dean's voice is crisp and annoyed. Mrs Williams bends her head to whisper something to the older woman.

"Are you sure?"

"That's what they said," answers Mrs Williams, as though she has suddenly been given permission to speak at a normal volume. "I just spoke to them."

"Well, we will just see about that! Come on."

"Where to?" Mrs Williams looks bewildered.

"Outside. I'm going to talk to them." She moves towards the door, her cream shoes clip-clopping on the wooden floors.

"*Don't* ... Vera!"

The children give a start. They have never heard their teachers addressing each other by their first names. They have never suspected that their teachers *had* first names. *Mrs Dean's name is Vera*. Alia feels the same sense of wonder she had once when she ran into another teacher at a supermarket. Teachers have first names and they buy food at the same place as her mother. *Vera*. Vera, in her floral dress and navy cardigan and cream shoes and bird brooch. Vera, who looks just as shocked by Mrs Williams' revelation as her pupils are.

The two women scuttle outside and stand against the patch of wall between two windows talking in fast, frightened tones. The children cluster close, trying to listen in.

Mrs Dean pokes her head around the door. "Get back to

your seats at once! How *dare* you listen in? Get back to your readers. Now!"

A few minutes later, she returns with a large tin bucket of water. Her face is pulled tight despite her puffy jowls.

"Listen, children, you are going to go home early today. There is no more school today, you hear? But I don't want you running out of here like mad things, you listening? *Are you listening*? You walk out in an ordered fashion and you go straight home. You don't act like hooligans. If you usually walk home, you walk *straight home*. If you take the bus, you go straight to the bus stop. Now take out your handkerchiefs. Out where I can see them! Wave them!"

Thirty small hands decorate the air with see-through bits of white cotton.

Alia sees a steam train pull out of an old station.

"Fazlin! Where's yours? *Don't cry!* Never mind, you can have mine. Here. Okay, now one by one, come wet your handkerchief in this bucket. Make sure it's really wet. Don't worry to ring it out. When you walking home, if you smell something or if the air looks cloudy and you can't see, you put this on your face. *Are you listening?* Over your eyes and your mouth and your nose. Line up and dip like so, like I'm showing Fazlin."

The girls do as they are told. While they stand, Mrs Dean continues, "I don't want you to leave in big groups. You listening? Walk in twos or threes. No more than that. And you come back to school tomorrow. Just like normal."

Mrs Dean keeps to her litany of instruction, but an unnamed fear has snaked its way through the children. It starts, Alia believes, in Mrs Dean's round thick belly and moves into her voice so that it quivers just a little, gliding silently into the throats and stomachs of the little girls until their armpits are sticky, and one child at the back of the classroom urinates in a tiny puddle of yellow shame. The other children shrink away. Mrs Dean takes the bucket and cloth to the back of the room, mops up the urine and sloshes the remaining water where the wood has darkened in a small oval. She places a consoling hand on the shoulder of the child while she squats in her cream shoes, trying to stop the already strong smell. The other children gather about her in a broken circle. They are standing like this when they hear the dog. First just its barking, quick and sharp and full of purpose, but then also the growls, low and gathering towards a groan. When Alia turns around, the first thing she sees is the animal's snout, tapered and wolf-like, poking through the door. And then its tongue, lolling across its teeth, saliva, collar and the leash attached to it, being held and jerked by an as yet invisible hand, and then a moment later, a boot and a man's voice.

"Are you here? Are you bladdy in here?! Because if you are, you better come out or you will fokken regret it!"

Mrs Dean rises from cleaning the floor, her full body precise. She cuts through the children and gestures at them to stay behind her. The man is now fully in the classroom, red-faced, sweating. Alia wonders if he is very hot underneath that thick greenish uniform. She has never been so close to a soldier.

"What do you think you are doing?" Mrs Dean doesn't wag her finger but it sounds like a scold. "You get that dog out of my classroom. You can't just come in here – you scaring these children."

The soldier yanks back at the dog that is in the doorway, advancing on the room and the children in it. "I need to search this room, Mam."

"Why?"

"We looking for the terrorists. Some of them ran down here. A boy in a purple top."

Alia feels her whole body wind in on itself. *Did this man*

know she had spoken to Purple Top's cousin? Should she tell him before he asks her? She raises her hand to tell him but stops because Mrs Dean is speaking.

"What are you talking about? You mean the *student teachers*? Well, no one is here except me and these children."

The man taps his baton to his leg, his free hand pulling back at the animal as it gags and dances against its leash.

"You tell the kids to sit down." He delivers the instruction flatly.

She holds his gaze for a long moment and then hustles her children to their seats. "Come now! Be quick about it! This gentleman needs to look for something. Mind you sit down and mind you sit still."

It seems to last for hours but really it takes a few minutes at most. The soldier roams up and down the desk rows, the dog before him, barking, sniffing, drooling, just a hesitation away from biting one of them. Mrs Dean walks a little behind him, as if she is showing him around, giving him permission. No one says a word. Alia's leg shakes a little under the table and she is surprised to feel Sheila's hand reach for hers and hold it tightly.

Alia keeps her eyes fixed on the soldier and the dog, uncertain as to who is really in charge. The dog scampers forward, black-brown paws with thick curved nails scraping to create cross-hatchings on the wooden floors. In its throat sits a low growl and every few seconds its mouth opens to reveal two long fangs. A bark flies from its neck into the air and through the children. The animal leads the man to the knitting cupboard, stacked with boxes of tightly wound balls of acrylic wool and nubby squares woven by small unskilled fingers, and then to the cleaning products where the man spends an age examining a bottle of disinfectant.

Once every cupboard has been overturned and every door opened, once the boots and the paws have roamed over every inch of the small classroom, the soldier turns to Mrs Dean and says, accusingly, "There's nothing here."

The curved lines between the ends of Mrs Dean's lips and the beginning of her cheeks deepen. The girls, attuned to all her expressions, know that this means she is getting very angry and they wait for her to explode. But there is only silence, and within it, the increased shallowness of Sheila's breathing and the heavy panting of the dog.

The soldier shakes his head as if the whole encounter has disgusted him and he turns to leave. He jerks at the leash and the dog follows him. Mrs Dean trails them both as though she is seeing them off. She is about to shut the door when he turns and says quietly, "I haven't inspected your desk yet."

Mrs Dean flinches as though slapped in the face. Her voice, when it comes, is just a few decibels above a whisper. "What is it you think you're going to find there?"

"I'm not accusing you of anything, Mam," says the soldier, his tone is coaxing, patient. "You just never know if some troublemaker is using this room to hide something."

He stands over her while she unpacks every paper, every folder, her medication for hypertension, her 1946 teaching certificate. The drawer is entirely emptied, her life laid out before her, her pupils watching. Alia looks down at her lap. She lets go of Sheila's hand and twists her fingers in and around themselves. She feels as if she has just watched Mrs Dean undress. Unable to remain still, the dog begins to shake and twist as if it has just taken a bath. Outside the weight and thud of boots against cement, the sound of gunshots being swallowed into the sky, a siren – the school's or the state's, who could say? – and again, the singing, this time threaded through with faraway shouts. The soldier, bored now, stands in the doorway, offering and asking for an update from the other men.

"There's nothing this side."

"They must have gone into the college."

"Look out for the one in the purple top – he's a troublemaker."

With the soldier gone, the girls sit in a hushed quiet waiting for Mrs Dean to tell them what to do next. When their teacher finally speaks her voice comes through in a whisper. She tells them to pack up their bags, re-dip their handkerchiefs in the water and to be sure to be at school the next morning. As the girls troop out of the room, they each turn back, as if by some unknown compulsion, to look at Mrs Dean, who remains at her desk, her thin tangerine mouth hanging open, her hand shaking as she reaches for her medication, the bird on her brooch seeming to droop at a defeated angle.

~

Alia wanders up the path next to the playground. The world seems different, something has broken, and the break has made a terrible sound. Everything outside is too bright, too bright as only the Cape sun can make things, and everywhere more of the same, more dogs, more soldiers, more children. The sky is duck egg blue and here is the same green for the grass and there is the District and the oak trees and the harbour and the playground, usually full of skipping feet—

"Alia! *Alia!* Why are you just standing there? Come! Give me your hand!"

It is Nasreen, her arm already tight around her sister's waist, her cheek pressed to hers. "Where's your handkerchief? Do you have it?"

Alia nods mutely and hands the damp scrap of cotton to her sister. Everywhere, girls in green uniforms and panama hats. If she lets go of Nasreen's hand or Nasreen doesn't hold onto her tightly enough, will she find her again? But here is the green grass and it is the same and there is the harbour and not far from here, home.

"Alia!" Nasreen is shaking her. "We have to go *home*."

And shot through the air, puffs of smoke, fat clouds of it and everyone coughing and wheezing. *Wheezing*, her mother had said when she was sick last month, *You've got a wheezy chest*. She is moving again, legs and black polished shoes through the smoke, with Nasreen forging ahead, her blue backpack bouncing from her pace, her eight-year-old legs giving her a slight advantage.

"Keep the handkerchief on your face," she turns to instruct her younger sister. "See how I have mine?"

Alia nods and coughs into hers, her eyes streaming. "I can't see! I can't *see*!" she cries.

"Don't worry about it. Just *run*! I can't find Imtiaaz! Have you seen her?" says Nasreen, cutting and weaving through the other children, sometimes pushing them, holding onto her sister's hand.

"No," says Alia and then, "Nasreen, where is the smoke coming from? Is it a fire?"

"No. It's teargas. Come. *Hurry*."

Up, up the steep school driveway they had skipped down that morning, and at the corners where the college, chapel and school converge come the boys, hurtling out of their classrooms like small uniformed missiles. Ties yanked from collars, blazers shrugged off, already swearing and picking up thin oak branches and acorns from the ground and hurling them at each other as they laugh and tumble through the gas and past the army trucks. And after them, their teachers, hands on hips, in cheap faded suits and polyester dresses, squinting into the fog and fumes, somewhere between concern and resignation. The soldiers stand next to the large army trucks, their boots grinding the acorns, their focus on the college. They let the children pass, let them teem through the gates in an avalanche of hats and handkerchiefs and white socks, so that the grounds will empty and they can begin their hunt for those angry eighteen-year-olds in earnest. One, a girl in faded jeans and a thin green T-shirt, has already been caught. A soldier is grasping her arm with one hand while the girl twists this way and that to avoid the sjambok in his other hand. Alia's feet are locked on the ground again. She stands and watches as the girl's lip is split open and listens to her howl as she cradles her face in her hands, her fingers growing sticky red from the blood. Nasreen has looped her arms around Alia like she did that day when they both feared the wind would carry them away.

"*Please*, Alia!" Nasreen is screaming now, "you have to *walk*."

And they do, crying and panting up the hill, their chests tight, eyes full, noses streaming with unchecked mucus. Their faces are streaked with dirt, they have wiped and re-wiped their faces so many times in the journey up the hill that at some point the tears have got mingled with snot and sweat and panic. They are nearly home, with one more hill to go, wondering how their mother could not have found them yet, how their parents could have let this happen, how it was possible that no adult has intervened and collected them in a car and shooed away the police and disciplined the dogs and reinstated order. But they are nearly home where things will be normal. Where Sylvia will have laid out their after-school clothes and their burkas will be ironed for madressa and, they tell each other, *Daddy will have a fit when he hears about what happened, an absolute fit! Those police don't know what's coming. He will go down to the station himself to complain! He will have a fit!*

Their chests are settling, and the further the sisters scramble from the noxious gas the better the air, the more their breathing calms into a rhythm they know, the more they calm themselves. They round the corner – *one last hill!* – and cut through a neighbour's garden full of yellow-orange kumquats, wild with purple nasturtiums. They stop only when they turn the corner and see the usually pristine cream wall of their madressa marked from one end to another with a red spray-paint message: STAY-AWAY JUNE and then an abrupt squiggle.

One of the women from the madressa comes outside, armed with a stiffly bristled scrubbing brush and a bottle of Jik. "What are you children doing standing here?" she says sharply.

"We just back from school, Auntie," answers Nasreen, her hand reaching once again for Alia's.

"Did you just come up from Zonnebloem?"

"Yes," the girls chorus.

"Well, mind you go straight home," she says, hunching onto her knees and setting to work to erase all signs of the command. "There's trouble about today, you should be inside. No madressa today. We'll see you tomorrow."

The sisters walk up the last stretch of hill until their street unfurls before them and with it the safety of their home. Sylvia answers the door and takes them immediately to the bathroom to wash their faces and scrub their hands clean of the awful mess of the morning. She guesses about the teargas without them having to explain anything; she has spent the last decade walking with and beside children, carrying a bucket of water and strips of cloth. She bathes the girls' eyes with infinite gentleness; she helps them rinse their noses without singeing them further. She hugs them close and makes them sandwiches of thick white bread and polony and then sends them out to play in the garden.

The girls climb trees and make mud pies, finding unexpected solace in the games of their nursery years, stopping only briefly when Nasreen says casually, "I don't think we should tell Mommy about what happened today," and Alia responds with nothing but a nod, the decision reached, the pact made.

But later, when they are sleeping, worn out by the day and its difficulties, it is Sylvia who tells Zarina what has happened, gives her a glass of water, sits her down, rubs her back, lets her cry. Two women standing in a kitchen, each knowing for once just how the other feels.

16

Monday, 6 September 1993

"I'm leaving you."

Anna stood in the middle of the lounge, her clothes stuffed chaotically into an oversized army tote. Three cardboard boxes packed with books, kitchen utensils and her Indian cushion covers were arranged in an ominous triangle at her feet. Waleed leaned against the fridge, arms akimbo as if he was protecting its contents from a marauding gang. They had been here before, the announcement had been made, the tote packed, but she had never got as far as packing her books and her kitchenware. He would miss the garlic press, he had told her, hoping to raise a smile. In reply Anna shoved a renegade jersey back beneath the bag's drawstring. She bent down to tape up one of the boxes, asking Waleed, as if to further demonstrate her indifference, to please pass her the scissors. He obliged, wondering how long they would play out this scene, how long before the tears started and the tote was turned upside down so that the clothes were in a pile on the floor to be joined eventually by the clothes on her back.

The argument that brought them to this point – *What was it now? Oh yes! Her thesis.* AGAIN. That all-consuming thing – at least for the person who is writing it. She had finished her first draft a few weeks earlier, or had it been a few months earlier? *Well done to her! What did she want? A medal?*

She had made him a copy to read, asking him to annotate it as he saw fit. He'd meant to read it, but things had conspired against him. "He had squandered time," he told her with a sigh, "the stuff that life is made of." He would read it tomorrow. Or the day after. At some point – fatally, he could not remember when – she had stopped asking him if he'd read it.

"Megan is coming to fetch me in an hour. I'd really prefer it if you were out when she gets here. I'm in no mood for a scene."

"Why would there be a scene?" Waleed sat down on the couch, realising that his protective stance in front of the fridge was not endearing. He passed a weary hand over his eyes. He was so tired. And she was so demanding. Why did everything have to mean *something*? He hadn't read the damn thing because he had shit going on. His family was in tatters, he was struggling to write, money was tight, he couldn't keep borrowing from his mother and he was in a state of panic about what was happening further north in the country between the ANC and the IFP, and no amount of people telling him it would all be fine, it was factional infighting, it was just old ethnic chauvinism having a last gasp, that it would all be fine, *it would all be fine*, could calm him down. He just kept thinking, *If people are hurting each other now, when we are at our most hopeful, what's going to happen in ten years, in twenty years*? So he hadn't read it. Didn't mean he didn't love her. Should he say that? Right now?

"Why?" Anna was answering his earlier question. "Because she thinks you're a *dick*, that's why." She shook her head while she wrapped a porcelain salt and pepper shaker set, bought in Kalk Bay one Saturday the previous year, in newspaper. She and Waleed had taken the train out there and spent the day at the seaside village, walking down its main road through a blustery, pitchy wind. They'd stopped at a bric-á-brac store where Anna bought a seasoning set. Waleed tried to ignore the way the shopkeeper first trailed him in the store and then refused to look at him when he stood next to his girlfriend at the till. Rifling through her bag for money, Anna didn't catch the look of disgust that swept over the older man's face.

"I don't understand what Miss California's problem is—"

"She's from *Detroit*."

"I'm just saying, she's American, isn't she? And we both believe that we are shaped by our social structures—"

Anna gave a howl. "Your point?"

"That she's meddling in something that doesn't concern her. Her intervention is not welcome. It was true of Chile, and it's true of this house."

Anna hunched over one of her boxes, hands gripping hair, looked slightly deranged. She directed her question at the box. "You just don't get it, do you? She's concerned because as a *woman*—"

"Oh, spare me."

"I'll say it again just to annoy you, *as-a-woman* she is completely alert to what's been happening here."

"Sisters under the skin, hey?"

"I understand your need to trivialise that sort of solidarity, Waleed. You have certain limits. It's not even your fault. It's partly narcissism, it's partly the result of systemic patriarchal privilege." Waleed suspected that she was gabbling Megan's words, gorging herself on them, and then spitting them back up: no surprise there, successful ventriloquism was one of the most subtle and devastating weapons of imperialism. She was *still* talking: "It takes genuine and sustained effort to overcome those things. Not everyone can do it."

Waleed could not fathom that Anna was attempting to

bludgeon *him* with a political weapon. It seemed ludicrous. "That's a completely unfair thing to say," he said, genuinely wounded. "I am a feminist. I pride myself on being one."

"You're not a feminist. How is it feminist to be intimidated by your partner?"

"Oh God, Anna." Waleed collapsed onto the couch, now utterly fatigued. "Please don't use that word 'partner'. It completely desexualises the relationship."

"Exactly! *Precisely!* You don't even know the language. You are so intimidated that you can't even read your *partner's* thesis because yours is sitting in a scrappy effortless pile in the study. I wasn't even allowed to talk about how it was going for six months because it was such a tough process for *you*."

"I thought you were being nice. Being sensitive." Waleed rearranged his body into tight angles.

"It wasn't *sensitive*. It was about swallowing my needs to protect your fragile ego."

"Writing a thesis is hard work, it's stressful—"

"I *know* writing a thesis is hard. I've just done one, *remember*? I had to change departments half way through for a host of reasons you were and probably still are supremely uninterested in."

"I thought you were handling shit."

"I didn't *sleep* for three weeks. I was completely freaked by everything. And all you could say was, 'Ja. Rosa Luxemburg. That's not a bad idea.'"

Waleed knew in his gut that this accusation was fundamentally unfair, he just couldn't for the moment remember why. Then, providentially, his eyes wandered over to a scrap of paper that bore a telephone number that Fozia had acquired for him. He seized the paper and waved it about victoriously. "*I* introduced you to Nazeem Desai. I organised that whole contact".

"That cost you nothing." Anna's face, now cut at hard gradients, was a map of her insides. *Winter on the Russian Urals*, Waleed thought, *could not be colder*.

"Fuck, Anna. I'm really sorry you've been nurturing this acrimony."

"Okay." She turned from her bag to look at him directly for the first time in several minutes. "What is the title of my thesis?"

"Oh, come on." Waleed tried to envision the pile of papers that had been shyly laid out on his desk all those months ago. He got as far as "submitted by Anna Catherine Mitchell for the completion of an MA in History."

"I'm waiting. The title. If not the title, what's it about?"

"Luxemburg and the Unity Movement," Waleed gabbled. "You're being absurd."

"Even my *mother* knows that much. I would bet that even *your* mother knows that. Tell me something else. Tell me how the hundreds of hours of backbreaking archival work actually mean something."

"That's ridiculous, Anna. I can't bequeath meaning to your work. You're asking me to solve a universal struggle around production—"

"No. I'm asking for facts. Specifics. What have I been doing?"

Waleed flung an irritated hand in the air. "I feel like I'm being tested. *Me*, miss! Pick me! *I* know the answer!"

"I can tell you everything about your thesis and it's not even written yet. I can tell you which authors, which *books* you think are central, fundamental. Which theorists are your lodestars ... I can tell you why you think you're stuck on Chapter Three and where you think the whole argument falls apart."

"Well, maybe you're better at that sort of thing than me."

"Better at what? At being in a relationship?"

Waleed suddenly froze as a terrifying thought occurred to him. He knew with horrible certainty what this was all really about. Everything locked into place with terrible clarity. "Are you having an affair?"

"What?"

"Oh, my God. Are you and Ben together?"

"Who?"

"Ben. From the English Department. Velvet jacket."

Anna allowed for a long silence, letting Waleed's accusation hang and sway between them. "I honestly don't know what to say to you."

"Why?"

"*Ben*? After what happened at the party?"

"I forgot about that. I take it back."

"You can't take it back."

"I can. I didn't mean it."

"So you just randomly chose some white racist to lump me with, and you accuse me of having an affair with him?"

"I wasn't thinking about that at all. I remembered that you knew each other. I just reached for something, okay? Not everything means something."

"You're amazing."

"Thank you." Waleed grinned when he said this, hoping perhaps to tempt her, just a little, away from the quagmire they had made for themselves. For all his self-styling as a feminist and all his experimentations with radical lifestyle choices, there were old-fashioned currents and stories that ran through Waleed's relationships. He took pleasure in being exclusive, in being proprietorial. He demanded monogamy though he didn't necessarily offer fidelity in return. There had been, he reminded himself now, other women, but they had been secret and only at the beginning, and anyway, there was no reason to go into all that now. He was intensely jealous of Anna's former boyfriends and on the rare occasions when they did bump into her exes he offered them thin scowls and barely disguised contempt. When he asked her about the affair with Ben – *with anyone* – he'd felt as if he were reaching into his own chest, pulling out his heart and stamping on it.

In a faraway voice, Anna was saying "I'm just so *tired*, Waleed, and I'm leaving because I find it impossible to say 'no' to you about anything and that's not a great place to be for anyone."

"If you want to blame a third person, blame your mother."

"Oh *this* again!"

As if on cue, Megan's car pulled up and she hooted to let Anna know she was outside and waiting. Anna hoisted the tote onto her shoulders, picked up one of the boxes and inclined her neck towards the other two. "Are you going to help me?"

Waleed's eyes were fixed on the floor, he was unable to look up. "I don't want you to go." But Anna was already several feet away, near the front door. He could hear her speaking to Megan.

"Jesus. He can't even help you with the boxes? *I'll* do it!"

But Anna stopped her, asking her friend to wait in the car. Waleed allowed himself the wild hope that this evidence of surviving loyalty, of protectiveness around their privacy, meant things were not actually over.

When Anna walked back into the lounge Waleed was crying quite openly, something he had only let her see him do twice before, and both those times, like this one, invited her into an intimacy that rivalled sex. Those two other occasions were now present in the room; the first night a weeping, drunken confession in which he had told her about Firoze. The second, the eight year anniversary of his father's death, a day when he had moved through everything in a foggy slowness and she had not known the reason until he mentioned, as casually as he could, that he was going to the graveyard. They had been together for two years, two years of countless meals and songs and talks and sex, and if either was asked to pick a few memories from those times, those two would be among them.

Waleed got up and placed both his hands over one of the boxes, weighing it down, making it impossible for her to lift. "Please don't go," he said.

"I have to. Megan's waiting."

"*Please*, An."

"Waleed, you want someone who is going to run after you and tell you you're wonderful and read everything you write and put up with your moods and be a conduit for all kinds of anger that's got nothing to do with me, and I just can't do that anymore. You keep me on some kind of emotional diet. I never feel full. And I'm so tired."

"An."

"No. Listen. This now, this focus from you is great, but it's wafer thin. Smoke thin. It could disappear in a few days. And then I'll have to go back to being mostly unnoticed."

"Anna!" A voice, full of awkward apologies, floated up from the gate and down the hallway. "I'm really sorry to interrupt, but I have to be in town in, like, ten minutes."

Waleed responded to the call by placing his forehead against Anna's. He closed his eyes and willed her to do the same. He put one hand behind her neck and reached his fingers into her hair, cradling her head. He repeated his earlier request, *stay*, he promised to read her thesis, to do better, to be better. He covered her eyes in kisses. He told her that the last hour had been nothing, *nothing* compared to what he felt, that the packed bags, the traded insults, the crude wrangling, all that could be undone. He asked of her what everyone asks in those terrible moments of being left, of being cast out, he asked her for just one more night. In response, she reached up and placed her hands over his. She moved them away from her head and placed them at his sides. Waleed offered no resistance: he had grown dazed with disbelief. He watched her gather up her things, making one, two, three trips up and down the thin, dark passage until eventually she slipped out the door into the blinding, bright light of day.

17

Thursday, 21 October 1993

Waleed had been nursing the same beer and the same dilemma for half an hour. He and Rashaad were sitting in the Heidelberg Tavern in Observatory, just a few short streets from Waleed's house. Every once in a while, cod-like, Waleed would open his mouth as if he was about to say something, only to shut it and wave a hand, dismissing his unspoken thoughts. Rashaad in turn stared off into space, focused on the cornered angles of the ugly bar, shifting his eyes every once in a while to settle on a stranger, never on his friend.

Waleed felt sorry for Rashaad. Dammit, this was a shitty predicament, no mistake. But he was also thinking back wistfully to the happy beer-padded joy of the previous hour, before this bombshell had been dropped.

They had spent the better part of the afternoon shooting some pool, trading a few new national conspiracy theories and then burrowed into one of the dark booths ready to embrace a cozy chat. Once they sat down, Rashaad seemed to grow fidgety, subdued, distracted. He nodded and said "Cheers" when he needed to, but there was something scratchy, something panicked about him. And then, in the midst of Waleed complaining about one of his students, he burst forth with an announcement. He was in love. "Colonised by love, ma broe. Subsumed if you will. Made *abject*, ek sê."

Waleed always responded to these kinds of declarations (of love, marriage or children) with a poet's heart. He would both thrill at the idea that someone he cared about could be touched by such profound joy and be a little jealous, not of the person behind the love or the birth or the union, but of the depth, the intensity of feeling that it had engendered. He had a simple equation: the more experience, the more feeling, the more writing.

He had raised his glass to Rashaad and wished him well.

"It's not that simple," Rashaad cried out, drawing the amused attention of two drunks at the bar. "This is kak serious, ma broe. I don't know if we can be together."

"Measured, as always."

Rashaad stood up abruptly.

"Hey, don't go, I was just joking."

"I'm not *going*, fool. I need another drink before I tell you. You want another Heini?"

Waleed nodded. While Rashaad was at the bar, he began to peel back the white label from the green bottle in thin serrated strips. Rashaad's girlfriend, Melanie, was nice enough. He couldn't imagine what the big deal was. Not that he knew her all that well. She had gone to a private school in Durban and seemed to know no one in the Cape their age, though her parents were from here. But she was sweet. Anna liked her. Maybe, he thought, it's about me? And here Waleed had a thought that made him colour a little shamefully after he learned the truth. *Maybe she's in love with me?* It wouldn't be the first time this had happened with a friend. It would certainly explain Rashaad's weird displacement activities throughout the afternoon. He thought carefully over his interactions with Melanie. They hadn't really said very much to each other, but could she be one of those women who loved him from afar? She was an electrical engineering student. Conversation was always a little lopsided. She made a huge effort to be interested in his writing – *Aha!* – but he could only reciprocate for a short amount of time. He didn't really understand the fundamentals of electricity (lights on, lights off) so their chats would usually fizzle out into cries for more drinks.

Rashaad ambled back to the table, beers in hand, shoulders rounded. Waleed in turn squared his; he would face the confession like a man.

"Ready?' he asked, his voice full of caring encouragement.

Rashaad squinted at him. "So last week, I go to her parents' house—"

"*Ja?*"

"And they live in Rondebosch East."

"Oh. Rondebosch *East*." Waleed was smirking now. So that was the problem. Rondebosch East people. Not *Crawford*, never calling it Crawford. Wannabe whitey parents. So it was time to eviscerate the genteel sensibilities of aspirational coloured families.

"Ja, man, Rondebosch East – that's the whole point of what I am saying."

"But, Rashaad, be fair—"

"Fuck it, man! Can you stop interrupting me?"

"Yes. *Okay*. Sorry."

"So we go there – to *Rondebosch East*," Rashaad almost snarls when he says it, "we go there and the house is really in the borderlands, man. Like smack bang in the middle of the two neighbourhoods. And it's this fuck-off house. *Huge*. With a massive garden and a pool. And I think it's all a little weird because Mel told me that her dad was a schoolteacher and her mom is some stay-at-home church wife or something. And I was already *mentally* preparing myself for some anti-Muslim onslaught from the mother—"

"Inevitably." Waleed shook his head, repulsed by this stranger's prejudice, and at the same time an image of Anna excitedly unpacking her purchases of scarves and spices from the Plaza rose in his mind.

"So I go in, and I meet them, and they're, you know, I mean, they are *okay*. No, that's a lie. They were fucking *awful*. The mother starts to talk about her garden and her porcelain figurines in these kak strangled tones, it's like she thinks if she pitches her voice higher she will sound more white, and we all know what Mel sounds like."

"Hey, *hey*, no judgement." Waleed still felt edgy when people mentioned private schools or women with white accents.

Rashaad pushed on, not acknowledging Waleed's interjection.

"We sit down, she's prepared this whole tea, with, like, sandwiches and then the father walks in. And he's all, like, fuck, man, jocular. He's got this neat suit on and he's got this coloured schoolteacher vibe, you know, that posturing combined with anxiety?"

"I know it well."

"But there's something else that I can't put my finger on and then, Mel says his name. She introduces us and all these things just click into place. And when she says it, she sort of looks at me, like she's pleading with me to understand and he reaches out and I take his hand and I shake it."

"You *killing* me, man. Who was it?"

Rashaad, who has been speaking rapid fire, suddenly stopped and looked away.

"It was Spielman. Oscar Spielman."

Waleed allowed himself a few moments to search for his voice.

"You're not serious?"

"As a heart attack." Rashaad stopped, recalling Waleed's father's cardiac arrest and felt immediately apologetic. "Sorry, bra, I didn't mean—"

"Never mind that." Waleed flipped the comment and the apology away. "Holy fuck. What are you going to do?"

"I don't *know*." Rashaad spoke as if all the talk had gone out of him. Waleed reached out and gave his oldest friend's hand a sympathetic squeeze.

"Does he know about us? That we were some of those kids?"

"Not yet, but I mean he must think chances are."

"Well," said Waleed finally, "you're not in love with *him*. His daughter is not him."

"Semantics." Rashaad had to breathe through the beginnings of his tears. He had always been the most emotional of the four of them. "How am I going to face Georgie? Or," he seemed to gear himself up, "Yusuf?"

"Who cares what they think? You worried about Georgie? Bra is *chill*, man. Nothing moves him except a plate of food."

"And Yusuf? That man is the reason he spent that first month in solitary."

"That's not, strictly speaking, Spielman's fault."

"Bullshit." Rashaad was indignant now. "He gave the order for them to be there. Don't try and sugar-coat this, Waleed, just for me."

"Ja, no, I understand. But what I am saying is that Spielman is not responsible for Yusuf's hearing." Waleed heard himself create a distance from his own oft-used logic; it's amazing, he thought, what love can make us qualify. Of *course* it was Spielman's fault. Of *course* he was culpable. From the lowly cop to his commander, to Spielman, to the prime minister, it was an unbroken chain of cruel responsibility.

Waleed found himself saying the unexpected. "Ja, well with family, man, with *family*, there is nothing to be done. You don't choose them, and sometimes they don't choose you." He grew maudlin very suddenly.

Rashaad pulled out a cigarette and asked, "How are they? Are things better yet?"

Waleed shook his head. Though he had raised it, he was still not really equipped to talk about it. He had been in isolation for months and months. Fozia shared Adam's wrath about his memorial behaviour and seemed, like Anna, suddenly weary of him. The fight after the memorial had somehow made him responsible for everything; it was his fault the girls had been there, his fault that his brother had been anxious, his fault that the gathering had turned ugly. At first he had been hurt by it all. He had, after all, been the one who for so many years had determined his relationship with them. He was used to swanning into Adam's house and being (pleasantly, he admitted now) swamped by enthusiastic women who wanted to see him, who longed to see him. He was used to turning up at his mother's when he needed pampering, when the piles of clothes and crockery became too much and he longed for the ordered domesticity of his childhood. Those two homes were just as important when he was not using them as when he was. They were always at the back of his mind, like the birth city of a man who is perpetually travelling, a place to return to if he needed its sounds and stories. So when the gates of that city were drawn against him and the doors of the two houses slammed shut and, unlike all the other times, no one was peering from the window hoping he would come back or knock harder, he was genuinely hurt. Initially his hurt took the shape of rage; he didn't care if they never spoke to him again, they were the worst kind of bourgeoisie, they never really got along anyway, he always felt uneasy around their compromises, their inconsistencies. Fuck them. He wasn't going to give an inch.

But after the rage had come regret. He missed them. It was an uncomfortable place to sit; it made him feel fleshy and vulnerable. And still, maybe more frighteningly, there had been no word from Anna. He had called just once, hanging up before she answered. She might not even have been home at the time.

"Anyway," Rashaad drained the last of his bottle, "there's only one thing to be done."

"What's that?" Waleed spoke carefully.

"Have to end it, don't I?"

It was a peculiar thing to say, half statement, half question, delivered with an almost hostile air, as though he was responding to an ultimatum Waleed had offered him.

"Yoh."

"What?" Rashaad jerked his head up at Waleed's response. "What kind of an answer is that?"

"I don't know what else you want me to say. I don't think you should end things because her father is Oscar Spielman." Waleed let out a chuckle as he said the last five words of the sentence, five words that would have damned anyone out of his life less than a year ago.

"You can't even say his name without laughing, boet," said Rashaad reproachfully.

"That's because I am thinking of his nickname," lied Waleed.

"Pielman," they murmured simultaneously and clinked bottles.

"Listen, bra, do you love her?"

Here Rashaad began to groan and settle his head in his hands. "Ahhhggg." Gradually he let his face emerge from where it was hidden beneath his hands. "I'm just picturing it. Having to listen to that man talk about how he was 'doing his bit from the inside.'"

Waleed drew out his pouch of Drum, pinched and worked at separating the damp strands of tobacco and then re-moulding them into a thin caterpillar that he deposited into the cocoon of the paper and filter.

"So," said Rashaad with a sudden grin, "what's up with you and these white kinders?"

"Not your finest moment of deflection, Rashaad."

"No, but seriously, ma broe. You always chasing the white girls. What's the story with that?"

"I went out with Kamiela for months!"

"Crazy Kami? With the—" he molded two orbs on his chest, "that was in Standard Six!"

"Still."

"Are they different? White girls?"

"I'm not answering that. That question is seven different kinds of fucked up. You've jolled with plenty of white girls and this is not an anthropology class."

"You the professor, ma broe. With a doctorate in white girls."

"Why you gotta lash out like that? Especially now? You cold, bra."

"Sorry. I need to take a piss."

Waleed watched his friend walk away and wondered how Yusuf would react. He found himself protectively rehearsing his defence of their friend's choice. Because Waleed saw in Rashaad what was worth protecting, worth saving. It wasn't just their friendship, it was the idea of it, the length of it, the time they had spent, the knowingness of it. There were fewer guarantees in long friendship than he had initially thought. The shared hysterics and shared flats of our twenties do not promise a lifelong commitment to interest or loyalty. Instead, the suffocating, compensatory closeness of those years, when friends were "one's family of choice" – a useless phrase that understands nothing of friendship or family – those years could make a lasting friendship impossible. Waleed felt something travel between his stomach and his chest, something he recognised as love, a word that neither man would speak, but flowed now and always, between them both.

Waleed paid the bill and suggested that they leave, it was getting late and they had people to meet, Melanie included.

They were walking from the cool gloomy wood interior of the bar into a hot afternoon, both men slightly but pleasantly unsteady, when Rashaad turned to Waleed and said, "I just wish I could stop being so fucking angry all the time."

"About?"

"Everything. The way it sits in you, this tightness, always. Listening for what someone's going to say, worrying about what's going to come out of their mouth, walking down the street, seeing how fucked everything is. Nothing is ever easy here, it's never neutral, a person can't even buy petrol without being in a panic about how the bra who's filling your car is going to eat tonight. If I have to take one more photograph of a starving child ... sometimes I just want to stop looking."

Waleed glanced around, knowing that before long the South Africa of Rashaad's description would present itself. The country did not disappoint; across the street a homeless woman shuffled along the pavement begging in a voice ragged with mania and meth.

"Why would you ever want to stop being angry about that stuff?" he asked Rashaad.

"Because it's exhausting."

Waleed offered his friend a non-committal smile, and the two men began to walk back to his place in a companionable silence. He didn't tell Rashaad that he hoped never to stop being angry, not because he wanted to live in a state of perpetual rage, but because the anger was a way of remembering.

18

SATURDAY, 30 OCTOBER 1993

Alia stood waiting at a bus stop, the same bus stop that, unbeknown to her, had first shaped her uncle's political consciousness, the same bus stop that had made her father swear he would buy a car the moment he could, anything to avoid the protracted humiliation of waiting and then being told *no*. Except it was no longer a bus stop. It had become something else. Something a little more cavalier, a little less regulated by schedules and passenger capacity. It was now a place from which to catch a taxi.

It was an early Saturday afternoon and her mind mapped out the route from the stop in Observatory to the one on Lower Main Road and from there to Wrench Road. She tried to recall her trips there with her parents, remembering that Waleed's home had a weather-worn wooden gate and a fig tree that dominated the front yard. It was a surprise visit, an ambush. She was going because there were words to be had between her and her uncle. Things had gone horribly wrong after Hani's funeral and she felt a responsibility to put everything right. She saw now that she had caused everyone a great deal of pain. She had infuriated her father, hurt Zarina's feelings, and possibly ruined things between her and Nick. She had engendered a rift between Waleed and Adam and, by extension, Waleed and Fozia. Every crosscurrent of this feud, she decided, circled back to her. She had heard from her grandmother just last week that Anna and Waleed had broken up and she wondered if this, too, was her fault, if the stress of this latest family fight had proved too much for Waleed and the relationship. When Fozia had told her about the break-up she had done so matter-of-factly. And this had surprised Alia; she had expected her grandmother to evince nothing but untrammelled glee, but the older woman had announced the news as though it was something she had been expecting for a while, as though she knew all possible outcomes for her family, and it was her lot in life to watch them fumble towards their fates.

Alia shifted the weight in her Karrimor. She had raided the fridge and packed the majority of last night's leftovers. She knew that this, along with any knowledge of the actual visit, would get her into trouble; Zarina had intended the leftover frikkadels for Saturday night sandwiches, and her father offered only a silent rage-filled profile at the mere mention of Waleed's name.

She didn't want to jeopardise the fragile peace that had taken up residence in the house for the last few weeks. The Dawoods had an almost carnivalesque response to grand family feuds. After the explosion, a certain calm would descend, a curious tranquillity would follow the ecstasies of an argument and a sense of normality would reign.

The taxi eventually pulled up in a cacophony of loosely jangling hubcaps, aggressively high-pitched announcements of "Wooooodstock, Mowbraaaayyyyy Kaaaaaap!" and the annoyingly exuberant optimism of a radio DJ to whom all Saturdays were occasions for ceaseless celebration. Alia alone had been waiting at this particular stop and she felt a sense of odd elevation, of singular responsibility, when the vehicle stopped just for her. Still, she peered uncertainly into the already overcrowded kombi, hesitating beneath the questioning gaze of the driver before actually clambering in.

This was only her second, possibly third journey in a taxi, certainly her first by herself. The vehicle's interior confirmed all of Adam's worst accusations and some of his more outraged suspicions. The over-packed seats sagged and Alia settled into the only available seat, just behind the driver.

Someone tapped her on the shoulder. She turned around, surprised to see a forty-something-year-old woman, her head wrapped in a cerise scarf trimmed with a matching crocheted border, holding out a cluster of coins between scrubbed-clean factory fingers. Alia smiled and looked at her uncomprehendingly. The woman thrust the coins towards her. Instinctively Alia took the money and faced forward but then turned again, saying rather plaintively, "What do you want me to do with this?"

But the woman had turned round and was collecting more money from the other passengers. "Betaal daar. Betaal daar," she was saying. Money travelled from the back of the taxi to the front, accompanied with a shouted command to receive change. Alia began to realise with mounting dread that for some reason all this cash was making its way, inexorably, towards her. Like those around her, she cupped her hands alms-like to receive the offerings, but realising that there was no one ahead of her to pass it on to, gazed out at the other passengers, bewildered, panicked, making a silent plea for their help. The driver swivelled his neck to look at her, his eyes off the traffic for several long and potentially critical moments, and bellowed out, "What you waiting for? Count out the fares there!"

But Alia was useless at even basic math. She was also bad at performing under pressure and this particular situation conjured a nightmarish merging of both shortcomings. She looked down at her now slightly quivering hands, terrified, until the woman who had started this *whole fucking thing* touched her arm encouragingly, saying, "Come now. Count there. It's ma' good for schoolchildren. You must practise."

"Um. I don't know how much everyone is supposed to pay." Alia hoped the practicality of this would exonerate her (it usually worked with her parents) but the older woman stared at her with a mixture of disdain and disbelief. Her announcement prompted a judging silence in the kombi broken only by the maniacally happy radio DJ. She continued to hold the coins, feeling her hands grow sweaty with stress. She was rescued eventually (humiliatingly) by a girl, who couldn't have been older than twelve, who grabbed the money and let her nimble fingers do the work of a calculator. Alia, suitably shamed, looked out the window and prayed to the gods of disappearance to perform their magic.

The taxi returned to a generalised discussion, and Alia began to feel soothed. They were hurtling along Woodstock Main Road and, with a bit of luck, she could remain inconspicuous for the rest of the trip.

"Driver! Someone didn't pay! Driver!" It was the twelve-year-old accountant, fresh from tallying up the money, her voice ringing clear and true through the taxi and over the radio. Immediately everyone began to mount their own defences, declaring their innocence with such hyperbolic vigour that one would swear that they had each been placed in the dock and that all potential sentences carried the threat of a hanging.

"It wasn't me, driver!"

"I gave my money to the lady in front!"

"I passed mine on to the toppie next to me!"

"It wasn't me, driver!"

"Ek het betaal! Iemand vat kans!"

Mercifully, the driver kept his eyes on the road and calmly asked the girl to recalculate. She obliged and then went one step further by conducting a headcount. She went on to dazzle everyone with her say-it-out-loud times-table skills and the entire taxi broke out into spontaneous applause.

The child ended her recount and announced in a slightly hysterical voice – *Had any twelve-year-old girl before her wielded so much power?* – that they were *still* one fare short. The driver slammed his foot on the brake, pulled over and announced with absolute finality, "We are not going anywhere until everyone has paid."

Cue fury from the passengers: *They had places to go! People to meet! They were already late! Who would do such a thing?* Alia wondered if all taxi rides were this intensely filled with drama. She glanced down at her watch and joined the shared hope that they wouldn't be long. She knew that Waleed usually stayed in on a Saturday, at least until mid-afternoon, and she didn't want to miss him. Around her swirled the others' anger. Everyone was announcing their hatred of the person who had not paid, everyone had been transformed into a suspect, and everyone agreed the driver was indulging in a fascist form of collective punishment. Alia, even given this opportunity to lend her voice to theirs, remained instead committed to out-the-window staring. It was only then when she realised with a dull thud of dread that in fact it was she who had not paid. In the bustle of being handed the money and the guilty dislike of the younger girl, she had somehow forgotten to contribute her two rand. She sat very still, in the clutches of terror. Her armpits flooded, creating two blurry carnation-shaped marks, a few shades darker than her fitted green top: she did not know whether to confess or remain silent. The mood in the car had turned ugly. The driver was still refusing to budge. Alia realised that she had two options: she could speak up and at least entertain the possibility of getting to her uncle in the next half an hour, or she could spend the rest of her life in this minibus, live out her days with these other fifteen people, all of them bound together by fate, money and the inexorable will of the driver.

"I think it's maybe my fault." She decided to whisper this to the woman who had first given her the money. She thought perhaps she could appeal to her motherly instincts.

"Was it you who didn't pay? My word!" The woman's booming voice coupled with her sense of outrage extinguished any hope Alia might have had about getting out of this with a minimum of fuss and focus. "Driver! Driver! It was *this* girl here! The one in front! It was *her* who didn't pay!"

From the back of the bus came a low whistle of disbelief, followed by the damning sentence. "It's now never the ones you think are going to try and pull a fast one like that."

Alia wondered if it was wise to at least try and mount a defence. "I didn't mean to—"

"They never do. They never do, my dear." This too, from the backbenches, an old-fashioned phrase, absurdly, from a woman in her early twenties, her hair ironed into obedience, a thin gold cross sitting at her throat.

"No." Alia called out to her. "You don't understand, I got confused—"

"Tell me another one! Driver, I hope next time you take a moment to look at the well-dressed ones."

"Man, I tell you. In this life it's now often the rich that do the stealing ... But blessed are the meek ..." Her proselytising drew appreciative and supportive sounds from the other passengers, even the Muslim ones.

But the driver had no interest in presiding over the moral dimensions of this case. He had his money; his taxi was full; all was right with the world. He started up the engine again and quickly, dangerously, rejoined the fast lane while Alia's basic character was roundly and thoroughly dissected, with a particular focus on the incongruity between the way in which she dressed and spoke and the way in which she behaved.

Stille water.
It's now always the sturvy ones.

When they reached the Observatory stop she limped off the taxi, exhausted and convinced that she'd actually aged several years. Although the majority of the vehicle's occupants had changed between the fare debacle and her final destination, a few of the core members remained, and with them the collective memory of her criminal behaviour. When she hopped off the still-running vehicle she held onto the illusion that she could somehow scrape together the tattered remains of her dignity by greeting the driver goodbye as politely as possible and turning to offer everyone else a small wave. Neither salutation was recognised or returned. One part of her mission was behind her, the next, the more difficult bit, still to come.

~

"What are you doing here?" Waleed's ability for unadulterated (and apparently unconscious) rudeness never ceased to astound her. He seldom said "hello" like a normal person and everyone just forgave him for it, shrugged it off like it was just his thing. If she ever acted like that her parents would flip the fuck out. Alia decided to stoop to his level. Perhaps it would be unexpectedly liberating, why bother with all the niceties if no one else did? The hard lesson of the taxi was still sitting inside her uncomfortably.

She wriggled the stiff little gate open and began to walk up the short path towards her uncle, who was unlocking the first of the three security gate keyholes.

"I'm here to see you," she answered, while waiting for him to master his own multiple safety precautions, and then with prickly vulnerability, "You said at the memorial to come by anytime, remember?"

Waleed did indeed remember. He had issued that invitation with a grandiosity that did not anticipate an actual acceptance. Yet here was the acceptance, standing on his stoep, looking up at him. The security gate was successfully opened and he stood to the side, determined somehow to rise to the occasion.

"Well, come in! Come in!"

He ushered Alia past him and pointed vaguely down the gloom of the wooden corridor, past the two rooms and directly towards the mouth of the living room, where every afternoon the sun made a sudden and localised appearance.

Alia walked ahead of him, glancing to her left into a bedroom. She wasn't sure why she looked, but felt there was something vaguely thrilling, something extraordinarily romantic about the idea of two people being together in it outside of the permission of marriage. There was, she thought now, a different kind of choice involved. It meant that people could, as Anna had done, just get up and go. It meant that every moment you were there was because you wanted to be there, not because you were being governed to stay.

"Do you want some coffee? I was just about to make some."

"I don't drink coffee."

"Why? You not allowed?" Two thoughts coursed through Waleed simultaneously: the first that he had somehow waded once again into possibly pissing his brother and sister-in-law off, the other was that this was probably one of their insane laws and rules.

"I just don't like the taste," Alia looked at him calmly as though she knew exactly what he'd been thinking, "and it makes me skittish."

Her uncle scratched round his fridge, angling himself in

the hopes of hiding the half-finished bottle of Chardonnay next to the milk.

"I've got some ginger beer." He held up the brown plastic bottle, swishing the remnants of the cooldrink around. "It might be a bit flat, though," he said a little doubtfully.

"I'll just have some water," said Alia, settling herself formally on the couch. She looked up at the poster in front of her. "Who's that?"

Waleed answered without looking up from the freezer where he was scrounging for ice. "James Baldwin. An American writer. You should read him. Actually, your father loves his work. Or he did. He's the one who first introduced me to him. Did you know that about your dad?"

"What?"

"That he loves to read ... anything he can get his hands on. He's not very discerning. But he's voracious."

Alia looked at Waleed, feeling a slim sense of outrage. *Of course she knew her father loved to read. What was Waleed thinking telling her this? She was the one who actually lived with the man.*

Waleed was slamming an ice-tray on the countertop. He seemed to have found a dozen ways of not looking directly at her since she arrived. She realised that the story about her father was really because Waleed found it easier to speak of Adam in the past tense than dig into the muck and difficulty of the present moment. She did what she could to meet him halfway. "Ja. I know."

Waleed handed Alia a glass of water, sat down opposite her and began to roll a cigarette. She made a study of her uncle. He looked terrible. His eyes were rimmed by sleeplessness, he was thinner than she had ever seen him, gaunt cheeks, a belt to hold up his jeans. His voice was deeper and hoarser than usual. She noticed the three overflowing ashtrays. *Was he living off his rollies? Should she ask for one?*

"How did you get down here?"

"Taxi."

Waleed stiffened slightly, and the next question came with all the hesitation that told the questioned that the expected answer was in no way desired. "Your parents know?"

"No."

Waleed snapped his pack of tobacco shut and leapt to his feet. "Right. Well. Allow me to escort you back from whence you came." He grabbed her by the arm and began to march her back down the corridor.

"What are you *doing*?" Alia squealed.

"I'm taking you home," announced Waleed, flinching at the easily reached decibel of her squeal and reaching for his jacket, all the while maintaining his grip on his niece as if she were a runaway who was about to make a dash for it. "I'm not going to go through another one of these things. You sneak off and I'm suddenly responsible. No way! This stops here."

"But that's why I'm *here*." Alia shrugged his hand off her elbow with unexpected force and began to walk back towards the lounge. "I'm here to sort everything out!"

"This is a full-on Fozia move."

"What's that supposed to mean?" Alia whipped her head back round at him, the gesture nothing more than an absolute confirmation of what he'd just said.

"Only that you're sticking your nose in things that don't concern you."

"Of course this concerns me! It's my fault." Alia perched herself on the edge of the low coffee table, shoulders rounded, a study of misery. Waleed propped himself up against the door frame. The girl's oscillating mood swings, now commanding, now despairing, were both exhilarating and exhausting. She moved her head deeper into her hands and her shoulders began, very slightly, to tremble.

Waleed read this with the care of a seismologist monitoring the onset of a quake. *What must he do if this child started crying?*

He gabbled a few easily reached responses, in equal parts truthful, comforting and unsettling. "It's not your fault, it's just the way things are. Anyway. Look. The point is I don't want to talk about any of it. Christ, I just want to be left alone." The last sentence was muttered towards his shoes.

Alia raised a tearless face towards Waleed. "You really don't like us, do you? You're really, really angry with us."

"I'm not!" He was getting crotchety and huffy now, an intimation of who he would be in his seventies, bushy-browed and perpetually annoyed.

"Mama said you and Anna broke up."

"Jesus! Is nothing in this life private?"

Alia continued relentlessly. "She didn't seem the least bit surprised."

"Well. Bully for her."

"Are you going to get back together?"

"What? No. I don't know … look … Why are you here?"

"I told you. I want to sort everything out."

Waleed was suddenly very tired, feeling himself strangely helpless in the face of the implacable will of a teenage girl. He sat looking at her, remembering himself in these feelings, that unshakeable, unconquerable belief that if we could all just sit down to talk, if we could get to a place where everyone feels heard and seen and understood, we could get to the bottom of things, smooth it all out, make it all work. He gave all these ponderings and his niece a rueful laugh. "That's not going to happen."

"Why?"

"Because it's not possible."

"Why?"

"Are you a toddler? How many 'whys' are you going to deploy?"

"I guess I take after you."

It was a playground retort, the last resort of the cornered. Behind the poor disguise of a sulky delivery sat Alia's hurt and Waleed felt a twinge of guilt. It was difficult with people at this age: so hard to work out what they were capable of digesting. One moment it was possible to trade verbal slings and arrows, the next they were out of their depth, paddling furiously to keep up with the adults, feigning a sophistication and knowledge they had not yet earned.

A quiet stole over the room and Waleed reflected that in this form the visit was actually quite nice. There was something lovely about having family just drop by like this, even if it was to effect an impossible reconciliation, even if it was fuelled by the relentless optimism of youthful passion.

Alia sipped her over-iced water, feeling that she should work out a way to fill the silence. Without Nasreen's presence she had lost some of what defined her behaviour around Waleed. She tried to remember now if she had ever actually been alone with him. When her older sister was about, she could relax, knowing that Nasreen was perpetually on the alert, alive to her misjudged statements, available to mitigate her inappropriate indiscretions. As a result Alia began, uncharacteristically, to bear towards the anecdotal. She started to tell Waleed about what had happened to her on the taxi, detailing individual responses, casting herself in a role that was self-deprecating enough to give the story a spine and movement. She delivered the last part deadpan and sparing (the image of her unanswered wave and greeting produced an especially merry laugh from Waleed), ending with,"The final discussion sort of examined the idea that it's often the rich who are the biggest crooks. 'Stille water,' they all kept saying, 'it's always the sturvy ones.'"

Waleed made her repeat the bit about the rich being thieves. It was the part he had enjoyed the most. And not just because at a fundamental level he believed it, but because it had only just occurred to him that there was an actual, if not fully formed, person sitting opposite him, and that, although he didn't give much credence to the idea that shared genes created psychic affinity, he was strangely delighted at the idea that here was someone, here was a family member, who maybe, just maybe, was developing the same sorts of ideas about the world that he himself had. After all, he reasoned, she had risked a lot to go to Hani's memorial. There must be something in that.

His own memory of that day and the terrible fight with Adam was governed mostly by his sense of outrage at being blamed for not safeguarding his nieces and by the pain and discomfort of his bruised rib. But he was recalling now some of the stuff of Alia's anger that afternoon. Something about needing to be kept informed and wanting to be a part of things …

"So will you call my dad? That's actually why I am here."

"I can't do that, Alia." Waleed felt a sense of contrition that surprised him. The girl had looked so hopeful that he had almost said yes just so that he didn't disappoint another woman in his life.

"I don't understand why you can't."

"It's complicated."

"It's not. It's actually really simple. You're brothers. So you should be talking." She sat back as if the beautiful simplicity of this was evident to anyone who would listen. "I could never fight with Nasreen like this."

This final statement hung like a challenge between them, and Waleed shook his head, his gesture, as always, preceding his words. "That's what you think." Waleed did not mean to sound cruel, but he felt this was really one subject on which he knew a little bit more; he had lived a little bit longer. How to explain to this child that of course he and Adam had had fights before. Awful, life-changing fights. Fights that had ended in scuffles and bruised egos and Fozia either shouting from the sidelines or landing her own smacks in an effort to separate them. But this kind of protracted silence had not happened since Firoze. Even now, as the boy's name floated to the surface of his thoughts, Waleed flinched as though the very sounds, soft Rumi-esque syllables, were razors scraping at an old sore. Could it be, he thought, that the two events were locked together? He and Adam had never spoken of the child. And they never would. But perhaps that was all part of it. All part of the fury and the silence. Once there had been only Adam in his parents' house. Fifteen. Almost a man by the time Waleed had been born. The first child, the one who had come quickly, with uncomplicated ease. His own birth, Waleed knew, had been full of worry, the ghosts of those two other unborn children keeping watch, animating Fozia's worst fears, forcing her out of bed to check compulsively on his breathing when he was fast asleep.

"I'm just saying, Nasreen and I would never do this," Alia said this with a sense of finality, of fervour. "We don't believe in being like that."

An uncle suddenly, he had the grace to let her hold tight to that belief. What good could it possibly do to tell her that a sibling relationship is an uncanny one, made up of different strengths of familiarity and strangeness, of love and rage? That knowing someone in that way, knowing their first versions of themselves, prompts not only the capacity for great love but also for unbelievable cruelty, that for now the fights that she had with Nasreen might be dreadful but they would always be resolved quickly, and not because they "would never do this" but because they still lived under the same roof. They *had* to sort things out. Once new homes were made, doors could be shut, telephones could be left unanswered. His niece was helping herself to more water, peering out into his garden.

"You know," she said, fastening the tap tightly to stop its dripping, and then, pointing inexplicably at his neighbour's palm tree, "you and Dad are no better than the Hassans."

"Who?"

"My mom's family. The ones who didn't speak to each other …"

"Oh, right. Well, hopefully our argument won't make the front pages."

Alia grinned. "Might not be the worst idea. Maybe it will get you talking."

"Alia, I appreciate what you've tried to do here. But it's really none of your business. It's also getting late. Let's get you back on a taxi. I'll take you as far as the Upper Cambridge stop."

"You don't have to come with me."

"I do. It's not a nice time to be on public transport by yourself."

"Okay," she shrugged, a response that masked her gratitude, "but before I forget …" she picked up her knapsack and began to unpack the foodstuffs. As she placed each offering on the kitchen countertop, she narrated its contents: *Frikkadels in squash, roast potatoes, carrots with jeera, tomato smoortjie.* She scratched, without permission, through Waleed's cupboards until she found dishes of his own to decant everything into. She washed and dried Zarina's Tupperware and then arranged the meal carefully onto a plate. Waleed watched her without a word. He realised, as she moved energetically around the kitchen with Zarina's purpose and Fozia's confidence, that he was tired, so tired, that the last few months without Anna, without his family, had been both full (days crammed with seeing friends, occasionally writing, nursing hangovers, pursuing compulsive flirtations) and empty (the rush of nothing, nothing really). But here was his niece. Here was Adam's daughter, with her story about the taxi, her obstinate belief that her own relationship with her sister was a mirror of his with his brother, here she was with food and love and talk and insistence.

She placed a steaming microwaved plate before him. He sat down, obeying her unspoken command, and ate with something approaching an appetite for the first time in weeks. As he finished, Alia reminded him that there was more in the fridge and began to make her preparations to leave. While she gathered up Zarina's Tupperware, he asked, "Were you and Nasreen ... you know ... *okay* after the memorial?"

"Why wouldn't we be? Nothing happened to us," said Alia, frowning at her knapsack.

As they left the house, Waleed was unusually careful with his niece, offering her a jacket to ward off the chill of early evening, pressing three books on her, and insisting on paying her fare in the taxi. Throughout the journey back he offered her wry smiles that told her he too was thinking about the madness of her earlier trip. They laughed together as one of the radio callers, an aged and frail-sounding woman, told a bemused DJ that she wanted to send a "shoutout" to her "girl Lasondra". Waleed glowered at a group of boys who were casting lascivious looks at Alia and felt an unexpected rage when he overheard snatches of what they were saying about her. She herself was impervious, but Waleed was surprised, uncertain even, as to what to do with this feeling of sudden, all-consuming protectiveness.

When they reached the stop close to her home he offered her a brief hug and realised that he would not mind if the jacket, the fare, the shared laughter, or the protective glares were relayed to Zarina and Adam.

When he returned to the empty quiet of his own home, he stood very still in his study for a long time, feeling the ache and mystery and companionship of all his books, and with that, the beginnings of the fragile, rare roiling that usually preceded the start of a story. But he surprised even himself when he sat down at his desk, and instead of reaching for his notebook, he placed his hand on the telephone, took a breath, and called Anna.

19

Tuesday, 7th December 1993

"Anna? It's Waleed. Again." Megan stood in the doorway to Anna's bedroom holding the portable phone between two fingers, the tentative grip a mark of disdain for the caller. Anna replied with a shake of her head, mouthed "no", and repeatedly jerked a thumb behind her to provide Megan with fodder for a lie. "She's not here, Waleed." Megan rolled her eyes for Anna's benefit. "Yeah, well, I thought she was, but she's not. I was wrong." Pause. "Well, we all make mistakes." Pause. "I guess I'm just being the bigger person, you know, admitting it."

Anna turned her head against a pillow to muffle a small, despondent laugh while Megan continued, "Sure, I'll tell her you called." A look of surprise, "I'm fine, thank you. Yeah. My work's going great." She pointed at the phone and flipped her hand palm up, making a charade of her disbelief. "How're *you*? Great. I'll tell her. I promise. I said I would, okay? *Okay*. You take care." Hanging up, she faced her roommate, "That's the fourth time this week. I don't mind being the keeper of the gates but you're going to have to speak to him sometime."

Anna shrugged, performing a cool detachment she did not feel. Leaving Waleed was, she had learned slowly, painfully, over the last few months, not actually about that big dramatic moment in his lounge. It was not about anything as easy and focused as the packing of boxes or emptying an underwear drawer. Rather, it rotated around the horrible and effortful process of not doing: of *not* calling him, of not taking his calls.

Anna lay back on the bed while Megan moved around the room: a small torpedo of purpose. It was exhausting just watching her. Lately it had been so much easier to sleep than to be in the world: to lie in bed for hours and hours and not stir, to leave her room to a clutter of messes, to shut curtains against light, to not eat but to smoke and smoke, to curl on her side and hug her knees to her chest, to not work on revising her thesis. Her parents had asked her to come home, her mother worrying for the first time that she was too thin, her father making a demonstrably restrained attempt not to say "I told you so," her brother turning up to visit, ostensibly to help put up new bookshelves.

SHE *had left him*, she argued with herself, *so why all this mourning? Why this cataclysmic grief?* She'd tried to explain it to Megan one night as they cooked and talked and Megan told her stories about growing up in Detroit and her factory mechanic father, his dread of the assembly lines, his class-stunted life, a life, Anna thought ruefully, not a million miles away from Waleed's, something he'd have realised if he'd ever bothered to have a conversation with the woman … Megan had asked her about Waleed, about apartheid, his family, and had listened, without judgement, when Anna had confessed that sometimes she didn't want to hear any more of it, that sometimes, even the listening was unbearable, endless.

Perhaps, Megan had offered cautiously, it wasn't *what* Waleed told her, but the *way* in which he told it. But Anna had shook her head, refusing this, knowing that for large chunks of their life together Waleed had stopped stories dead in his mouth, or dressed them up in comic rags to amuse her, that there had been whole parts of his past that he had hidden from her.

On insomnia-plagued nights, she told herself that she could have learned to live with and inside those stories, she would have found a way to meet them, offer to bandage him up, return him whole to himself. It was only much later when she realised that it wasn't the stories, it was the constant fluctuation between being showered with attention and then abruptly ignored, being loved with a totalising force and then treated with an arctic disregard. It was the knowledge that, at any moment, she could be made invisible: that terrible swing between being alive and dead.

And then, of course, there were the other women, the affairs both emotional and physical. Though this she only admitted to herself in the smallest, scarcest of whispers. She knew about them without proof or reason, following only the thinnest thread of intuition: not all the slammed doors and long absences could be about his mother or his past. But she couldn't think about that now, and besides, in place of that initial fury, the burst of proactive energy, was a deep and lingering longing for the man in all his forms.

When she had told Megan that she had been thinking about leaving Waleed, her housemate had looked just a few degrees shy of elated. "Relationships with narcissists," Megan had pronounced, "are best ended." Anna had puzzled over that word and its intentions. Did Megan mean narcissistic in the sense that Waleed couldn't see others? Megan had shifted uncomfortably in her seat and then crowded in to face Anna with an intensity that embarrassed her. "I mean narcissistic in the sense that" – here Megan paused to let the full weight of her inversion sink in and she began to separate the words as though she were taking her cues from a metronome – "He. Can't. See. Himself." She then had led Anna to the sagging couch and had offered her a highly convincing, very cogent reading of her relationship.

Waleed, she had told Anna, almost regretfully, was the kind

of man you had to love without expecting consistent reciprocation. His devotional energies were geared towards himself and his work, and that meant that she would always be second. Always. And it wasn't even entirely his fault: systemic patriarchy had fed him a looped myth that this was acceptable. "Who he was in the world," she had said, her brow furrowing with an apparent effort to remain careful, remain measured, "was not who he was in private. He could not always move ideas of equality from theory to practice." What she, Anna, needed to do, Megan counselled, was decide if this sort of life, a life when she would often only appear in hazy outline on Waleed's peripheral vision, was going to be enough. "Some women could manage it." Megan's shoulders had enacted an exaggerated cinematic shrug when she said this, a movement meant to offer Anna the solace that she would still like her, maybe even still respect her, if she decided to stay.

Anna had heard herself offering a string of predictable sentences: "He's not always like this. When we are alone ... And his MOTHER ... she's just Jocasta on speed." And even as she recited the easily reached-for script, she couldn't take her eyes from her unread thesis, which sat on the coffee table between her and Megan, a silent, reproachful reminder. It had been the rejection of said thesis, the thing she realised she had done in large part to get closer to him, to understand all his stories, that had hurt more than anything else.

Megan peered now into Anna's face, a puzzled look on her own, apparently repeating a question. "I said, do you want a cup of coffee or something? And then maybe get up? We can go for a walk?"

Anna nodded. With Megan gone, she turned on her side and stared at the thin undulations of the net curtains. Her window looked out onto their apartment block's long, corridor-like balconies: she could see her neighbours pass back and forth, the single mother with the two noisy boys, all three of them with the exaggerated, unblinking eyes of a Manga cartoon, the young couple at the start of their relationship – Anna loathed having to hear their excited chatter – the old woman who lived alone, the cautionary tale, confined to the horrible cliché of having only cats for company.

The doorbell rang and Anna sank further beneath the bedcovers: these days, when she wasn't sleeping, she was pretending to. She heard Megan answer it and speak for several minutes to a man: "Don't you want to come in," she heard her flat mate ask again and again. The murmur of voices continued and Anna, unable to keep a sustained focus on anything, lost interest and resettled on the pillow.

"Anna? You dressed yet?"

"I'm in bed."

Megan opened the door, "Waleed's here. Wants to know if you'll see him, but won't actually come in until he gets your go ahead. Says he trying to respect your boundaries."

"Oh, God."

"He's a few seconds away from Cusaking it, standing in a trench coat, blasting us with a stereo."

Anna began, reluctantly, to pull on her jeans and make a half-hearted search for her hairbrush. "Sometimes it frightens me that our pop culture references are almost identical. The reach of your country is terrifying."

"She says to come in!" Megan shouted towards the front door.

"Did I?" said Anna with only mild reproach. She was still on the bed, gathering up her hair – ratty and unbrushed – when Waleed appeared behind Megan.

"Hi."

"Hi."

"Bye." Megan waved a hand to indicate that she was leaving not only the doorway but also the apartment.

"How you?"

"Good. You?"

"I'm fine." Anna stood up, and though the day was warm and the room hot she pulled on a cardigan. She folded her jersey-clad arms beneath her breasts and waited.

Waleed, still in the doorway, still at the threshold of being welcomed in or cast out, scanned her unusually untidy room, his eyes settling on the reassuringly repetitive geometry of the parquet floor. "Were you out last night?" he asked eventually.

"No. Why?"

"Looks like you haven't gotten up yet."

"I don't see how that's any of your business."

"Oh, Jesus. I didn't mean—"

"Why are you even here?"

"You wouldn't take my calls."

"And apparently you can't take a hint. I just want to be left alone."

In answer, Waleed slipped his leather satchel from shoulder to floor and crouched down to retrieve something from it, while Anna, who had still not relinquished her stance, began to drum her left fingers against her right elbow. Waleed pulled two files from the satchel. He placed one file on Anna's desk – there was just a small space to do this, every bit of real estate was taken up with fresh and dirty laundry, strings of beaded necklaces, books, three deodorants, all only half-used – and held the other file up towards her in offering. "I came by because I've read it. Well, as much as I could find … the sections you left. I don't know if what I've got is properly up to date. But that's mostly what I've been doing for the last week."

Anna raised her arm to push back at her fringe, but she didn't take the folder.

"It's really good, An. I mean that. It's strong and cohesive … and this is only an early draft. I've made some notes, I don't know if they'll be helpful at all." He moved towards her slowly, cautiously, opening the file and taking out pages made bright and merry with dozens and dozens of Post-it notes. She took it from him and silently trailed a fanning finger over the coloured paper, creating a soft whirring. "Don't get freaked out by the Post-its, I know it looks like a lot, but they're not all suggestions, some of them are comments, just me saying, This is really good or I liked this. I'd love to read the final version."

Anna held the pages flat against her chest. "What's in the other folder?"

"My stories." He looked embarrassed.

"You finished?" Anna put her thesis down next to his work and traced a hand over the manila folder: she could not bring herself to congratulate him.

"I thought maybe you'd read them? If you had the time."

Anna felt a sense of wonder at the scene unfolding before her: not just because this was what she had longed and hoped, but because now that it was here, it didn't feel or taste like anything she had expected. There was no sense of triumph or mad joy, no whirlwind emotion, no desperate need to keep him in the room, no terrible desire to kick him out. Instead, there was Waleed, looking a little thinner and less aggrieved than usual, entirely readable and very human.

"Okay. I'll read them. I'd like to anyway."

"Thank you."

"Have you eaten?"

"No." He offered this along with a hopeful grin.

"There's some leftover pasta from last night."

They walked towards her galley kitchen, passing a small hallway table. On it, a collection of wonky blue-glazed ceramics: a vase with an indented middle, an ashtray with uneven resting places for cigarretes, a lopsided container with a pressed-in centre that could have been for anything, but in this case was filled with paperclips. In a flat otherwise sparsely furnished, it was impossible to pass them by without comment.

"Fucking hell. What are these?"

Anna felt slightly sheepish. "I made them."

He picked up the vase and turned it upside down as though searching for a signature that could disprove her claim. Anna knew that Waleed found it excruciating to witness these sorts of amateurish attempts at self-expression: the only thing worse than this sort of crafty-nonsense-as-product, he often said, was the new tide of cringing soul-baring poetry starting to take place at open mics all over the city. There had been several occasions when, together, they had excoriated any friend's or family member's attempts at any such endeavours: laughed, teased, been merciless, ruthless. *This person's macramé, that person's crocheting, this person's rhymes about their roots and routes.* That Anna had long had these sorts of pastimes had been kept secret from Waleed.

She took the vase from his hands and placed it with much more care than it warranted back on the table.

"They're incredibly ugly."

"I know. I made them after our break-up, so you're witnessing a relationship between form and content."

Waleed smiled and moved the vase slightly to the left, so that the more deformed of its bulges was hidden from immediate view. Anna walked ahead to the kitchen, not bothering to turn around when she asked if he wanted some salad as well as the pasta. These are the ways, he thought, in which she will mark and re-mark her disdain. Unseen by her, he leaned weakly against the wall trying to swallow past the myriad of feelings, mashed and jagged, that had gathered in his throat, stopping any number of things he wanted to be able to say. Anna, absorbed with opening a bag of lettuce and shaking its contents into a shallow wooden bowl, did not notice that her body, slack and tired for so many weeks, was moving easily, swiftly through the room, the thick dullness of the morning edging its way out.

Picking up the paperclip container, Waleed steeled himself and walked into the kitchen, saying, "This one's not so bad." He knew it was a fairly feeble attempt at subtext, that the gesture was anything but subtle or sophisticated, but that didn't stop him from being infinitely grateful that when Anna looked up from squeezing a lemon, instead of ridiculing him, she smiled and handed him cutlery, asked him to set places for them both at the kitchen table.

20

Friday, 31 December 1993

Fozia only pulled out photographs of the District, of her old life, when she needed to show her granddaughters where she believed they were from: she did it as an antidote to *that* school, as a way of reminding them that they were foreigners in that other world.

This is your father in his first Labarang Eid outfit. This is our whole family watching the Carnival. The Big Days, she would tell them, her mind a whirl of quick images and blurred memories, *the Christmas choirs, the nagtroepe, the Carnival, satin, two-tone everything, ghoema drum, dhoof, dhoof, dhoof, klopse, trellis balconies, pitchfork devil, shrieking children, laughing adults, steep hills of the BoKaap, skirts flying upwards, drum majorettes, drum roll, ghoema drum, dhoof, dhoof, dhoof, tafel, watermelon with a million seed eyes, pots of breyani, sweat smells, people smells, dagga smells.*

She looked for those old photographs now, telling herself that she was cleaning, tidying, that it was not at all an act of sentimentality, of longing. But the old envelope was not where she'd left it. *Waleed had probably taken them, that child, so full of love and anger, always scratching through the past.* If she went to his house one day, she decided, she'd probably find them all framed and hanging in the hallway, like some kind of altar to a life he barely remembered. She gave up looking. The pictures would only tell her a story she already knew: Tweede Nuwe Jaar in the District, standing on Adderley Street, watching the Carnival surge and heave and snake its way past them. Abe to Adam, pointing out the troepe, and the moffies and the Atja Americans with their crazy headdresses like tropical birds. Abe taking his son to meet the men dressed all in white, the workers from the bread factories who spent their days covered in a fine film of flour, smelling, like women, of yeast and comfort. Sometimes he would turn to his wife and say, "Let's leave before it gets too crazy," with a wary eye on the wild dancing and easy knifings, but she would walk through the crowds and twirl her skirts and laugh when Aapie the dwarf would climb on someone's shoulders and grab their hair. Fozia remembered how she had thought it was a big joke until Abe had told her that Aapie was a known murderer and that that was his move, to jump on you from a height, slit your throat, rob you of your weekly wages. But during the carnival, none of that mattered. On that day Aapie was not a killer, and they were all free, and life was good and full of music, and even though the air was sick with the smell of sweat and dagga and spilled brandy, the District didn't seem to stink as badly as usual.

And even as she thought this, she knew it was not true. She knew that what she had wanted back then, when it felt like they would live there forever, was the *option* to leave. That she'd found the noise and the filth and the constant nosiness of the neighbours unbearable, that she'd wanted to be able to visit for the Carnival. She'd wanted windless seasons of trees and land and space, the Kirstenbosch home of her girlhood, before they'd been moved from there too. But she kept the longing a secret, knowing its impossibility, knowing the law's indifference to her preference. She kept it from her husband, from the other girls in the factory. She hid it fiercely from her sons: there was no sense, *no kindness*, in letting them know that there was more to life than this, that it was all right, it was okay, to want other places, other people.

It was only when the removals came that she really began to love the District, only when it was taken apart brick by brick that she had wanted to stay, not move, just set herself on the steps of the stoep and not go anywhere. It was worse, she had thought furiously, helplessly at the time, for her boys. She sensed what was to come from Adam's teenage fury, from Waleed's incessant questions.

Not because it was such a loss, she told Abe as she packed up her kitchen, but because when you take something from someone when they are young, they don't remember it properly and suddenly it's a fairytale, suddenly it's Xanadu, suddenly there is a hole, there is an ache that they can't make sense of, there's this thing that will hold them back, or make them afraid to love, make them bound to the past, always looking over their shoulders, always trying to work out a way to patch it up, make it better; or worse: always making them look for the person who did it, putting them on a lifelong hunt for the perpetrator when she believed, then, as now, that there was no such thing. Not really. That if you try to hunt down the guilty party, you only end up tugging a thread that comes loose at the very beginning, and that no one ever really knew when the real beginning was anyway.

~

Alia lay splayed out on the floor in Nasreen's room while her sister deliberated between two New Year's Eve outfits: a long black dress with brass-studded clogs or a grey halter-neck top paired with jeans and clunky jewellery. The top had been brought into the room with great solemnity by

Alia who, at fourteen, was still not allowed out past eleven. Alia had decided to bear this purdah stoically: if forced to celebrate New Year's with her parents, she would ensure that at least her new top had a good night out.

The small room was hot, as though it had collected a year's worth of heat: Alia sat up and lined her spine against the cool of the wall.

"New Year's is always terrible," said Nasreen as she stepped in and out of the clogs, taking the measure of fashion over comfort. "It's this hideous pressure to have a good time. We just end up running from one criminally boring party to the next, desperate for the night to improve."

"More boring than staying home with the parents?"

"You win," Nasreen conceded and then, "though it could be worse. You could be hanging out with Mama."

"Mama's cool – she'd let me sneak one of her smokes. Anyway, it's fine, I don't really want to go anywhere anyway." Just a few weeks before, Nick had left: to be out in a crowd of people would only emphasise her loneliness. She had not gone to the airport with the crowd of forty-strong friends and relatives to see the family off.

"Mom said you got a letter?"

"Ja. His parents are thinking of coming here on holiday next year."

"I thought they left because it was so dangerous—"

"I know! I know!" Alia broke into a bitter laugh. "That's what I thought! If it's so *dangerous*," and here Nasreen chorused with her, "if it's so *dangerous*, why do they want to come here on holiday?"

"Standard expat bullshit." Nasreen shook her head, appalled and amused at the same time. "Top or dress?"

"Top. Allow me some presence on the scene."

~

Waleed always called Fozia a few hours before midnight on New Year's Eve, and by eight in the morning on New Year's Day. It was a ritual that Fozia had invented in his teenage years that meant he checked in with her before going to do God-knows-what-God-knows-where and that he told her he was safe and sound when God-knows-what God-knows-where was over. Long after his father died and well into his years of living alone, Waleed had kept up the phone calls. Like all parent–child rituals it was instigated delicately, threaded through with euphemisms that dulled the truth of its purpose and alluded only a little to the facts of his nocturnal movements ("Yes, Mama, a small gathering with friends. No, Mama, none of them drinks") and its promises ("Of course I'll be home by twelve. No, I'm not going to run around with any hooligans"). Waleed felt guilty about lying, but he played a relativist's game with himself that worked well and piqued his sense of fun: *I never said which "twelve" I would be home by. I never said who doesn't drink what.*

He had used these kinds of excuses during high school and while Fozia had raged against them, Abe had shrugged in weary resignation. He had given up trying to discipline Waleed years before and, also, perhaps, felt a grudging thrill at the boy's commitment to the pursuit of pleasure.

Waleed's call that evening had been more loaded than usual. The action was dutiful, even as he chafed against the wording: "We're just going to be in Obs tonight – we may go into town. Me and the boys. Ja, Ma, obviously Anna is going to come with us … she says hi by the way …" Anna, who had said no such thing, broke off in the middle of packing away Waleed's groceries to smile over at him. "Yes, she is standing here. Do you want to say hello? Well, suit yourself then. Okay. Bye. Happy Happy. I'll call you in the morning." Frustrated, Waleed returned the receiver to its cradle, just a degree short of slamming it, while Anna came up and stood behind him, her head resting between his shoulder blades, her strong thumbs massaging his neck.

~

"Why don't you give your brother a call?"

Anniversaries, birthdays, the advent of a New Year's, all these things drew out the reconciliatory part of Zarina. The couple were sitting on their balcony, watching the last hours of 1993 fade into the harbour. Adam drew a pair of binoculars up to his face and inspected a docking cruise ship with great care. "Why should I call him? Why doesn't he call me?"

"Well, you're older—"

"Precisely! Some respect would be nice."

"*Adam*—"

"Zina. Listen to me. He put my girls in danger. Again. Anything else, I could probably forgive. But not that. Okay?"

~

Fozia stood at her gate, her fingers trailing absently back and forth across the iron. The street was still full of children, but her loneliness, along with the evening, was about to fall. Perched on a rickety assortment of rusted wheels – rollerblades, skateboards, bicycles – they counted in unison: "On your marks ... On you marks ... nee, kyk hie, I'm calling it ... On you marks ..." then flung themselves down the road in a race towards the harbour. In the fading heat, on the last day of the year, they had stripped down to their shorts, and their young, brown, gangly limbs swung carelessly as they glided down the hill. Fozia watched them for a moment, remembering her sons playing a similar game in which Adam pulled at a wooden fruit crate affixed with wheels while Waleed sat in it, saluting the neighbours like a little emperor. The memory had all the trickery of nostalgia – longing, loss, ache – and Fozia folded her arms above her chest to steady herself. That memory, she was sure, was like all those photographs she couldn't find, a pretence, a stand-in for other moments that were not caught on camera: *It's not proof*, she told herself, *it's not proof that they were once close.*

The boys were beginning to make their way up the hill, preparing, once again, to descend it. She kept watch over them and suddenly saw herself through their eyes: an old woman in a doek and a house-dress standing at a gate, making inquisitive, interfering noises, worrying about other people's children, using their lives to cover the cracks and fault lines of her own. She took a sharp breath and turned to go back inside. She shut the door behind her.

Saturday, 1 January 1994

It was the day after the year before. At first Fozia had not understood the news item. It was as though her brain had stalled working to digest the first bits of information. *Bomb blast. Terrorist act. Heidelberg Tavern.* Her mind seemed to have made the decision that her heart could not handle the information and had simply stopped processing any of the details. As she watched the reporter on television stand in front of the cordoned-off area, the red and white tape making it look like a candy-ribboned gift, she tried to focus on the scraps of story as it unfolded. A woman, presumed twenty. Presumed dead. APLA maybe. AWB maybe. Fozia felt her breath begin to pan out into little shallow gasps. The Tavern was just a street away from her son's home. Wasn't this the place he meant, but never specified, when he said he was just going down the road?

Fozia knew that she should call Waleed, that he would answer and laugh down the phone and say that it was all fine, that he was *fine*, that he hadn't been there at all, that she was panicking for nothing – as usual. But there was something happening in her chest and she couldn't move. There was something heating up from the bottom of her lungs; an iron clasp had locked itself beneath her breasts and was squeezing the air from her. She swayed, reaching for the chair she knew was behind her, but missed it and her body began to fall about the room, hoping it could navigate a soft landing. Everything took on the mottled swirl of the front door's glass. Even the figures on the television and the voices that claimed that they "could not believe what had just happened," were tinny and distant. She reached towards her chest, hoping to unlock the iron belt, just a little, so that she could let some air travel between her mouth and lungs, but her arm froze in mid-air. She stumbled down the corridor, past a photograph of a young smiling Abe – *Where the bladdy hell are you when I need you!* – and managed to unlatch the front door and stand for a moment on her stoep before collapsing. As she had hoped, the street-racing boys saw her and rushed over, their shouts of worry drawing neighbours from stoeps and shaded bedrooms and gardens towards Fozia, now a crumpled floral heap on the welcome mat.

21

Saturday, 1 January 1994

"Goddamit, why won't this *bladdy* man answer his phone?" Zarina angled her neck to meet her shoulders, keeping the phone in place, leaving her hands free so that one could be placed on her jutting hip and the other could crook a finger at a red-eyed, tearful Alia, a shorthand request to be handed a pen. "It's just ringing and ringing."

"Maybe he's not there," said Alia, looking up at her mother through a film of tears, "maybe that's why."

"Of *course* he's there," snapped Zarina. "Where else would he be on New Year's morning? He's probably bladdy hung—" She stopped herself short, seeing her daughter's shock. "*Goddamit*. This means we'll have to go down there."

"Just try again." Alia reached into her pocket and drew out a crumpled soggy tissue. "Mom?" she began, her voice shivering a little.

"Mmm?" said Zarina, her fingers tapping out a redial. "Don't use that old tissue, Alia, here's a new one."

"Mom?"

"What?" Zarina frowned while she checked her dialled numbers against the information in her little maroon telephone book, muttering the digits out loud.

"Is Mama going to be okay?"

Zarina hesitated a fraction before hanging up and then

answering slowly, "I don't know, Alia. Come. Dad and Nasreen are waiting for us."

Zarina hurried Alia out the front door, touching her shoulder briefly, distractedly, a gesture closer to ushering than comfort.

Daughter and mother sat in the car on the first day of 1994, their eyes squinting against the deep blue of the late morning sky. Within minutes Zarina, who could trip about swiftly in her little car when occasion demanded it, had negotiated the tight streets of Woodstock and was speeding along the Main Road to Groote Schuur Hospital.

"I thought we were going to try Uncle Waleed first," said Alia.

"Fuck," murmured Zarina loudly and unusually, "I'm sorry." She was badly shaken. The news of Fozia's heart attack had ushered in worry, pity, anxiety, and, tumbling beneath and between, dread. She was frightened and prematurely heartbroken for Adam, concerned already about the deep grief lying in wait for him, awed by the thought that this time it would be collective, referential pain, and beyond that, she trembled at the genetic implications of both his parents suffering from serious cardiac problems.

Alia's tears were gathering momentum, falling through Zarina's tissue supply and onto her lap.

"I know you're upset, but try and get a hold of yourself. We'll be there any moment now and you'll see for yourself that she's okay."

Zarina was speaking to them both. She navigated the deserted roads of New Year's morning with a menacing speed, barely waiting for the traffic lights to change, flicking her indicator after turning, chasing through streets made emptier by the signs of last night's revelry. She came to a reluctant brake at a four-way stop notorious for accidents. To their left, a collection of homeless drunks, who had collapsed around the bottom of telephone poles in a heap of snoring and filth, were waking up as one to do battle over the dregs of a bottle. To their right, a group of street children, growing every day in hungry numbers. The children moved quickly to the front of the car to beg, their faces streaked white with traces of glue or snot. Zarina reached automatically for her purse, one hand on the wheel, and scratched around for a few coins, handing them to the child without a trace of optimism. The municipal trucks had begun to make their rounds, and just behind them the newspaper boys clambered onto poles to hang the first headline of 1994 in thick unfurling letters: BOMB BLAST KILLS FOUR. MASSACRE AT HEIDELBERG TAVERN.

"Mom," Alia said as Zarina turned into the hospital parking lot, her voice hoarse, "Mom," this time more urgently, "there was a bomb at that bar, the Heidelberg. Isn't that down the road from Uncle Waleed?"

"What?" said Zarina. She pulled up the handbrake, grabbed her purse, rummaged for a tissue while she pushed her sunglasses up on her head and pulled them again onto her face, anything not to meet her daughter's eye. "Now don't panic, Alia," she said, fighting to keep the shrillness from her own voice, trying to stop her mind connecting the violence of the headline with the endless unanswered ringing of her brother-in-law's phone. "Let's not get hysterical, okay? Let's not leap to any conclusions."

At the hospital, Alia trailed just a little behind Zarina, who was walking purposefully through the entrance with unconsciously squared shoulders, sandals clacking on old linoleum. Alia looked about her, taking in the sharp smell of disinfectant, the smell of effort without love, and remembered the last time she had been there, when her grandfather lay dying on a thin plastic mattress designed for a small child.

"Are you coming?" Zarina, already a few metres down the wide corridor, had turned impatiently to find her youngest child rooted in a vague trance.

Alia scuttled up to where her mother stood, pressing impatiently, repeatedly, pointlessly at the lift button as though continual pressure could speed up its arrival. "Now listen, Alia, I don't want you to get a fright when you see Mama, okay? She may seem a little different. Sometimes when people experience a big shock like this they need to rest for a long time, and sometimes they can't talk properly."

The lift arrived with the rattled thud of the outdated. Alia stepped inside it and turned to Zarina. "I know what happens when people have heart attacks. You acting as if I wasn't around for Papa's funeral."

Zarina tucked her hands under arms she had folded across her chest. "You were so small when that happened."

But Alia remembered. She remembered what it was like to have someone there and then, apparently, without warning, to lose them: to wake up one morning to a life that had all the signs of being yours, but with a deep gash in its centre as if someone had taken a long-nailed malignant hand and scratched through the delicate web of love and support that your family had taken generations to spin. She remembered what it was like to watch her father weep, to see him and Waleed collapse into each other's arms at the funeral, clinging as if they were lost at sea, each holding to keep the other from drowning, to prop him up on the crest of the wave, to give him another breath. She remembered how Fozia had not left the house for a month and how, overnight, she had become full of old woman smells. How for a year after Abe's death she had made unreasonable demands on everyone, had all but insisted that Adam move in with her and that for a long time all three, Fozia, Waleed and Adam, spoke about Papa as if he was still alive.

Daddy loves mince curry.
You father really takes care of that car.
Papa won't mind if you take his jacket.

It took years for them to move him from the present to the past tense.

Zarina and Alia reached the cardiac ward. The elevator doors opened and deposited them a few steps away from a sparse arrangement of waiting-room chairs and thick plastic flowers where Nasreen and Adam sat, one reading a torn magazine, the other staring ahead, tense jawed and wide-eyed. Behind them, unseen, came Waleed and Anna, charging down the corridor, out of breath and dishevelled, whatever mad revelry of the night before sitting like a blurry film over their persons. Zarina and Alia felt a mirrored relief: here was Waleed with all his limbs. *Breathing.* Adam and Nasreen had not seen the headline; all their energies were reserved for Fozia.

Adam leapt out of his chair and moved towards Waleed in a wordless re-enactment of their father's funeral. They stretched their arms towards each other and when they met, each reached for the other's back and began to pat and soothe it. Zarina stood watching them, her face without a trace of the indulgence that Alia expected to see.

"You see this," she remonstrated to a startled Anna, who had removed her velvet hat as though she had entered a church or a courtroom and had been offering the scene a tremulous, tearful smile. "This is just *typical*. This only happens in a crisis. Why they can't admit these feelings when things are calm is beyond me."

"Is she okay? Is she okay?" Waleed was asking Adam, still clinging to him. "I spoke to her last night, she sounded fine, I just can't believe this happened—"

"She's stable," said Adam, drawing reluctantly away from a full embrace with his brother, but keeping one arm wrapped tightly around his shoulders.

Alia went to stand beneath the vacant shoulder and leaned against her father. "Now don't forget," he went on with a kind of rouse-the-troops fervour, "we are at one of the absolute top heart places in the world," adding, because he drew comfort from any association with the famous, "Dr Barnard did his transplant here."

"Have you spoken to the doctor?" asked Zarina.

"Not yet, he said he'll come and find us. She's out of danger, we know that."

"Well, then." Zarina sat down and picked up a magazine.

"Should I go and pick up some coffee or something?" said a disembodied voice. It was Anna, standing awkwardly, hidden from view, just behind Waleed.

"From where?" answered Zarina sharply with misdirected impatience. "This isn't a private hospital. They don't have places for that here."

"I could go to the corner store? I mean, I *really* need some coffee."

"That would be great, Anna, thank you," said Adam, looking pointedly at his wife. "Perhaps later. Let's just wait and hear from the doctor."

Waleed turned to greet his nieces with kisses and long-held hugs, ushering them, too, into this rare and charged moment, where affection and vulnerability could flow freely between the Dawoods. He belatedly introduced them to Anna, taking care to mention that Nasreen was university-bound and that Alia, too, could not bear rugby. They all sat on the unyielding plastic chairs, with Waleed taking Anna's hand and pressing it to his lips in a display of affection that made his nieces blush.

When the doctor found them, he smiled broadly with the good news that Fozia's heart attack was not a heart attack at all, but an angina attack and an extremely rare form of it at that. Prinzmetal's angina. Apparently she had been very pleased to hear it was so rare, but less pleased to hear she would have to give up smoking and change her diet. The doctor laughed obligingly but then pulled back into professional seriousness.

Adam made a show of shaking the doctor's hand before the man went off on his next rounds and then dispatched Anna to get some much-needed coffee.

"I'll go with you," Nasreen offered. "You won't be able to carry everything."

"There's my girl," said Adam, kissing the top of Nasreen's head. "That's some smart thinking."

Nasreen accepted the kiss and the compliment with a very un-Nasreen-like smile, and called over to Alia, "You want to come with us?"

Alia shook her head. "I want to see Mama as soon as we allowed."

Her sister replied with a little shrug and turned to Zarina to ask for some change for the coffees.

Alia found a seat next to her father and listened as he and Waleed spoke in the charged excited voices of long-lost friends who have found each other at a school reunion.

"You should have heard her on the phone yesterday: 'You just tell Yusuf that I see his mother by Golden Acre all the time and if I hear of any funny business I will pass it right on to her.'"

Adam laughed appreciatively and continued to ask interested, focused questions about Waleed's friends. He heard about Rashaad's exhibition, and his new discovery about his girlfriend's family. ("Nothing wrong with that – not her fault, you people better not make her feel a thing about it.") He grasped Waleed's shoulder in warm congratulations when he found out that his thesis was nearly done – the one positive result of being ignored by everyone – and somehow found the generosity to ask about how his own writing was coming along. He insisted on a celebration when he heard that Anna had handed in her thesis and conveyed the news in a raised voice to Zarina, who replied, without looking up, that she knew, and that she and Anna had already had a celebratory tea at the Mount Nelson. Waleed chatted enthusiastically about everything and everyone; he warmed under the glow of Adam's attention, he felt invigorated by his mother's survival.

Alia watched and listened to the ease of their conversation, how they leaned in to one another, exchanged frequent touches and clasped hands, patted shoulders, how their grins remained fixed, their agreeing nods eager, as if there had never been a fight, had never been a terrible door-slamming event, never a cold, unforgiving silence. As if Waleed had simply been out of the country for the last seven months and this was their catch-up time, their precious chance to reconnect. Occasionally Adam would look up at his family as if to invite them towards the *wonderment*, the *funniness* of Waleed, as if his brother's gift for amusing storytelling were a talent that he had only just discovered and it would be churlish of him not to share it. He would turn to Alia and repeat Waleed's sentences, laughing heartily, rendering his youngest just one inhibited movement away from applauding. Adam even tried without success to rouse Zarina from her magazine, but she remained resolutely determined to read and reread an Afrikaans article on South African folk music.

Eventually, puzzled by her refusals to join in, Adam asked, "When did you become such a boeremusiek aficionado?"

"I'm not," came the terse reply, "but it's better than watching the two of you and your spectacular hypocrisy."

The two men looked at her, bewildered and hurt, in an alliance older than Adam's marriage.

"What do you mean?" said Waleed after a long pause.

"What I mean is that this is *insane*. You haven't spoken in seven months. Seven months! And now, because there is a crisis, you can talk and catch up and act like nothing happened? It's crazy."

"Why?" asked Waleed aggressively. Whatever it was that was flowing between him and his brother felt precious and possibly fragile. Some kind of peace had been brokered and a part of that peace was the fiction, at least for now, that the battle had never happened. For the first time in a long time, he thought of Zarina as an outsider.

"Zina, I don't see the problem here – this is a good thing. We're *talking*."

"You don't see the problem?"

"NO."

"Well, then I give up."

But by now, both men were intrigued. They began, as one voice, to ask her in a legalistic, hectoring tone, precisely, no *precisely*, what she meant. They dragged her fights with her own mother into the frame as evidence of her inconsistencies, they cited her warring family, the Hassans, as proof, and they both insisted, testified, that even in the darkest moments of this latest falling-out, they were both always assured of the other's love.

"Even when Adam told you never to come to our house again?"

Waleed flinched and Adam slammed his hands against his thighs. "Why do you have to go and bring that up? Jesus, Zina."

"Because it's *there*. It was said. And it's festered. I'm sorry you don't understand that."

"Mr Dawood?"

Both men looked up at the doctor who stood in the waiting room, clipboard in hand, and then grinned at each other as though the shared name was further evidence of their new closeness.

"Yes?" they answered, still each other's echo.

"You can see your mom now. She's been asking for you both."

"Can I go too?" asked Alia.

"I don't see why not," the doctor answered kindly.

They trooped after him into a ward with six beds, four of them occupied. Fozia was lying beneath a regulation floral sheet, her heart monitor registering a steady safe beat, grey hair peaking through a loose scarf. She offered them all a weak smile and submitted to a flurry of embraces and kisses.

Alia looked at her grandmother, absorbing her in fragments: arm punctured by a drip, eyes wide and unfocused, the hospital bed with its familiar function and unfamiliar steel bars.

"We didn't bring you any flowers," she said.

"Where's anyone supposed to get flowers this morning?" said Fozia.

The men shuffled their feet and Adam began to straighten Fozia's bedclothes and inspect her hospital chart as if he could decipher it.

"We so relieved you okay, Mommy," Waleed said ardently. "How you feeling?"

"I was so worried about you," Fozia said, not answering his question, and then, to her great surprise, began to cry. "I thought something happened to you … I saw the news … about that bar … by your house …"

"Oh, Mommy, I'm so sorry about that—"

"I don't even know why I'm crying."

"It happens after a big thing like this," said Zarina with great tenderness, and then, "You have to take it easy."

"I'll be able to take it easy after I've said a few things."

The brothers looked uncomfortable.

"What you want to fight for?" Fozia continued. "There's enough fighting in this country. What you got to be so angry for? You think your anger does anything for anyone? You think holding onto something someone said long ago means anything?"

Adam, always the more traditional of the two, merely listened. His mother was lying in a hospital bed, she was an old lady, she had just come close to what he had feared was death, this was not the time to contradict or disagree with her. But Waleed felt his head take over, remembering the conversation he had had with Rashaad all those weeks ago. "Mommy, sometimes being angry means people change, and remembering is also important, look at here, look where we come from—"

She cut him off with a sigh and danced her good hand in the air.

"No, no, *no*. I'm *sick* of talking about everyone else and everything else. I only want to talk about us, about you and about you," a nod for each of her boys. "Before this happened to me, I was thinking about the past, how upset you both are about the District ... still so upset ... no, don't start denying it, I know ... and I thought I must say to you that you can remember bad times and bad things, but don't let it hold you, don't let it sit on your neck like Aapie." *Who*? The men looked at each other. "Don't let it grab you and slit your throat, don't twist your neck looking back. Like with your daddy, he wasn't always easy, but I don't want to think of that ... you understand? And places are like people in that way ..."

Nasreen walked into the ward carrying a steaming styrofoam cup. She handed her coffee to Adam and kissed Fozia hello.

But Fozia was still talking in this disconnected way, her sentences shaped by the inconsistent headiness of post-shock, her mind still reeling from her body's earthquake. Her thoughts ran circles around her logic and her throat seemed to gurgle independent of the words she managed to form. Her pupils were wide, dark and glittery from the sedative, and she fixed them on her sons as she reached out a hand to each of them. Though her breath was papery and shallow, she gripped their hands with the inexplicable strength of the very weak, a concurrent squeeze that put them both somewhere between bent-knuckle pain and acute relief. *Surely this strength must speak to other reserves?*

Adam returned his mother's squeeze and hoped that his boast to his daughters was true, that they were in the best hospital possible. He mentally re-landscaped his property, paved over the pool and built an annexed cottage for his mother. He did not pause in this fantasy to discuss the renovations with Zarina.

Fozia knew, for her part, that she was close to raving, but she had also lived long enough to understand how old women are elevated by illness, how those close to the end are held sacrosanct. She knew that her boys would do anything for her now, that her granddaughters would remember what she said and parse the words apart in the years to come, that Zarina, whose parents were both alive, looked at her and Abe as a rehearsal for her own grief. *There is*, she thought, *such power at the end*. She focused her dark eyes on her youngest, unblinking as a cat, and said eventually, "Is that girl here?"

Waleed took a breath. He looked at Adam, who offered him a tiny, almost unreadable shake of his head, no. Fozia's face was paling a little and her lips suddenly seemed cracked. There was a rattle in her voice as she asked the same question: "Is that *girl* here?" Waleed nodded.

"She doesn't want to come and say hello?"

The room held the moment. The standing Dawoods looked at each other, faces redrawn in astonishment, bodies made still by wonder. A patient in another other bed let out a sleeping groan, whatever pain she was in had reached deep through the drugs to rattle her.

Waleed darted towards the door, his face wide and open. Even Zarina, who was doing her best to refuse the day's theatrics, felt her throat gather a little tightly.

At the foot of the bed, Nasreen and Alia flanked their mother until Fozia motioned them both forward and placed a hand on each of Alia's cheeks, pulling her down so that their faces were parallel, and said, her voice clear and full of delight, "Not even *God* can change the past ... you hear that? You hear that?"

~

In the parking lot, that little phenomenon known in all driving cities from LA to Cape Town unfolded; just six people made their way to three cars. Adam walked ahead purposefully, the stride of a man who had dodged grief, who saw before him a calendar of easy days. His mother had outrun death. It was a moment like this that gave meaning to all those hours spent in prayer. Waleed ambled behind him, his hands twinned with Anna's. *So, this is what it is like to love with permission.* Anna, for her part, was in a daze: *So that was Fozia. That* was the monster who had occupied a central place in her bed and her head for so long. That little woman with the scarf rimmed in sweat around her brow, who had grabbed Waleed's hand so tightly that her hospital gown had slipped to reveal her wrinkled shoulder blade. *That* was her.

Zarina held both her daughters towards her, releasing them only when it was time to unlock the car. She called out to the rest of her family that everyone should meet at theirs for breakfast, and she looked pointedly at Waleed and Anna when she offered them an English fry-up (no bacon).

"Is no one driving with me?" asked Adam in a wounded voice. Alia volunteered, and for a moment the six of them lingered outside their vehicles: to get into them would break the spell of unity that had been cast. Better to stay here among the petrol fumes and the ugly emptiness of a grey and black hospital parking lot than risk losing this feeling of togetherness.

"Hey!" said Adam suddenly. The rest of them started from their reverie. "You won't believe who I saw yesterday."

Waleed, to whom the question was directed, pulled out his pouch of tobacco before saying, "Who?"

Adam gave a slight pause before the reveal: "Auntie Ragmat."

"*No.*"

"Yes."

"Really? Where did you see her?"

"By the shop. There by Marwaan's."

"But I mean, can she even walk nowadays?"

"Hah! Can she ever!"

The two men laughed, shook their heads from side to side, their memories running in parallel lines down a disappeared street.

"Auntie Ragmat from the Kamaldiens? I thought she was bed-ridden?" asked Zarina with a laugh that her daughters, who were feeling roundly excluded, could not place.

"Please. Do you know of *anything* that could keep that auntie down?" said Adam.

Here Zarina turned directly to Adam, but instead of answering him she raised her fists and then placed one hand on a jutting hip and made as if she was throwing a dishcloth over her right shoulder.

"*Net soe, ja! Net soe!*" said Waleed, while Adam and Zarina laughed too long and too much: the morning stress insisting on a little levity.

"So, as per usual Auntie Ragmat has now all the news nè—"

"What did Daddy call her again?" Waleed interrupted Adam with the eagerness of a small boy, "Rightful Ragmat?"

"Right*eous* Ragmat!" corrected Adam, "So listen man. I'm just about to make my getaway and she stops me by the door to tell me she has the latest update … on *your* family." He directed the possessive at his wife.

In response, she cradled her forehead and shielded her eyes, "Oh no. *Please*. What? What have they done now?"

"Well, apparently there was an attempted break-in at the Hassans—"

"What? When? I didn't even know about it—"

"Well, I'm telling you now—"

"Is everyone ok?"

"Yes man, everyone is fine. Just *listen*. So there is a break-in last week. And the thieves got in because of all the renovation work they had to do after the fire, probably an inside job—"

At this, Waleed rallied a little, "Look, let's not accuse people—"

"Hell. Can I *finish*?"

"Sorry."

"Auntie Ragmat tells me that Auntie Waarda told her they got right in there by the front door – just *waltzed* in – easy as anything, and went straight for the safe. But what they didn't count on – these *fools* went out the front door – can you believe that? What they didn't count on, was Taariq next door being up early. Crack. Of. Dawn. He was leaving on a cross-country trip. So they on their way out and they still counting the cash – greedy bastards – and Taariq sees them while he's putting his suitcase in the boot, he works out exactly what's happening, so he grabs his gun, you know he's got that Glock man—"

"I know his wife is not happy about that – she's told him time and time again it's dangerous to have that around the kids," said Zarina.

Adam waved an airy hand at this, fretful that his story's rhythm was under threat, "And you know Taariq, nè, he now always has to be dramatic, he waits for just the right moment; for them to get onto the street and only *then* he cocks the gun and he calls out, 'Ahoy there! Stand and deliver!'"

Waleed, who had been smoking for much of the story, exhaled in a spluttering fit of laughter, "And then?"

"So naturally, they get a fright and they start to run. Bladdy fast too, and Taariq knows he's on the backfoot now, so he jumps in his car and he follows them—"

"No!"

"Bladdy right!"

"The one runs right up into the mountain but the other one goes down the street and Taariq hightails after them like he's Steve bladdy Mcqueen until he corners the guy in who else's but Auntie Ragmat's driveway. Talk about getting yourself onto the local news channel. And knocks the man a little with the car—"

"Oh my God! Was he okay?"

"Yes man, nothing serious, they just connected on the hub. It was just a bump. But this man is now *paaping* and he actually climbs the bladdy *tree* in the front garden! Can you believe that? He climbs that short guava tree and waits there, as if Taariq suddenly can't see him. And he's still holding onto the cash. Taariq just gets out the car, with the Glock, makes the man come down, takes the money back and gives him a few smacks before he lets him go. And who witnesses the whole bladdy thing? *Yes*. Auntie Ragmat. Up early as usual and watching *everybladdything* from her bedroom. She guesses what's going on, and as the man is running off, she leans out her window and all she says to Taariq is ..." here, Adam paused and slammed a hand on the boot of his car as if providing the drum ending of a vaudeville act, "Kwaai. *Kwaai.*"

He allowed himself a slight smile, while Waleed and Zarina rewarded him with shrieks of congratulating laughter on a story well told, it's final phrase disarmingly delivered. Anna, in turn, had watched the scene with the befuddled joy of a traveller observing a tribal dance. Her usual reservations about vigilante justice were banked; she was at once earnest, invested and encouraging, nodding along, hoping for enlightenment, for inclusion. Waleed caught his breath, waited for Zarina to calm down before saying, "Huh-uh ... Auntie Ragmat ... she was now always baie lailai."

At the last word, Adam and Zarina laughed with renewed energy. "Oh goodness ..." this, from Zarina, "I have not heard that word in forever."

"What's 'lailai'?"

The adults' laughter died down and in the emerging silence one daughter repeated the other's question. "Hey, seriously, what's 'lailai'?"

Zarina, Waleed and Adam all caught each other's eyes, their expressions fusing derision and amusement.

"These kids have gaps in their education, Adam," said Zarina, as if the day of reckoning about St Michaels was finally upon them.

"I don't know either," smiled Anna.

"It's not *la-lie*," said Waleed, cruelly distorting Nasreen's pronunciation to sound as white and as clueless as possible, "It's 'lai-*lai*'." He turned to his niece with a grin and offered her further instruction. "Say it like you going to smack someone."

"Okay," said Adam, gearing up to transform this into a teaching moment. He shifted as he began his narrative, planting his feet at an authoritative angle, his hands held up in front of him as if he were already detailing the story. "So this auntie, Auntie Ragmat, before she lived in Walmers, she was opposite us on Nial Street in the District, and she used to stand on the stoep everyday from one-thirty after lunch until just before magriep and she would stand there and—"

"So?" said Nasreen, impatient to hurry things along, to get to the dictionary bit, to stop her mother from making Waleed laugh continuously just by swinging some imaginary dishcloth from one shoulder to the other.

"So let me finish," snapped Adam. "So she would stand there and watch the kids playing and keep an eye on them and if there was any nonsense or interference from the gangsters she would roll up her sleeves like this, and she was a big woman, hey, *dik*, and she would say, 'Nou kom! Nou kom!' Now *she*, she was lailai." Adam ended with a flourish that consisted of him leaning triumphantly against the car door, one leg crossed over the other, while his daughters looked at him, bewildered. Anna nodded vaguely and supplied the expected laugh though she, like anyone else who had not grown up in District Six circa 1950–1970, could not understand the punch-line.

It was Alia who eventually broke through the puzzled silence. "That's a story," she announced with authority, "not a definition."

"Arguably the same thing," said Waleed.

"See that? Listen to your uncle." Adam flashed Waleed a grin that his brother was quick to return.

"Very nicely done, Adam," said Zarina, placing a congratulatory kiss on his cheek, "That sums it up perfectly."

"One time," said Waleed. "I wouldn't kiss you for it, but

that's it." He licked his rizla to seal the tobacco and laughed softly, repeating, "Lailai, lailai."

Alia offered Nasreen a shrug and her sister returned it with a raised set of eyebrows, each gesture allowing, with only partial resentment, that some histories were not inheritable, some mysteries could not be untangled.

The family climbed into their respective cars, this time, Alia with her father. She felt she should confirm what everyone else seemed to find obvious, "Dad?"

"Mmm?" Adam's fingers were tapping jolly on the steering wheel.

"Does this mean that they are talking again? That everything is fine?"

"Of course everything is fine. After what happened, how could it not be?"

"So Uncle Taariq went to the rescue, and now everyone is friends again?" she could not stop the creep of sarcasm in her voice, hearing, as Adam did, how she had become Zarina's impatient echo.

"Ali— Nas— *Nalia—*"

"*Alia.*"

"Alia." Adam pronounced those three syllables with an aggrieved finality that both refused to entertain further comment and suggested that a show of gratitude, not interrogation, at the advent of family peace was in order, "That is *exactly* what it means."

22

THURSDAY, 12 MAY 1994

Dear Nick,

Your letters are taking ages and ages to get here, or have you just stopped writing?

Has your accent changed yet? You know what they say about Capetonians, we only need to fly over a country and the transformation begins. Ha. Ha. That was awful of me. Sorry. I just miss you so much.

Have you read any good books in the last months? The hunt for Nat Nakasa continues – nothing yet, but it's led to a host of others, Themba, Rive ... The Drum Decade looks incredible, cool suits, everyone smoking, jazz clubs, Defiance Campaign ... must have been amazing, apart from the oppression, obviously.

Anyway, here, as promised, is everything I can remember about the 27th:

I think everyone in Walmer Estate registered at my old school, Zonnebloem. I hadn't been back since I left and there was something incredibly weird about walking through those gates again. Everything looked the same: uncollected acorns everywhere, steep driveway, chapel, boys' school. I remembered my classroom really clearly, the girl who sat next to me, terrified of our teacher, Mrs Dean. It was as if there were two things going on at the same time, what I was seeing right then and there and then also what I was remembering. Maybe it will be the same for you when you come home?

We went down together: my parents, me, Nasreen and Nasreen's boyfriend Zubair (more on that another time, but they've been seeing each other for an entire year! Who knew? Not me. None of us did). Waleed and Anna were registered in Observatory and we picked up my mom's parents and my Mama along the way. People queued all the way from the Training College where the voting booths were, to right outside. I thought everyone would complain about the wait, especially the older people (there was a light rain, nothing serious) but it was like a reunion for them. My dad kept running around greeting friends he hadn't seen in ages and people came up to my grandparents, which was nice for them. Uncle Sammy was there too with an international news crew. They filmed him coming out of the voting booth and he threw his arms up, waved them about and gave a Churchill 'V' for Victory salute. ("Kak old school, ma broe," said this guy standing next to me.) My Mama got into a fight with her neighbour Auntie May because Auntie May announced really loudly that she would be voting for the Nats, which we now know (sickeningly) is how most of the Western Cape went. She kept saying, "Better the devil you know, Fozia. Better the devil you know."

Nasreen and I decided to walk home: people were hooting, shouting out their car windows and you could smell braais and hear music from every house. And all the adults kept saying "I just can't believe it" and also "Now the real work begins." Which didn't make any sense to me at all. What does that even mean? That everything up to now has been a holiday?

Farouk's parents were throwing a party so I went there for a while: lots of music, lots of being dragged into a dance circle by insistent uncles, lots of laughing from Mikhail when this happened. Some idiot started going on and on to me about how we should forgive the Nats because that was what "The Lord" wanted us to do. Christians, man … (joking). And then I came home and watched some TV coverage of the day: nothing you wouldn't have seen, Madiba beaming, aerial shots of miles-long queues, all the commentators talking about the 98% voter turnout. I called Lizzie. I could barely hear her above the music in the background. She invited me round, she said Gugs was *hopping*, mad with joy, and I begged my mother to drive me there but she kept saying she was tired.

Waleed has been spending more time with us lately. He takes Nasreen and I for long walks, we hike up Lion's Head or make our way up through the forest to the Constantia dam. Last week he took us to one of the kramats in Camps Bay – we walked up a path thick with the smell and scratch of fynbos, and at the top, the most incredible view of the ocean. It's good to talk to him: I think he's helping me understand everything a bit better, even though I don't always like what I'm understanding. Is there much poverty in Australia? Lately, it's all I see here. Waleed says "seeing" is one of the things that's going to happen, that's *got* to happen: that we'll start to see it, no one will ever be able to say again that they "didn't know". He says the hope is that everyone will see and do something, not see and just learn to live with it. He says you can't be really free if there is food everywhere but you are always kept hungry. This is a sad place to end. I don't mean it to be. But it's always like that here, isn't it? Both things at once.

No PS for this letter, except to say, write. Please write.

Love always

Alia

23

FRIDAY, 27 MAY 1994

They drive there in Zarina's car, Adam having decided not to embarrass his brother with the chrome flourish of the Mercedes. The air is cool with a crisp autumn thinness. Zarina unwinds the window a fraction, turning her face towards the city and its coming season. Around her shoulders, a shawl of deep maroon. She'd spent the morning at the hairdressers and later, kept her family waiting while she fussed with her makeup. The girls are both in jeans, T-shirts and second-hand jackets – there had been a mercifully brief fight about who would wear what.

As they emerge from the car, a Dawood from each door, Nasreen pins an ANC victory badge on her jacket's lapel. Adam notices and begins to say something, but Zarina stops him; she can do that these days, with just a look, or a hand held up flat against the air.

Alia reaches into her pocket to assure herself that she is carrying, as always, Nick's latest letter. In it, he tells her that voting in Brisbane was an empty experience: "It was awful, Alia. My aunt put out bowls of biltong and stuck mini flags in every conceivable place. My parents had these frozen smiles when she took photos ..." Alia will keep the letters long after Nick stops writing back, long after it becomes clear that he is never going to come home.

It is a still night in Cape Town. The kind when one

cannot imagine its terrible winds, its past pains, when everything feels new, just-born, a history made up of stories, gentle and good. It is that sort of night, when, if you stand in the centre of the squat market square, press your feet against its cobbles and strain your ears towards the wide steep streets ahead, you might hear the women in the BoKaap calling their children in from the streets, notice a club owner carrying decks and vinyl for tonight's DJ, see a group of students, newly friends, but already bonded, tumbling from a open door planning the evening ahead and the years to come. And if you stay in that place, feet on rounded stone, you may also hear the murmurs of a family as they gather to eat, feel their chairs scrape and steps patter on thinning wood. You could turn your head and see, in a forgotten alleyway, street children scrambling into tight corners, catch the notes of a song you think you remember, notice a woman in an apartment laughing into a telephone, greedy for love, unable to say goodbye. It is that kind of night when the city refuses its past, when it holds none of its present secret.

The Dawoods walk towards the address, finding at it a corner bar with the broad doors and stain-glass swirls that mark it as a remnant of the city's brief affair with all things Art Nouveau. The family stands for a moment on a step that merges with the pavement until Adam lets out a small and lovely laugh. "I don't believe it. I know this place. I used to listen to jazz here." His daughters draw close, waiting for more: in his sentence, a world. He has been doing this lately, telling them things, pointing places out.

Inside Fozia is counting out the pies, laying them on a side table, arguing with the café owner, a tall, skinny man with dirty blond hair and a half-hearted, unfinished tribal tattoo who is trying to convince her that people will want the chance to try his Italian coffeemaker. But Fozia remains unmoved. "Listen here, no one has fancy coffee with my food. It's tea, or Frulata or mix-drinks or nothing."

The man looks cowed, defeated. Between them stands Anna, soothing Fozia, placating the owner, while Megan, still here for a few more months, helps arrange the seating. The room is dotted with claw foot chairs and sofas upholstered in patterned velvet and small wooden foot-stools decorated with thin leather straps woven into blocks. It could be Fozia's lounge were it not for the 1920s French Bistro posters and the rows of alcohol behind the counter that she will somehow, through sheer force of will, manage to not notice for the entire evening.

Waleed is testing the mike on the makeshift stage. Rashaad, cool in a Che beret, photographs him. The girls kiss their grandmother and hover uncertainly near their uncle. He smiles them over. "You guys remember Rashaad, don't you?" Rashaad offers them a funny little salute he thinks matches his cap, while Waleed taps at Nasreen's badge, his smile growing a little. "Your father seen this?" he asks. Alia he catches around the shoulder in a half-hug. She tries to stay there, to extend the moment, but he has already turned to greet his brother.

The bar begins to fill up with Waleed's friends. Zarina and Adam stand to the side, shy, overdressed, in this room of sloganised T-shirts and unlaced Doc Martens. There are familiar faces, though ("Howzit," "Slamat," Adam says to boys he bullied and protected as a teenager), and strange faces (friends of Anna's, people from university, those who populate Waleed's other life).

Fozia moves on from tormenting the bar owner to collecting about her a group of her son's friends. She shocks and feeds them at the same time, offering them snacks and her thoughts about the new government in one breath: they eat both up, between chokes of laughter – it's always funny when it's not your family.

Waleed walks towards his mother, holding a drink he has just taken from the barman. 'It's *lemonade*, Ma," he says, answering her unspoken accusation. "Here, taste."

But Fozia purses her lips and shakes her head; she has brought her own cup and her own Frulata and that is that.

Someone opens the doors and a small sharp rush of cold fills the room. Alia sees that dusk has drawn close and little circles of smokers have formed, their cigarettes glowing and bobbing in the gathering dark. Rashaad asks Adam and his family to call everyone in, they are about to begin. Others arrive: Lizzie, who'd insisted on an invitation, behind her; Melanie, slightly late, trying to keep to herself, for her and Rashaad's relationship had not been received as enthusiastically as Waleed had hoped: Yusuf refuses to speak to Melanie, so Rashaad refuses to speak to him. Tonight will mark another polite but painful orbit of avoidance: from bar to couch, from doorway to bathroom, faces will be turned, greetings will not be offered. After Melanie, Nasreen's long-secret boyfriend, Zubair – tall, thin, slightly gangling, infinitely gentle, nineteen years old, an architecture student – appears. Nasreen calls him over to where she is sitting with Anna and Georgie and he slots in easily, asking them questions about their work, about the election.

Waleed has planned the order of his reading. "No introductions," he'd said to Anna earlier. "No framing, none of that. Just words, that's all. Just the stories." But once there, once he looks out into the small crowd and sees in that crowd the faces of his family, his own face in theirs, he finds himself saying something quite different. He has raged for years against readers assuming the biography of his work, saying that it is a ghettoising tool for women, for people of colour. Always, he's refused his own life in his work. But now he sees that there is no shame in acknowledgement. *No, none at all*. He looks at the page and then at the crowd, focusing, not by design, on the wide mouths and deep-set eyes of his family: *Adam, Fozia, Nasreen, Alia*. On Zarina, who has taken him aside and said quietly, "Your father would have loved this, really" – glossing the truth, giving him what Fozia and Adam could not. He sees Anna standing with his nieces, and his boys gathered as if to cheer him on at a match. Each page a story and each story a life, his, others, blinking up at him. And he tells the crowd that they are of and from his life, without denial or chagrin.

And then the words begin, and with it the walking. Waleed walks across the stones of the District into the rubble of the West Bank, through the endless sunburnt roads of the Karoo into the caves of Table Mountain, across the deep blue of the bay to the Island, through the groves and orchards of the Cape and up the hills of the BoKaap. He walks towards his mother's kitchen, plunges his hands in the samoosa dough and eats a plate of tomato bredie run red with sweet oiliness. He waits in a back room while a woman speaks of djinns and smoke and holy oil, he watches as the walls of his childhood home turn to dust and weeds and forgetfulness. He listens as mothers ask where their children are, and he rushes towards a friend to cradle his head while his ears stream blood. He sits in a taxi, pressed between passengers and the thump of the kombi's subwoofers, bound for university, the city tumbling about him and through him. And at university, he walks through the library, past the shelves full of old stories, feeling the want of new ones. He finds himself in his brother's house, seeing for the first time the frail, faint shadow of Firoze: the ghost boy stands in the doorway saying nothing, offering the silent comfort that the death has been quick, the final hours lasted just a moment, the border between now and then a breath, nothing more. Then, walking with women, the ones who have given him gifts of food and notebooks and coffee and new pens and perfect poems, and difficulties, and bus rides and Anna. And finally this moment, in this autumn, when the world has been born anew and his stories hold everything: the past, a present full of urgent hope, and the dead, who circle a frayed edge between dreaming and waking with their melancholic warnings of the griefs and betrayals still to come.

~

Waleed looks out at the small world he has gathered, at those left standing in the ruin and the new, and at the end of the reading he raises his hand to show he is finished, but from where she is watching, Alia thinks it is a blessing.

ACKNOWLEDGEMENTS

This book was written in three cities I've called home and in all three I have had the gift of family, friends and colleagues who have kept faith with me and with the work. Thank you to Leila Davids, Carol-Ann Davids, Quanita Adams, Patrick Flanery and Ina Roux for their detailed readings of the first draft, their insightful, encouraging comments, their perceptive criticisms. Thank you to everyone at the Wylie Agency: especially Charles Buchan, who gave this book the most extraordinary amount of time, focus and support: Charles, all the aunties salute you! Thank you to Sarah Chalfant for her wisdom and guidance. Thank you to Rustum Kozain for his exquisite poem *The Blessing*: in many ways this novel is an unwieldy response to what he was able to say in just a few pages. I am grateful to Alison Lowry who understood the work deeply and fully from the beginning and then edited it with such grace and patience. Thank you to JM Coetzee. Thank you to Ledig House for a residency that came at exactly the right moment. Thank you to everyone at Random House Struik, but especially to Fourie Botha, whose combination of care, enthusiasm and generosity is the sort of thing every writer hopes to encounter.

Special thanks to my parents, Joe and Shereen Davids, for their love and support, and to Ilyas Tomás Davids Gutierrez, bringer of unimaginable luck and love.

This book is dedicated to John Gutierrez because he knows why we must make new worlds but still write the old ones.

NADIA DAVIDS is an award-winning writer who works across a range of forms: plays, articles, short stories and screenplays. Her theatre works, including the well-known *At Her Feet* and *Cissie*, have been staged in South Africa and abroad, and her writing has appeared in various newspapers and short-story anthologies. She lives between London and Cape Town. *An Imperfect Blessing* is her first novel.